PENGUIN BOOKS

WEIGHT LOSS

Upamanyu Chatterjee was born in 1959. He has written three previous novels – *English, August: An Indian Story* (1988), *The Last Burden* (1993) and *The Mammaries of the Welfare State* (2000), which won the Sahitya Akademi Award for writing in English. He is married with two daughters and lives in India.

UPAMANYU CHATTERJEE

WEIGHT LOSS

PENGUIN BOOKS

PENGUIN BOOKS

Published by the Penguin Group
Penguin Books Ltd, 80 Strand, London WC2R ORL, England
Penguin Group (USA) Inc., 375 Hudson Street, New York, New York 10014, USA
Penguin Group (Canada), 90 Eglinton Avenue East, Suite 700, Toronto, Ontario, Canada M4P 2Y3
(a division of Pearson Penguin Canada Inc.)
Penguin Ireland, 25 St Stephen's Green, Dublin 2, Ireland (a division of Penguin Books Ltd)
Penguin Group (Australia), 250 Camberwell Road, Camberwell, Victoria 3124, Australia
(a division of Pearson Australia Group Pty Ltd)
Penguin Books India Pvt Ltd, 11 Community Centre, Panchsheel Park, New Delhi – 110 017, India
Penguin Group (NZ), 67 Apollo Drive, Rosedale, North Shore 0632, New Zealand
(a division of Pearson New Zealand Ltd)
Penguin Books (South Africa) (Pty) Ltd, 24 Sturdee Avenue, Rosebank, Johannesburg 2196,
South Africa

Penguin Books Ltd, Registered Offices: 80 Strand, London WC2R ORL, England

www.penguin.com

First published in Viking by Penguin Books India 2006
Published in Penguin Books 2007

1

Printed in England by Clays Ltd, St Ives plc

ISBN: 978-0-141-02953-5

For
Sara & Pia

CONTENTS

WOMANISH

'Only when you die will you cease to feel ridiculous,' announced Anthony the Physical Education teacher, swaying gracefully on the balls of his feet, rapping his baton against his thigh.

April 16, 1970, a terrible—but typical—day in one of the best years of Bhola's life. He had then been eleven. The years that he spent in his Jesuit school became in retrospect truly the happiest of his existence. Even when he had lived them, he recalled later, he had experienced a sense of brimming over with sap that had enabled him to enjoy even his unhappy moments. Of which there had been countless.

12.25 to 1.35 was a Double Sports Period. Out in the cricket field, the class had just finished staring at the sun while inhaling non-stop for the aeon that Anthony took to count till ten, holding their breaths for another ten and exhaling slowly and without pause while he barked out the numbers till twenty. While the class recovered its breath before the next round, with a moan, Dosto in the second row keeled over. Sunstroke, he would have explained had he been asked. Anthony strutted up, pulled him up by the ear, boxed him a couple of times and made him all right again. 'Ridiculous,' hissed Bhola at Dosto from just behind him, hoping thus to attract Anthony's attention. An expectant hush amongst the files of students, faces contorted with the excitement of an imminent second thrashing, as Anthony swaggered up to Bhola, smiled, dug his nails into his ear and dragged him out of the line. Then he sneered, like a Nazi commandant of a concentration camp in an English film sneers at noble good-looking honourable witty Allied soldiers caught trying to escape. 'So, my little woman, you've been learning big words.' He rocked back and forth a couple of times. The entire school referred to him as Cleopatra.

'Sorry sir no sir slip of the tongue sorry sir—' mumbled Bhola, eyeing Anthony's lips stained with years of tobacco and screaming silently at him, Beat me, pinch me, you bitch, make me bleed.

'Ridiculous. Only when you die, my woman, will you cease to feel ridiculous.' With his thumb and forefinger, he began kneading the soft armflesh between Bhola's left tricep and armpit. 'You'll find time enough later in life, my boy, to learn big words.' The pain puckered up Bhola's face and propelled him up to the tips of his toes. 'No sir please please sorry sir—' Anthony abruptly released him. Bhola stumbled to his knees, his upper arm jerking convulsively. Above him, Anthony spread his legs, thrust out his crotch, snarled and called him womanish. 'Womanish' was his favourite adjective with the younger students of the school. With the seniors, he, while stooging their cigarettes, exchanged jokes about the females on the staff. Bhola's classmates relaxed, happy that he had drawn away so much of the teacher's attention and, looking at their watches, calculated how much time was left before the bell. Bhola remained on his knees till Anthony entangled his fingers in his hair. The boy then made to get up and butted his head into Anthony's crotch. 'I heard Cleopatra's balls go *plich*,' he later told an envious Dosto.

The teacher toppled over with a gasp that the class rejoiced to hear. Bhola tripped against and sprawled over him, rubbed his nose in the crook of his throat, pushed his knee into Anthony's abdomen and scrambled up before he could gush out in his trousers. Anthony turned over on his left, both hands cupping his testicles, knees drawn up, eyes shut, face screwed up, teeth bared. Bhola knelt beside him, one hand tender on bicep, a second on hip. 'Please sir what's happened? Please sir sir are you all right?' He trembled with the moment's perfect pleasure.

The class broke up to cluster around them. 'Sir is dying,' announced one voice joyously. Anthony slowly turned to face the sky and almost immediately curled up onto his right, his face still a snarl. The boys, momentarily disturbed, gathered around again like vultures. Bhola, his head thudding with the drumbeat of his heart, resisted out of fear the temptation to straddle and squeeze the life out of his Sports Teacher with his thighs. Some of his urgency, by a process of osmosis, transmitted itself to Anthony, for he soon pushed away the boy's hot hands, sat up, licked his lips, shut his eyes, inhaled deeply, then laboriously—like a mythical figure awaking— stood up, blinked and looked about him. His students gazed carefully and expressionlessly at the world surrounding them— the cricket pitch, the tennis courts, the grey Junior School building, the red tiles of the roof of the changing rooms of the swimming pool, the school buses revving up at the gates, the cricket bats heaped up like corpses for a mass grave outside the Sports Room. No one dared to look Anthony in the eye. He eventually focussed his eyes on Bhola, the veins in them filled with blood and his two slaps drove lust out of the boy's mind for a while. 'Cleopatra is back to normal.'

Almost, for he had to hobble across to the bird-shit-spattered bench alongside the Sports Room. The boys reluctantly returned to their places in the sun, eyeing from time to time, with diminishing hope, the hunched-up teacher. 'Stick Drill,' croaked Anthony. He had meant to bark. The boys, glad of any opportunity for undisciplined movement, broke ranks and rushed to beat one another to pick up their wooden sticks. In the mêlée at the open door of the Sports Room—with those without nudging and shoving to gain access and those with sticks poking those without—any boy unmindful enough to stray within arm's length of Anthony on the bench was out of habit slapped hard by him on the buttocks. By the time that each student had got hold of a stick—each two feet long and painted in one of the Ludo colours assigned to each of the school's four Houses—and returned to his spot, Anthony was truly back to normal, up and strutting about, snapping and snarling like an exhausted bitch. The dull stick-lifting and manoeuvring began. Bhola remained warm at the memory of having touched Antony's body. When one set of exercises was over, he absentmindedly threw his stick down. 'Oh sorry,' he yelped and bent down to pick it up, but time enough for Anthony to push his knee into his buttocks. At that stage of his life, Bhola had been tall, soft and almost Kashmiri-white, with large jiggling hips that had a life of their own.

Having once been bitten, Anthony did not try the second time to pull the boy up by his hair. But when Bhola did get up, Anthony held his left nipple through his shirt and tweaked it hard. Bhola shrieked and, his head throbbing, jerked back out of reach. 'So you find the stick too heavy, Womanish?'

'No sir not at all sir I—'

'Give it to me.'

The slow thwack of the stick against Anthony's thigh was almost drowned out by the thudding in Bhola's skull. He pushed Bhola's chest with the stick. 'Just look at you, Fatty, soft and fat like an old diabetic female. At your age, you look like your mother.'

'Sir.' It seemed a safe answer.

'What d'you mean, sir! How old are you—twelve, thirteen?'

'Eleven, sir.'

'*Eleven*! You look at least twenty-five.' Dosto snorted, short and sharp like a fart. Anthony glared briefly and murderously all around. 'You look older than me, fat boy. How old do you think I am?' He looked thirty and was actually forty-one.

'Fifty-three, sir.'

Bhola's classmates thrilled at the sight of the stick being broken on his head. Anantaraman, however, a pale, sensitive, shy, nervous and complex boy, passed out. Anthony sneered at being distracted from his labours in so amateurish a fashion and walked across to loom, hands on hips, like a supervillain in a comic, over the bespectacled heap. He bent and nudged the body with the part of the stick that remained in his hand, then, straightening up and looking around, commanded the group, 'Here, some of you carry the ninny over to the Dispensary.' Bhola, scalp aflame, stumbled forward to volunteer, to escape, for he found Brother Dr David Tolaram at the Dispensary sexy too in a different, hairy sweat-and-cologne kind of way. Some of the boys snickered at seeing him lift up Anantaraman's left leg but he had correctly—though instinctively—gauged that with one fainted student and one stick broken on another's head, Anthony had sated himself with violence for the day—or for the afternoon, at any rate.

'Sir sir there's blood coming out of his nose!' squealed the alarmist at Anantaraman's left arm. The four bearers halted near the Sports Room, manfully resisting the urge to dump their burden with a thud on the concrete, and waited for Anthony to react. He came up reluctantly, with a frown, glanced down at the unconscious boy, swivelled about athletically and hollered at the class, 'You shirkers are to continue with the drill is that clear!' To the four coolies, he appended, 'C'mon c'mon careful with the weakling.' Fifty paces later, huffing and gently puffing, Bhola turned back to see that the abandoned Physical Education session had begun to resemble some picnic or a boisterous fair, joyous white figures on a stretch of uneven green.

Brother Dr Tolaram was much more intrigued by the lump the size of a toothpaste cap on Bhola's hairline. He was squat, dark, balding, with long tendrils of grey hair that, in search of some support to cling to, swayed in the air like a new form of mutant plant life sending out feelers. Anantaraman, who had disappointed his porters first by coming to before they entered the Dispensary and then by insisting— screaming shrilly, jerking to free his trapped limbs—that he walk, the doctor had dismissed with an icepack and two glasses of Electral solution. The boy, exhausted but calm, sat in the corner with the second glass held limply in his hand, gazing at nothing. Anthony and the other boys had left by then.

Like several other students, Bhola liked the Dispensary— its polished teak doors, the rows of dark-glassed bottles, its smells of disinfectant, the trays of cotton—and felt secure in it. He sat demurely on the metal stool and, when Brother Tolaram neared him, inhaled deeply to get a whiff, then sagged gently against the doctor's thigh while he examined his head.

'Brother Sir, Sir Anthony beat me just because I can't do those exercises.'

'No no,' disclaimed the doctor absentmindedly as he daubed the lump with mercurochrome. 'You know that it's only for your own good. He wants you to grow up to be fit and strong like a man should be. The child is the father of the man, as you know.'

'And Brother Sir, then Sir Anthony,' continued Bhola, not cramped in any way by Anantaraman's presence, 'sat on me piggy back and beat me repeatedly on my head with a cricket ball while screaming Womanish! Womanish! into my ear.'

'And what do you all call him? Don't, don't tell me, I don't want to know.' The doctor, a little oppressed by the boy's weight on his thigh, gave him a farewell pat on his shoulder and stepped across to his other patient. While he proposed to Anantaraman that he lie down and rest for the remainder of the Sports Class, Bhola surreptitiously eyed the wall clock. He still took quite long to read the time and particularly hated it when the two hands overlapped or were close to each other.

'No no you should return to your class.' Brother Dr Tolaram was quite firm. 'Anantaraman no doubt will rest better without you.'

Bhola ambled off in the direction of the swimming pool. The second half of Sports was generally swimming unless Anthony decided that the boys were not leathery enough and couldn't be rewarded with a swim and made them jog in the sun instead. He stopped after a few steps and decided to measure the remaining distance by leaving no space between treads, by placing one foot directly in front of the other so that heel touched toe. He lost his balance at the tenth step and stopped beside the open gate of the open-air stage. He hated swimming and displaying his body before others. It was hot and his scalp burned. He was scared and ashamed of himself for not being aroused by women. With his friends, he snickered and joked about breasts and cunt but he—they all—had the vaguest notions about the second; about the naked female form divine he was curious without feeling for it any desire. He had noted, for instance, that his stepmother's breasts were large but nothing within him had stirred at visualizing them.

He heard from a distance the sounds of clumsy splashing and the screeches of Anthony's whistle. He peeped through a gap in the bougainvillea that surrounded the wire mesh fence of the pool. The handful of good swimmers, Dosto among them, had been set to doing breadths—without pause and till they died—across the deep half of the pool. The learners gasped for survival in the shallows, blubbered with terror on the ladder or, hugging themselves, trembled with fear on the jute matting that bordered the pool on all its four sides. Anthony, in his yellow cap and his red Cleopatra-is-showing-half-his-arse codpiece swimming trunks, strutted about amongst his charges like a tourist in a bazaar in Paradise, thwacking a turnip-shaped head here, pushing a boy into the water there, communicating only through the shrill stridor of his whistle, and grinning permanently.

Not quite knowing how to kill time till the bell, Bhola wandered off to the changing rooms. They were deserted. He stole across to the partitioned-off section reserved for Staff and found on a hook beneath Anthony's blue trousers his underwear. He smelt it and was disappointed. In a sudden, feverish rush, he took off all his clothes, abandoned them in a heap on the floor and put on the briefs, soft and warm with use. He was elated. He walked around the room, imitating Anthony's strut. His exhilaration vanished when he saw himself in the mirror. His breasts dangled like two soft white mangoes. Puckered up with depression, he took off the underwear, replaced it beneath the trousers and put on his clothes. He then stole a couple of notes from Anthony's wallet and sidled out of the rooms. Outside, Anthony was doing pushups on the jute matting. For a brief while, Bhola watched him go up and down.

With the pilfered money, he bought chocolate, ice-cream, envelopes and scented writing paper. Over two afternoons at home, while his father and stepmother were still at their offices, he, with glue, scissors and a month's supply of *The Statesman*, laboriously, practically with tongue sticking out with the effort, composed three letters to Anthony. He had wanted to do a dozen, one for each month of the year, but was exhausted after two and enervated beyond belief by the third. The first read:

> *I am a boy and you are my god. I saw you once and can't get you out of my mind or body. I want to worship your strong manliness and feel your great hard buM forever over my face. Please my god meet me on the 13th at 7pm at the North Gate of the Centenary Stadium. I want to be your woman. From your slave.*

Oddly enough, *bum* had been particularly irksome to compose. Nowhere amongst the headlines had he found *bumpy, bumper, bumption, bumpkin* or *bumblebee*. Dissatisfied and unhappy with himself at having to make concessions, he finally, the next day, broke the word up into two.

He dated the second letter the 13th and snipped and glued together:

> *You did not come, you sexy ditcher* (from '*last ditch effort*' and '*cropper*', both from the same headline over a report on the failure of some NATO legerdemain). *You will torture me by not meeting me. I love it but I love your body even more. Please please meet me on the 20th.*

In the letter of the 20th, he threatened suicide and to leave behind a note implicating Anthony. He posted these letters on the appropriate days. In the days that followed, whenever he saw Anthony, he would feel strange, as though they were meeting each other in disguise.

Three long days after he had posted the first letter, daydreaming in school during Geography, suddenly, in a panic of passion, he was convinced that he had miscalculated postal lethargy and incompetence and that his letter would never reach Anthony in time. Hiding his exercise notebook with his atlas, he tore out a page and wrote one more note to the Sports Teacher, this time in careful, trembling capitals:

> *IT'S ME. IF YOU LOVE ME, WEAR YOUR BROWN PANTS TOMORROW SO THAT I MAY KNOW.*

During First Break, he gobbled down his jam sandwich, rushed down the stairs from the second floor and trotted across the football field and basketball court to the sports complex to slip the note beneath the locked door of Anthony's room. While returning to class, sweating with the exertion and warm with the easing of successful execution, he spotted his loved one beside the cricket pitch march-pasting the senior classes and again felt that the two of them led their real lives elsewhere. But Anthony wore blue the next day and Bhola was half-relieved.

They had their Sports Period that day too. Anthony announced that the class wouldn't play any games because one of them was a thief. Everyone relaxed with relief. 'During Sports last week, one of you stole some money from my wallet. I am ashamed to have to stand here and make such a statement.' He had accused each and every class that he had taken that week.

Someone in the back row snorted at the news. Anthony for the next few minutes slapped the entire row trying to find out who it had been.

'Sir how much money was there sir?' asked Dosto.

Eyeing him suspiciously, Anthony replied, 'About seven hundred rupees. Why?' Ohhhh you liar, shrieked Bhola silently, not more than two hundred and fifty.

'Sir, we all could have contributed and repaid you,' continued Dosto, incoherent with nervousness, 'but our parents would never give us any extra pocket money.' He was cuffed twice, for being both confused and frivolous, and then detained after school and made to jog—more hobble—round and round the football field for an hour with his arms up in the air. Bhola stayed back with him to watch from the shade of the jamun trees that divided the field from the basketball court. In any case, there wasn't much at home in the afternoons for Bhola to go back to and he liked the rides that would follow in Dosto's father's chauffeur-driven Ambassador car.

Dosto was Bhola's best—practically his only—friend. He was a little strange—Bhola thought so too—warm-hearted and excitable. He was so openly happy that Bhola had elected to remain after the school buses had left that he seemed to convert his punishment into a long victory lap. Each time that he passed Bhola under the trees, he grinned, waved, wriggled his hips, flashed vee signs and blew kisses at largely-invisible and adoring spectators, amongst which he included the sullen gardener in charge of the cricket pitch, even more vinegary that afternoon at having been ordered by

Anthony to keep an eye on Dosto while he himself went off to have lunch, smoke and relax.

Dosto's father's driver, Hiralal, joined Bhola under the trees. He repelled and fascinated the boy. He was dark and running to fat, moustached, with knowing and permanently bloodshot eyes.

'Shall I run with you to keep you company?' shouted he across the field. They—Dosto and driver—got on so well together that they embarrassed and obsessed Bhola.

In the car, as always when there was nobody around who would object, Dosto sat—lay down, more accurately—in front, his head in Hiralal's lap beneath the steering wheel, snuggling up and prattling away, red-faced, sweating, lost in Paradise. Bhola sat at the back and laughed and joked along, but always conscious, almost envious, of the intimacy between his friend and the driver.

'Whoever swiped Anthony's money should steal some every day so that he is flat broke and has to beg outside the school gates.' Dosto chortled delightedly at his own idea. His disembodied voice seemed to float up from Hiralal's stomach. All that Bhola could see of him above the back of the front seat were his knees, rhythmically parting and then gently thudding against each other.

'We could start a secret society called The Mark Anthony Club with only him as target. Each member does something to him every day—whacks his cash, pisses on his clothes in the changing room, writes him dirty letters, whatever. The Club will also have a weekly timetable just like the one in our diaries.' Bhola paused, pleased at the hoots of delight emanating from Hiralal's nether regions. The car swerved as Dosto squirmed his head against the driver's abdomen.

All things must befall one before they can pass. Thus Bhola at thirteen was fantasizing about his new Class Teacher Miss

Jeremiah even though she did not dispel any of his womanish myths. One faction of the class called her 'Hip-hippo-ray' and another, more straightforwardly, Jiggletit. She was not the kind of woman whom any boy could admit to being in love with. 'It's like wanting to sink your nose into the pussy of a bad-tempered pig,' mused a very senior boy in the school bus. She was fortyish, usually wore skirts and had vast lemon-pale, soft-rubber thighs. In class, she generally sat in a voluptuous slouch in her chair alongside her table, her ankles crossed, legs spread wide, patches of sweat on her beast of a paunch, arms linked overhead to display armpits that were vast and grey wastelands of talcum and stubble. She tended to look down at her own body when she spoke and all the while, quickly and steadily, her thighs twitched open and shut, open and shut, like an eye blinking, mesmerising the entire front row, 'as though she needs to breathe her own puss musk to live,' whispered Bhola to Dosto.

'Even I want to breathe.'

'I want her to close her thighs around my ears like that.'

'Me too.'

Dosto was an appalling student but the son of an influential parent. On the first day in the new class, Miss Jeremiah had asked everybody what their fathers did and Dosto had ceased to be part of the blur when she discovered that his father held a position of some importance in the Ministry of Communications. Within a week, she got her home phone connection and his marks in the weekly tests from the very first began to show a significant improvement over his performance in the previous years.

When she had wanted the facts about the financial health of the families of her students, she hadn't minced words.

'How much does your father earn?'

Bhola had no idea.

'Does your mother work too?'

'Yes, Miss.' He never voluntarily divulged to anyone that

his father had married twice. He then hazarded, 'I think that they earn about a thousand rupees each.'

'Per month or year?'

Bhola had no idea. The class tittered but money had never bothered him. He had hardly ever lacked it and had never felt the pinch, not even when he didn't have any.

Dosto even began going to Miss Jeremiah's house three afternoons a week for extra Maths and Science. 'Yesterday, I saw Jiggle's pantie for two hours straight. She sits in a low chair and cootchie-coos to her armpit while her pantie winks at me. How do they expect me to study integers?'

'Well, phone her and tell her to stop it in the public interest.'

Dosto liked the idea very much. 'Especially since I got her the phone.' He dialled, with—as he had learnt from the crime thrillers that Bhola had begun to read—a handkerchief over the mouthpiece. 'If it's her stupid deaf grandmother, we'll ring again.' Someone picked up. Dosto panicked and disconnected. 'Here, you do it. She might make out my voice. She doesn't even know you exist.'

Which was true and Bhola hated Miss Jeremiah for it. In class, he would gaze at her knees and thighs and his skull would swell with lust. Look at me, he would scream silently, show me, let me lick.

Once Sad Beri brought new pencils to the Geometry class. They were pink, yellow and green and perfumed. The class felt that Sad Beri believed that he would get more marks with scented pencils. Bhola had inhaled deeply because the smell had seemed to emanate from Miss Jeremiah's orifices. In later years, whenever, unexpectedly, he had smelt that fragrance, he had remembered a hot classroom with a green blackboard, an enormous beehive just outside the rearmost window, and beside the teacher's table Miss Jeremiah with her armpits and thighs. He at first had been disappointed that the smell was sweet. He had wanted it to be harsh and strong.

He had seemed to exist for her only once, when she had slapped him hard for a Social Studies essay that he had written. He had cried then, out of pain and rage, disappointment, loathing and lust, and she had grinned and slapped him again, saying, 'Here, don't be silly, only girls cry. You aren't a girl, or are you!' Then the class had chanted in a chorus, 'Miss! Miss! Sir Anthony calls him Womanish!'

The Social Studies essay that had so infuriated Miss Jeremiah had in fact been written to impress her with Bhola's knowledge of the world. The topic given to the class had been 'My Neighbourhood'.

The local United Ganga Jamuna Saraswati Bank is housed in a building just four doors down the street from us. Two Fridays ago, late at night, its guard, a scavenging dom by caste, got drunk. A neighbourhood warder rushed up in the dark, excitedly announced that a king cobra had been spotted in the vicinity of the local park and asked whether the dom would help to catch it and thus do society a favour.

'Certainly, certainly,' responded the dom and, armed with his second bottle of hooch, went off to the park. After much swilling, shouting and strategy, he caught the cobra live in his hand and held it up to his face so that he could chat to it eye to eye.

'Hiss or kiss?' asked the dom of the snake. 'And show me the permit that allows you to wander about in my neighbourhood. And while you're about it, let's also see whose poison is stronger.' He got the snake to bite his arm, sucked the blood from the wound, spat it into a glass, added some hooch and drank the cocktail down. Then he glared at the snake for a while, bit it once in return and hammered it to death with the hooch bottle. Fortunately, he himself died soon after. The warder was aghast at the turn of events because he had wanted the cobra alive so that it could be worshipped in a neighbourhood temple that, beginning as a cane basket on the pavement in front of the bank, would gobble up surrounding buildings to eventually become an illegal four-storeyed edifice in white marble.

The guard's corpse was taken to his house somewhere in Pahariganj where it was kept for six days becuse he was a dom and they can never die of snakebite. His wife, naked, would lie on him and chanting some hymns, press down her stomach on his. With each effort, bubbles would appear at the corpse's mouth. That was the poison, they said, being forced out.

On the sixth day, they took the body to the river and threw it in, thinking that as it floated downriver, the water would dilute the poison. They had not reckoned with the other varieties of poison from diverse sources already in the water. When the police finally arrested the whole lot, they still did not think him dead. His missus, however, probably looking to replace him at the bank on compassionate grounds, has been spotted of late in my neighbourhood.

Bhola dialled with Dosto beside him, his tongue and teeth worrying his lips. 'What're you going to say? Make it throbbing.'

Miss Jeremiah picked up. 'Hello.'

'Hello.'

'Yes?'

Bhola cupped his hand over the mouthpiece. His nerve had failed him, despite his feeling buoyant that afternoon at having successfully sweated over for four days on his father's typewriter and finally dashed off to the Reader's Digest an article entitled, *I Am John's Arsehole.* He stared at Dosto for a second, blurted 'armpit' into the phone, replaced the receiver and with a sense of having crossed a threshold in his life, watched his friend, moaning with near-hysterical excitement, cavort all over the room. He himself felt warm and full, tense but triumphant. This was much better than writing letters with newspaper headlines. He dialled again. 'Say you want to suck out all her juices from her armpit.' Dosto couldn't keep still but danced from desk to cupboard to bed, gurgling ebulliently and waving his arms in the air. 'Tell her it's the Armpit Vampire calling.' The phone rang and rang, rang and rang and rang. Once the deaf grandmother answered.

'May I speak to Miss Jeremiah please!' shrieked Bhola into the receiver, his head ready to burst with rapture. 'I'm calling from school! My name is Anthony!'

For the Annual English Elocution Competition, he chose the most emotionally-charged passage from Patrick Henry's 'Give Me Liberty, Or Give Me Death.' Miss Jeremiah was amused. 'A funny poem would suit you better,' she decided.

He was hurt. 'But Miss, I want to do a serious piece.'

'What nonsense.' She indulgently uncrossed her thighs and poked through their Poetry book. 'Here, do "The Owl Critic."'

They argued a little. She won after a slap or two. Snivelling throughout, he, with appropriate dramatic gestures, recited the stanzas. The class and Miss Jeremiah snickered from beginning to end but not at the poem. So he phoned Miss Armpit that afternoon from home.

It was a pattern that he sustained for several months. Whenever she was sarcastic and violent in class, and later, when anyone offended him in any way, when *anything* went wrong, if he didn't get tickets for a movie or he cut his finger while sharpening a pencil with a razor blade, he would call her and say, 'Good afternoon, Miss, how is your armpit today?' or one of its variations. He would disconnect immediately, for he could not bear to hear her stridently demand his identity for fear that he would wilt into giving himself away. Thereafter, in the classroom or the corridor, or on the stairs, whenever he met her, passed her or sensed her, he played out his sham life with aplomb, with eyes, now a little crafty, turned away when he greeted her, terribly conscious of the down of adolescence on his upper lip.

Bhola's concern with weight loss dates from round about the time of his infatuation with Miss Jeremiah. It could have been called a phase in his growing up had it not remained a hub of his life for virtually the next twenty-five years.

As part of his weight loss programme, he began to jog clandestinely after dark, wildly, stumblingly, over footpath and across main street and neighbourhood park, not enjoying it overmuch, harried by a stray dog or two, observed en passant by itinerant vendors of fruit, and pickles and papad, in a hurry to finish before he was discovered. He was determined that no one must know. To reveal a desire to be physically trim was to confess to shame and inadequacy and to be laughed at. Any exercise in the morning was ruled out by the school bus that arrived at bloody 6.40. With friends, he snacked the expected mammoth amounts but at home, after some weeks, even his stepmother remarked on the self-disciplined frugality of his diet. He had to admit, though, that the food at home—invariably of the day before, cold, smelling of cockroach shit, served in steel plates on last week's newspapers by a depressingly unsexy middle-aged female servant with red teeth and paan breath—the food at home helped him in his efforts not to overeat.

He lost weight for twenty-five years but was never content. When, at the age of twenty-two, he learnt that muscle weighs more than fat, he was torn for months between muscle gain and weight loss. No matter what he tried apart from jogging—swimming, situps, cycling, pushups, walking with weights, chinups—there always remained a tyre around his waist and pale blobs on his thorax. The girth of his chest never exceeded that of his hips. His torso remained a cylinder and never became a vee. When, at the age of nineteen, he first read Marlowe's *Dr Faustus*, he felt that he himself would quite willingly have sold his soul to the devil in return for some divine pectorals. All shapes more attractive than his own galled him. Even the ridiculous Dosto with his swimmer's body became an object of subtle envy. In the school changing rooms, as Dosto flexed himself before the mirrors and drew the attention of the world to the ripples beneath his skin, Bhola behind him noticed the hideous contrast with the dollops of fat on his own body and saw his reflection become a distorted, watchful and depressed double image.

Do not eat when you are not hungry. It took him years to formulate his first axiom of weight loss. Rather, he didn't have to formulate it; it crept up and revealed itself instead, honed and polished, when he was ready for it. It was admittedly easier to follow at the dinner table at home than elsewhere. Its simplicity and profundity struck him with renewed, epiphanic force each time that he reflected on it. In the ensuing decades, three to four times a month, he wished to have it tattooed in obverse on his forehead so that he could focus on its wisdom while shaving. Do not eat when you are not hungry.

He was puzzled—one of the thousand things that puzzled him was—how people who had clearly not believed in the axiom for a second had turned out nevertheless to be sexually so arousing—Miss Jeremiah, for example. Conversely, it was also curious that after much strenuous self-denial, one could well become slim without becoming irresistible. One simply became more acceptable to oneself, that was all. That was important, but that was all. Besides, in the case of Miss Jeremiah, what was even more baffling was how no one else seemed to desire her in his hard, self-abasing way. For Dosto and the others, their lust for her appeared to be cursory and comic. Either they quite genuinely preferred the slim women in girlie magazines or they dissimulated. For Bhola, in contrast, the second most erotic experience of his life till that point— almost rivalling the moment when he, aged seven, had seen for the first time and fondled the blood-red cord that wound itself around the abdomen of the family cook and factotum and dangled down to run through his pierced foreskin—the second most memorable event had been trailing in a trance Jeremiah on the school picnic day in the Jahanpanah Public

Gardens, hypnotised by her hips swaying like a duck's in skintight white slacks, he as helpless and out of control as one of the stray dog suitors around a bitch on heat in a neighbourhood rubbish dump.

It was a relief, though, that Miss Jeremiah was female. At last, within him had kindled longing for a woman—even though Miss Jeremiah's womanliness was really quite open to question. He felt as though huge shutters within his mind had been flung open to let in miles and miles of guiltless blue sky. His lust for Anthony hadn't disappeared; instead, it had been complemented, given a certain depth to. It looked as though desire for woman was the next phase in life's progress after a temporary retardation and further, that it represented the sunny side of existence because, as the months passed into years, Bhola, analysing himself, remarked that his physical longing for Anthony or one of his sort—a bus conductor or an itinerant ear-cleaner—was strongest when he himself was in a blue or black mood.

Gradually, his programme of weight loss expanded— much like dawn mist on a hill road sending out white feelers amongst branches, around lamp posts, over cars—to cover his entire existence. The maxim that one should shed what one does not need implies that one should tend well what one does. Money just for the sake of it did not interest him, but it was never to be sneered at. So he began to keep painstakingly accurate accounts of every paisa of his pocket money—and later his earnings—that he spent. Ditto for every minute of his waking hours, for time was a platinum Cartier watch studded with diamonds.

His first trial with maintaining a record of his weight loss programme lasted two days. On sheets of plain paper every evening before going to bed, he parcelled out the day to come. To fit everything in, he noted down that he would have to wake up at four in the morning. Bhanu, his elder brother, came upon his schedule just when Bhola in bed was breathing deeply, with his abdomen, as a countdown to deep sleep.

4–4.20: Walk on grass, barefoot, briskly and bouncingly
4.20–4.30: Pray to the sun

'There is no sun, arsehole, at 4.30 in the morning! And if your alarm clock—or *you* wake me up while banging into things in the middle of the night, I'll simply fuck you.'

On the third day, Bhola's stepmother nudged him out of bed at six twenty-five, just in time for him to dampen and plaster down his hair, put on his uniform and scamper off for the school bus, his shoes in one hand and a sandwich in the other. Being woken up more than two hours after the alarm clock had rung felt so much nicer that he realized with relief that he would have to be firmer with himself while drawing up his wild plans for a more disciplined life.

Dosto introduced him to chain letters, that is to say, Bhola received one in the post and correctly deduced that it had come from him.

Do you want to be fit and worthy for the man or woman of your dreams? Do you want him or her to think of you with as much longing as you feel for him or her? Are you tired of being alone even in your dreams? Then post this letter!!! Instantly type or write in your own hand and post copies of this letter to ten people you know who need love! Do not hesitate. It is the chance of a lifetime to improve your life!

Hey Jude! Don't make it bad! This wisdom comes to you all the way from Brazil. You can't buy me love but you can win it by correctly interpreting your dreams. A forty-year-old in Nairobi posted ten letters within a week of receiving one himself and within ten days, his childhood

*sweetheart phoned him out of the blue after twenty years to
state that she was on the verge of a divorce and could they
have lunch somewhere next Thursday?*

*A thirty-seven-year-old woman in Manila threw her
copy of this letter in the wastepaper basket and that same
evening, caught her maid trying on her—the mistress's—
fancy lingerie before the latter's admiring husband.*

*So go ahead, stoop low and take the plunge! Post these
ten letters to win peace of mind and the man or woman or
humble servant of your dreams! Remember, in the words of
the Guhyasamaja Tantra, that perfection can be gained by
satisfying all one's desires!*

'How does this shit work? Is it your dad's Postal
Department that's organizing it or what?'

'I don't know,' confessed Dosto, 'but you can't send one
back to me. That's against the rules.'

Bhola made terrible, amateurish copies on his father's
typewriter and sent them to Dosto's mother, father, Anthony,
Jeremiah, his own elder brother and some of those teachers
and classmates whom Dosto had not included in his own
mailing list. Next day, no doubt as a consequence, he had a
bizarre sexual experience.

On the way back home from the school bus stop in the
afternoon, alone because his elder brother had stayed back for
cricket practice, in the dead, dusty open space between the
milk booth and the Community Centre open-air badminton
court, he met a sadhu, the sort of person who makes one
marvel at the variety of homo sapiens as a species.

It was a hot day early in April. There was no other living
thing in sight except the two of them and a stray dog sighing
under a tree. The sadhu, short, slim, dark, bearded, was
dressed entirely in yellow—turban, kurta, lungi—and carried
a yellow shoulder bag. Three rows of beads and one reptile
garlanded his neck. The fingers of his left hand played with

a red cord as with a rosary. Its other end disappeared behind his kurta.

He accosted Bhola with some holy gibberish. He had full, purple lips and even teeth. He was so verbose that Bhola wasn't even sure whether he was being asked for alms... 'Just as the space within a jar, my child, does not differ from the space without, so the individual soul is identical with the Universal...' He held Bhola's hand to prevent him from escaping and asked him why he at so young an age looked so sad. To cheer him up, he twined the cord in his other hand around Bhola's index finger.

'Pull it with love in your heart, have pure thoughts and you will see a miracle.'

Automatically, with his mind elsewhere, trying to pin down a memory of childhood that had been stirred like some brute creature beneath the mud of a lake, Bhola tugged at the cord as at the string of a kite. Out from behind the folds of the lungi emerged a rather phallic-looking leathery cosh into the edge of the tip of which had been pierced a golden ring through which passed the red cord. Instantaneously he recalled his first love, Gopinath the family cook, and realized that the cosh *was* the sadhu's phallus with a perforated foreskin. With a grunt of surprise, he jerked the cord off his finger, stepped past the sadhu and strode rapidly on towards home. His chance acquaintance, comfortably keeping pace two steps behind, followed him, continuing his discourse in sonorous Hindi.

'Whatever are you running away from? Friendship between strangers is more beautiful than the love act—which indeed it resembles in its give and take. Our savants have often noted that the giver has to first make ready the taker, exactly like the woman in the love act, whose arousal has poetically been compared to luring a pet snake out of a hole by offering it milk.' They crossed the badminton court and began to scurry along the boundary wall of the Central Government dispensary. They passed children in the uniform of some other school grouped around the cart of an ice-cream vendor. 'The intensity of friendship can even be measured by how far the snake moves out from the hole. Of course, it can enjoy the milk even with its body halfway out of its lair.' Bhola was scared but a minute part of him nevertheless noted that his pursuer's breathing had become audible. Something cold and clammy touched his right elbow. Emitting a squeak of fear, he rounded the corner of the dispensary wall and began to run. His school haversack bounced up and down on his back like a rider holding on for dear life to a runaway horse. The sadhu appeared to pick up pace too. The exertion of the chase fortunately seemed to prevent him from lengthening his discourse. Bhola involuntarily slowed down a fraction at the gate of his house, realized at the last minute that in the circumstances he simply couldn't enter, stumbled in his hesitation, righted himself and continued on.

Dosto had a joke, he remembered haphazardly, about a man whose penis was so long that he had to wrap it round his neck like a muffler or a snake and have its mouth pout out between two buttons of his shirt like a pink carnation; at a party, a society lady admired the flower—'Oh what a beauty!' she exclaimed—and lightly stroked it with her painted fingernail and that's how the man strangled himself to death.

Bhola was running in the heat without purpose. There was nobody following him. He slowed down a little on sighting Makhanlal's cigarette shop—a three-by-two hot plywood box plastered over with posters of Hindi film actresses that had rippled in the heat, festooned with garlands of empty packets of foreign cigarette brands. He slowed because, seeing Makhanlal's swarthy and venal face puffed up in the heat, he suddenly felt real and safe. Before he even turned to check, he knew—because his back felt free—that the sadhu had slid back into the yellow afternoon. All at once, there remained no cause for alarm, so to ignore his feeling haywire, he ran up to the cigarette kiosk as Alan Davidson the great Australian cricketer and pelted down a perfect left-arm outswinger that snicked the off bail and the follow-through of which brought him up against the enormous brass tub in which floated Makhanlal's paan leaves.

'Six for forty-four, boss Makhanlalji.' How aghast his father would be to hear him chat in so friendly a manner with someone of the lower orders but he liked debasing himself. The forty-four was a meaningless addition tacked on for the pleasure of hearing the music of the jargon of cricket. At the end of the day, bowling unchanged from the Maidan end, Sonny Ramadhin had given away just forty-four runs for his six wickets. For Bhola and his elder brother—the single interest in fact that they shared—the joy of cricket lay entirely in its statistics and esoteric vocabulary. Nineteen for ninety. For years, gooseflesh had tingled Bhola's skin whenever he had heard either number, for both had recalled cricket's greatest bowling performance ever, that of Jim Laker of England in 1956 when he had taken nineteen Australian wickets out of a possible twenty. For a brief insane period, in class tests in Sanskrit and Maths, Bhola had even deliberately written one wrong answer so that he could get nineteen marks out of twenty.

Makhanlal therefore correctly understood that with some of his pocket money, Bhola wanted to buy six loose cigarettes, Wills Filter Navy Cut. The boy lit up with the help of the booth's makeshift lighter, a smouldering cord that dangled along the edge of the plywood wall. 'Don't inhale when you light your fag,' Dosto had time and again advised him, 'breathing in the fumes of the burning jute or hemp or whatever of the rope gives you cancer.' In turn, Bhola had counselled him not to smoke in public when in his school uniform. 'You are an arsehole but your school is not,' he had elaborated when Dosto had continued to look blank. Ignoring his own precept, he leaned against the gulmohar tree that gave the kiosk its shade, contemplated the lane of houses, lying straight before him, up which he and the sadhu had sprinted together—or so he had imagined—and drew prodigiously on his cigarette to impress any passerby with his Marlboro manliness. The snake's cold, hard-fat body had kissed his elbow, of that he was certain, but of not much else, particularly since everything in front of him looked so dull and normal, the blind white houses that shut out the sulphur-coloured afternoon, the Ambassador taxi—an old, black-and-yellow oven—parked under a tree, a servant boy in pyjamas and sleeveless vest ambling at snail's speed on an errand. He shuddered despite the heat. With the next puff, however, the cigarette smoke caught his throat and made him feel both nauseous and high. He could visualize the sadhu and himself spurt up the lane as in a relay race; he was distracted then by his own particular version of the relay, in which the runner behind had to touch the anus of the one ahead before the second could go full pelt.

The sadhu had been both sexy and scary; Bhola dreamed and daydreamed of him for months. His mouth widened to engulf and suck on Bhola's skull and at the end of the red cord jerked a fat, rigid snake, its sausage tongue twitching in and out like the head of a penis. The sadhu joined the circus that had been performing nonstop in Bhola's head for the last several years. Its lead performers included Gopinath the cook, Anthony, Jeremiah, a couple of others and sometimes even Dosto in his swimming costume. They all uniformly behaved far more outrageously than they would have in real life. Each of them had his or her characteristic, typical setting but the stage that Bhola most favoured, on to which all his fantasy lovers eventually drifted, was the rooftop terrace, where, in the company of Gopinath, he had spent some of the most contented evenings of his life.

If the next day was a holiday or if his father and stepmother were out, then after dinner and after the cook—his de facto ayah—had cleared up, Bhola, then aged seven, tense with anticipation, would accompany him to the terrace to be with him and watch him unwind.

He had been a gentle and restful soul, Gopinath, with the modesty not of a maiden—in whom the trait is partly two-faced—but of a drug addict in whose brain the parts that relate to coquetry, ardour and avarice have been smoked dry by hashish. Gopinath needed nothing. Bhola would sit in his cot and watch him slowly change into another being, but one who exhibited all the characteristics of the cook simply in a more honed form. Humming, not very tunefully, to himself, he would first squat on the floor, burn a black ball of hashish to soften it, knead it into a palmful of tobacco, fill a clay pipe with the mixture and then, with a sigh and a creak of surprise from his knees, stand up to stroll about on the terrace to smoke it. Fitfully, he would continue to warble and croon snatches of lyric—folksy refrains, with an air about them of festival song sung in chorus—and, after he had finished his pipe, to dance a step or two to their beat, one pace forward, a half-step sideways, a flick of the wrist, a soft clap, a gentle pirouette, second foot forward. He would rest in a squat on the jute mat alongside the cot, completely immobile on his haunches. After a while, he would wash his hands, feet, face and neck at the cistern and courteously suggest to Bhola that they should descend because it was bedtime.

'I want to stay here with you. Teach me how to dance?'

Gopinath would chuckle away the proposal. He had a warm, gap-toothed smile in a manly face. His sparse hair was grey. His manner, however, and the way in which he carried himself had a woman's rhythm. It embarrassed Bhola dreadfully to hear his friends in the neighbourhood refer to Gopinath as a eunuch but on those occasions, he, scared that his face would disclose his infatuation, dutifully snickered the loudest.

'What does he have in his pyjamas? Have you tried to look?'

When he did, he hadn't meant to, not premeditatedly. A bridge tournament had taken his father and stepmother to Gwalior and they were to return the following morning. Gopinath had been instructed to sleep indoors with the boys but Bhola's elder brother, half-delirious at the opportunity, had decided to spend the night at a friend's house.

'Okay, sure, don't be silly, why should I snitch to them?'

Bhola fell asleep on Gopinath's cot on the roof. He was woken up in the wee hours by the cold and a squadron of fighter-pilot mosquitoes. The cook dozed on the jute mat on the floor. The crotch of his pyjamas was a white hillock and his shirt had ridden up to reveal the hair on his abdomen. Still scratching the bites around his ankles and elbows, Bhola descended to kneel beside him. His palm brushed against the hillock. He whimpered with impatience while fumbling with Gopinath's pyjama strings. He first pulled the wrong string, then the right string the wrong way and actually added another knot which he then tightened by yanking vigorously at both strings. He wanted to snip them open and then plunge the scissors deep into the full abdomen. Not caring whether the cook awoke, he crouched over his waist and tore at the strings with his teeth. One canine was almost wrenched out of his mouth. Unrewarded, aroused yet depressed, with aching jaws, he halfheartedly tugged the pyjamas down and, not having reckoned with those full-bellied adults who loosen their nightwear to breathe more freely during sleep, was taken aback to have Gopinath's loins pop into view, dramatically, like a black breakfast sausage—with accompaniments—produced by a magician. It was then that he noticed properly for the first time the red cord that he had seen a thousand times before around the cook's waist, how it descended to pass through a demure golden ring that pierced the foreskin of a tumescent penis. Entranced, the boy settled down beside the sleeping figure to observe, examine and then play horsey-horsey with the red cord, to pluck at it and

watch the phallus prance. When, without warning, sleep
swamped him, he caved in in a heap alongside the object of
his calf love, a hand reposeful on the other's hairy stomach.

Gopinath disappeared from Bhola's life some six months
after. He went home on his biennial leave to his village a
thousand kilometres away and never returned. Everyone
pined for his cooking. His substitute, a middle-aged female
by the name of Phorania, a paan addict, red-toothed,
tuberculous and periodically jolly, cooked well only when she
felt that she had been adequately praised for her previous
efforts. If only I could remember one of the tunes that
Gopinath used to hum and dance to on the terrace, thought
a frantic Bhola for several weeks, he will return. His
stepmother's explanation, that Gopinath needed to be
physically present in his village to prevent his brothers from
doing him out of his rights to their father's nine square inches
of land, was incomprehensible.

It continued to be so even when Bhola grew up,
experienced at first hand life in a typical Indian village and
became old enough to ruminate on the human need to sink
one's roots somewhere and other such questions. For his own
part, ever since the age of seventeen, when he had left home
for college without experiencing any unbearable pangs, he
seemed to have felt most at home in inconspicuous and
unfamiliar railway stations and later, in the transit lounges of
shabby airports. Not seeing it as a deficiency, he blamed
nobody for his rootlessness. He had been born and had grown
up in the new residential areas of a city that themselves had
not been older than him. They had no history. From the day
that man had been some kind of tadpole till the nineteen
sixties, they appeared to have remained wild pasture lands,
dotted with dung, for stray malnourished cattle. They had
been prettier untamed, though. Gopinath's attachment to a
dot of land that in quality must not have been noticeably
different was puzzling. Better to reign in one hell than serve

in another was one reasoning that offered itself. Bhola acknowledged that the matter was more complicated than his analysis of it but in the initial months, he had sorely missed the cook and had felt bitter at not seeing any sign of reciprocal affection.

Gopinath was illiterate and had to have his two letters a year written for him. Even Bhola at the age of eight and then nine was appalled at the quality of literacy and the penury of thought exhibited in them. They were postcards on which the letters of the alphabet—large, ugly, staggering drunkenly in all directions—had been etched by a ball point pen seemingly wielded as a knife. *I am well* (even when he wasn't, naturally). *I trust and pray that God has kept you and the family in good health,* by which time, mercifully, the end of the card had been reached. Actual news was conveyed by means of manic, almost indecipherable, scribbling around its edges, resembling an embroidered border for the benevolence expressed in the main text.

'Can't we go and visit him?'

'What a funny idea. Whatever for?'

To learn that tune, responded Bhola silently and despondently.

He did visit Gopinath, they eloped and lived together, he became his servant's servant and his cook's cook, all in the prodigious and enduring fantasy that he, in haphazard fashion over the ensuing years, detailed in the back pages of his school exercise books, in the unused diaries that his father gave him for his Maths roughwork and in the hand-me-down class texts that he inherited from his elder brother and that became obsolete by the time that he was ready to use them because the syllabus had changed in the meantime. *Pater*— Baba became Pater and Ma Mater; the elder brother was erased out of existence—*came into the room and caught Bhola in Gopi's arms. He was horrified. 'Let go of my son instantly!' he shouted at the servant. 'I can't, sir,' retorted Gopi simply, 'for he is my life,' and holding Bhola hard till the boy felt that he would stop breathing and ascend to heaven, kissed him full on the lips. Gopi's tongue tasted of sweet paan and sweeter mango. In this way, living in the cook's ancestral mud hut in the village, Bhola became a diabetic.*

He taught Gopinath how to read and write English and how to hate Maths and Hindi. While Gopinath went off every morning to till the fields, he worked at home on his manual typewriter writing witty articles for the *Junior Statesman* and *The Illustrated Weekly Of India* that he then sent off before lunch from the village post office. The cheques and grateful notes from the editors arrived every Friday. The entire village was illiterate but cute—Malgudi-like, in brief—and undemonstratively adored its quiet adolescent who had become an internationally renowned man of letters at the age of thirteen. Bhola had no idea what tilling the fields meant and was not interested in the operation; he only demanded of it that it send Gopinath back at midday gorgeously sweating and macho so that he could then bathe and revive him.

With the appearance of Miss Jeremiah in Bhola's life, in his ever-flowing adventure chronicles, the personality and physique of Gopinath underwent some changes. Bhola's memory of him dimmed with the years, naturally; the family had no photographs or belongings of the cook to help the boy conserve and embellish the details; he thus correspondingly idealized the inexact but predominant impression that he retained of a masculine form with a maidenly bearing, brawny yet sweet-mouthed, not the eunuch of the neighbourhood but the possessor of a body that was a human mosaic of yin and yang. In his daydreams and fantasies therefore, at the height of passion, Bhola would tug at the red cord around Gopinath's abdomen, and the latter, bashfully averting his eyes but at the same time blushing with pleasure, would, through a marvel of yogic control, retract his penis and testicles to reveal a full, purple vagina.

He managed to reach the stop just in time that evening to catch the last bus to the village. He sat opposite a large fat woman whom he hadn't seen before. She wore a funny shirt and skirt and had sweat patches at the creases of her paunch. She lifted up her arms and suddenly screamed at him to come and worship her armpits.

Creating in this manner, in bits and pieces, an epic fantasy and making it swell with his longing for all sorts of odd people—divesting himself completely in it of all the indispensable comfort that one takes for granted—a home nest, the cocoon of the family, school, companions—and replacing it with a hard, harsh and hysterically sexual imagined life—that too, though Bhola didn't recognize it for years, was a weight loss programme since it helped him to lessen the load of the lumber in his head. Living would have been insupportable without the therapeutic outlet that it provided. He kept the stray pages in a maroon cardboard suitcase beneath his bed. Periodically, during some calmer moment of a still afternoon, he would sift through them and, frightfully embarrassed by their nakedness, tear into tiny bits and chuck into the garbage sheavesful of them.

'Check at home,' he whispered to Dosto during Social Studies, 'whether anyone has received any of the chain letters that I posted. They don't work. The sadhu I met yesterday is not the woman of my dreams.'

'How do you know?' countered Dosto in a louder hiss. 'That kind of shit takes time.'

'He belongs to a sect the members of which have their foreskins pierced like ears.' Bhola filled in the details during Second Break. The nuggets of information enthralled Dosto more than gold does a dowry-hunting mother-in-law-to-be.

'Even I'm going to join them and tug at my red cord all day long during class,' he vowed with shining eyes. 'Where are they headquartered?'

'How much money can you lend me?' asked Dosto in a whisper over the phone.

'I have eight rupees left over. They are to see me through till next Wednesday.'

'Can you ask your mother-in-law to lend you some?'

'You mean, stepmother,' corrected Bhola coldly. 'How much and whatever for?' He was not enthused about helping someone who used words and phrases as loosely as Dosto.

Dosto paused for dramatic effect and to muster up both courage and arguments to overwhelm Bhola's hoots of disbelief. 'About four thousand rupees.'

It was the last Thursday of February, 1973. Bhola was then fourteen and Dosto some six months older.

'Look, can't we discuss this tomorrow before Assembly? It's seven-thirty already and I've to bathe and do my homework before dinner.'

The doorbell rang at a quarter to nine. While Bhola's father wonderingly grumbled about neighbours who had absolutely no idea about social etiquette, his stepmother went to answer and demanded through the shut door an identity. Nobody answered but two minutes later, the bell rang again, briefly and softly, like the mewl of a scared cat which nevertheless has urgent business to transact.

'*Don't* open the door!' advised Bhola's father in a shout from his bed on which he had prostrated himself with his *Manusmriti* and other books, his magazines, biscuits and cups of tea ever since his return from office at six. 'It's the neighbourhood Welfare lot scouting about for donations for Holi or Shivaratri or something.'

'Or maybe the Deaf and Dumb Relief Association,' suggested Bhola and continued when no one seemed to get the point. 'You see? That's why they can't answer your question. Or a telegram to announce the death of...' He was still casting about for an appropriate personality when his stepmother unbolted the door to reveal a pale and tense Dosto.

With Bhanu, Bhola's elder brother, timorous and bilious while studying for his final exams in their common room, there was nowhere to go for a private chat other than the terrace. Under the stars and amongst the mosquitoes, Dosto finally hinted that he needed some money so that he could elope with his father's driver.

'Wow. But why four thousand?' To gain time to think, it was easier to ask the simpler questions first.

'Not exactly four, stupid,' snapped Dosto, happy to find an outlet for his anxiety, 'Just sufficient money so that Harilal can start something new.'

'What? He's quit his job?'

'My father's fired him.'

Bhola felt fearfully excited. Yet he couldn't reveal to Dosto or anyone else the welter of his thoughts. Harilal was too swarthy and dirty-looking for his taste but to run away with Gopinath had been his ardent dream for years: at the same time, he had in his heart always known it to be a fantasy, to be encouraged and toyed with only as a dream.

'Boy. Whatever for? What did he do?'

'Lots of things,' responded Dosto airily, even proudly, happy to be able to babble. 'For ages, he's been stealing petrol and selling it to some taxis. Then this morning he talked back.'

'I think you're crazy.' He glanced at Dosto's face and sensed more than saw in the dark its tragic, heroic, all-for-a-grand-passion expression. 'What'll you do about school?'

'*School*?' Dosto was again glad to be given a subject on which he could pronounce with illimitable scorn. 'Harilal's going to teach me how to drive and then we'll open a garage or something.' He abruptly heaved himself off the charpoy. 'I have to go. He is to meet me downstairs at nine-fifteen.' He stood over Bhola, raising himself up on his toes, rhythmically thwacking his left palm with his right fist. 'How much money, then, can you give me?'

'You mean you're going *now*?' Bhola struggled to stand up and make sense of the proposition. 'Do your parents know? Otherwise, they'll have that Harilal bugger arrested for kidnapping or something.'

'I've left my mother a note.'

'Yes, but does it make sense, your note?' Bhola was aware of Dosto's literary skills. 'It'll be full of spelling mistakes and grammatical errors—' he began dimly to visualize it—'and won't make any *sense*. You've probably put my name in it somewhere.' He moved to the edge of the terrace to lean on the railing and gaze down at the street lights and the lane below. 'I don't see Harilal anywhere—unless he is fondling his balls somewhere in the shadows.'

'Thanks a lot, you cheap little miser!' exploded Dosto suddenly in a loud and tearful whisper before he turned and scurried off the terrace.

'Hey, Dosto!' Bhola followed him till the head of the stairs and then peered into the well to hear the thumping of his shoes recede into its dimly lit shabbiness. He would have descended too had he not been feeling full and vaguely ill after dinner. Excited and nonplussed, he returned to the railing to watch Dosto trot off into the shadows of the lane. 'Farewell, friend, and good luck,' he dramatically whispered into the night to ease his anxiety and foreboding. He wanted to quote some famous line to applaud his friend's courage and spirit of adventure, to salute him for haring off to live out his, Bhola's, own fantasy, but he could think of nothing other than what he had last heard his father recite from *Manusmriti*; singularly inappropriate but he cited it anyway, arguing with himself that what mattered more than the chosen text was the solemn tone of delivery: 'No redemption is prescribed for a man who drinks the saliva from the lips of a servant woman or is tainted by her breath or begets a son in her.'

Timidly rang the doorbell at a quarter past ten. From the sofa in the drawing room, on which he had begun to doss down a few months after he had started to masturbate, Bhola reached the front door in a couple of leaps worthy of a ballet dancer. Dosto looked distressed and red-eyed with weeping. Bhola was overjoyed to see him.

'It's okay,' he shouted into the house at whoever might be listening, 'it's only Dosto and his parents!' Few other statements would more effectively ensure that his father and stepmother, both acutely unsocial and inhospitable beings, remain in their rooms pretending to be asleep. He put his arm around his friend's shoulder and ushered him in. 'Dosto's father has lost the key of their house,' he yelled conversationally into the dining space as he shut the door between the drawing room and the rest of the house, 'Not to worry—*they* are going to some friend's house but they were wondering whether Dosto could spend the night here!'

Dosto sat on the sofa and snivelled and blubbered and wept. Bhola perched on the armchair opposite and watched him with a mother's tenderness. Words were unnecessary; there was nothing to say. However, five minutes later, when Dosto still hadn't stopped, Bhola asked a little impatiently, 'Shouldn't you phone home?'

Sniffing and sobbing, after a pause, Dosto answered, 'In the note I've said that I was spending the night at your house.'

'God. All I need now is for Harilal to ring the bell at midnight.'

At the name of the loved one who had jilted him and made off, moreover, with a suitcase full of his things and as much of the housekeeping money as the boy had managed to lay his hands on, Dosto's features registered the pain of a fresh stab. Continuing to fuss maternally over him, Bhola settled him down on cushions on the floor. He himself slept wonderfully well that night.

At the age of fifteen, Bhola in the kitchen at home on a Saturday morning bemoaned his stepmother's strategy of never hiring any sexy servants. His entire life was to be a quest for sex on tap and on payment with females and males of the lower orders. The innumerable successors of Phorania, the red-toothed cook, had all been crones and halitotic dotards, short-tempered shirkers, negligent, slatternly and unattractive filchers of sugar, milk powder and petty cash. Bhola sipped his tea and bit into a cream biscuit covered with red ants and ruefully accepted that his stepmother's domestic policy was probably going to force him to leave the nest early.

Even though he viewed them as an additional source of protein, the ants were not a regular item of his weekend breakfast. It was just too bad for them that they had found the packet of cream biscuits. Making the best of a bad bargain was how he saw it—though within limits, of course. He wouldn't, for instance, relish a rice and lice pudding, the lice dotting the cream like black cumin, or crisp, deep fried-and-dried cockroach legs. Ants were admissible because they were clean and industrious like mindless workers in an ideal communist state. He recalled that just the previous year, when they had returned from a trip to Simla one humid July afternoon and had opened his stepmother's bedroom to find the walls damp with rain that had seeped in and the room teeming with hundreds and hundreds of black ants crawling in single file over everything, the first thing that he had been reminded of had been the luxurious English-language edition of Maxim Gorky, brought out by Progress Publishers, Moscow, that his father had recently bought—not to read, though, but to place on the drawing room shelf alongside the National Museum clay replica of the Gandhara Buddha.

The front door bell rang. He heard his father leave his newspaper and tea to get up and answer it. The caller was a woman with a reedy, supplicating voice but Bhola couldn't make out what she said. Then suddenly he heard his father raise his voice a little. Biscuits and ants in mouth, he rushed to spectate.

'Are you here as a guest? To have tea with us? This front door is not meant for vegetable vendors. Go round the back at once and don't make the mistake again.'

His father was proud of the fact that he almost never lost his temper, that he could make those not in a position to answer back tremble merely by the judicious use of his cold and controlled whip of a voice. For Bhola, observing his father's incivility with people who didn't matter was a sado-masochistic show. It was his father's way of getting back at life, at the small mess that he had made of it. As a man, he was incapable of being happy, was in fact suspicious of happiness. He considered himself a sort of stoic, impervious to both pleasure and pain; in reality, however, he was impervious only to pleasure.

The face of the vegetable vendor reddened and fell. A man in his mid-twenties stood beside her—perhaps her brother, for he seemed to have her features. The spectacle that Bhola wished to see would only start if she dropped her mask of servility and snapped back at his father; when she revealed her true coarseness in language, gesture and expression, his bowels would simply melt. But she nodded her head submissively and turned away. Bhola found the faces of the couple, brother and sister—or husband and wife, or lovers—the high cheekbones and small noses, the cheeks that stretched flat and taut to tight, round and full mouths—distractingly attractive, like an athlete's tanned, sinewy buttocks.

His father had returned to his newspaper. 'Come round the back,' beamed Bhola and gestured vaguely at the boundary wall. 'We need all the olisboi you have—gourds, green bananas, carrots.' Except for the word *olisboi*, he spoke Hindi. He had recently discovered the word in one of his father's books, an encyclopaedia on Hinduism, and loved it because it even *sounded* like a dildo. He used it often as an inventive adjunct in phrases—in Hindi, Bengali and English—and no one noticed or cared. 'Well bowled, Olisboi!' and 'Our new Chemistry teacher is called Mrs Hema Olisboi.'

On his way back to the kitchen and the rear of the house, as he passed his father in his armchair, he was thankful that things had not been worse, that his father had not forbidden completely the new vegetable vendors from selling at their gate. He could well have. He was fiercely protective of the inviolability of his house and frequently stood guard at the corner where front gate met boundary wall, ready with a handful of pebbles to throw at all those passersby who paused to piss—or even contemplate pissing—against the wall. 'Hey you,' he would hiss across it, 'button up and move on. Life is short.'

Oddly enough, though humans pissing in public was disgraceful, pet dog fucking was not. Banerjee their neighbour would often halt during his evening stroll with his mongrel on a leash to chat with Bhola's father from the lane that bordered the wall. Very often, the dog, while exploring the neighbourhood garbage dump and sometimes while still on his leash, would sniff at and subsequently mount a stray bitch after snarling the competition away. Banerjee and Bhola's father would look on while desultorily continuing to complain to each other about those of their fellow citizens who lacked civic sense.

Bhola opened the door in the rear boundary wall and waited for the vegetable vendors. The pushcart seemed far too wide and heavy even for the two of them. They struggled at the corner to turn it into the alley. A monstrous pumpkin, dislodged, landed on the ground with a dull thud. Wife squawked at husband in an unfamiliar tongue. The man enveloped the vegetable with his arms and torso and struggled to lift it up. His bony and under-nourished haunches were clearly outlined in his once-white pyjamas. Wife clumsily steered the cart through the weeds and the undergrowth, past the two open manholes and the washerman's lean-to shed and over the ruts, the stray plastic bags of refuse and the other litter that the neighbours had flung over the walls of their houses when they had felt too lazy to walk to the dump.

Her face was warm and red and she was gently panting when she pulled the cart to a stop before Bhola. The short sleeves of her blouse disclosed stout, powerful upper arms that he wouldn't have minded having himself. The patches of perspiration at her armpits extended to her breasts. With the edge of her sari, she scrubbed away at the exudation and heat on her upper lip, cheeks, neck and throat. He wanted to lick the sweat out of her cleavage, wondered how many dozens were fucking her and then felt dizzy when he thought of the moist heat in her loins.

'You are new.' Their part of the housing colony had been the territory of another vegetable vendor, a rheumy-eyed male much given to grinning and displaying his three yellow teeth.

'Yes. Kaduram now has set up shop near the municipal market beside his house. I've taken over his beat.' After a pause, to establish her bona fides, she added, 'We come from the same village.'

'And where is that?' He liked the way in which the two of them stood opposite each other, pressing with their loins against the shorter sides of the cart to keep it stationary, thus leaving their hands free to pick up a carrot or—as in the case of the man—scratch the lice in one's hair. To restrain himself from loutish conduct, Bhola briefly surveyed the diseases that he could catch from intimate contact with the couple—syphilis, hepatitis B, tuberculosis, leprosy, herpes—and what he could pass on to them in return. Incessant incontinence, probably, life was a perennially leaking tap. Otherwise, he was in the pink of health.

Her reply didn't register with him. 'On weekends, you can turn up at this backdoor whenever you want but during the week, would it be possible for you to make your rounds after four?' In response to her blank gaze, he continued, 'I'm at school till 2.30 p.m.' To make polite conversation, he then turned to the man. 'And you? Have you ever been to school?'

The man grinned bashfully and resentfully from ear to ear. Bhola in reaction pressed his loins too against the third side of the cart. 'Of course he did as a child but now he helps me. How else will I manage?' retorted the woman for him.

Bhola moved his head towards her in the hope of reaching her body odour. 'But he can read and write?' The husband nodded vigorously and several times like a puppet, an answer so emphatic that Bhola was almost certain that he couldn't. 'And you?' He turned back with his charming man-of-the-world smile to the wife.

She grinned broadly too. Her face crinkled up and her eyes became crescent gashes in the skin of an overripe banana. 'Of course. I'm Eighth Pass,' she, drawing herself up a little theatrically, retorted pertly. The phrase 'Eighth Pass' was in English.

'That's very good.' He edged sideways a step and reached out for the spinach because it was the vegetable closest to her loins. He would instantly ascend to Heaven, he knew it, in a golden chariot drawn by milk-coloured steeds if he could slip his hand, palm outward, in between the wood and her wedge. 'And where do you stay? I mean, what's your postal address?' he continued with elaborate offhandedness, holding the spinach leaves in front of his face, pushing his snout out at them and frowning critically. 'That is to say, suppose we buy some vegetables and don't have enough money to pay you just at that point. We can always send you a postal money order later in the day. And seeing that you can read and write, you can sign without any problem. Give me two bunches of these.' His hand brushed against hers as he handed over the spinach.

While she busied herself with weighing the bundles on the scales, the man, irresolutely tossing a potato from one hand to the other, answered, 'We stay with Kaduram, he being my relative, in Ambedkarpuri.' Bhola had heard of but never seen the area, a new housing colony way beyond the extreme southern suburbs created to relocate the citizens of the razed slums of the city's centre. If some of the newspapers and right-wing parties were to be believed, almost a third of the population of the colony comprised refugees from Bangladesh.

'But the house and Block numbers?' Bhola spoke to both of them but had eyes only for the subcutaneous swell in the woman's upper arms as she adjusted the kilo and five-hundred-gram weights on the scales. 'And the postal code?'

Husband and wife smirked faintly at each other. She then glanced at Bhola's face for a second before responding, 'May we tell you tomorrow? I think it's 14/443 but I'm not sure.' She heaved the spinach off the scales and set it aside. 'Would you like something else? Carrots and green bananas, you'd said.'

From the kitchen window, sharp as scissors, the voice of Bhola's stepmother nipped the formation of the ménage à trois in the bud. 'We have enough vegetables for today and tomorrow, Bhola! There isn't any more space in the fridge!'

'Spinach!' Bhola shouted back, grinning conspiratorially at the vendor woman. 'I need folic acid and iron!'

After he had got her name and address, he sent her two anonymous, handwritten love letters in Hindi. They were a challenge. They made him sweat. For one, no English-to-Hindi dictionary was available at home.

'We don't need one,' snorted his father. 'Ask your teacher or better still, ask me. Anyone with any knowledge of Sanskrit can clear your elementary doubts.'

Ram the back of my head against the edge of your cart with your wedge. Smash the bridge of my nose with the disdainfully powerful thrusts of your pussy muscles while my palms palpate with trembling adulation your breathtaking buttocks. While olisboi topple all around me, let me, inhaling the aroma of your vagina, swoon into oblivion.

Bhola had no idea—and didn't much care—whether the letters ever reached her, whether she read them or— acknowledging the abysmal level of her own literacy—had them read out to her by a genuinely lettered neighbour, whether she understood them, or they amused, embarrassed and angered her. He saw her and the man four or five times a week for about a month. After four in the afternoon, they would wheel their cart down the back alley, clanging, to announce their arrival, the spokes of the cart's bicycle wheels with the aluminium curtain rod that they used to shoo stray monkeys away.

By that time of day, both they and the produce on offer looked the worse for wear but that of course did not matter. Bhola gave them cold water from the fridge and bought with his pocket money some sad-looking vegetable or the other that he later placed before the cook of the month as an item in his weight loss programme.

'These turnips are rotten,' she would announce, ready to fling them into the garbage and later, surreptitiously, to retrieve them and take them home under her sari.

'Roughage. Boil them, covered, in salt water on a low fire for an hour. Don't look at them, don't criticise them, just boil them.' At the dinner table, on the rare occsions when the family ate together, he even impressed his father with the relish with which he munched the boiled olisboi of the day. A concern for his own well-being was a sign of maturity in the boy.

The vendor team of husband and wife was unfailingly glad to see him and seemed to enjoy the roles that it played with him. To his lustful smiles and ardent eyes, they reacted by bashfully simpering, giggling, turning their gaze away and tenderly overcharging him. 'You buy too little,' the woman would deferentially chide him, 'never enough for the whole family.' Then she would extract a tiny purse from somewhere in her blouse and he would imagine that he could smell on its faded cloth surface, and the petty notes inside it, her breast sweat.

'They are terrible meateatarians, what to do.' For a certain sum of money and if he made the right moves, she would lie down and lift up her sari and he could lose his bloody virginity, of that he was sure but not of how much money and what moves. Now he freely touched their hands and forearms during their exchanges, thumped the man between his shoulder blades, squeezed his waist in brotherly affection and tested his Maths by lobbing sums at him. Their camaraderie was in some senses even more fulfilling than sex because it was comparatively innocent and therefore increasingly uninhibited; further, sex with wife or husband or both together was likelier to be more explosive in his head than in reality. He was thus after a fashion content with his day—the Jeremiahs, Tolarams and Anthonies during school hours and then the afternoon to look forward to.

On the first Monday of May, he waited and waited but didn't hear the clanging on the bicycle wheels. He opened the rear door a dozen times in fifteen minutes but all that he saw were the wrinkled, swollen and exploded plastic bags of garbage and the undergrowth of the back alley incinerated a dead brown by the sun. He rushed up to the terrace and surveyed the neighbourhood in forty-three degrees Celsius. O God, where the fuck are they? he asked himself as his bowels became hollow and cold. An accident. Illness, heatstroke. It could not be that they had decided to bypass the back alley because they'd felt that the few rupees that they picked up from Bhola were simply not worth the effort. He scanned the suburban middle-class houses, the grey trees and the parks the colour of dust for three more days. He started at every sound from the street. He was the first to reach the front door when the bell rang. It was incredible that there was nobody in the locality whom he could ask except Makhanlal the cigarette seller—and him he didn't want to because he would never be able to keep his longing and his anxiety from showing on his face. And at home, he was both irritated and relieved that no one noticed that he hadn't had his boiled vegetables for four days. Of course, the vegetable vendors had entered his diary within a week of his making their acquaintance; they had stayed a while in the hut with him and Gopinath, but that was a poor substitute for meeting them in the flesh.

On Thursday evening, before his father and stepmother returned from office, he set off on his bicycle for Ambedkarpuri. He had often spotted public buses with Ambedkarpuri Bus Terminus written on them and he vaguely knew in which direction to go. He liked adventures up to a point, and particularly when he had finished whatever he had to during the day. It took him a little less than an hour to reach the outskirts of the suburb and he was almost mowed down twice in that period, once by a truck laden with water coolers and the second time—when he asked a cyclist while overtaking him whether he was headed the right way—by a white government car. Both times, he was more scared of how angry his father would be were he to find out—through the police, to boot—just how far—and on what dangerous thoroughfares—his son had gone traipsing about on his bicycle. It was fun, though, to weave one's way through cycles, mopeds, cattle, autorickshaws, bullock carts, motorbikes, cars, two-wheeler scooters, horse-drawn tongas, minivans, pushcarts, pedestrians, buses, trucks and one procession of elephants.

Ambedkarpuri was ugly, dirty, crowded, smelly and unfinished. Bhola felt that people looked at him strangely because they knew that he did not belong and that they leered at him because they knew the purpose of his visit. Navigating a course past the whisking tails of buffalo, the multicoloured wires of varying widths dangling like festival decorations from illegal electricity connections strung across the lanes, the residual mounds of earth from permanently incomplete road repairs, the dung and excrement, the hawkers of peanuts, popcorn and icecream, the cyclists and the several varieties of two-wheelers, he diffidently searched for the objects of his desire.

'14/443?' He couldn't remember what 43 was in Hindi, so he very soon began enquiring for 450 instead. 'Lane 14? House Number 450?'

Nobody that he asked seemed sure. 'Which Sector?' demanded a paanwala quickly in return, like a debater scoring a point off his opponent, his hands busy all the while spreading lime on six paan leaves ranged evenly before him like playing cards.

'Sector?' repeated Bhola with sinking heart. 'I don't know. I didn't think there were sectors.'

Without a word, the paanwala with his limestick pointed the way down the alley into the bowels of heaven.

Those were the hot and squalid byways where Bhola had always longed to be, amidst the low life when it was at last itself—on a string cot, for instance, cuddling up to three men, two in sleeveless vests and string drawers, smoking and playing cards, the third barebodied, displaying sad and scrawny muscles, intently shaving his armpits and intermittently scratching his balls. The women, hair all awry, some in blouses and petticoats, washed clothes and vessels at a communal tap; others, screeching small talk at one another, ferried buckets and pots of water back to their ten-foot-wide but three-storey houses, newly built but already threatening to fall in on the alley, their walls painted in once-bright colours, mustard, green, livid red, rose. Transistor radios and tape recorders everywhere caterwauled terribly happy Hindi film music. Imaginatively designed signboards, placards and handbills—with some of the flavour of popular art—hammered above doors and pasted atop the Municipal Corporation roadmaps, advertised the offerings of dhabas and the services of tailors, plumbers, barbers, masons, repairers of all music systems, electricians, exclusively ladies' tailors, carpenters and masseurs. Lanes sliced one another with bewildering disorderliness; overhead, fat black wires crisscrossed from building to pole to dead tree trunk as though providing a model for the chaos below. Domesticated street dogs, stray pigs, a goat or two, wandered about everywhere, around overflowing rubbish dumps and under the awnings of food stalls; naked urchins excreted into open drains and then used its black, viscous water to wash themselves. Everyone—adult, infant, stranger—gazed at him with unabashed curiosity. Some grinned, eyebrows raised enquiringly. To those he found attractive, he swathed his way up through the fleas, flies and mosquitoes, smiling and blushing, to ask for directions. He did not receive any that were of help. 14/443 did not exist. Lane 14 seemed to stop at 384B but it did not matter. He had had his dose of the lower orders—indeed, had almost forgotten the purpose of his visit.

With his fetish for hierarchy and gradation, he wished, on his way back from Ambedkarpuri, to rate the ten sexiest people that he had seen in it. Eventually, a brazen-eyed matron baking rotis at a tandoor and an almost-adult male torturing his dog tied for the first slot. She had had jet-black eyes—the colour of night, of hell and knowledge—a swollen, domineering face, purple puffed-up lips, and while sitting, legs splayed like tree trunks, beside the gaping mouth of the clay oven, had abruptly lifted up the edge of her kameez to fan herself and then, indulgently, with a couple of beringed, bloated fingers, half-scratched, half-massaged through her salwaar her vagina. The adolescent, in contrast, had been underdressed in just faded green underwear. He had repeatedly dragged out from under the cot his pet, a well-fed, even sleek, off-white mongrel and, in requital for some misdeed, thrashed it savagely with his slipper. The bulge in his underwear had seemed to grow with each wallop.

'A seller of vegetables and her husband. He seems a bit retarded. They owe us some money. Their names are Titli and Moti and they stay with Kaduram in 14/450. Perhaps you know them? Know why they haven't done their rounds these last few days?'

The eyes of Bhola's interlocutors would flicker momentarily at hearing the word 'money' but for the rest, they remained completely apathetic. Titli and Moti sank slowly and sadly down to the seabed of his memories.

At sixteen, Bhola, a few months before he was to pass out of school, got thrown out of it. For a variety of reasons, he had been going through a bad patch for quite a while. He regretted for one having picked two years ago Economics instead of Biology as his first optional subject. At the time of choice, while he had been hesitating, Dosto had scornfully protested, 'Are you crazy? Biology types have to stay *back* after school *three* times a week to cut open frogs and sniff their gonads while Economics types are flown to Bombay once a term to be wined and dined by the captains of industry.'

'Only people like you who don't have the marks for Bio take Eco.'

In the end, a reluctance to remain behind with several bespectacled, turnip-headed classmates after his friends had left, waving, on the school bus—and that too three out of five days a week—tilted the balance in favour of Economics, a subject that eventually bored him so much that for the rest of his life, his mind became the calm ocean within the being of some Himalayan ascetic the instant that it heard, read, saw or sensed the terms deficit finance, demand graph, marginal utility, diminishing returns, inflationary spiral and value added cost.

He, feeling that he had outgrown his friends and their concerns, also suffered at that stage of his life the routine pains of adolscence. His sexual life—that it took up so much of his thoughts without getting him anywhere—appalled him. He felt depressed that pusillanimity restrained him from making an irremediable pass at some improbable person, from taking other similar steps to set his sexual career off the mark and rollicking away on some uncontrollable rollercoaster ride; at the same time, he was also downcast by the inescapable quality of bizarreness in the people who attracted him sexually. Nobody else, he was certain, would ever find them appealing in the same way. Consequently, he couldn't even discuss his sexual itches with anyone. His desires, several dozens of them, were his dark secrets. The latest in the list was an old eunuch, one of a group that had barged in past the gate one hot afternoon in search of gifts, tips and donations. They were black, loud and menacing and their leader had chucked him under the chin the moment he had opened the front door. Somehow the heat and his own boredom had prevented him from being intimidated.

'Hallo pretty boy.' The first one, in an orange, see-through-because-wet-with-sweat salwar kameez, rested his outstretched arm on the doorpost not far from Bhola's shoulder. 'No one home?'

'No, there's only me,' and added in a murmur to himself in English, 'just daydreaming about being buggered.' It was the third eunuch who held his attention. He was tall and rangy, ebony-coloured, in a dark green blouse and light green nylon sari pulled tight across his flat buttocks. He, puffing away at a bidi, hovered near the gate as though on guard. His eyes were large, black and kohl-ringed, his nose sharp, straight, perfect, the sort that one would demand of plastic surgery. The lipstick on his full lips was an outrageous pink.

'Where's the child?'

'Whose? I'm the only child that I know of in the area.'

Bhola responded with his eyes on the eunuch at the gate and wondered what there was under that green sari. A hairy scrotum and a purple scar in lieu of the penis chopped off in infancy?

Who wrote the bestseller *Russian Torture*? *Ivan Kutyokokoff*.

According to Dosto, they let you peep at a price. How to ask? Particularly with the cook snoring on the floor not thirty feet away.

Feeling no doubt that he wasn't being paid enough attention, the eunuch at the door lightly ran his fingers across Bhola's cheek and throat. Bhola moved back a little, taken aback at being titillated. The eunuch smelt of a kind of incense, sweet and heavy, vaguely familiar, nudging a memory in him. 'Is the baby that's just been born yours?' he asked with a smile. Some orange lipstick had stained his teeth. 'We've come to bless it and to share in your good fortune.'

'I'm not married.' Bhola resolved to try on one of his stepmother's bras at the next opportunity to see how it felt when you didn't need one. He would have liked to amble over to the gate and chat up the eunuch in green but feared that if he abandoned the doorpost, the others would slip into the house and start their hideously raucous clapping and singing.

'Ohhhh so sad. Why aren't you married?' enquired the second eunuch, shorter, balder, bulbous-nosed, scratching his navel, his pupils like huge full stops in a red lake fringed by fronds tinged silver-grey by eyeshadow.

'Who would marry me? No money.'

'Why, I'd marry you. We all would marry you.' The second eunuch, grinning broadly, stepped forward like a suitor. The other two contributed exaggerated affirmative nods, seductive sighs, a winsome smile, a voluptuous lurch against the doorpost. Bhola caught the acrid tang of sweat compounded with older sweat.

Almost reflexively, he retorted, virtually snapped back, as

though trying to keep them at bay, 'But who would marry *you*?'

'Who'd marry me?' asked the first eunuch of the second, looking around at his partners, for the moment nonplussed by the adolescent's composure.

Bhola hurriedly changed the topic. 'I thought that you only collected money to bury your sister eunuchs,' he opened, instantly wondering whether 'bury' and 'sister' should have been 'cremate' and 'brother' instead.

The first eunuch yawned hugely, flashing his tonsils. 'One sister of ours did pass away day before yesterday. We need funds for that too.'

The second eunuch, sensing that Bhola was about to retreat and shut the door, suddenly reached forward and lightly patted his crotch—'Just checking the growing boy's needs,' he simpered—and then pulled his lungi away. Exaggerated exclamations of pleasure and awe followed; then they all mockingly but tenderly praised his tumescence. For the seconds that he stood naked in front of them, he was embarrassed but also faintly thrilled. Before he could close the door, the first eunuch pressed his fingers to his own lips and then touched them to Bhola's mouth. Bhola again felt humiliated by the tremors of his response.

Three days later, on Monday, he still had not fully recovered from the eunuchs. At school, Economics at twelve noon was succeeded by Sports. Between the two, he hurriedly smoked three cigarettes—his first taste of Craven A—behind the basketball courts with a couple of the wicked boys and felt both nauseous and an urge to shit. Anthony had over the years picked up an Assistant in the Sports Department, male, Rath by name, bulky and handsome despite being frog-eyed, but so dull that Bhola disliked him because it was a waste of good looks to gift them to a grey cow.

So there stood Bhola at twelve-thirty, on the fringes of his disorderly class, undecided about which of the two games on offer, basketball or softball, he detested less, daydreaming still about the eunuch in green, wishing that he hadn't smoked, wanting to excrete and to throw up and trying to will both the urges to disappear.

Without warning, Rath began barking at the class to range itself in some sort of order. Immediately, with comparable suddenness, as though startled into losing control by the abruptness with which Rath himself had lost his calm, Bhola's sphincter threatened to give way. Mumbling an excuse that nobody heard, he turned and stumbled off in the direction of the school buildings. Three steps later, realizing that he would never be able to reach the toilets there in time, he turned towards the swimming pool. He staggered rather than ran, buttocks tight, back stiff, legs splayed and paralysed, pointing out to himself that his distress felt like male rape but in the opposite direction. En route, he remembered, when he knew that even the pool changing cubicles were too far away for him, that the Sports Teachers' Room had a toilet in it. Huffing and hissing with relief, he opened with a crash the door of Anthony's office, hobbled across to the lavatory, tried to open it and found it locked. 'Bastard. Only perverts lock their loos.' Frantic, at the same time sad in a corner of his mind that he had lost the epic struggle, but for the moment desperate to avoid soiling his underwear and trousers, blubbering gibberish to himself in a sort of comic panic, he unclasped his schoolbelt, unbuttoned his trousers, pulled them and his undie down and squatted on the floor to relieve himself, on the grey cement between desk and faded carpet, in a series of noxious explosions. He remained in Heaven for a minute.

A new man, he shuffled around the room, pants and undies still crumpled up like a cabbage about his ankles, looking for material to clean himself with. One possibility was the frayed curtain that covered the one window. Another was the framed photograph on the desk, appropriately of Anthony himself, smiling, in his only, black, foam-leather jacket, beside his motorcycle before the gates of a public park. The desk top was of scarred green rexine. On it, besides the photo, sat a defunct table clock, a JB Mangharam toffee-box containing pencils and ballpoints and a school library book on weightlifting. It was an outrage against the goddess of wisdom to tear pages out of a book, particularly to wipe your arse with. Yes, even a book on weightlifting. He was thus half-bent over the desk, the photo of Anthony folded in two in his left hand behind him, poised at the cleft of his buttocks, a mound of pasty, malodorous excrement a couple of feet away from his shoes, atop which lay—inadvertently—the void photo frame that had dropped from his fingers—he was thus in the midst of wiping up when he heard the sound of a toilet being flushed and almost immediately saw the lavatory door open and Anthony, belting his trousers, step into the room.

Next morning, a peon from the Principal's office entered during Maths class with a letter for him. It was addressed to his father and requested him to meet the Principal at 10.30 a.m. on Thursday, two days hence, an appointment both unexpected and unwelcome. Close to tears, Bhola had spent half the afternoon of the previous day apologizing several times to every authority that he had met. Uncontrollably bad stomach, he had reiterated. To questions about Anthony's photograph, he had kept quiet, but uncontrollably bad luck was what his silence had meant.

He was apprehensive, though, about the Principal. He had met him only to receive prizes and pats on the back. The Principal was called Chhipkali by the entire school because of his reptilian eyes and snout. The rest of him was small and plump. The thick lenses of his spectacles magnified his eyes like a dragonfly's, and he tied his trousers an inch or two beneath his nipples. Bhola liked him because he considered him—for lack of a better word—a gentleman. Discussing his shameful act with him and his father *together* was simply inconceivable.

Focus, you cow's arse, he exhorted himself all of Tuesday morning, focus on the problem. He focussed like hell till two-thirty when he reached home and then decided that instead of the problem, perhaps he should focus on the damned solution.

'Do you know any forty-five-plus-year-old man who speaks English and who'd be willing to be my father?'

Dosto was impressed with the idea. 'It might even work.'

'I don't think anyone in school has ever met or seen my father. My stepmother's attended one or two PTA meetings, that's all. It's a pity that we need an English speaker. Otherwise, I'd thought of the butcher who home-delivers our mutton. He has a distinguished face and could in the right clothes pass off as a Bengali Brahmin. On second thoughts, maybe he's a little too red and swarthy.'

Too tense to numbly wait for Dosto to come up with a solution, Bhola accosted the meatwala at the gate at four the same afternoon. 'Do you want to do a small role for me? Enact a part? You'll have to wear a pant and shirt and say in English, Good morning, hello Mister, how do you do...' He observed the uncertain grin on the man's face increase with his befuddlement... 'It's nothing, just a small private joke at school...okay, forget it, just forget it.'

On Wednesday afternoon, while Bhola haphazardly contemplated suicide, Dosto phoned to excitedly announce that he had unearthed a father figure after all. He was Swaraj Chacha, a distant uncle, a cousin of Dosto's father, a black sheep of some kind, a bachelor who had in the fifties been a Hindi movie actor of sorts and thereafter had done no work but had been sustained—ever since—by a part of the susbstantial rents of diverse family properties in the upmarket areas of the city. Bhola cycled over to Dosto's house at six. Dosto's father's office car deposited the two boys before a large mansion in the fashionable Jahanpanah area, the ground floor of which was occupied by one maiden aunt of Dosto,

Swaraj Chacha's elder sister, and their ninety-one-year-old mother.

Swaraj himself owned a flat a five minutes' walk from his sister's house. He detested almost all his relatives, but was even more terrified of being alone. He was to be found at his sister's at all hours. He drank all day and bickered patiently with her, justifying his presence in her flat with the argument that he had just popped by to check whether his mother was still alive and if she had moved on, to whom she had bequeathed her apartment. When in the mood, he made gentlemanly passes at whichever of his mother's nurses was on duty, and dined off whatever was available before shuffling back home to his own flat in the ill-lit gloom of evening. He was tall, thin and bald, with an alcoholic's paunch and a noble nose in a bloated, crimson face.

They sat in the dolled-up front lawn amongst the mosquitoes and drank tea. Swaraj's mother, a soothing presence, a smiling zombie in a wheelchair, and her nurse, pert, with a tight body, kept them company. Swaraj was quite happy—indeed, magnanimously willing—to play the role of Bhola's father the next morning but he didn't want to hear any details. They would cramp his style, put brakes on his performance. 'Just the broad outlines—where, when, what and before whom. A dance step or two, if you wish. The rest you leave to me, my son,' he assured Bhola but, leaning forward in his garden chair and displaying large, even, yellow teeth, looked and smiled only at the nurse. Bhola was abruptly relieved and proud to have the father he had.

He was also overwhelmed with disquiet about the appointment the next day but didn't see how best to control events. A dance step or two—a sinuous twitch of a shoulder, a ripple across a hairy belly—before the Principal. 'My father is a senior administrator in an academic organization. He is usually cold and civil. He would be aghast to hear of my misconduct but would carry himself correctly.' Swaraj held

out a plate of salt biscuits to the nurse. 'You do know where
the school is? You'll be able to make it there on time? Please
please don't be late because then they might phone home or
my father's office.'

He tossed and turned in bed all night. All morning, he
waited in class on the edge of his seat, knees pressed hard
against each other, the fist of apprehension in his belly
threatening to turn his bowels to yellow water. A peon arrived
from the Principal's office at eleven-fifteen. Bhola
accompanied him. It took him a couple of seconds to recognize
Swaraj loitering in the first floor corridor, looking like a fifties-
Hindi-film villain in a dark blue suit and a maroon *bow* tie.
Even his face, though still red, looked less dissolute. He did
not place Bhola till he and the peon stopped in front of his
chest.

'Hello Mister how do you do and where were you? I
thought that you'd be present at our meeting.' Swaraj's eyes
fidgeted like a squash ball in play.

'You mean it's over?' Bhola's mind seemed to become a
cold and grey, carrion-dotted field above which, in a twilit
sky, circled vultures. How could it be over? Leaving the peon
to flop down and scratch his balls in his chair outside the
Principal's office, they straggled off together in the direction
of the stairs.

'I naturally didn't know why your father had been
summoned. You hadn't cared to tell me. So when I learnt that
you—uh—went to the toilet on the floor of a teacher's room,
I didn't have to feign either my surprise or my disgust. I
nevertheless dutifully—and forcefully—protested. Boys will
be boys, I pointed out, and need to be given a new lease of
life with the long rope—very vigorously argued.' He nodded
several times to himself in appreciation of his cameo, wafting
to Bhola in ripples the whiff of gin and after-shave. Then he
abruptly paused on the last but one stair and stared for the
first time into the eyes of the adolescent on the step above

him. 'However could you do it? The Principal was really quite adamant. He seemed to hint that he wanted to expel you from school. Frankly, I approved of his decision and also added that I felt that you should spend a week or two in jail. Dosto's father needs to be told about the company that his son keeps.'

Bhola couldn't restrain himself. 'My god, you've fucked up good and proper.'

Swaraj was genuinely taken aback at the coarseness of the boy's language. 'Careful. I'm like a father to you.'

All at once, Bhola about-turned and rushed up the stairs, then, as though struck by the thought that he had nowhere to go, halted at the landing, looked back and demanded in a voice screechy with strain, 'But what did Chhipkali *say*! Finally! What's the verdict, you bald buttock, what's the bottom line!' He began to cry.

Swaraj gave Bhola a long, poisonous look and then turning, straightening and shrugging off his shoulders the memory of a performance unforgettable for the wrong reasons, mooched off towards the car park.

'May you have an accident on the way back home, arseface!' hissed Bhola after him through his tears. Then he wandered about the school in a daze, bitterly regretting not having confessed to his father, for having chosen as impersonator a cretin who had been moreover pickled for decades in alcohol, trying to visualize what could have transpired between Swaraj and the Principal, every now and then speculating once more about the least messy means of suicide, wondering how on earth he was going to face the world—his class, the school bus—again. When the bell trilled for Lunch Break, he realized that he was tense, depressed, scared, exhausted and hungry.

Dosto was petrified that his uncle had given the game away and that he would be implicated as a consequence. 'But didn't the bastard give you any details?' Behind the basketball courts, they puffed away frenziedly at their post-tiffin cigarettes. 'I mean, did he say who he was or who *we* said he was?' He was close to tears. 'If my father finds out, he's going to belt me.' Oddly, it calmed Bhola to observe the panic that his friend was in. Then briefly, perhaps owing to the expression on Bhola's face, the predicament that he was in dawned on Dosto. 'You relax. They expel the poor turds, not the bright sparks. He'll probably give you a stinker of a letter, that's all, written in red ink or something.'

Bhola received that letter within the hour, shortly before school closed that day, from the Principal in person. It was short and typewritten and signed in blue ink by Chhipkali himself. They all seemed to know its contents in advance— the peon who arrived during Hindi to summon him, the Principal's Private Secretary in the outer office, Sister Stanislaus the Student Councillor whom he came upon at the door of the sanctum sanctorum—and save for Sister Stan, who was paid to beam at the students, they avoided meeting his eye. They glanced at him askance and he caught them hurriedly looking away when he gazed at their faces. Their shunning him filled him with dread, as though he had become the vector of some contagion.

'I am sorry that we have had to expel you,' said the Principal to the glass paperweights on his massive table. 'We had no choice. You gave us none.' His face and voice were completely expressionless. Bhola unobtrusively pressed his thighs against the table and leaned on it because he needed to sit down and hadn't been asked to. He felt on the edge of being effaced and yet somehow wanted to abase himself still further. 'Your father was encouraging and positive this morning. He gave us hope of your improving yourself in the future.' Through the open windows, Bhola could see the tops of the gulmohar trees of the car park and hear the school buses revving up as they came in at the gates. Now he couldn't commit suicide because he'd have to stay alive to murder Swaraj Uncle.

Then followed seven utterly bizarre, almost frightening, months. He did not show either his father or his stepmother the letter from the school. He simply could not inform them of his expulsion from it. Every morning therefore at the usual hour, feeling totally unreal, he dressed for school and trudged off in the direction of the bus stop with his bag and his tiffin-box. Long before he reached it, however, he strayed off to a municipal park or to Hafeez Market to smoke cigarettes, windowshop, munch his sandwiches, timidly decline the homosexual advances of strangers and while three hours of his life away. He returned to the house at ten in the morning when it was void of its other inhabitants, his father and stepmother having left for work by then and his brother for the university. Ten days passed in this manner. He was careful to keep an eye out for the post. There were however no letters from the school.

He revealed to no one—not to Dosto, not to any of his acquaintances—that his family continued to be in the dark about his rustication. The less said, the better. With time, moreover, the need to inform the world of the developments in his career receded. Life had gone on as before. Why complicate it? His subterfuge worked for seven long months because he was a loner in a family of loners, each immersed deeply in himself. His father and stepmother had no friends amongst the parents of his ex-classmates. In fact, they had no friends at all, they only knew some other couples who played bridge. His brother, fortunately at that point of his life in the university, dreaming of money, loss of virginity, cannabis and the wider world, in any case remembered that he had a sibling only about once a fortnight, on the occasion, say, when the family ate together and he realized that he'd got less fish or egg curry only because of the number of insatiable male maws at the table.

The nights were difficult, though. In the dark, Bhola's guard was down and his future black and blank, without forms save for the ghosts of his libidinous past—Gopinath, Anthony, Jeremiah, Titli, Moti—their figures and faces increasingly fuzzy, banteringly unreal; passionate physical contact with all of whom had been objectives that faintheartedness, it seemed, had prevented him from attaining. They provided no consolation. He simply had been as much of a failure with them as with the rest of his life. However—he asked himself, mesmerized by a dread of the future, with one eye clamped tight against the pillow and the other wide-open, staring at the blurred contours of the book on the night table and seeing nothing—however could things have come to such a pass? Then abruptly, the extent of his fall from grace, the sheer distance that he had plummeted, would strike him with fresh force and he would sit up in bed, nauseous with panic.

During the day, however, by the second week, in some park, smoking, eyeing the passersby but averting his glance before they stared at him lolling on the bench in his school uniform, he sometimes felt as though he were on vacation. Things could be cool. Even when one was outcast and lived in the shadows, one only needed to look around with a tranquil, receptive and open eye to note the simple pleasures that could reaffirm one's faith in life. That short, plump woman in a nurse's uniform, for example, trampling down the path towards him with the outlines of her meaty thighs winking, slowly and bewitchingly, at the world through the skirt with the ponderous rhythm of her gait—someone like her would make anyone feel as upbeat as the Charvakas that he had read about in his Ancient Indian History school textbook. 'The Charvakas,' he recited, grinning to himself with tension as the woman advanced, having suddenly laid bets with himself that he could not cite the entire first paragraph, without faltering, at normal speed, before she passed his bench and that if he could, everything would turn out all right, 'are the only truly optimistic school of Hindu philosophy. They strongly opposed the Buddhist preoccupation with suffering, holding that although pain exists, it is transitory. In the pattern of pleasure and pain that constitutes life, pleasure is just as abundant and more beneficial and can predominate over pain if we will it so. In any case, should one throw away the rice because it is covered with husk, or refrain from eating fish because of its prickly spine?'

More than the face, perhaps it was the rear that he recognized. She had looked at him once, dismissed him instantly as a wastrel, a lonely heart about to whistle at her, and moved on with her heavy, rolling tread. 'Titli.' She didn't hear his gasp. She had put on weight—substantially—and doubtless some of the fat had clogged up her ears. 'Titli!' He yelled, jumped off the bench and strode after her, all in one movement. Overjoyed to see her, he, unthinkingly, held her by the shoulders and kissed her on the lips. They didn't yield as they were supposed to so that he could bruise them with his. Fortunately, he thought for a nanosecond, since they smelt of sweet tea and garlic. Instead, his cigarette singed a wisp of her hair above her right ear and she automatically wiped her no-compromise lips with the back of her hand. Nevertheless, she looked delighted to see him—and his elation too—and, almost instantly, a little embarrassed at her own response.

'It's been more than a year! You just disappeared where have you been no word at all I even went once to Ambedkarpuri to look for you!'

She no longer braided her hair and let it hang down her back like a rope to encourage his masochistic fantasies with. It was now a neat, tight bun at the nape of her neck. It suited her, as did the uniform. Her face was smoother, paler and looked less deprived. She had clearly climbed a couple of rungs of the class ladder and he was fleetingly jealous that it had not been because of him.

Her explanations made no sense to him. He returned to

the bench to pick up his school bag. Then he fell into step beside her and they continued to walk on in the direction in which she had been heading.

'I don't understand. How can you become a nurse on Wednesday when you've been selling olisboi on Tuesday? Who is this doctor?'

Across the park and past Chamatkar Cinema Hall, they sauntered on, he enchanted to have met her and wondering whether passersby noticed the class difference between the two of them. It was her mien, the lack of assurance in it, and how she spoke. Perhaps he should walk ahead a bit. He would have preferred to drop back, though, and amble just behind her for a better view. It was true that because she had grown fatter, she seemed to have become a little shorter. I love you, he screamed silently, suddenly, guiltily and rapturously at her docile profile, for your trudge up the social ramp, you make my heart quicken and my loins jump, you and my lust for you make me belong in the workaday world of unfiltered cigarettes and matches, samosas and sweet tea, and Hindi film songs on the radio. Outside on the footpath, where he would have turned left to go home, they turned right.

She was not used to explaining, to description. To talk precisely in response to his intense and brazen questions lightened her, made her blush and laugh, showing her gums; it flattered her, this display of curiosity on the part of another about her cheerless inner life and her dismal past. 'We used to do this part of the colony with our vegetable cart round about noon.' Her face dulled for an instant at the memory of a grimmer life.

It galled him to think that for more than a year, she and her husband had lived not more than a fifteen-minute walk away from him and had not cared to tell him of their whereabouts. How selfish she is, he grimaced at her spongey profile with distaste and lust, a man invites her into his house—but only to be his maidservant—and she forgets instantly the rest of the world. 'But you could've told me where you were!' He broke out accusingly. 'How easily you forgot me.'

She had the intelligence to simper contritely. The houses in that sector of the colony were more spacious. They stopped before one painted and tiled in pink and chocolate, two storeys high, its frontage only partly redeemed by two tall palms and a monstrous pink bougainvillea that reared up the central wall to the roof before flipping backwards in a suicidal gush of colour. A large painted board affixed to the gate announced Dr Vijayendra Borkar, MBBS, General Practitioner, and his timings.

'The doctor isn't in right now,' Titli spoke uneasily. Bhola received the impression that she wished him to disappear before any inmate of the house spotted them together. 'He's gone out. He dropped me off in the car on the other side of the park.'

'You look good in your uniform,' he responded, warming up belatedly. 'How do we meet?' as though to a lover. Losing and finding her—both so unexpectedly—had liberated him from the niceties of social conversation. 'Maybe I can drop by with a sore throat or something. Where's Moti?'

'He helps out in the clinic. He wears a uniform and everything. I insisted. Then he goes to night school.' She grinned—a blaze, like firewood catching fire—at one of the sunny things in her life. 'His exams are on at the moment. Uniform...exams,' she repeated, half to herself, amusedly marvelling at the unforeseeable ways of the world.

He supposed that it was only fitting that even Moti, who at the age of twenty-six hadn't known what nine sixes are, was at school. Some fluid that kept his body buoyant nevertheless seemed to sink down to his ankles, leaving his head and torso heavy like cement, numb and cold. Moti hadn't known who the President of the country was and he was now sitting for an exam. Well, fortunately, not having a school to attend at least freed him, Bhola, from the dreary anxiety of those periodic tests and terminal papers. Except for the Board exams next year, of course, the last oh my god oh my god. He looked at Titli, suddenly breathless with panic. Her lips were moving but she seemed to have been cut off from him by a blurry glass wall. Without a word, he turned around and began to run home, his school bag thumping clumsily on his back and ruling out speed. He needed to speak to someone of his world, someone who would be aware of the civilized concerns beyond food, clothing, shelter and sex oh my godgodgodgodgod.

He had to wait till three. To calm himself down, he smoked cigarettes, masturbated and listened to Jethro Tull on his brother's new stereo system. From his last James Hadley Chase thriller, Bhola's brother had learnt to tape one strand of hair to the side, towards the rear, to both lid and base of record player—a tripwire, a triphair, to catch the unwary. When he was fed up of listening to rock music LPs, Bhola, all the while abusing his brother, took almost forty minutes to locate and retape the hair. He knew that he would be caught out no matter what. The fucker even folded in a certain way the rag with which he wiped discs. He kept them cleaner than his own dick, bloody prick. At two-thirty, Bhola left on his cycle for Dosto's house.

'Sure you can sit,' Dosto assured him as they played cricket, with a hockey stick and tennis ball, in the humid heat in the rear verandah on the first floor, wolfing down in between overs chicken curry and rice from steel plates balanced on the ironing board, 'the Board exams privately. I know. My cousin sat them. You have to go,' he suffixed hazily, 'to the Board office and fill out a thousand forms.' Unlike Bhola, who out of habit after school used to change out of his uniform immediately, either to dump his clothes to be washed or to hang up his shirt and trousers so that he

could wear them again the next day, Dosto remained in his
school clothes practically all day, perhaps because he wore
them only once before tossing them in the bucket kept in the
kitchen for the laundry. Seeing him in them, Bhola felt
deprived and depressed, like a child of the slums who has
stopped going to school because he has to stay at home and
tend to his siblings while his mother goes off to scour and
scrub in the posher houses across the railway tracks. 'You
would still need to be,' added Dosto even more vaguely,
'affiliated to the school,' and settled down to face Bhola's
bowling across four metres of cement flooring.

'Would your Swaraj and I have to meet Chhipkali again?'
Bhola gripped the tennis ball from underneath between
thumb and middle finger as he and his brother surmised the
Australian bowler Jackie Gleason had held it. When he spun
the ball overarm with that grip, nobody—not the batsman
and certainly not Bhola himself—knew which way the ball
would turn after the bounce. 'That'd be tough because I'd've
murdered him by then.' Dosto chuckled and his mood
marginally elevated, Bhola began to sing as he released the
ball:

Dil karé fuck fuck
Bombay se Baroda tuk

Not having heard that parody of a Hindi film song before,
Dosto cackled, taking his eyes off the ball and allowing it to
go through and hit the laundry bucket that did for the wicket.
'That's cheating but that's good,' he acknowledged, in one
breath criticising Bhola's tactic but applauding his compostional
skill. 'How does the rest of it go?'

Hum Sub tub tuk
Karte rahen fuck fuck hmmmm hummmm.

Bhola's parodies were almost always bilingual.

The heart goes fuck fuck
From Bombay to Baroda.

The original has an onomatopoeic Dhuk dhuk instead of fuck fuck. The heart goes dhuk dhuk from Bombay to Baroda. In the film, the singers are in a bus and the hero is wearing falsies.

We all till then
Will continue to fuck fuck weeeeeeee weeeeeeee

Invariably, Bhola it was who thought the spoofs up and Dosto who sang them loudly and elatedly in school bus, classroom and playing field, pretending, in Bhola's absence, to be their lyricist.

Bhola returned home before sunset, gloomy anew because once more alone and becoming progressively bluer the further he cycled away from Dosto's. Impulsively, he decided on a longish detour to pass by Dr Borkar's house in the hope of catching a glimpse of either Titli or Moti. In his mood of that moment, he would have preferred the man. Thinking of him pepped him up. Abruptly, in a fit of self-assertion, a rush of blood to the head, he began to cycle faster and more aggressively, 'When-the-heart-goes-fuck-fuck,' he exhorted himself to the rhythm of his feet thrusting down on the pedals, 'snap-out-of-this-muck-muck.'

NEAR-SEX EXPERIENCES

'Why do you always sleep with your back to me?' asked a shy, thin female voice that Bhola hadn't heard before. Then it giggled, belying its diffidence.

He was on a cot on the terrace, alone at eleven in the morning, naked and with his eyes shut, basking in the October sun, allowing it to burn him, supposedly meditating and actually daydreaming, hoping that if he muttered the right Vedic mantra—part of his father's conditioning—the right way, the energy of the sun would bore into and sort out his life for him. While he admired the flame-coloured interior of his eyelids, nagging him at the back of his mind—and dimming his pleasure—was the notion that he could more profitably have been spending the same time catching up on his medieval Hindi poets or his Coordinate Geometry.

His abstractedness and woolgathering had increased—with reason—since his expulsion from school a month ago, almost as though there were a certain number of reveries that he had to carry through and dispose of before the year ended and for which he was horribly behind time. Not much had gone his way in the preceding weeks. Out of inertness, he still had not enrolled himself through his school as a private student for the Board exams. His family continued to remain ignorant about his rustication and most dismal of all, Titli and Moti had vanished yet again.

Four days after meeting her in the park, Bhola had returned to Dr Borkar's house undecided, for pretext, between a headache and a backache. Both were good in that neither exhibited any external evidence. He had finally determined to leave it to Dr Borkar's sexiness. If he was a bomb, it would be an ache in the anus.

The house looked shut up. The doctor's board on the gate had been replaced by a smaller blue tin plate that stated: *Beware of Dog* in both English and Hindi and exhibited a painting of an Alsatian suffering the process of meltdown. Bhola's heart settled down with a sigh on his diaphragm like a small, punctured blimp. He rang the bell on the wall beside the gate. After a couple of days, a small, thin, old woman, a suspicious grandmother type, opened what appeared to be a bathroom window and exhibited cautiously a bespectacled left eye. At the same time, she switched on a tape recording of a dog barking.

Bhola loudly explained from the gate. The eye gazed at him for half a minute. The woman then reluctantly informed him in clumsy Hindi that the doctor had permanently left the city for the hills.

Thinking at the speed of Superman rushing off for a superleak, he elaborated that while he did have a frightful backache, he also needed urgently to meet the Doctor's nurse because—he continued in response to the question in the eye's distrustful and baleful expression—she owed them four thousand rupees from the time that she used to work in their house. One fine day more than a year ago, she had melted into thin air and they had had to go to the police who had instantly blamed them for not registering their domestic servant with them in the first place.

The eye disappeared from the window. With no evidence to support his conclusion, Bhola nevertheless knew—a gut feeling—that the woman had *liked* what she had heard about Titli. He listened to several squeaky bolts in a door being drawn back. The woman cautiously stepped out on the driveway. She was really very small. She shuffled up to the gate in Kolhapuri slippers that seemed on her feet as large as hand baggage for a flight. 'She and her husband or whoever he is left with the Doctor.' Her tone made it clear that she knew only too well who had seduced whom in the trio. In her hand fluttered a torn-off piece of a used envelope. Bhola presumed that it had the Doctor's address in the hills and that it was meant for him. 'Thank you,' he said in English and reached out for it.

Dodging his fingers, she held the scrap of paper with both her hands over the gate and flat under his nose. *Resident Medical Officer*, it read, *M.K.M.Z.A.P. Graduate College for the Sciences and Humanities*. It had everything down to the telephone extension number and the postal code. Bhola had the fanciful impression that that was all that the doctor had left behind of himself with his family, that the rest of him had been swallowed up by the yawning orifice of his maidlover. 'I know it,' he grinned gratefully at the old woman. 'It's quite well-known and enjoys a good reputation, in fact, particularly its Humanities wing. Thank you for being so helpful.' For a second, the eyes behind the spectacles looked less anxious, less hostile.

'Why do you always sleep with your back to me?'

The voice had come from across the wall. The terrace on which Bhola lay daydreaming—the entire house, in fact—shared one wall, its eastern, with the adjoining house. On the terrace, an arm's length away from the cot, it stood ten feet high, plastered over, once white and featureless, and over the years scrawled and furiously etched over by the brothers with graffiti. Neither their father nor stepmother ever mounted to the second floor. Only the maid of the month did with the washing and, biennially, some odd-job man to scour the inside of the water tank. With the rubble of red brick as crayon, at several places on the wall had been drawn sets of wickets, as though to indicate that several cricket matches could well be in progress simultaneously. The dried smudges of damp tennis balls generously dotted the entire four hundred square feet of surface. Across and under them—and over and through the pierced hearts, vaginal footballs, incubuses and King Kongs, cartoon torsos, phallic columns and cricket bats— could be read the slogans that recorded the brothers' ripening. *Make Love, Not War. Make Money, Not Love. Light My Fire. Light Your Own, Baby. Be Indian, Buy Indian Dope.*

'Hello! I sleep with my back to you because—hello! I can't see you—I don't want us to breathe one another's exhalations.' To a decorous giggle from behind the wall, he turned over on his left to modestly hide his crotch from view and offer for the voyeuse's consideration his bum. He was past caring. God alone knew for how long she had been peeking at him—one hour, a couple of days, one week—God alone knew. He felt neither rage nor embarrassment. To be spied on was both disquieting and flattering. She had watched him masturbate, sing *Hey Jude* in the nude at Woodstock, make love to an old cushion when it had become Jordana ben Canaan of *Exodus*, chat with and chuckle attractively at the wall, tug fetchingly at a nonexistent forelock, narrow his eyes the Marlboro way against the drift of cigarette smoke. He had nothing to hide from her.

With the sun baking him, he waited for the female to say something, to reveal herself. He would give her a couple of minutes before returning to his make-believe world. That had already been delineated in some detail. In it, when occasion demanded, his parents—that is to say, his father and the mother whose face he didn't remember—whisked him out of Gopinath's hut and packed him off to the Chesterfield International Academy, simply the world's best school located in a balmy island in the Pacific. He had good friends there, warmer, wittier, more suave, cosmopolitan, modern and racially integrated versions of Billy Bunter's companions at Greyfriars. His parents themselves had changed beyond recognition and

become intellectual giants, truly astride East and West, dhoti-
and sari-clad but Professors nevertheless of Sanskrit and
other related, awe-inspiring subjects—Oriental Philosophy,
Comparative Religions—at the Winston International
University, situated a couple of islands away from Chesterfield.
They had originally taught at Harvard. Later, however, when
Bhola learnt that Abhijit, one of his elder brother's college
acquaintances, small, bespectacled, pimply, and near-moronic
in worldly matters, had left to join Princeton University in the
US to study something or the other, he regretfully had to give
up his Ivy League institutions and create one of his own a
rung or two above any the world has ever known.

His fantasy parents had also been given correspondingly
rich pasts. His mother, depending on the plot of the day, was
either upper-class Muslim or lower-caste Hindu. Being terribly
independent-minded, she had faced acute problems of social
adjustment in conservative Dhaka. No one had wanted to
marry her despite her demure but stunning beauty and her
unobtrusively formidable intellectual accomplishments. At
the same time, she had been giggly and bouncy and full of
enthusiasm as directly opposed to her husband-to-be who
was shy and reticent, hiding deep within him a reservoir of
coruscating and sagacious wit that had to be teased out with
patience but was well worth the effort. After their marriage
and several trials and tribulations worthy of Jesus Christ
Superstar, his parents, simultaneously ostracized and hounded,
had had tearfully to flee to the West where, in painful
contrast, they had been welcomed with open arms by J.
Edgar Hoover.

He had dressed and was about to descend when he saw
her, a head peeping and smiling at him from behind the wire
mesh between the end of the wall and the water tank. He
walked towards her. Despite a certain empty expression on
her face, as though a filter behind her eyes had been removed
for repairs, she was pretty. He stopped beneath her. She

looked older than him. He had expected someone younger. She had an attractive snub nose and a round face topped by a hemisphere of short—but thick—curly hair that made it appear even rounder.

She stood behind the wall on a platform of some sort—a table perhaps—and gently oscillated backwards and forwards, each time lightly touching her forehead to and flattening her nose against the six inches of wire mesh. The stink of a chicken coop wafted across to Bhola from the neighbour's terrace. 'You people have recently shifted in, haven't you?' began he to break the ice. 'I saw a huge truck before your gate last weekend. Also some sweaty-looking cops.'

She laughed with disproportionate gaiety. 'I sometimes see your brother exercising in the mornings.' She spoke an easy mix of Hindi and English. In his entire life, he did not hear her speak even one full sentence exclusively in one language, unadulterated by the words and phrases of another. 'I want to ask him what exercises he can show me for my stomach.'

'I can too if you wish.'

'You? But you've already shown me so much!' She trilled and laughed with such excess that she pretended to topple off her perch.

He liked her faked madness. 'What's your name?'

'*Anjaanaaaaaaa*!' she sang abruptly in response in the manner of the popular Hindi film song, drawing out the last syllable and letting it hang in the air like an echo in the mountains, and ducking underneath it to disappear from view till the following morning.

Anin was short for Anindini, Sanskrit for one who does not speak ill of others, or one who is not spoken ill of. Bhola had never come across the name before and thought that she had got it wrong. 'Nandini I've heard of and Anindita, and even Annadata and Anna Karenina, but Anindini? A Nandini Satpathy. Had it been A*nan*dini, it would have meant one who is *not* a dutiful daughter, which is nice.'

She pouted. 'My real name is Kaushalya. I hate it and never respond to it. I renamed myself years and years ago. Which do you prefer?'

She grinned with pleasure at hearing his name. 'Ohhh, such an unsexy name for such a sexy person!'—and flung back her head to send her laugh fluttering up into the sky. Bhola, feeling flattered, smirked till he realized that by sexy, she had meant not sexually attractive, but highly-sexed.

She was at the spot of the day before, behind the wire mesh, gazing at him like a caged bird on the lookout for some means of escape. 'Why don't you hop over and show me your stomach exercises?'

Her concern for losing flab warmed his heart. 'Certainly, but how?'

She was surprised that there wasn't on his side of the wall a metal ladder riveted into the brick like the one on one of the rungs of which she at that very moment stood. 'Oh. What a nuisance. Will you wait a bit?' Some minutes later, she flung a rope ladder across the wall. 'I've tied one end here to this pipe. I'll hold on to it too. Come on!'

It was the first time that he had climbed a rope ladder and was taken aback to find that it was not easy. 'I should do this more often. It seems to be great for the arms.' He paused for breath astride the wall. Their part of the housing colony lay spread out beneath him like an urban sprawl before some invading colossus. He recalled the hot afternoon of the previous year when, unmindful of the febrile weather, he had scanned the same view for a sign of Titli and her man and had felt that he would burst in an explosion of semen and sorrow and his nothingness would merge with the dust of the quietly hideous landscape confronting him. No longing was sacred; they were only cyclical and time took care of them all.

In contrast with Bhola's, Anin's terrace was untidy and crowded, half-covered with tarpaulin and asbestos to provide some shelter for a chicken coop, an Alsatian guard dog, the family washing, a goods shed for hose pipe, plant tub and rope ladder, and a getaway place for the daughter of the house. 'That damned dog is twice my size, you know.' Careful not to lose his balance, Bhola tried gracefully to about-turn atop the wall, changed his mind and hopped and slid backwards on his bum till he reached the metal ladder. Anin and the dog waited for him at its foot. 'Why isn't the monster barking? I hate the strong and silent type.'

Anin made little effort to hide her pleasure at his arrival. Without moving her feet, she danced in brief, jerky movements to some music in her head. She wore a blue track suit bottom and a loose, long orange khadi kurta. She was short, he realized when he stood beside her. The beast came up and sniffed his crotch. His balls curled up and became raisins. She giggled. He wanted to know whether she was older than him but didn't know how to ask. 'When a woman is piling on like crazy and you want to slow her down,' his brother had advised him in the manner of elder brothers, 'you can start by asking her her age.'

'Which school do you go to?'

'I don't. I study at home. And you?' The three of them moved towards a striped rug spread out on the floor alongside the goods shed.

He peered into the chicken coop with elaborate casualness while answering, 'Me too. I'm sort of meant to be studying on my own.' He would have told her the truth had she pressed him to be precise. It would have been a relief to lay open at least one of his cumbrous secrets. 'How many hens do you have? I can't see any in this gloom.'

'Seven, and two roosters. They should all be there somewhere—unless Corbett's been shirking his duty and the neighbourhood cats have carried them off.'

'And why do you keep them? For the eggs?' He watched the dog flop down on the rug.

'What d'you think? For the stink?'

'I don't know—maybe to ensure that you all wake up on time every morning—' The Beatles song *Good Morning, Good Morning* ran in his head as he continued—'No, I mean, isn't it simpler just to buy lots of raw eggs from the market?'

'My father eats dozens and dozens of raw eggs,' she explained vaguely, gazing up at the hot grey sky as though anticipating rain, 'and drinks tons of raw egg soup.' She stood over the dog, arms akimbo and waited for Bhola to join them.

'Does the beast too want to learn some new stomach exercises?'

With a brief yelp of a laugh, she lay down on her back beside the dog, legs aligned, toes pointing upward, hands pillowing her cranium, and with a composed face, spoke to— and with her eyes fixed on—the tarpaulin roof above her head. 'I raise my head and legs up at the same time, bend my knees and twist my torso so that my right elbow touches my left knee.' Without looking at Bhola, she demonstrated the exercise once. 'Then I return to the original position and jerk up again to touch my *left* elbow to my *right* knee. The hands remain clasped behind the head throughout.' She repeated the manoeuvre four more times, turning, from the waist up, left once, then right. After the last, she swivelled a little and in one smooth motion, lay down with her head pillowed on the dog and looked straight, even a little challengingly, at Bhola. 'The book recommends forty-four stomach jerks in sixty seconds but my best so far has been twenty two. On the days when my back is stiff, I can't even get up off the floor.'

'You should listen to your body. If you can't get up off the floor, it means that it doesn't want you to.' Sitting down gingerly beside her feet, half off the rug, reeling off any old rubbish that came into his head, careful not to touch any part of her, not sure whether he was expected out of passion to kiss her instep or something, extremely depressed because of how little he had been aroused by her even though he liked her—how his eyes in fact had strayed more often to the dog's balls and prick—he showed her the peculiar sit-ups that his brother did on Mondays and Thursdays. She tried them and liked them.

Without specifically planning to, they began to meet on Anin's terrace twice or thrice a week. He would return at ten in the morning from his charade of having gone to school in his school uniform in the school bus, change his clothes and mount to the terrace to smoke cigarettes, listen to Hindi film songs on the transistor radio, read trash and—if Anin was not at her station behind the wire mesh—chat, chuckle and playact with his ghosts. If she was, he, quite happy to be disturbed, would cross the wall.

On the street, they did not recognize each other. For one, outside the house, they never met alone. Anin did not step out without a chaperone, usually her mother and sometimes the maid, a dour-faced but handsome, middle-aged woman. Anin's mother Bhola recognized because he spotted her daughter's snub nose on her face. She had otherwise a long, more-unhappy-than-ugly face that was at variance with her large and flabby body. When they had first come upon each other in the lane that led to the milk booth, Anin had looked right through him and at the same time managed to convey, through some furious wriggling of her eyebrows and lightning sideways flicks of her pupils, that he should greet her mother and simply pretend that she herself did not exist. He had smiled and mumbled something polite-sounding at the mother who had nodded and smiled back.

That Anin was special was obvious but peculiar in what way he did not especially want to find out, particularly since he was quite sure that he would not be able to grasp the subtleties of her dysfunction. Whatever could she have done that kept her at home? He had imagined the worst and enjoyed it. Perhaps she too had shat a mess on her school Sportsmistress's feet. Or she had fellated her dog before the Principal's eyes. Well, he had toyed with that kind of image himself, of a being in an orange kurta and with Anin's head cackling away above, and with the dog's loins below, erect and implacable before Bhola's face. He liked her. What he was indefinably apprehensive about, however, was that people like Dosto would come to learn that he and an attractive girl spent three hours a week together all by themselves and did nothing either exceptional or exceptionable. She spoke of the Binaca Hit Parade of Hindi film songs on Radio Ceylon and played endless rounds of Rummy with him and Patience with herself. They played Rummy till he wanted to vomit. Then she, enthusiasm unabated, switched back to Patience while he marvelled at her continuing to be bewitched by the capriciousness of the cards. Her fascination for them depressed him, the delicious suspense with which she turned each face up, tut-tutted or exclaimed with delight at what it declared to her, the concentration and facility with which she handled the deck. He feared that his will-lessness would suck him down to the level of his emotionally brittle, half-witted companion and then, feeling guilty at thinking mean things about her, he would himself propose another session of Rummy.

It was partly his disgust with the two card games that caused him to suggest that Anin meet Dosto. 'He was named after the famous Russian writer whom his father, who claims to know the language and the culture, loves. But then the parents decided to restrict themselves to the first two syllables of the name because they could never agree on the spelling thereafter.' Anin, not having followed, tittered politely. 'You know, if we had him as a third hand, we could play Auction Bridge.' There were other reasons too. He had been a little surprised to see the almost-spellbound repugnance with which she had observed him smoking his cigarettes. He had offered her one and had been refused with vehemence. 'Dirty dirty,' she had protested, wrinkling her nose and turning her head away, pushing even the space between her and the packet away with her beringed hands. One thing had led to another and he had soon thereafter discovered that she had never tasted alcohol in her life.

'Chhee chhee shame shame.' She had shut her eyes and vigorously shaken her head to rid her immediate surroundings of the noxious spirituous fumes emanating from the very word. Intrigued by the vigour of her reaction, he had mooted that alcohol wasn't so bad, was in fact beneficial, if drunk at a propitious moment and in judicious quantities. 'Besides, you have all your rings to protect you.'

She had laughed, almost snorted, meaninglessly and then, to reassure herself, brought up before her chest her hands, side by side and palms down, and scrutinized her rings. She wore two on each hand, coral, amethyst, opal and jade, so she had elaborated more than once to Bhola, though he couldn't tell one from the other and was quite blind to their beauty. Gems are the congealed influences of the planets and heavenly bodies, she had expounded—her wide-eyed solemnity transcending his scepticism—the crystallized products of invisible rays operating within the crust of the earth. They therefore retain the powers of the planets in a highly concentrated form.

She had looked at him archly over the tips of her fingers, suddenly smiled coquettishly and demanded, 'What kind of propitious moment?'

They finally decided to wait a few days and celebrate with alcohol Bhola's registering himself as a private student for the Board exams. The manoeuvre necessitated a second visit to the school with Dosto's Uncle Swaraj and, what was trickier, getting his real father to sign on the forms and make out a cheque. Bhola accosted him at his morning tea, a time when he would be least displeased at being disturbed. 'I've decided to offer Sanskrit as an extra paper at the Board exam. Do you remember suggesting it more than a year ago? I've brought the forms.You have to sign at a couple of places. And it's expensive. If you could either give me the cash or write out a cheque. I just hope that the last date isn't over.'

As he had anticipated, Dosto was intensely intrigued at the suggestion that the two of them drink his father's alcohol with a strange girl on her terrace on the quiet on a weekday during the forenoon.

'Why not add, while standing in the sun on one leg and shagging off with your left hand after it goes round your back and inches down on your cock from the right?'

'Don't be a yogic anus. Nobody else that I know of regularly steals his father's whisky. Even rum would do. She wouldn't know the difference.'

'Are you fucking her?'

Bhola correctly interpreted the question to mean whether their thighs touched when they sat side by side on the occasions when she read his palm. 'Sometimes.'

'It'll have to be after five p.m. You're crazy if you think I'm going to cut school to drink rum with strangers at eleven in the morning.' It did sound absurd even to Bhola when phrased in that manner. 'Besides, I have Maths and Hindi tuitions every afternoon, all week.' Bhola's heart flinched when he saw the distance that he had travelled, in just a few weeks, from the routine of a normal adolescent's life.

In the end, they drank together several weeks later, early in November, in the evening well after five, with the grey sun retreating at the end of a blue day. The day, a Monday, chose itself. Anin's mother had gone off to Lucknow for a few days to participate in some family crisis. Monday was usually Bridge day for Bhola's father and stepmother. They didn't get home before ten. Mindful of having to play host to a stranger, Anin, nervous and giggling without cause or pause, offered to receive Dosto at the front door of the house. 'It's his first time, silly,' she explained when Bhola's comically exaggerated frown made it clear that he hadn't followed, 'It'll look funny if, to get to my terrace he has to walk up to the second floor of *your* house and then climb a rope ladder. What does he look alike?'

She had placed three plastic chairs, two red, one blue, around a table under the tarpaulin farthest from the chicken coop. She had switched on the naked bulb in the shed but shut its door. Through the tiny ventilator above it, the bulb cast outside a reflected, softer light. She had lit anti-mosquito incense in saucers at three almost-equidistant points around the seating area. On the table were arranged different varieties of salt biscuits, glasses, a packet of paper napkins and a saucer with slices of lemon in it and next to the blue chair, on the floor, stood two bottles of water and a hideous ice bucket shaped like a wooden beer keg. Alongside the door to the stairs sat a crate of Thums Up and Limca.

Dosto arrived quietly, a guest unsure of his welcome. He mounted the stairs behind Anin demurely, smirking shyly and knowingly at everything—the dog, the reproductions on the wall, the terrace. He carried in his school knapsack rum, Indian whisky and two bottles of beer. Ceremonially—and at the same time grinning like a conspirator at Bhola—he undid the bag and stood the bottles on the table. Then one by one, he turned them several degrees about so that the labels all faced Anin. It was his way of saying hello properly. To oblige him, she sat down, read them out aloud and asked him what she should begin with.

'Beer. Beer after whisky, very risky. Whisky after beer, never fear.'

She seemed to like the couplet and repeated it to herself a couple of times, smiling and nodding approval at its pithiness, stopping only when Bhola asked her whether they had a bottle opener with them because they would need one both for the beer and the soft drinks. No, they hadn't, and she didn't wish to go down to the kitchen because she didn't want to disturb either the maid or her father and besides, she wasn't certain where they kept theirs.

'Your father's back from office?' Fathers were universal bad news.

'Yes,' she admitted, balancing the cold beer bottle on the dog's head.

At last, Bhola climbed the metal ladder, crossed the wall, descended the rope ladder on the other side and went to look for his bicycle keys, the chain of which had a bottle opener attached to it. After he returned, he, feeling excited, tried to drink some whisky neat and Anin and Dosto, heads together, peered into the gloom of the chicken coop and she explained that the birds probably would have to be relocated in some warmer corner of the house before the onset of winter.

She tried them all, generously and adventurously, mixing rum with Thums Up, beer with Limca and towards the end dashes of whisky with both. She had a memorable evening. She was relieved that Dosto turned out to be nice in a way different from Bhola, and the unexpectedness of the pleasure, of spending an agreeable evening drinking with two attractive boys, went a little to her head. It didn't help at all that rum mixed with Thums Up tasted so much like Thums Up and beer with Limca was practically Limca.

For the boys too, the experience was novel. Neither had ever drunk alcohol before with a girl other than Dosto's sister and she didn't count as memorable because, in the afternoons after school, while quaffing in her presence Dosto's father's diluted cognacs and puffing away at his beastly cigarillos and hating both, they both simply had been waiting for her to evaporate. Unlike her, Anin was an unknown quantity. She was older, more attractive, freer, unpredictable, apt to get tipsy and start swaying, dreamily and alone, to some tune audible only behind her eyes. 'What's the matter? Aren't we celebrating Bhola's registering for the Board exams? Why don't both of you get up and dance?' She rapidly executed some elementary Kathak steps and twirled away across the floor of the terrace.

The boys reluctantly left their chairs to amble a few steps after her. 'Well, I can't dance,' confessed Bhola with a smile that tried to minimize the importance of the disclosure. He paused to allow Dosto too to concede that he couldn't but while *he* hummed, snorted and hawed, Anin, near the enormous frangipani that threatened to split open its tub, pirouetted once, seemed to slow down, gasped in surprise as she lost balance, reeled and fell heavily, with a dull thud, to the floor. The boys and the dog rushed up. For an instant, she lay flat on her back, wondering at the darkening sky. Then embarrassed, trying to giggle it off, she, repeatedly exclaiming, 'Oof, oof,' attempted to rise but was held down by Bhola's hand at her shoulder. He felt her bra strap beneath her kurta and unbiddingly, the thought entered his head, If she doesn't wriggle her shoulder out of my grasp, it means that she'd like me to get physical. The idea filled him with dread. 'Take your time to get up,' he urged her. He squatted on his heels beside her as though shitting atop an Indian loo.

Anin was pale but looked happy, as though she didn't care that she didn't feel well. 'Do you want to vomit?' asked Dosto with his face quite close to hers, his eyes large with anxiety. 'I vomit all the time. It doesn't matter. It feels great, like into that heaven of freedom, my father, let my country awake. Maybe you drank too much too quickly on an empty stomach. It's like sailors crossing the Equator for the first time. Do you want Bhola to push two fingers down your throat?'

'I'll just lie down somewhere, I think.' She belched, apologized and holding on to them, got to her feet. Not letting go of either hand, she swayed a bit, perhaps a little too long, as though she wished to start dancing again, giggled unexpectedly and then, gently shrugging off all assistance, shuffled across to the rug by the door to the stairs and laboriously, in slow motion, lay down. The dog flopped down beside her. It had a hardon. She immediately—but slowly—shifted so that she could pillow her head on its neck.

Vaguely feeling, with their hostess incommunicado, that the party was over in half an hour, Bhola helped himself to a second whisky and Dosto to a third rum. He took a sip of his drink, looked at his glass like a Shakespearean suicide at the cause of death, changed his mind about the soliloquy, glanced at Bhola and muttered, 'I gotta go. Is she sleeping or dead or what?' He abandoned his unfinished glass on the table. 'I really gotta go.'

In his friend's place, Bhola felt that he too would have fled early the scene of the crime. He helped Dosto top up with water the bottles of whisky and rum, screw tightly their caps, wrap them up, one in Dosto's swimming towel, the other in a teeshirt, and place them carefully upright in the knapsack. 'We should really learn, Dosto, how to dance. There must be some bugger somewhere in some dance school who gives lessons. Not that Mohiniattam-fox trot crap, but you know—just what to do with your damn hands and feet when the music starts.'

Dosto swung his bag onto his back and shambled off a little guiltily towards the door. 'You'd better hang around till she wakes up. What if she's raped or dead or something? It isn't safe to leave her alone with that dog. It's sick that I gotta go. Don't tell her that I left right away because it doesn't look nice, like rats deserting a sinking ship or whatever.' At the head of the stairs, he got cold feet, paused, looked back and asked in a low voice, 'What if I bloody meet her father or the maid?' He turned about and stepped back out on the terrace. 'Hide those beer bottles somewhere—take both across the wall. I'll wait until you return.'

'I'm not going to ascend and descend that rope ladder a thousand times like a monkey while drunk. Just relax and fuck off. Nothing is going to happen.'

Dosto descended as surreptitiously as he had arrived.
Bhola shuffled across to the front of the terrace to observe
him negotiate the guard at the gate. At a loss for action, he
returned to the table, finished his whisky—without much
wanting to—in two large gulps, and feeling flushed and
adventurous, stepped over to gaze down in the gloom at and
fuzzily contemplate the recumbent Anin and wonder why it
couldn't have been any of the others—a porcine, imperious
female teacher, a vegetable seller with prominent collarbones,
a stupid bank guard in a tight uniform.

She tugged slowly at the hem of his trousers. He almost
fell, he was caught so unawares. Obediently, he sat down
crosslegged alongside the dog's huge head. With her eyes
shut, she changed her pillow from the beast's neck to Bhola's
lap. In a daze, he felt her head shimmy about on his thigh till
it found repose against his crotch. Some moments later, he
could sense her exhalations against his jeans. Almost
involuntarily, he stroked the hair off her forehead. Her cheeks
were wet. He couldn't remember whether it was biologically
possible for human beings to weep in their sleep. The notion
depressed him. Perhaps she was crying because she had X-
ray vision and could see in his undies his gloomy, Hamlet-like
one-incher peanut. In a couple of minutes, his right leg went
off to sleep. He needed to shift position. He had no idea
whether the next move was to be his. He couldn't imagine
her going any further without some kind of encouragement
from him. He wanted to go home and settle down in bed
with an Agatha Christie written before she became senile.
Maybe if he unzipped himself, then took off all his clothes
and rubbed and brushed his penis against her skin, and
pranced it about all over her body like a lizard on the prowl
and at the same time thought furiously of some sexy things,
it would balloon up to a respectable size. And yet she was
pretty, that was what was so horrible, he thought, stooping

over with yogic ease and kissing her temple, she was attractive, warm and lovable, even if it was infuriating how she couldn't speak one full sentence in any one language correctly.

He had reached for the buckle of his belt and then paused, deciding for the moment not to disturb the head in his lap, to reflect instead a little more on this and that, on the universe eventually being sucked back into itself and how anyone could admit to being born after 1960 when, without warning, the dog noiselessly arose and glided in one fluid movement to stand sentinel at the door to the stairs, a menacing murkier shape in the darkness. Bhola, with panic aggravating the clumsiness of his movements, lifted Anin's head and placed it on the ground, got up, staggered, with one leg asleep, to the table, picked up the bottles of beer and hobbled off to squat, practically without breathing, in the patch of black between water tank and chicken coop. 'Tchaah,' he exclaimed to himself immediately, got up, switched off the light of the shed and returned to his position.

The maid appeared first and for a moment was silhouetted in the doorway against the streetlight that filtered in through the translucent glass of the stairs window. The dog wagged his tail twice and went back to stand behind Anin. Someone switched on a light in the stairs. A man of middle height and middle age, bespectacled, with thinning hair, was visible behind the maid on the second step from the landing. 'She's here,' said the maid over her shoulder to the man, 'I think she's asleep.' 'Asleep?' The man climbed the steps and stood for an instant behind the maid with his hand on her shoulder. 'How could she have fallen asleep at this hour?' He brushed past her despite there being enough space between her figure and the railing and stepped out on the terrace. 'Anin?'

'Yes, Papa?'

'What are you doing alone in the dark?' He came and stood over her, hands on hips, not more than ten feet away from the concealed Bhola.

'My meditation exercises.' Her voice was subdued and slurred. To Bhola, it sounded so false that to show that he couldn't bear it—the compound of the strain of concealment and her bad acting—he wanted to rush out sobbing from his hiding place, in passing contemptuously flick his fingers against the father's loins, tumble down the stairs to the feet of the maid, push his face deep into her crotch that doubtless exuded the warm smells of maternity and beg forgiveness for being who he was, for being alive. He watched with an affectionate sneer Anin sit up on the rug, stretch and look about her like a tourist on a magic island. Her clumsy dissimulation somehow freed him from fear. The huge clot that his heart had become melted. If her terrible performance was not objected to, then neither would his presence on the terrace. Perhaps it wasn't inexplicable in the least, his being there, perhaps Anin had told her father that she had invited some friends for tea that day and his jumping up and secreting himself away had been totally unnecessary, merely the instinctive, primordial blue funk of one of the lower animals and Anin gazing about her in the light from the stairs was simply a hostess searching for her missing guests so that they could be introduced to someone who mattered. Still undecided, Bhola cautiously half-raised and waved a hand in the dark of his nook. He could barely see it himself.

Father, daughter and dog left the terrace. At the doorway, the beast paused once to look straight back at Bhola. He gave him a thumbs-up sign in gratitude for not having forgotten. Rolling the beer bottles under the water tank, he arose, stretched, lit a cigarette, trailed around for a while and then wondered how he would get home since there was nobody on Anin's side of the wall to hold the rope ladder tight when he lurched down it on the other side. It was no use just tying the rope to the rungs of the metal ladder; they had tried that several times before but their knots had simply not been strong enough.

He dawdled till he had smoked the cigarette down to its filter, all the while dreaming up ever-giddier ways of reaching home. In the end, he had almost decided on creeping down the stairs barefoot when he saw that the dog was back at the doorway, again an ominous black form in the darkness. 'Hey hey you you get off my cloud,' sang Bhola pleasantly to it. In Anin's absence, the brute was altogether another matter. Bhola flicked the cigarette butt in its direction, skipped away to the metal ladder, climbed it, sat astride the wall and looked down to find the dog a foot beneath him, silent, with forepaws on the middle rungs, the huge head intent on striving for his calves. His insides melted into mucus. He snapped his leg up out of reach, tumbled over and hung down the other side. For a second, the thought that he had left behind on the table his bicycle keys distracted him, making him lose his grip. Scraping his shins, knees and elbows against the wall, he fell. He landed ineptly, a sharp pain in his right ankle making him forget even the dog.

The next morning, it had swollen up and become red. He hobbled out of bed to inform his stepmother that he would have to skip school that day. It was surprisingly painful, particularly when he poked it or tried to place his weight on it. In the evening, his father accompanied him to the doctor. Though the ankle was not broken, it *was* sprained and would have to be plastered. He was advised rest for a week.

The sprained ankle calmed him down and set him right. It gave him a reason for stopping his mentally debilitating sham of dressing up every morning for school and departing with his school bag and tiffin box without having a school to go to. For hours, he lay in bed gazing at and dreaming of nothing, soaking in the balm of relief. Later in the week, he got down to organizing himself. He loved being methodical. Slow and steady never won the race but it was the only way to run if one wanted to be sure of finishing honourably.

'Listen, Dosto, if there is some Trigo or Cood Geom that

I can't follow, will you ask your afternoon tutor?'

'Sure. The ape will wonder, though, how I on my own've arrived at the stage when I can figure out that I can't figure out a particular problem.'

November became February as the weeks hurtled by. Bhola was surprised to learn from across the wall of the terrace that Anin too, though older than him and Dosto, was sitting the Board exams with them and, like Bhola, privately. Her subjects though were strange. Of the five, he hadn't heard of one—Home Science—and hadn't known that two others—Physical Education, Pali—existed as options.

'We could study Civics together,' she proposed, standing on the ladder and pressing her nose flat against the wire mesh alongside the water tank.

'Only if you kill that dog first,' responded Bhola, 'and skin his head and gift it to me so that I can wear it as a mask for the exams.'

She smiled without humour. 'He's right here, Corbett,' she observed, looking down at her invisible feet.

The evening that they had drunk together turned out to be the last that Bhola spent on Anin's terrace. For the first few weeks, of course, he couldn't cross over because of his sprained ankle and then later he discovered that he didn't especially want to. The dog, it was true, was a genuine deterrent but he also felt uneasy at the thought of Anin's physical proximity. He wasn't ready for it. They didn't refer even once to the events of that evening, to her falling down and then dropping off with her head in his lap. He moreover locked away in his skull the images of her father standing, invisible to his daughter, with his hand on the maid's shoulder and then brushing past her when there had been no need to. Anin on her part didn't press too forcefully her invitations to him to traverse the wall, appearing quite content to chat with a wire mesh between them. When Prep Leave for the exams began, Dosto joined Bhola on his terrace on some mornings to waste everybody's time so that all three eventually dispersed ridden with guilt and worked better thereafter.

Bhola sat his exams in a sunny Municipal school surrounded by dust, cobwebs and rat droppings. His fellow examinees all looked like retarded grocers and door-to-door salesmen of water purifiers. The results were announced and published three months later. He was placed fourth in the country out of ninety-five thousand students. It was the first time in the history of the exams that a private candidate had found a place in the top ten. His father, stepmother and brother were elated, proud and puzzled.

'Private? In all the newspaper announcements, why have they written "pvt" in brackets after your name?'

'Because of Sanskrit. Pvt doesn't mean private at all, it's a Sanskrit word for—well, pure Sanskrit. You remember that I'd decided to offer it and had had to fill up those forms?'

'But Sanskrit isn't even mentioned as a subject against your name.'

'That's because they only choose the top five. It's a top five system. TFS, they call it. Pvt—oh now I remember—means TFS in Sanskrit.'

'It's odd that your school doesn't seem to be mentioned even once anywhere.'

'Why should it be? The credit is mine—and yours, of course. You were so supportive and all that.'

Bhola's father's perplexity increased when he learnt that his son wanted to leave the nest some years earlier than expected and go off to a hill station several hundred kilometres away to pursue his studies in something called the M.K.M.Z.A.P. Graduate and Post-Graduate College for the Sciences and Humanities.

'What is it? *Where* is it? What is wrong with Presidency? With your marks, you'd get in anywhere for any course.'

Dosto was even more intrigued, almost outraged. 'This is obviously The Case of the Alluring Armpit, my horny boy.'

Their Perry Mason days were not yet over. 'The body parts of some unknown are drawing you up there. I need to chat with your father. They teach English Literature in Hindi there, is what I'll tell him.' Dosto himself and Anin, having done reasonably well in the Board exams, had both applied for courses in Political Science, History and Psychology in three or four of the local colleges. There was talk of Dosto's parents, who had been dreading all the while that he would fail, rewarding him with a Java Yezdi motorcycle. It was one of the two reasons why he did not consider going Bhola's way. The second was Anin.

Bhola himself wanted to get away even from them, be on his own, free to lead a life of social and sexual anarchy, if possible be driven principally by lust. His self-discipline in the months that followed his expulsion from school and the unexpected manner in which it had borne fruit—the way in which, because of his performance in the exams, things had suddenly righted themselves—had boosted enormously his self-confidence, his sense of his own worth. He wanted to test the waters because he was now confident of wading through.

It galled him vaguely that Dosto and Anin had hit it off well enough for them to meet each other, apparently quite often, independently of him—leaving him, as it were, to the company of his own depressing self. His pride—particularly his new sense of self-esteem—made it impossible for him to even hint at his mild bitterness at the feeling of being excluded. It was easier to mask his emotions beneath an amused, slightly superior—but nevertheless agreeable—smile. It was evident that Anin had physically and mentally improved considerably with the tension of the Board exams having receded. Whatever it had been that had kept her at home for several months on end—mental collapse, nervous breakdown, attempted suicide, whatever—it was clearly now a thing of the past. No longer cooped up, she was free to laugh and chat with Dosto before her parents in the drawing room and go out to the movies with him. It stunned Bhola when they came back from seeing *Kabhie Kabhie* together.

'Sorry man what to do but she watches only Hindi films. This was her sixth viewing of that damn film. She knew all the songs and sang along during the show. Everyone around us in the hall shushed her. Me too. I pretended not to know her.'

Expectedly, Bhola's father made enquiries about M.K.M.Z.A.P. College and was surprised to receive a favourable report. Its results had been consistently good. It had recently been granted the status of Deemed University. It was run by a private Trust packed with vegetarians that also managed a hospital and a College of Dentistry in South India. Its alumni usually became, in diverse fields, successful moneygrubbing vegetarians. Most important, his father unearthed someone who could keep an eye on Bhola, the younger sister of one of his stepmother's college acquaintances. The sister herself worked in some administrative capacity in the same college and he could even board and lodge with her. 'Home food and home life will be better than the fare of some ghastly college canteen and sharing a hostel room with unclean unknowns,' his stepmother had elaborated.

Before taking the plunge, he returned once to Dr Borkar's erstwhile house in the neighbourhood to find out whether the doctor—and Titli and Moti—had struck root and were still up there in the hills. He had tried to book a long-distance call from his father's office only to be told by the operator that the number that he had given her did not exist and that to get the correct number of the college, he would have to phone another number which later turned out to be unremittingly either engaged or unattended. The college prospectus that he had received by post listed another doctor, a Dr J.P.Maheshwari, as Resident Medical Officer, but it could not be relied upon because the main body of its text dated from

1973. Nobody that he knew of knew anybody who had attended M.K.M.Z.A.P.

The house itself had changed, been repainted. The pink and chocolate had given way to grey and cream. In the tiny patch of lawn squatted two boys seedier and younger than himself pestering a litter of pups. Neither the grandmother-type nor the *Beware Of Dog* sign were visible. He guessed that the house had changed hands. 'I'm looking for Dr Borkar.'

As though in response, one of the boys stood up sniggering and without a word held up for display a brown-bodied, black-faced, clearly unhappy pup. Urine dripped from it as from a leaking faucet. With a squeak of excitement and makebelieve disgust, he, misjudging both direction and distance, flung it at the other boy. The pup hit the side of the parked car with a deep thud and, screaming at the heavens, dropped to the ground. Continuing to squeal in agony, it slithered forward on its abdomen for the safety of the underbelly of the car. Bhola watched its three siblings scurry after it. While the boys observed him, he waited for the shrill howling—and the sharp, sympathetic yawps of the other pups—to drop a couple of decibels before turning around and leaving.

In the weeks before his departure for M.K.M.Z.A.P. College, at times when he stood outside at some distance and observed himself, he was appalled at the deranged manner in which he had taken one of the important steps of his life. How old would Titli be? Twenty-three? Perhaps younger. She might not even be up there. Perhaps the world had swallowed her up again. At other times, the lunacy of the decision and the uncertainty of his future were in themselves exciting and she merely a pretext for getting away and moving on. Had the village of Gopinath the cook been located next to some educational institution that offered courses in something or the other—Vedic Psychology or Anin's intriguing Home Science—he would have weighed even them as possible options.

Leaving home without suffering the twinges of departure was however impossible. He began playing chess two or three times a week with his father and discussing the Bridge and Recipe columns of the newspapers with his stepmother. His brother had already left to study Hotel Management in Bombay and had more or less forgotten home; predictably, he had phoned just once in six weeks and that only to ask for some more money. His father was fifty-five and his stepmother forty something. They would suddenly be alone but surely they'd be okay.

'I want you to promise me something. Check,' said his father, sliding his rook down to the end of the board.

Bhola's king minced away a step to hide behind a bishop. 'Yes, sure, what?'

His father gazed down at the game for an age without speaking. The overhead light gleamed dully on his thinning scalp. It was a favourite technique of his, to distract his opponent with boredom before making his move. Slowly and menacingly, he stretched his hand out for his remaining knight, paused in mid-air, looked Bhola straight in the eye, said nothing, changed his mind and nudged a pawn forward two squares with his index finger, sat back in the chair in a slump, took off and dropped his spectacles in his lap, rubbed his jaw as though caressing his evening stubble, sighed and suddenly unburdened himself in a rush, 'You should consider carefully—when you marry—whenever that is—there's no hurry, of course—your duties towards maintaining a line— your responsibility to your blood and your caste.' He stopped as though deprived of breath but continued to stare defiantly at his son, daring him, as it were, to protest or frown or guffaw or snicker.

They were alone at the dining table; they played there because of its right height. 'Sure, whatever,' agreed Bhola, smirking nonplussedly, even nervously, at the board without

seeing any of the men. He felt for a moment that he had
become someone else, somebody to whom such a request
would sound quite reasonable. He himself didn't know his
own sub-caste—what kind of Brahmin he was—or even the
names of his great grandparents. Surely that wasn't a lapse on
his part? Sneaking a glance at his father, he commented, 'It
sounds a little like a Hindu Macbeth, though—maintaining a
line and blood and all that.'

Shakespeare was usually a safe subject with his father.
'Whose turn is it?' he asked, raising his spectacles against the
light on the wall to check how clean the lenses were and then
absentmindedly replacing them on his nose without wiping
off the specks and smudges. 'Mine,' responded Bhola and
aimlessly made his queen's knight prance forward in the
general direction of the other's king. He doubted whether his
father would have broached the subject in the presence of his
second wife, a Bihari Catholic brought up in Calcutta. He
wasn't even certain that he had understood what his father
had intended to say because he felt that he couldn't have
meant what he seemed to have said. 'What about Bhanu?' he
deflected in response. 'Has he promised too, to do the right
thing by his caste?'

Then suddenly, while he smiled at his father to take any
possible sting out of the question, just from the way that his
father looked at him without either smiling or speaking, from
far away, with sorrow and a father's tenderness in his eyes,
and with anxiety pulling down his face in pouches, Bhola
knew that he knew of his son's sexual proclivities. He knows,
he knows, my God, hey Ram, God knows how but he bloody
knows. Reflexively, to hide his face, Bhola began massaging
his eyelids with his fingertips. Perhaps it was one of those
weekends when he had decided to supervise the reorganization
of Bhola's things, to see what his son should leave behind. He
must have come across a stray scribble somewhere, a page
torn off on which Bhola would have recorded his passion for

what he called the Owl, the Object of that Week's Lust: *Went fishing this evening. The market stank like rotting corpses. Peeping Tom sat behind his prawns and rui, his lungi tucked up around his crotch, flashing his black thighs at his clientele, his tom practically peeping out. The odour of fish wafted up out of his lungi. He had nicked himself at the knee with that monstrous knife while dressing some fish, no doubt also monstrous. Bury my lips at Wounded Knee. The fucker knows. He sees the lust on my face and smiles and overcharges me.* From behind his palms, Bhola asked his father, 'Why now? It's a bit early, isn't it? Rest assured that at M.K.M.Z.A.P., I won't be smitten by true love for some low-class, low-caste, dark female.' To himself, he added an afterthought, *And what if he now says: It isn't the females that I'm worried about?*

In the few days that remained before his departure, he prayed that his father would not enter upon the subject of his marriage again. He also remained on his best behaviour, eliciting from his father a corresponding response, above all because he wanted to carry away with him a pleasant memory of home.

'Remember that stupor is the greatest sin,' began his father once more on the morning of the last Sunday, standing over and supervising—without following anything—the local mechanic while he tinkered with the car.

'Not to worry, Baba. The lad of action is on his way to becoming a man.'

From the claustrophobic, air-conditioned, second-class compartment of the train that took him out of the city, he gazed at the hot, humid greyness beyond the windows and wondered how any condition other than stupor was possible in a climate such as theirs. People were like the land they inhabited. They were formed by it. There was some substance in the colonial notion that the defeatism and detachment of Hindu thought could only have emerged from a brain pickled by the warmth of the tropics.

When his mood lifted, however, he decided that he could do worse than follow his father's advice. The life of every man must be lived in accord with some standards. As long as nobody knew, he could set his own.

HINDI LESSON

He arrived to start his college life in a daze on the morning bus that he had taken from just outside the railway station on the second Saturday of July, two days before the new academic year was to begin. Throughout the journey, he had felt slightly breathless whenever he had daydreamed about his newly found freedom and what he could do with it. When he alit from the compartment in the rain, he couldn't recall whether Mrs Manchanda, his landlady-to-be, or her son Vivek, was to meet his train down in the plains or his bus forty kilometres up in the hills. With the help of a coolie whom he willingly overpaid because he was attractive, Bhola, thinking parenthetically of Moti and his wife, hauled his unwieldy luggage—a monstrous steel trunk, his bedding, two grips—across to the bus stand.

There were other occupants of the bus who were clearly students headed for the same destination but, during the one and a half hour drive, neither Bhola nor anybody else made any move towards making new friends. He for one was tired, wet and disoriented; moreover, the sullen sky, the mist-like rain against the downcast trees, the scarred and self-absorbed hills and overriding them all, the roar of the bus as it struggled to master the steep, nauseating hairpin bends—everything seemed to discourage contiguity and contact. He shrank into and huddled up in his shirt and intermittently, in flashes like lightning, allowed himself to pine for home.

Mrs Manchanda met him at the hill town Inter-State Bus Terminus. She was pale, soft-spoken, bespectacled and separated from her husband. He didn't know how to react to her. They rode to the college in a hand-pulled rickshaw, under umbrellas in a fine drizzle. His luggage, tied down and covered with a plastic sheet, wobbled magically behind them in another. Having little to say, they smiled shyly at each other whenever their eyes met. The rickshaw, hard, tiny and uncomfortable, with sharp metal edges at unexpected places, jolted them gently but completely over the uneven roads. In the rain the town looked pretty and the green of the trees washed. Alongside a pink clock tower, the wooden buildings of a government school disgorged its students dressed in white and blue, cackling and chattering excitedly. The twenty-minute ride to the college campus was made longer by the puddles, the pace of the baggage-laden rickshaw and a detour occasioned by a minor landslide. He enjoyed watching the easy, loping gait of the old rickshaw puller and wanted a couple of times to reach over and, massaging his shoulder blades, advise him not to ruin his lungs by smoking while running. Hoping—and wondering meanwhile what the mathematical chances were of thus fulfilling at its start the objective of his adventure—to sight Moti and his wife, he scanned the faces of pedestrians—Nepalese labourers, Tibetan monks, ordinary citizens about their business—and of passengers on other rickshaws—tourists, students, honeymooning couples from the plains—doubting all the time whether he would—even if he saw them—recognize those known faces made unfamiliar by context and time. As his fatigue and feeling of strangeness lessened, he began to like what he noticed of his surroundings—the absence of noisy traffic, the greetings exchanged by passersby, the colonial-style bungalows spread out like sated royalty amidst terraced field and wooded incline, the goats on the slopes of hillocks, the prospect of hill after hill after hill dissolving into cloud. Further ahead, when they were clear of the town, the lanes turned quieter, more winding, leafy, undulating, ideal for a steady and endless cross-country run at the end of which he would emerge perfectly thin, free of dross, pure.

M.K.M.Z.A.P. occupied almost twenty acres of a portion of a valley and some chunks of its enclosing hills. The rickshaws paused at a bend in the lane for them to admire the view of the campus from a crest and for the rickshaw pullers to light fresh beedis. Mrs Manchanda, doubtless having no wish to gasp with wonder at the sight of her workplace, asked them to hurry up in a tone that made Bhola thankful that he wasn't her domestic help.

'I sometimes,' he began in a mix of Hindi and English as they started their descent, 'have a bad back.' He turned and smiled shyly at her downy forearm and the hand that still clutched the open umbrella even though the drizzle had stopped five minutes ago. 'Perhaps I should visit the college doctor before classes open.' He felt that he should kick off his search early. The umbrella served also no doubt as a kind of purdah against the sun.

In response, she smiled at a flock of goats on the verge of the road. He, completely nonplussed, could think of no more subjects of conversation with her for the next four weeks. As they neared the main gates of the college, they passed bookshops, secondhand furniture stalls, cyclostyling kiosks, congenial cafés, stationery stores, the appurtenances of academia. Mrs Manchanda snapped her fingers at the rickshaw-wala and spat out in Hindi, 'Go ahead and take the third side entrance to the Administrative Staff Quarters' Block.' Even he, alarmed at the gratuitous peevishness in her tone, missed a step.

They stopped at the gate of the ground floor apartment on the left. It had as a bonus a tiny, manicured lawn. Vivek, Mrs Manchanda's only son, opened the front door. He was tall, rangy, personable and about Bhola's age. When awake, he hummed to himself, virtually without pause, one of three sixties-early-seventies Hindi film tunes. They didn't change in four years. Over the succeeding months, Bhola, analysing them, felt that he could discern in them a pattern; like the ragas of classical music, Vivek's choice of tune could indicate his mood or just the time of day or even—more simply—his plans for an afternoon. For instance, he always hummed *Jaag Dil-e-Diwana* from the film *Oonche Log* when he went to answer the doorbell or when he put on his boots before traipsing off for football. Sometimes, when the two occurred together, his humming became loud enough to rival the volume of the radio.

The apartment comprised one sitting room, two enclosed verandahs, one bedroom and three black holes—a toilet, a bathroom and a kitchen. Bhola was to occupy the servant's room that jutted out from the back verandah. It had its own primitive, Indian-style toilet and, more significantly, an independent rear entrance that gave on to a kitchen patch half the size of the front lawn.

Vivek helped him with his luggage. Between panting and sweating over the trunk and pushing and cursing it when it got stuck in the doorway of the room, he revealed without rancour, 'This was my room. We need the extra money, so I had to move out.'

'But you can use it whenever and for whatever you want,' responded Bhola without enthusiasm. They dumped the trunk in the middle of the room. It wouldn't go under the bed. Bhola hated it. 'Where is the nearest STD phone? I need to call home to tell them that I've arrived safe and sound.' At least the room and window panes were clean and there was nothing ghastly on the walls save for a college calendar depicting the forts of India. 'And do you know whether Dr Borkar is available on Saturday afternoons?'

'Borkar? You mean Maheshwari.'

Lunch was late, vegetarian, simple and delicious. Bhola gorged like a college student at the Sunday buffet of a new 5-star hotel when somebody else is paying. Mrs Manchanda had to cook a second round of rice. She didn't eat with them. 'None of the males in my family,' disclosed Bhola to Vivek sitting opposite him, 'have been known ever to refuse any food, no matter what time of day or night and no matter what the food. It's quite an obstacle to overcome when you're serious about losing weight.' Vivek didn't even look up from his plate. Bhola was famished because he had had nothing since the tea and biscuits on the train. He was upset that nobody seemed to have heard of Borkar; he wanted to hide his reaction and needed time to figure out what to do in the immediate future.

'Maheshwari is a strange person and not a competent doctor,' Vivek declared as though that was what they had been talking about, 'friendly though but strange.' He ate rapidly, convulsively swallowing mouthfuls—his Adam's apple bobbing—between phrases. 'He is a Leave Vacancy appointment who's here to stay forever. People say that he isn't really a doctor and that his medical degree from Ulhasnagar or wherever is faked.'

'I see. But Borkar. Who could tell me about him?'

Nobody, ostensibly. The College Dispensary Office would not open till Monday. Further, Dr Maheshwari turned out to be old, dour, taciturn and virtually deaf to questions that did not concern him.

'I've never met Borkar-Shorkar. And there's nothing wrong with your back as far as I can make out.'

Classes began and Bhola in his habitual daze, dreaming of other options and other lives, busied himself in adjusting to a new rhythm and world. His classmates, in general industrious and serious, at first appeared difficult to relate to and seemed indistinguishable one from the other. None of them exhibited any of the cynicism, moral insensibility or worldweariness of Bhola's big-city set. Since they too were new, it was pointless of course asking them about Dr Borkar. Bhola's search for him subsided to just beneath the surface of daily existence,

its questions ready to pop up like toast whenever he was in
the mood. Whom didn't he ask? Teachers, waiters in the
college canteen, hostel attendants, the newspaper vendor,
neighbours in the Staff Quarters Enclave, Rana the cigarette-
and-paan-wala at the gate. They all either recalled nobody by
that name or dimly confused him with somebody else. The
frailty and volatility of public memory never ceased to bemuse
him. 'Ah yes I think I've seen a doctor's board with that
name—now where was it...' It depressed and shocked Bhola
that Borkar could have either lied to his family about where
he was going or changed his mind en route about his
destination. The second notion, with its indications of a truly
vagabond spirit, beguiled him momentarily too. On his bad
days, therefore, he found it galling that someone like Borkar,
who played such a major role in Bhola's mental life despite
his not having seen him till then, had so successfully shaken
off his pursuer without even knowing that he had had one; it
made Bhola feel stupid and useless. To anyone even mildly
curious about his connection to Dr Borkar, Bhola, lately
occupied with trying to avoid having Hindi substituted for
History as his first Auxiliary Subject, would lucidly explain, 'I
need him. He was the best Hindi teacher that I've ever had.'

College life was novel and interesting. On his good days,
therefore, he didn't mind waiting a while to discover Titli's
whereabouts. The delay would test his self-discipline. Besides,
he had located others in his surroundings to distract him. He
liked the sensation of going about his business while the
Borkar trio went about theirs out there in the town somewhere,
waiting passively to be unearthed at a suitably dramatic
moment. Ambling about the alleys or jogging in the lanes in
and around the town, in company or alone, he kept an eye out
for a signboard announcing the timings during which the
services of one Dr Borkar, Medical Practitioner, could be
availed of—and when, without warning, the thought taunted
him that the objects of his longing, having forgotten him

completely, were probably leading happy and fulfilled lives several hundred kilometres away, he would stumble, then straighten up, grit his teeth, jerk his head away to clear it, and force himself to increase his pace to elude the bogeys of the foolish decisions of his past.

Then, in the middle of March, 1977, almost eight months after the start of the academic year, Anin and Dosto came up to visit. Bhola admitted to himself that he wasn't looking forward to showing them round M.K.M.Z.A.P. He did not want to hear that as an institution, it was not top-notch, that he was wasting himself in it, that he had made the wrong choice. Of course he was and he had, he knew it, but he didn't want to be commented on by anybody else. He had gone home twice during the intervening months, once in October for the autumn break and then around New Year, met everybody and found that things—people, relationships, he himself—seemed to have changed. He preferred living alone and with strangers, for one, to staying at home and feeling unloved. It wasn't too bad waking up in his tiny room in the cold, eating Mrs Manchanda's alu parathas and dahi for breakfast and panting up the paved footpaths to class at eight o'clock. It took him over four hours to digest the grease of the morning, so he usually jogged at lunchtime.

Slowly, as the weeks glided by like a river, a sort of routine, founded on the kind of person he was—obsessed with keeping physically and mentally trim, with standing back, as on the bank of a watercourse, to slow things down—crept up on him. He jogged, attended class, read, kept to himself, helped Vivek with his English Comprehension, joined the Chess and Cinema Clubs, and turned eighteen. Though young, he was demoralized, nevertheless, at the unambiguous manner in which time was running out. The days swirled by without either affording him any pleasure or revealing anything of value. Almost insidiously, as though trying to hide from the hard core of his loneliness, he began anew a daily programme of acts that progressively helped him to define his day, to mark the passage of time and eventually to slow it down.

By and by, he began to refer to his programme as the Secret Seven. He had started with a total of four obligatory daily acts and the number over the years went up way beyond seven to touch thirteen at one point, but it had remained at seven for several months. The activities were secret because he knew them to be ridiculous and retarded for someone of his age and because he never disclosed them to—leave alone discussed them with—anybody in his entire life. They were meant to give shape to his day (and thus to his life) in the manner in which his plans of weight loss were meant to give shape to his body. Naturally, some physical exercise was the first of the seven. With time, the others came to include:

ii) *The Reading of Non-Shit.* Not lolling in bed with a Harold Robbins but sitting upright in a straight-backed chair with Freud's *The Psychopathology of Everyday Life* or something comparable before him on a desk in proper lamplight.

iii) *What the Fuck Did You Do with Your Day?* An account of the day in a diary. Predominantly sexual, reminiscent of the earlier Chronicles of Gopinath but more open to recording diurnal events, how Kumkum Sharma the Assistant Librarian revealed that she knew that the college called her Cumcum and how fortunately she didn't seem to know what it stood for, and how he saw an early Tarkovsky at the Ciné Club, boy, heavy.

iv) *Relax. It's Good to Think of Nothing for a Minute.* He tried almost every day for twenty years to truly empty his mind and think of nothing—blanker than pitch black—but he didn't succeed beyond a few seconds at a time. For his birthday, he asked for and received a stopwatch with which he would time himself till overwhelmed by a sense of preposterousness.

v) *Keep Mum.* Hold your tongue. You've nothing to say. To be silent is the first step towards being mistaken for an intelligent being.

vi) *Skill Sinister*. Use your left hand for some act or the other for which you normally use your right and thus exercise the unused parts of your brain. Vanity of vanities, do not forget that the world's most impossibly elegant cricket players have all been left-handed.

vii) *Get Out of Yourself Once a Day*. Make contact with others. Help Vivek Manchanda with his essays and vocabulary. Notch up a plus point or two with Karma the Boy Scout god.

Those for years formed the core of his daily round. He saw that they were absurd and fatuous, yet he persisted with them. They nagged him and made him uneasy when he ignored them for a day or two. Indeed, from time to time, with something of the periodicity of the waxing and waning of the moon, he grappled with whether he was excluding from the Seven some crucial notations. Should he not, for example, *measure* the amount of water that he drank every day? Did he *laugh* enough? What about a minimum of four therapeutic belly laughs? Then things that he read about in the Health columns of newspapers would intrigue and inveigle him for days: Was he *Listening* to His Body at all?

By the time that he got Anin's card wishing him luck for his exams and announcing that they would like to visit him for a lightning weekend *before* they started, he was so enmeshed in the rhythm of the Secret Seven that he was actually quite dismayed at the news. There was nothing to be done, though, except to grin and bear it and reserve a room for Dosto at the College Guest House. Anin was travelling with her parents and naturally would stay with them.

Dosto caught the slow train and then the late-afternoon bus, turning up well after dark on the second Friday of the month. Anin and her parents reached by car the morning after. The parents evidently did not know of Dosto's arrival in the hill town the previous evening. To extricate Anin from the clutches of her family without arousing either comment or suspicion, the services of Devika, a student of Economics at M.K.M.Z.A.P. whom Bhola knew by sight and who had been Anin's schoolmate for some years, were roped in.

For two whole days, the four of them, as a quartet or in pairs, walked the mountain lanes over the last of the winter snow, taking care to steer clear of the Institute where Anin's father had been invited to be Chief Guest at some prize distribution ceremony, watched—and hooted throughout—some rubbishy Hindi film in the college auditorium, munched peanuts and pakodas and drank litres of tea at several dhabas and cafés, rode horses—depressing, half-dead beasts—in the Exhibition Grounds beneath the Bus Terminus, staggered up Fatman's Hill and were appropriately intimidated by the monkeys on it, and took reel upon reel of photographs. Bhola abandoned the Secret Seven for two whole days and didn't mind in the least—indeed, when he recalled in flashes what he would have been doing at that particular time of day had he not had visitors, he almost blushed with embarrassment and slammed the door shut on the memory of the drudgery and silliness of his self-imposed routine.

The visit depressed him out of all proportion. Anin and Dosto looked complete in each other's company. Whenever either spoke, he or she glanced often at the other as though seeking approval, checking whether he or she was saying the right thing, and the other would nod agreement or smile in encouragement or add an explicatory phrase or two. Nothing that one of them said was news to the other. They seemed to have done very little singly and meeting them made Bhola feel that he had been bypassed completely by the warmth of companionship.

Neither Anin's face nor body had changed noticeably, and yet she had become positively attractive—less vacuous, more independent and sure of herself. No doubt the cause was partly Bhola himself, simply remarking what he hadn't taken note of before—the likeable way in which she, for instance, responding just to the inflexion in his voice, would begin to smile in anticipation, well before he actually said something witty or funny, and then happily, at the right moment, in stages through giggle and chuckle and chortle, let herself dissolve luxuriously in her rich laugh. Her laugh had always been uninhibited and agreeable; only of late did she appear to have known it herself.

The new Dosto befuddled Bhola.

'What're you planning to do when your three years here are over?' he had asked Bhola authoritatively—a bit like a serious but well-intentioned elder brother a heedless younger one—on Friday evening after he had installed himself in his Guest House room and they had ambled out of the campus gates and automatically, because its slope was downward, wandered off towards the Tibetan shacks selling chhang and chowmein a hundred feet below.

'Well, first of all, I want to improve my yoga and do the Scorpion Pose perfectly. That's going to take some time. Right now, I can barely pronounce it in Sanskrit correctly. Vrischikkasana. And—' feeling that it was expected of him to reciprocate '—you?'

'Oh I have plans.' He shot Bhola a look, clearly disapproving of his silliness at trying to be witty all the time and synchronously apprehensive of his reaction to a grandiose statement. 'Life is short and I have plans.'

'Do they include losing weight?'

They did but not for himself. Dosto could not provide further details of his blueprint for the future. Things were hazy in his head and, to properly assume form, would need the charged ions of ideas from others.

On the rocks and the dead sentinel trees, and alongside the lanes that snaked through the Himalayan foothills, the winter snow had yet to melt fully. At eleven in the morning, they were out walking. Bhola should have been attending his Auxiliary Law class but the fine weather had drawn them out like a spool being unwound.

The crack and crunch of dead branch and gravel under boot, the drip of melting ice on moss, the birdcalls of early spring, the occasional frantic ringing of a bicycle bell, in the distance a truck stuck in the slush roaring like an entrapped beast and Dosto panting and prattling away beside him. Fortunately, the tourists were still two months away. One could really tramp and eat up bend after bend in the road. Had Dosto not been with him, Bhola would have jogged for the second time that day.

'These hills are great for the lungs. Shall we stop somewhere for a cigarette?'

'Only if you also stop going on about Anin's maidservant's body and the outline in her sari of her mother's backside.'

'Why? Hearing me on sex is the nearest that you've got to the real thing.'

Bhola laughed openly. Dosto was a terrible human being but wonderful company. He had always been popular with women for much the same reason. He made them feel good, he made them laugh.

'There, that bench. If it's free of birdshit and other droppings. That's an attractive title for a book of poems.'

They crossed the lane to mount the shoulder. The bench, placed between two trees, looked down the gently descending valley to the sloping roseate roofs of M.K.M.Z.A.P. When Bhola turned to accept Dosto's light for his cigarette, a flash of red behind his friend's left ear distracted him for a moment. Some sixty metres away, a figure in a maroon sweater and orange muffler had conspicuously hidden himself behind a sickly eucalyptus tree.

Since the bench was in the shadow of the trees, they chose to stand in the sun a few paces from it. A hint of a breeze tingled the sheen of perspiration on Bhola's forehead. Dosto suddenly began jogging on the spot, raising his thighs waist high. He stopped after a few seconds and started to pant theatrically like a dog, letting his eyelids droop and his tongue hang out.

'The perils of a vegetarian physique—despite being a beefeater, you,' commented Bhola, 'The vegetarian ideal is the outline of one of our classical male statues. Wide, flat, womanish hips prominently—and incongruously—adorned with male loins, narrow waist, narrow chest, no pectorals at all, but strong—and wide, almost two-dimensional—arms and smooth, the skin smooth. No veins, no bulges—and the masculine torso rising proudly out of the female hips like a mermaid's.' He waited for Dosto to gibingly retort that he, Bhola, with his soft hourglass form that he had been trying for years, through diets, prayers and physical effort, to metamorphose into the undulations of Greek sculpture, had only been describing an ideal for himself.

All at once, the man in the maroon sweater stepped down from behind the tree and determinedly began walking up towards them. Bhola, recognizing him, felt his insides turn to warm liquid and his legs begin to tremble. Moti neared, caught Bhola's eye, was caught off-guard by the disbelief, the rapture, on his face, simpered with pleasure and at the same time looked away with a jerk of his head, almost lost his balance, righted himself, marched on past them, head held high in air to hide his embarrassment, all but stumbled over the root of a tree and losing his nerve, turned the next curve of the lane virtually at a run.

Leaving Dosto to listen to his own sentences, Bhola set off after Moti. Dosto automatically accompanied him without however ceasing his patter. 'Hey Ram, what an oddball. He seemed to know you, though. Does he?' Whenever Dosto used the phrase Hey Ram, he, a Roman Catholic, meant Jesus. The substitution dated from his last year in school, from the month before Bhola was expelled from it. Ostensibly short of pocket money, he, to needle his parents, had proposed to them that they, to inculcate in him the truly secular spirit, should give him a rupee each time that he remembered Ram in place of Jesus, subject to a reasonable maximum of two hundred rupees per month.

'Vaguely. He owes me some money.' Dosto had found Moti attractive too. Bhola could sense it in his elaborately casual, faintly off-key voice and see it too, in the slight widening and brightening of his eyes. 'But he's been shadowing us for a while and it could hardly be that he's itching to repay me. It's probably your sex talk that draws him in. I've often felt that what must have wafted out of the orifices of the Pied Piper of Hamlin was the odour of fish.'

The groundswell of hills before them had once been lush and virginal green; human spoliation over the decades, however, had rendered them bald and scab-coloured, forsaken even by their mud. They were appropriately peopled by the forever alien, poorer Tibetan refugees, by retired Defence personnel who had learnt too late that puffing up and down slopes day after day did gout no good, and by the students with infertile minds who ascended from the plains every July. In the months that he had spent in those hills, their barren and enduring contours had frequently dispirited Bhola, upset him with a sense of time's fruitless passage, of a wasted life, of his shrivelled, empty and friendless existence. In that mood, he had from time to time felt that he wouldn't mind never seeing again even Dosto, his only friend. Yet, just the sight of Moti's rear ten paces ahead altered everything, gave the world bounce and exhilaration, reddened and warmed up his ears and cheeks, blurred the surrounding landscape into an Impressionistic fuzziness of brown and green and dust, and honed his life down to revelling in the tingling in his thighs as he vowed never again to lose sight of the figure in red.

Dosto and Bhola had set out for their ramble with no specific destination in mind. The forenoon was wide and free save for a rendezvous with Anin at eleven-thirty; it would take her that long to give her parents the slip. Almost automatically, no doubt because it was the road most frequented, they had found themselves heading for the village of Manaspeth. It boasted of a medieval Shiva temple but neither of them was religious. Halfway to Manaspeth, however, some four kilometres from the Training Institute, the road cut through a small plateau with a hillock on its left and a gorge on its right. The tableland above the gorge, officially christened Pundit Shiromani Aflatoon Chowk and popularly known as Suicide Point, offered an impressive view and was a minor tourist attraction. The hillock was dotted with the buildings of Limbersting, one of the country's poshest schools for girls. When the sun was out, male tourists dawdled for hours at the terrace cafe atop the gorge with their backs to it, eyeing the hillock in the hope of spotting some of its residents. When the sun was in, they sat indoors, all glassed in, gazed down at the gorge and the valley beyond and, honouring the weather, contemplated suicide.

They spotted Anin at one of the tables, hunched over a Bombay film magazine to avoid the curious stares of passing males. 'Moti,' said Bhola before they crossed the road, needlessly squeezing his shoulder, 'You wait for us here. Don't disappear.'

'Hi, Bitchie-Rich!' exclaimed Dosto, punching Anin lightly on the forearm, 'pushed your family into the ravine yet or do you have to rush off somewhere at eleven forty-five?' They sat down on either side of her, Bhola stealing a glance behind him to ensure that Moti was still visible, there, fifty metres away before the side gate of the school, sitting in the sun on the pavement amongst—and sharing a smoke with—the rickshaw-walas.

'I thought that nothing was going to tear you away from

the joy of being sprayed by Tiwari,' smiled Anin in greeting at Bhola. Though he had known her longer than Dosto had, and though they got along well, neither was moved to touch the other or publicly display his or her affection in any way. It was Dosto who lived his life as though it were a spectacle, inviting everyone to share and admire every grain of it. By familiarly touching Anin's forearm before the world, he claimed her in full view of it. He didn't however stop there. On Bhola's last visit to the city during the winter break, through indelicate suggestions and clumsy innuendo, Dosto had revealed to him—and God alone knew to how many others— that she had lost her virginity to him. He had held forth on her body and face when softened by desire and then flown into a rage at seeing that he had discomfitted, embarrassed, amused and entertained—but not impressed—Bhola, who in any case hadn't believed a word of it. Dosto had in fact provided his audience evidence of a universal truth, namely, that the male typically needs to fall in love with an object that he wishes the entire world to acknowledge as beautiful. When attracted to someone not conventionally good-looking, he tries even harder to convince his group, through tiresome reiteration of the object's virtues and redefinitions of beauty, that he has picked out a showpiece.

'On the contrary, it was Tiwari's spray—and the sun outside the window—that made me slip away,' said Bhola, getting up to button his jacket only so that Moti could—just in case he had for the moment lost sight of him—spot him more easily. He was careful to speak evenly, to hide from the world his rapture, how his innards were threatening to explode with desire.

Tiwari taught him Constitutional Law. He was a short, bald and choleric man. He lectured peripatetically, pacing incessantly before the students, glaring ferociously at the inattentive, spraying non-stop with spittle the first two rows. When he had first suffered it, Bhola had actually thought that a fine drizzle was falling inside the classroom and had, gazing stupidly at the windows five metres away, for an instant wondered how. Tiwari never failed to fly off the handle whenever he saw a trainee lying low in his chair, crown of head level with top of backrest, cowering, as it were, beneath the span of fire. He usually stopped directly in front of the slacker, pulled him up within range and gave him a talking-to that left him feeling sticky for a week. Attendance in Tiwari's classes tended to be low.

'Can we sit closer to the wall? It's a bit windy here, isn't it?'

Anin looked across at the table that Bhola proposed, thought for a moment, nodded her okay, picked up her handbag, her shoulder bag, film magazine and sunglasses and rose from her chair. She seemed to have grown a little in height. Though subtler than Dosto, she too liked being discussed and being the centre of things. She flirted with elan. At least Bhola privately called it flirting, her habit for example of unexpectedly disclosing to him—when they were alone—terribly personal things about the completeness of communion that she and Dosto enjoyed and from which he, Bhola, was excluded. Unwarranted, she was apt to blurt out in her peculiar mix of Hindi and English: 'Ever since last January, after we've...done, Dosto goes off wearing my underclothes (laugh, a nice laugh she had). The first time I thought he'd made a mistake and I felt insulted, thinking to myself—surely my pantie size is smaller!' At such times, Bhola disliked her for lying, for colluding with Dosto in faking the nature of their friendship. It was inconceivable that they could be speaking the truth. He knew them and their proclivities. He could feel her mishmash of emotions for him, the lust of curiosity, her suspicion that he saw through her, her greed for his attention. Bhola had at times wanted to beat her till she confessed to her ugliness.

She was good-looking, he realized anew; with her round

face and snub nose, she did resemble a little the comic strip character Ritchie Rich. While she stood next to the table beside the cafe wall deciding where to sit, Bhola slipped into the chair under the kitchen window so that he could enjoy an uninterrupted view of Moti smoking with the rickshaw-walas.

'It's terrible, incredible, disgusting,' whined Dosto, flopping down into the third chair and putting his feet up on the fourth, 'that even after countless months here, you can't produce a single female acquaintance or fellow-student who speaks decent English and to whom you could introduce us.' When idly content, he wanted existence to be—or at least *look*—ideal, two male friends going steady with two female friends, a quartet for a cigarette-and-instant-coffee ad, laughter and pearl teeth with head thrown back against the firelight.

Bhola looked away because he felt that there was no need for him to answer. Most of the tables on the terrace—which was about the size of a badminton court—were unoccupied. A high, wire-mesh fence cut off the cafe from the drop of the cliff. From where they sat, they could see the mists of the valley dormant like fleece amongst the low, bald and black hills. Kites soared and loop-the-looped against a pale sky.

A waiter appeared, the swarthy adolescent who interested Bhola. They ordered tea. 'O-o we have company,' grinned Dosto, gazing at the knot of rickshaw-walas outside the school gate.

They watched Moti cross the road and climb the steps of the terrace towards them. The orange muffler had been tied in a knot around his waist. He looked less shabby and gaunt, almost dashing. He strode in a determined straight line, his cats' eyes staring fixedly at Bhola. Like a comic in a C-grade film, he walked straight into a chair and almost toppled. He paused at the table next to theirs, gripped the back of a chair and said to Bhola, 'May I speak to you alone, please, sir, for a minute?' in Hindi.

'Yes, of course.'

Moti's face was pinched and grey, his Adam's apple monstrous in a grimy throat, but the eyes were startling. The skin seemed to have been pulled back tight from his cheekbones. From a distance, his figure might have suggested a stripling of seventeen but his expression was maturer, perhaps even a thirty-year-old's. He himself had no exact idea of how old he was.

'Alone, sir, for a minute,' repeated Moti.

Bhola glanced with mock helplessness at his friends. Dosto openly leered back at him. Anin eyed Moti steadily, as though trying to plumb him. 'Yes, of course,' murmured Bhola again and rose from his chair.

'No no, not now sir!' exclaimed Moti, grimacing in panic, left arm outstretched to discourage Bhola from moving forward.

'When then?' demanded Bhola, faintly irritated.

They settled on nine o'clock that evening, after dinner, in Bhola's room in Mrs Manchanda's flat. Casually, as though giving directions to a monument to a tourist, he explained to Moti how to get there. Moti nodded frequently throughout Bhola's delivery, yet at the same time gave the impression of not having followed a single word. He then clicked his heels, saluted like a cadet, turned about and walked rapidly away.

Dosto insisted on being present at the meeting—'in the cupboard, under the bed, somewhere. That young man is a prostitute and he's going to sell you the secret of his slimness. I want to be present to see how you goof up so that I can take notes for the future.'

'You should let him be, Dosto.' Anin smiled without humour and put on her sunglasses before continuing. 'If Bhola chooses to chat up a stranger who looks desperately ill with TB of the kidneys or something, then you should allow him to sink alone.'

'You will freeze,' Bhola addressed Dosto as though Anin had not spoken at all, 'and the chattering of your teeth will give you away. I should check with my father first what the caste laws have to say on the delicate subject of fellatio. There must be some regulation—who bends and who doesn't, size and texture of organ—it's simply a matter of finding the right text. But do not forget that I switch my lights off at nine-thirty. Any noises thereafter will be you groping for the secret of that bugger's slimness.'

It was true that Bhola continued to be obsessed by thinness, by balanced weight loss as a principle to live by. His lights went off at nine-thirty because he assiduously tried to give himself eight hours of sleep. He felt—almost religiously— that one must take care of one's body because it was the temple of residence of one's soul. His self-discipline, his adherence to dogged, self-imposed, physically and mentally demanding—and fundamentally pointless—routine irritated Dosto greatly. Whenever he had pressed Bhola to put his feet up, let his hair down, skip his evening jog to go and have a couple of beers instead, Bhola had ruffled him further by reminding him for the umpteenth time of the Parable of the Dark Brown Corduroy Jeans.

'Once upon a time, Dosto, a young man, on his first trip abroad, bought his younger brother a pair of perfect dark brown corduroy jeans. They were expensive—and symbolic because they were the first and last gift that he ever bought his younger brother. Be it noted that buying the jeans in the first place had been a mistake in that he should have bought a larger pair. However, once bought, they couldn't either be thrown or given away; they needed to be made the best use of. Be it also noted that they enjoyed a reputation for lasting forever—and indeed, looking better with age, less new and more your own. The younger brother therefore decided to shape up so that he could get into and remain in them. Ditto for everything else, he found. One must lose weight to fit into one's circumstances. Then, when you have made the effort, the circumstances too seem to adapt to you.'

'Now *that*,' exclaimed Dosto, inclining his head forward

to indicate a group of Tibetan schoolgirls on the road, 'is what I'd call slimness. Wow-ee-ee-ee-ee. Bodies unwashed in protest since the Chinese aggression of 1962. Hindi-Cheeni bhai-bhai, Hindi-Cheeni bahenchod. Inhale deep, my friends. If the wind is right, you can smell them from here, the musk of heaven on earth.'

Both Anin and Bhola were used to and ignored his egregiousness. Not many could. Dosto was in many ways like an excited child on a see-saw, thighs gripping wood so hard that the muscle strain inched up to stab the loins, impervious to all other sensation, ascending and plummeting faster and faster out of fear that the fun would stop and the heat ebb away.

Abruptly, Bhola was depressed and felt that he was wasting his time, drinking sweet, thick, milky tea that he hadn't wanted in the first place, waiting unthinkingly to see what other ways his friends would find to waste more time and in the meanwhile suffering Dosto's insecure and tiresomely overpowering personality. Since Moti had left, he could see nothing in his head but him loping further and further away, up and down the hill roads and out of his life once more. He wanted to get away too, run after and spend himself on him, and then read an uplifting book, play some chess, clean his fountain pens, browse through his diary of unforgettable recipes.

He signalled to the adolescent waiter for the bill.

'Hey! We've just got here, you cad! You rotter!'

'I must say that your eccentrifulness is jolly terrific!'

Anin and Dosto in their Greyfriars-Billy Bunter mood never failed to send Bhola's blood rushing to his forehead. 'I have to go. In any case, Dosto will drop by tonight and we'—with a grimace of a smile at Anin—'meet tomorrow morning.'

When the waiter appeared with the bill, Anin and Dosto laughingly ordered more tea. Bhola stopped him from going away with, 'How much is one tea? I'll pay my share now.'

'Your miserlifulness is disgustific!' giggled Anin. 'Pay the entire bill, you bounder!'

Bhola did, muttering, 'Daylight robbery is the price of freedom.'

'And promise, promise us that you'll let *us* pay up next time. It isn't fair, your generosity.'

Dosto tapped on the rear door of Bhola's room that evening at a quarter to nine. He looked like a happy and excited clown in a maroon beret that was too small for him.

'Am I too early? Too late?' he asked in a stagy whisper, his eyes sparkling intoxicatedly.

Earlier in the evening, Bhola had successfully avoided his friends by having dinner in the hostel's communal dining room at seven with the first batch. Eating with them sometimes helped to uplift his mood. The first batch usually comprised the feral eaters with no social life. They wolved down, off almost clean plates, the hot food of a dreary menu and subsequently wrote reams in the Complaints Register. It was their way of redeeming their course fees. They hated the cold and habitually wore monkey caps. They never skipped class and hardly ever did well. On the days when she liked to dine early, Mrs Manchanda—the College's Administrative Officer and Bhola's landlady—was often to be found among them.

He had sat beside her. The tablecloth before them had been grey and dal-stained.

'Good evening. Is this place taken?' They had conversed as usual in Hindi.

'No no—oh, hello—please sit, you're most welcome.' She had smiled up at him and unobtrusively taken off her spectacles.

'It's cold today.'

'Yes.'

'Even though it was sunny this morning.'

'Yes yes.'

'It's good to eat dinner early.'

'Yes.'

Bhola helped himself from the rice bowl, idly wondering what other sparkling things he could say. It's good to eat dinner early, he *quipped*. She was so pale, demure and correct that she had intrigued him from the start, made him wonder from Day One what steps an experienced philanderer would take with her to seduce her. They chomped away in silence, looking pointedly either at their own plates or at that of the lone, unknown diner facing them. In a few minutes, he obliged—and all seemingly in one movement—by gulping down the last of his potatoes, tossing off his glass of water and without a nod, smile or glance at anyone, pushing back his chair and leaving the table—and behind on it, a mess akin to that around a trough abandoned by a sated boar. Bhola glared at his back till he exited from the dining hall. Mrs Manchanda however relaxed perceptibly and turned to Bhola with a smile.

'All well at home?'

'Yes, I'm sure. No news is good news.' He had hesitated for a second, been in two minds whether he should try and be witty by asking her to clarify. Home for him was her flatlet a five minutes' descent away, which he had been occupying for the preceding eight months, where he was likely to stay for another thirty and where he had just wasted a couple of hours daydreaming about what diseases Moti might have picked up in the intervening period. He seldom thought of his father and stepmother when he was away from them. 'I haven't seen Vivek for a couple of days.'

She flashed him a glance before responding. 'He's gone down to Lucknow and should be back on Monday. His father called because his elder sister—Vivek's favourite aunt—so she'd like to think—has apparently been diagnosed with TB.'

Mrs M's cheeks were faintly pitted with the dots of smallpox. Bhola liked her unaffected gap-toothed smile. His hand brushed against hers when he reached out for the salad plate.

'Oh, I'm sorry to hear that. TB of the what?' He paused, plate poised in his hand like a frisbee seconds before the flick, remembering how that very morning, Moti in a matter of seconds had become shatteringly unsexy when Anin had attributed to him tuberculosis of the kidneys. 'For a long time, I didn't know that TB could affect regions other than the lungs.'

'Let us just hope that Vivek doesn't return with it.' She often spoke of her son as of an embarrassing discomfort, a painful boil in one's private parts.

She seemed to welcome the arrival of the waiter. He took away her plate, sloppily wiped the trough area with a damp, stained, grey and revolting dishcloth and placed before her a steel bowl containing the dessert of the day, two testiculate gulabjamuns, one a darker brown than the other.

'No, thank you. Please take it away,' she said in Hindi.

'No, don't! I'll have your share too—that is, if you don't mind.'

She laughed. Warmth tingled through him. He began to gulp down his food so that he could leave with her and then suddenly asked, not quite sure of what he was saying, practically directing his question at the first half of the second gulabjamun, 'I was wondering—if you have the time, whenever—if you'd help me with my Hindi?'

Moti didn't show up that evening. Dosto and Bhola waited for him till a quarter to ten. They listened to deafening music on a portable cassette recorder. They smoked a couple of joints. They tried to be witty at each other's expense. They got on each other's nerves. At nine-thirty, Bhola began trying to evict his friend.

'He won't turn up. He came to the door, overheard your jokes and left, appalled.'

'Appalled. He'll be back. He went off to get his condoms. He remembered at the door that you have a pussy.'

Bhola's short fuse was lit by then. 'Please fuck off, you. I've told you I've to get up early for my run.'

At six the next morning, when it was bitingly cold and still dark, Bhola, in woollen cap, mittens and tracksuit, opened his door to find Moti waiting in the tiny kitchen garden, bareheaded, hands in pockets, shivering in a thin pullover. The unexpectedness of the sight first hit Bhola like a jab below the heart and then flooded him with a hot mix of rage and lust.

'You are nine hours late.' To warm up, he began to jog lightly on the spot at the threshold and then past him. 'I can't talk now. Come back in an hour.' He was irritated to see Moti striding rapidly after him. He stopped. 'Stop fucking my mood up at six a.m.' He glared into Moti's wide overawed eyes, at the fleshless face, the mouth that jutted out sensually. 'You're not going to follow and disturb me. You look ill. For all I know, you now have TB of the anus. You can't jog, okay?'

Moti said nothing but continued to stare unblinkingly at him. Bhola suddenly reached out, held his jaw and shook him gently. His skin was ice. Bhola noticed then that Moti's hair and clothes were wet. He exuded an odd, not unpleasant, smell, a mix of perfumed hair oil, damp wool, tobacco and something thick and sweet like incense.

The apartment blocks were built at—and protruded out of—the base of a hillock. Bhola negotiated the track between the flats, reached the level of the main walk to the blocks, exited and began the ascent up the cemented path that led to the main administrative buildings of the college. He paused at the crest of the hillock to look down on the dawn darkness of the valley, the spectral trees, the mist that bedimmed and dampened the glow of the lamps on the path. At its bottom, he spotted Moti doggedly making his way up.

He slowly loped off down the driveway to the north gate and once out of the premises, turned left towards the town because the road was better lit and its shoulder surface wider and more even. In summer, when it became light at five o'clock, he invariably headed the opposite way towards Limbersting. He was panting lightly after four hundred metres and felt more virtuous for it. He would follow the loops of the road, its ups and gentle downs, its almost aimless meandering for two kilometres. Once past Liberty Cinema, he would turn off at Fatman's Hotel, climb up Bhulbhulaiya Hill and then reward himself by taking three kilometres to descend the four hundred metres to the level of Gas Link Road. At the fork in the road at Fatman's Hotel, he was intrigued, almost impressed, to spot under the streetlamps Moti shuffling and stumbling along a couple of hundred metres behind him.

Staggering about like an intrepid traverser of some desert in a comic strip, almost crumpling up more than once but never giving up, sustained more by willpower than by lungs and legs, Moti was there trailing Bhola both on Bhulbhulaiya Hill and on Gas Link Road. It was just turning light when Bhola reached his room. He unlocked his door and left it ajar. He stripped completely before the electric heater. He was excited by Moti's doggedness. He felt as though he had been pursued by an implacable lover. He heard him panting outside the door before he saw him. 'Come in and shut the door,' he ordered. He met him completely naked, just like in his dreams. Moti couldn't have cared less. Gulping air down with the expression of a goldfish, he collapsed on the floor.

'Don't die here. Take your clothes off. Pneumonia after tuberculosis, that's how your bio will read.' He gently pulled Moti up. The young man looked sickly pale and swayed on his feet. His eyes didn't seem focussed. His breathing filled the room. Bhola pulled his sweater off his head and then one by one, the rest of his wet clothes. Moti began to shiver faintly. He didn't either resist or react when Bhola unbuttoned his trousers and later pulled down his underwear.

Bhola loved Moti's nakedness. He didn't have a centimetre of fat on his body. His was the slimness of malnourishment. His stomach sank inwards, his hips were wide, flat and high, and his thighs wiry, brown and hairless. Bhola would have loved to have a body like Moti's, weight lost to the maximum, ribs standing out tight under the membrane as though against a sail in a high wind, nipples indistinguishable protuberances, the navel a tiny dip in the undulation of smooth, small muscles. The poor and dispossessed, Bhola had often mused, had much nicer bodies than their fat, soft fellow-citizens above them on the ladder. Their faces aged terribly early, though. Moti hugged himself and turned an uncertain face to Bhola. Bhola wanted to whistle at the absence of fat, the clean lines. 'Here, let me warm you up.' Unable to resist himself, he gently pushed Moti on to the bed, lay down atop him and pulled a quilt over them. He felt like an ascetic testing his endurance by lying flat on a glacier. At the back of his mind, he wondered who was more far gone. He kissed Moti on the lips. His mouth tasted of exhaustion. He spurted out in seconds. Moti's expression darkened faintly with a sort of surprised tenderness.

'Put these on.' Bhola handed Moti a pair of pyjamas and a kurta. He himself dressed in jeans and teeshirt and—'You should drink something hot'—shutting carefully the door behind him, went off to the tiny kitchen to put on the kettle.

When he returned, it didn't appear to him as though Moti would recover normalcy in a hurry. Leaving him to die on the bed, Bhola collected towel, soap and extra clothes and traipsed off past the dining table to the bathroom that was so tiny that it could contain nothing that wouldn't get wet. He liked bathing early and in a dry bathroom. Neither Mrs Manchanda nor Vivek were up at that hour and neither was silly enough to bathe every day in that weather. He had fobbed off a couple of snide remarks on his habit by alluding vaguely but nobly to caste compulsions. He was disoriented after his first sexual experience and didn't even know whether it had been memorable. It had certainly been quick. A quickie, like a fast bowler at cricket. When he returned to his room, he saw that Moti had rolled off the bed onto the rug and had dragged the quilt down after him. Bhola didn't like messes. He was sure that Moti had wiped his—Bhola's—spunk off himself with the quilt. He wished that Moti would disappear before the rest of the household awoke. Moti looked up at Bhola's entry. His face was still ashen but his eyes had lost their look of wanting to roll up and disappear into the top of his head.

'Did you drink some water? Look, I have to have breakfast and then go for class and all that. What did you want to see me about? And where do you and Titli stay? Tell me now. Soon my landlady will be up and then you can't talk.'

Moti said nothing. His gaze followed Bhola around the room as he went about collecting his books, notes, keys, pens and other stuff for the day. The sight—and the notion—of Moti in the clothes that he himself had slept in the night before titillated Bhola anew. 'If you don't want to talk now, okay, we can find some other time. You'll have to push off pretty soon anyway. You can return my clothes later if you wish. And if you want some money, I should tell you at once that I'm a Below the Poverty Line person.'

'May I have some water please?'

'Help yourself.' Bhola indicated the jug, glasses and flask on a tray atop the chest of drawers. 'Mix hot and cold.' While he put on his jacket and combed his hair, he watched Moti drink without touching the tumbler to his lips. Holding it a couple of inches above his mouth, Moti downed a full glass without pausing. Bhola watched his Adam's apple bob up and down convulsively, its rhythm the slow beating of a spasmodic heart. Moti put the glass down and looked around uncertainly, as though searching for an object to stare at. Bhola waited for him to pick up his clothes and leave.

Clutching damp sweater and shirt to his chest, with a supplicating glance at the windows behind Bhola's left shoulder, Moti mumbled, 'Can you lend me some money, sir?'

'How much?'

Both his gaze and voice dropped to the rug. 'I don't know. A thousand rupees?'

'Why? Unless you don't want to tell me. Or is that your fee?'

With the trepidation, guilt and trauma of one who has raped, murdered and then eaten his mother for dinner, Moti confessed that he needed the money for an operation. Bhola was piqued at the manner in which his expectations had been ridiculed.

'It's a lot of money. What operation?'

Extracting answers out of Moti proved to be not much easier than extracting his teeth. He winced before each response, gazed all about him for ways of escape from the questions and answered only when all other recourse seemed to have failed. 'It's for my health in general. I have a problem. It'll help me to stop smoking.'

'But you don't reek of tobacco. Have you started smoking something else?'

The tone of Moti's reply suggested that he for the moment couldn't think of anything else that could be smoked. 'I need to pay the doctor today. He won't start without an advance in his hand.'

'First of all, we can go down right now—even before breakfast—and you show me where you stay. Unless your wife's become another person, she would be happy to see me.' Bhola tried to conjure up a picture of Titli as he had last seen her in the neighbourhood park, plump and meaty-thighed in a nurse's uniform, but couldn't hold on to the image for long.

'I'd like to pay today,' repeated Moti. With time, he

appeared to have aggrandized both Bhola's wealth and his munificence. Besides, Bhola 'had always had a fine, kind face,' added Moti without a change of voice. Bhola was ashamed. 'Not your friends. They have the faces of schemers.'

Bhola switched off the heater. 'Do you want to wear something else? A sweater or jacket?' Moti shook his head vigorously. Bhola placed his hand on the small of his back and gently steered him outdoors. He bolted and locked his room. Hugging his wet clothes like a mother her retrieved infant, Moti accompanied Bhola to the path.

'Last night,' he revealed abruptly, with a hint of pride in his voice and of a smile on his face, 'I sat under the cold water tap in the bathroom till six this morning.'

Bhola glanced at him, feeling that he hadn't heard him correctly. 'With the tap on?'

'Of course.' Moti stopped looking smug. He disliked being disbelieved.

Bhola felt something lurch inside him. But this is winter, he protested silently. 'And Titli and your Dr Borkar? They slept through the sound of water falling all night in the bathroom?'

Moti eyed him a little scornfully. 'They? They have no role to play other than to encourage me.'

'It isn't possible to squat under running cold water in this weather for'—Bhola tried to calculate—'I don't know—eight hours, ten. Have you done this before?'

'Yes, several times, but last night was the longest.'

'Does she sit too?'

'Of course not. She doesn't need to.' Frowning, Moti then used a couple of Sanskritized Hindi phrases that Bhola wasn't sure that either understood fully. 'The austerities that we practise should be in accord with the season.'

'Yes, of course.' The image of Titli shivering in see-through wet sari and blouse distracted Bhola for a moment. 'And what do you do in summer?'

Intimidated perhaps by the presence of passers-by—a couple of whom greeted Bhola affably—by the daylight and by their imminent return to the normalcy of a daily routine, Moti however clammed up. His face resumed its sullen haunted expression of an outcast animal. He even dropped a couple of paces behind.

Five minutes later, Bhola halted before the shutters of the travel agents' kiosks beneath the Romantic Rendezvous Restaurant and waited for Moti to draw abreast. He had grown tired of the other trailing him like a dutiful Hindu wife her husband. 'I still haven't understood why you want the money.' He scanned the other's wan, exhausted face and was aroused once more by the awfulness reflected in it, by Moti's hopelessness, his gutter world and the distance between the two of them. He wanted to see him, for once in his life, in an unabased position. 'I don't *have* that kind of money—and would you like to earn some of it? You could massage my back two or three times a week. It acts up sometimes because of too much jogging.'

Moti nodded without having heard the offer. Looking at the top button of Bhola's jacket, he then mumbled, 'I want to be operated on soon. I want you to be there.' Bhola waited for him to elaborate. Moti remained silent too, clutching his clothes, almost relieved at having gotten the truth off his chest.

Bhola was again riled at not comprehending. 'Look—I've changed my mind. I'll meet them next week. You turn up at four o'clock on Monday afternoon for a massage—and we'll see about the money in instalments or something, okay?'

Moti's eyes darkened and glared briefly at Bhola in anger and frustration. Without a word, he swung around and stumbled off in a clumsy run back in the direction of Fatman's Hotel. Bhola made no effort to stop him. He would find him and his wife again, of that he was suddenly certain; he wished, though, that he could be as sure of his clothes.

It snowed that night, a freakish and unaccountable event. The effect of its whiteness the following morning was amnesiac, enabling Bhola to bury the encounter with Moti, to treat it as unreal and fanciful—much like the snow. Winter, it seemed, had slipped into a deeper winter before struggling up to display the shoots of spring. The bathrooms couldn't be used for two days because the water froze in the taps, briefly prodding loose in him the reflection that even Nature could most unexpectedly intervene to prevent the silliest self-imposed atrocity. The mental picture of Moti sitting in a dry bathroom under the tap, eyeballs rolled heavenward, imploring his gods to be kind and arrange for a thaw—the image even made Bhola laugh out loud a couple of times. It was one characteristic of innocence to force joy and comedy, however warped, even out of sorrow, to refuse to recognize it as sorrow even when it grazed one's heart.

Seducing Moti took six pleasurable weeks. They met on the average once every five working days in the afternoons in Bhola's room after lunch, that is, after Mrs Manchanda had returned to office and Vivek had wandered off to smoke cigarettes, play football and waste away what remained of his day. He never could stay alone at home. He was scared of empty apartments. On the days of his assignations with Moti, Bhola would therefore announce after lunch. 'Okay, I'm off to the Library,' and exit from the back door of his room. Within ten minutes, unfailingly, Vivek would leave from the front, humming one of his tunes, loping off on twinkling feet and not looking back. Bhola always gave him an extra five long minutes before re-entering.

He paid Moti fifty rupees per encounter—or per massage, because that's how they started and officially, that's what it remained. He himself stripped progressively as the weeks passed and, once Moti was comfortable with rubbing him down in the nude, focussed on disrobing the masseur, proposing at successive sessions that he would be more at ease without his sweater and that he should be careful about not letting the oil stain his trousers. The first time, Moti had reddened with pleasure at seeing the cash. Later, when the sex began, he had even tried—halfheartedly, a couple of times—to refuse accepting payment, and an irritated Bhola had pushed the notes into the breast pocket of his shirt. Finally, when he had got used to the relationship, he accepted the money expressionlessly and without demur and even maintained an account in his head, that is to say, when, on occasion, Bhola told him that he would pay him next time because he didn't have change, Moti, at their subsequent meeting and with a faintly embarrassed smirk, reminded Bhola of the arrears.

'Where have you all been all these months? Do you know, I've been searching for you for more than a year?'

On the Monday after Anin and Dosto's departure, therefore, in the late afternoon, after his first vigorous oil massage and well before either Vivek or his mother returned home, Bhola accompanied Moti back to Dr Borkar's clinic. He would never have found it on his own. It was on the lesser slope behind Fatman's Hotel, in an untidily winding, perennially unfinished lane of new, shabby single-storey houses, quite a few of which appeared to have been converted to commercial establishments; he noted two grocery stores and one Fair Price Shop, a typing school, a depot for domestic gas cylinders and mounds of gravel and sandstone dumped by construction trucks. He had passed the mouth of the lane times out of number on the jogging route that he followed on Mondays, Wednesdays and Fridays. No doubt he had been spotted by Moti when he had panted past on one of those occasions. Dr Borkar and his adopted family shared a tiny, orange-painted house with a Learn-English-In-Thirty-Days Institute. They had the two front rooms, of which the larger,

a twelve-by-ten, was the clinic-cum-drawing room. No board
on the gate or above the front door or anywhere proclaimed
the availability of a doctor on the premises. Four ragged-
looking patients from the nearby slum that housed the
labourers working on the hotel's extension—dark, depressed
by affliction, dull-eyed as though unable to stare the healthy
in the face—waited their turn on a bench in the minuscule
verandah.

He was surprised at how happy Titli was to see him and
how plump she had become. He wanted her to sit on his face
immediately and grind his jaws into dust with her pussypower,
right then and there in front of her husband and the woman
patient whom she had been bent over, syringe poised to
extract blood from her sickly left arm. With a soft gasp of
surprise, she abandoned her and came forward a couple of
steps to greet him, syringe still in hand, grinning from ear to
ear, pushing her fleshy cheeks up and out till they made slits
of her eyes. She wore a white cotton coat over a pinkish
synthetic sari and looked virtually lower middle class. She
had fortunately got rid of that ridiculous nurse's skirt. In
greeting, he wanted to reach out and massage her mound
with the heel of his palm. Horribly tense, he prayed to God
that he would find Borkar sexy. They exchanged idiotic
pleasantries. He touched her elbow affectionately, then gently
nudged her into an about-turn-and-returning-to-work. The
patient, emaciated, her hair rusted by henna, flinched when
the needle punctured her skin. Still smiling and simpering
over her shoulder at Bhola and carrying on an empty
conversation, Titli drew out what looked like a cupful of
blood.

The room was tubelit. The panes of the single window
that gave on to the verandah were translucent and let in
almost no light. A stretcher in the corner became at night
Moti's resting place. Alongside it stood a metal table, with an
aluminium canteen chair behind, and a metal stool—on which

slumped the patient—before, it. Next to the orange table fan mounted on the wall hung a photograph of a man with a pale, open, squareish, blunt face, short hair and large, rectangular spectacles. For a moment, Bhola thought it to be an enlarged snapshot of the pop singer Elton John at his ugliest. It was the first fan that he had seen in the town. The calendar above the stretcher showed Kashmiri damsels before a lake and beneath them, the June of the previous year.

Important truths are not arrived at either through the study of books or independent intellectual contemplation, but through inheriting wisdom from correctly inspired leaders. Dr Borkar spoke almost entirely in Hindi. *For the seminal verities to be effectively transmitted, both guru and disciple must be aroused and made ready.* His figures of speech were predominantly sexual. *The appropriate guru alone can inflame the unlit wick of the pupil, duly dipped in the oil of the master's teachings, with the spark of real knowledge.* He babbled almost incessantly, particularly to Bhola, practically from the moment that they met, clearly finding him a more worthy receptacle than either Titli or her husband. He was the man in the photograph on the wall.

He looked sad, worn out, older than his years. When he took off his spectacles—which was often—to rub his eyes or cover them completely with his palms, presumably to rest them—he looked different, nearly good-looking. He was lanky, almost a head taller than Bhola, and stooped. His eyes looked aged, as though nothing could jolt them any more. He was quite open and welcoming, and Bhola didn't have to trot out his bad back as a pretext for the visit. From the other room, a grinning Moti brought out a second aluminium canteen chair for him and then he too put on a white coat, much like a costume in a school play. Bhola sat and watched the trio attend to their patients.

He felt completely at ease, as though he belonged in that room as much as the incongruous furniture around him. He noted that the functions of the three had been hierarchically apportioned. Borkar did not look at a patient until he had been seated by Titli and his previous prescription or report arranged on the table top by Moti, who did not cease to grin—a nervous, humourless snarl—for the entire three hours that Bhola spent with them. The two handed Borkar the things—torch, blood pressure instrument, thermometer—that he needed during his examination but he left the winding up—putting eyedrops, dressing a sore, dousing a child with cough syrup—to Titli. Since his assistants were effectively illiterate, Borkar wrote the prescriptions, but in an appropriately illegible hand. Between patients and for long after he had finished with them, he chatted with Bhola about politics and the state of the nation, religion and its demands on the individual, the ethical life and twenty other topics. Bhola did not hesitate to ask the meanings of the Sanskrit words that he did not follow. Each time he did, Titli broke into a smile and Moti's snarl broadened momentarily. They all drank innumerable cups of tea made by Titli on a gas stove in the next room. Once, in mid-sentence and mid-patient, Borkar disappeared with Titli and without a word into the adjoining bedroom-cum-kitchen, from where, through the peeling, plywood-like door, they heard, within the minute, his soft, incontinent, delirious moaning. Bhola felt as though, after years of wandering, he had at last—and quite serendipitously— come home, the place where he had always longed to be.

For some time after they debouched from their quickie— that was what Bhola thought it had been till some months later when, under his determined probing to find out what kind of lover Borkar was, Titli, playing at being embarrassed, disclosed that she didn't have to do very much to please the doctor, didn't have to shed her clothes in the cold, had to just stand, stare at the wall and maintain her balance while he bruised his lips or his groin against some part of her—for some time after they debouched, Borkar remained subdued, went about his business slowly and quietly and responded to

Bhola's questions in the monosyllables characteristic of the
calm after the storm. Titli too was her usual composed self,
not looking anyone in the eye for fear of appearing too brazen
and of being understood for what she in fact was, a sort of
demure prostitute. It was while glancing around and enjoying
himself that Bhola realized that the one truly unhappy person
in the room, unable to mask his misery with his grimace of a
smile, was Moti. Aroused without warning, the torment of
one soul by another nudging loose a related memory, Bhola
could not control himself from asking,

'Could you tell me a little about the notion that the
austerities we practise should be in accord with the season?
That in winter, for example, to control the senses and our
bodies, we should subject them to intense cold—air, water,
earth? Sit under a cold water tap all night and things of that
sort?'

Borkar glanced once expressionlessly at Moti before
replying, all the while continuing to scrawl out the last
patient's prescription. 'That was a special treatment thought
up for himself by God's greatest gift to womankind.' He
stared briefly at Bhola with his eyes that had seen the world.
'His impotence is a typical psychosomatic case.' Moti, following
the female labourer out to the verandah, shut the door after
him. Titli was at the stove in the bedroom-kitchen. It was
clear that her husband avoided the doctor's company in his
wife's absence.

'Oh, I didn't know that. Is it…dangerous? For him, I
mean.'

One of the several things that he liked about Dr Borkar
was his self-centredness. He was so absorbed in himself, he
with his thick lips and rich voice, that he didn't much care to
know what Bhola's relations with Titli and her husband were,
had been, how they could know each other despite the
obvious social divide, what on earth he saw in Moti in
particular, for the man was almost imbecilic in his

inarticulateness. There would be several times in the near future when Bhola, in response to a question that he would never be asked, would want to photograph a nude Moti, chop off the stupid head with its staring, unhappy eyes and present the rest of the snap as an ideal, in hairless brown, of male fatlessness.

Titli saw him out till the steps of the verandah the first evening. 'I like him, he's good,' appraised Bhola her master and lover for her without being asked. She, happy that they had got on well, smiled in the gloom and responded, 'It was very nice to have seen you again after all these months. Please come and see us frequently. Are your parents fine?'

With Moti hovering behind her like a visitant, it was difficult to touch her, make a pass, get sexy. 'You must come too and have tea with me in the college one day,' he said, wondering what he was talking about. 'You and Moti. Or Moti alone, like today. Or even you alone, why not?'

'Can't you get him a job somewhere?' Her tone changed in instant response to his attempt at intimacy, became aggressively wheedling. 'Any kind of job. He's a good and steady worker.' Moti stopped fidgeting and came and stood almost at attention beside his wife, as though ready to be interrogated and physically examined.

'Aren't there any Adult Education classes here that he could attend? And before he becomes decrepit, he should enrol himself in a driving school so that he can get his licence to kill.'

Titli shambled forward to get even further away from the shut door of the clinic, through which could be heard, faintly but distinctly on the radio, some Armed Forces' Listeners' Letters kind of programme—a woman announcer chuckling over the requests of and flirting with her admirers ten thousand kilometres away atop some Himalayan glacier. Bhola bent his head so that he could be titillated by her hot breath in his ear. 'Doctor and he don't like each other.'

'What do you think is the reason?' He seized the occasion to whisper into her ear, have his nose tickled by her hair and the lice in it. Behind her, he could see that Moti had edged closer, that his right hand alongside his thigh had balled itself into a fist.

'I don't know.' He again offered her his right ear to be brushed by her lips. 'I thought that maybe he could learn to be a doctor's assistant but it's not working out. Doctor is tough with him.'

By the end of April, by which time the last of the snow had melted, to celebrate, as it were, the completion of Bhola's First Year exams, he and Moti became—for lack of a more accurate word to describe their relationship—lovers. He doubted whether they could in any sense be called a couple, whether the togetherness of any other pair in the world was as loveless as theirs but he did not care as long as he got what he wanted. Each week when they had met for his massage, he had encouraged Moti to undress a little more and had flattered and touched his slimness. When Moti was completely nude, in April, the massages stopped altogether and Bhola got down to business right away. Every week, Moti did obey all his instructions, but with a grimace of a smirk on his lips and a nervous shine in his eyes. So Bhola was never certain whether Moti enjoyed their assignations or was terrified of them. He, Bhola, climaxed early—after a minute—or late—after fifteen—depending on what time it was and when either Vivek or Mrs Manchanda were expected to return. Moti's body, however, registered no heightening of desire; his penis remained half a kebab of dough but Bhola couldn't have been bothered. After spending himself, he wished Moti to die, to disappear instantly and not return to Bhola's surroundings for a week or two, a period that he could use, following the laws of Manu and were he so inclined, in consequent penance and fasting. *Should...a man...eat semen, urine or excrement, he should undertake the Painful Vow...eat in the morning for three days, then in the evening for three days, (then) for three days... food that he has not asked for, and for the next three days he should not eat.* When the sap in him rose again, he would walk down to the clinic, hear Borkar on sexual power and the mysteries of the human body, make eye contact with Titli and with elaborate artlessness arrange the next rendezvous with her husband.

'Why don't you apply for a second telephone connection, Doctor? This one's out of order all the time. The father of a friend of mine works in the Ministry of Communications and could help.'

He wanted to breathe sex into Titli's ear when she held the receiver against it. He would never be able to match the quality of Borkar's sex talk but that was not important. No one followed Borkar in any case. It was not what he said but how he said it. His fat purple lips contorted themselves over the words like the vagina of a circus performer. *The concept of man as a microcosm reflecting the greater cosmos was as fully developed in India as in ancient Greece. Much of Hindu thought is based on the belief that every individual is a 'minute world'. Whatever exists in the universe exists in the human body.* Besides, when Bhola went home for the vacations, he wanted to phone to keep in touch with the trio, for he feared that they would drop out of sight again. In a matter of weeks after he began having sex with Moti, in his fantasies and during his Secret Seven meditations, he started to oscillate between the masseur and his wife. In his head, she lay naked before his face, pale, giant thighs parted and her vagina, wriggling and writhing like Borkar's worm-like lips, emitting with its heady sewer smell the words of wisdom of the doctor. *You develop your potential by controlling the natural forces around you, but man's signal triumph is the understanding and control of the forces within; in them are comprehended all the powers and potencies of the cosmic plenum.* Her thighs and loins would start to pulsate, slowly and domineeringly, blocking out the world, like a beast in control. *All truth is within; all states of heaven and hell, the universe with all its objects and localities, space and time with all their dimensions, divisions and subdivisions. Hence in man are also found all the contradictions and conflicts of the universe.* Her freshly-shaven mound would start to leap out at him, to thud against and bruise his upper lip. *These opposites may be perceived in the dual nature of human sexuality, for every individual is both male and female and within himself can achieve fulfilment. At the same time, in the physical world, the male and female genders symbolize a dichotomy that exists in the Absolute as Shiva and Shakti, Krishna and Radha, Buddha and Tara, and the bodhisattva Vajradhara and his sakti Lochana. The heat of desire and the power of lust sustain the cosmic order.* He would taste blood in his mouth, hers or his own, he couldn't tell but it'd taste rich and he'd gulp it down. *There is an intimate connection between cosmic creation and the primal urge of men and women; and differences are resolved and harmony achieved between the macrocosm and the microcosm through sexual union. The sex act therefore, properly regarded and approached, is a channel for the highest spiritual experience, a means of salvation.*

In that phase of Bhola's life, everything seemed to coalesce in his head and form a recognizable, coherent pattern—his hourglass figure, Borkar's chatter of the divine as a cosmic union of male and female forces, and the swings of the pendulum of his desire between male and woman, husband and wife. To learn even indirectly that his unusual sexual proclivities had divine sanction was greatly reassuring. He would have liked in addition to hear of some human precedents, though.

In 1977, Bhola was not worried about AIDS—it was still remote—but he did off and on think about venereal disease— that is, when he wasn't puzzling over his Secret Seven activities in general or his weight and his jogging in particular. He would have been quite embarrassed had anyone found out how many hours he spent during the day mulling over footfalls, the short stride, the firm but relaxed knees, the landing on the heel, the forearms parallel to the trunk. He often wished that he could constructively pass a fraction of that time reflecting on his future or his relationships or on VD the time bomb. Before he expended his passion with Moti—and later, with Titli—he would be aroused by the notion that they could be the carriers of some loathesome infection; instantly after, bemused and disgusted with how bestial, how helpless, lust rendered him, he, flagellating himself, would begin to recall that one never knew whom one's sexual partners might have had—or have—sex with before—or after—one had had the misfortune to seduce them, that he had read somewhere or learnt from somebody that the period of incubation for some sexually transmitted diseases could be a decade or more, a long long way for him to tread before he could begin to expiate his sin of the lack of self-control.

'Which other human beings have you had sex with?' he demanded of Moti, not very delicately. 'Other than your woman'—literally, she whom you have at home.

'There was a girl in Gorakhpur,' replied the twenty-eight-year old, reddening and with a shy, triumphant smile.

'How old was she?'

Moti had no idea.

'How old are you, exactly?'

'Round about twenty-five?'

'Have you told anybody about what we do? Your chowkidaar friend of that Learn-English Institute whom you smoke cigarettes with? Your wife? Is she really your wife?'

Instead of dramatically exclaiming, No one, by God, Moti said quietly, 'Only God, you and I know.' While Bhola gazed at him sceptically, he held his Adam's apple between forefinger and thumb in what—Bhola understood—was a gesture akin to placing one's hand in court on the appropriate religious text.

Moti would have liked to while many an afternoon away

in Bhola's room because it was comfortable inside with the heater on and he had simply nowhere else to go. Sometimes Bhola, surmising that Borkar had the preceding evening attacked him for beating up Titli, let him stay for a bit. Moti's was not an interfering presence. He seemed to merge into the room like a cat. Most of the time, he lay on the rug on the floor, reposeful, content to gaze at the cobwebs and the stripes of whitewashing on the ceiling.

'If Mrs Manchanda or Vivek turns up, we'll say that you've come up from home with some snacks and sweets, okay? Oh but then I'll have to produce some to offer them. Or you pretend to dust the desk or sweep the floor and we'll say that you're the black sheep of the clan of the family servant or some such shit and that you've been packed off here to jobhunt or something. Any ideas?'

'Why don't you buy some cassettes of new Hindi film music?'

'No money. Why don't *you* buy some with the vast sums I pay you? Why don't you read instead?'

Moti apparently kept the last advice in mind because a couple of occasions after, he showed up with a magazine, some Hindi porn pulp called *Karamchand*, but reading matter nevertheless. Surreptitiously, Bhola watched him struggle with the page and realized that he could not read, not in the sense of comprehend. He could recognize the letters and after a brief struggle the words but they didn't connect in his head with their meanings. Then he recalled, with an obscure sense of shame at the divide, the contrast, that not so long ago, when he himself had been a little over *half* Moti's age, *half*, he had swooned over the verse of Andrew Marvell.

'Which other human beings has your dear-wife-at-home had sex with?'

Moti did not reply. He paled and became tense instead, like a student anticipating the swish of the cane in the school Principal's office. Suddenly contrite, Bhola reached out and wriggled his hand through layers of clothing to place a repentant palm on the warm skin above Moti's thumping heart.

To Borkar, however, over tea—thick, sweet, like a syrup of molasses—and in the presence of some passive, tuberculous ragpicker on the patient's stool, Bhola's questions would be more theoretical. 'Should the loss of semen, Doctor saab, be construed as weight loss, a good thing, or as essence loss, something bad?'

Semen was a subject dear to Borkar's heart since he lost so much of it so quickly and so often. In fact, discussions about the human body exhilarated both of them. Pleasure illumined and made young the doctor's face and he forgot the patient of the moment in his joy at initiating a disciple. His delight infected his listener. Even the shabby surroundings—the tubelit walls, Borkar looking like Elton John in the photograph alongside the mounted table fan—seeming to catch a little of his ardour, ceased to depress and began to glow instead with the cosiness of a nest. The presence of Bhola's lover and lover-to-be—each unaware of—or at least refusing to acknowledge—the other's position in the triangle—added to the warmth. Both wife and husband—their loins, Bhola daydreamed, tingling perhaps at being desired, snug in the heat of his gaze—simpered as they sloppily went about their tasks, one ear cocked to sift through the quack's discourse to pick up any snippet that could affect the fragile stability of their lives.

'The bindu is a drop or globule.' Bhola was immediately distracted by the word into thinking of the Hindi film starlet of the same name. He could recall Bindu's gross, sequined, shimmying body in an impossible cabaret number but, try as he would, not her face. 'The bindu is a metaphysical point out of time and space, the zone in which samadhi, spiritual weightlessness, is experienced. It is a sacred symbol of the universe, written as a dot or the sign of zero, and in the

human body symbolized and materialized in semen.' Borkar's
hand trembled while scribbling out the illegible prescription,
perhaps with the enthusiasm generated by the subject.
Leaning over the desk, he held the paper under the patient's
nose and with his left index finger jabbing at the remedies
proposed, professorially explained the cure to the droopy and
uncomprehending woman. He returned to his exposition of
the globule at the core of the cosmos even before she had
taken two steps towards the door. 'Semen is the quintessence
of all manifested things. You will find that the *Brihadaranyaka
Upanishad* says: Verily, of created things, earth is the essence;
of earth, moisture; of moisture, plants; of plants, flowers; of
flowers, fruit; of fruit, man; of man, semen.'

'Oh. What about women?'

Borkar grinned like a pugilist who likes opponents with
spunk. 'Women? Coition is a sacred rite and woman the
sacred place.' He took off his spectacles and tossed them on
to the table. They landed with a clatter. He looked blinded
by hankering as his eyes followed Titli about the room. Moti
mumbled something and slipped into the bedroom-kitchen.
Relishing like a lip-smacking snack the phrases that he
enunciated, directing them at his maidservant's body, the
doctor continued, 'Woman's hips and haunches are the
sacrificial ground; the mons veneris the altar, the pubic hair
the kusa grass burnt in the ceremony, the moist labia the
soma press that provides the juice of the gods, the yellow
vulva the prepared fuel, the red-headed phallus the ember,
lust is smoke, penetration the mystic chants, orgasm the
living flame, and semen the oblation.'

'Can you repeat that? I want to write it down.' Suddenly
both rose as one from their chairs, Bhola to move towards the
desk to look for pen and paper, Borkar to slouch off towards
the adjacent room to shut himself up for half a minute with
Titli. 'An emergency,' he whispered in passing, his lower lip
trembling. Moti shot out of the doorway, the aluminium

kettle of molasses tea in his hand. The doctor grunted unpleasantly at Moti before the door closed on him and Titli. 'It'll just take a second,' breathed Bhola into Moti's ear, 'He's examining her stomach pain. Come on, let me examine yours too.' Neither the explanation nor the offer seemed to register with the distraught husband who exited through the door to the verandah, kettle still in hand.

They egressed soon after, Borkar downcast, Titli with her features still with shame. Her sari seemed to stick to the skin at the rear of her left thigh. Had Bhola been less aroused, he would have left immediately. Borkar sat down again behind his desk. His shoulders sagged and his body became a puckered balloon.

'Semen the oblation.'

Borkar didn't appear to have heard. Then, after a minute, looking at Bhola with crimson eyes, 'Where's that imbecile?' he asked.

'He's just gone out to water the plants.'

Borkar contemplated the floor between his feet for a while, then placing his hands on his knees, seemed to wonder whether the effort would be worthwhile before sighing and getting up. He lumbered to the front door, opened it, let in the cold and 'Oye!' he called out into the evening. He stayed in the frame of the doorway till Moti's figure appeared behind him.He moved aside a little—but not enough—so that Moti had to brush past him to enter. Borkar turned, gazed at the other's back till he disappeared into the bedroom-kitchen to put back the kettle, then bolted the door, slouched forward a couple of steps and halted in the middle of the room as though waiting for Moti to reappear. Moti, uncertain, paused in the doorway of the second room for the doctor to decide first where he would place himself. Borkar yawned audibly and protractedly and shuffled across to the stretcher bed. It creaked and squeaked as he wearily mounted and stretched out on it. He covered his eyes with his left arm and seemed to fall asleep instantly.

'Doctor is tired,' explained Titli in an unnecessary footnote. 'More tea?'

'Semen,' declared he, slowly and distinctly without uncovering his eyes, 'is believed to have an irresistible adhesive and magnetic power, particularly when it is retained in the body and made the centre of a field of force. The man who desires to attract men and women to himself should first deliberately practise celibacy by concentrating on the power stored in and generated by his unexpended semen.'

Bhola glanced at his lovers to see what they had made of the Sanskritized Hindi of the disquisition but it was evident that they had decided that it didn't concern them. Titli wandered about the room, picking up stray teacups and rearranging slippers while Moti dipped again into the second room and through it to some toilet-bathroom zone, for Bhola soon heard water thundering into a bucket somewhere. He should have been on his way back to the college but his hardon wasn't a tail that he could simply tuck away between his legs. What he wanted was a kind of calm orgy, for Borkar to temporarily die so that he could lie down in peace between Titli's thighs with her husband atop them. He arose from his chair and walked across to stand over the recumbent doctor. With the hand that Borkar wouldn't see even if he suddenly dropped his arm and opened his eyes, Bhola reached out to stroke the back of Titli's thigh. She moved out of reach as smoothly as a snake.

'I don't understand, Masterji. How can both coition and the retention of semen be advised at the same time as viable approaches for achieving spiritual strength? Wouldn't the success of the second, Baterji, negate the mystical pleasure of the first?'

Borkar lifted his arm to open his eyes, dark with repose and love, and smiled at Bhola with maternal indulgence. He looked immeasurably tranquil and grateful, as though he had awakened from the sleep of a fairy tale at last to enjoy the presence of a disciple thoughtful enough to ask the right questions. 'When you meditate on gods and goddesses joined together in union—what do you think—is the god spilling his precious seed six times a day like a fourteen-year-old fistfucker? He doesn't know how to enjoy coition without emission, you suppose? How else will his thrusts goad into motion the cosmic dance?' He was intoxicated with doctrine and while expounding it, disliked being reminded that not the entire world was paying attention. He frowned at the din in the background that was clearly dissonant with his thoughts. 'Somebody should shut off the water, Titli. The bucket must be overflowing.'

'He's gone to bathe, I think,' she answered, using the pronoun to refer demurely to her husband and the gentle voice that she usually put on along with her nurse's coat. Without waiting for a reaction, she shuffled off in the direction of the bathroom.

'In cold water?' asked Bhola of the room and then of Borkar in particular, 'Is this one of your ideas to test God knows what in that man?'

The doctor had covered his eyes again and appeared to be mentally preparing himself to doze off. 'What is there to test in him? No semen. Dead loins. And the brains of an ant without its industriousness.' He spoke without ill-will, lazily. 'He bathes on a winter evening in cold water for the same reason that he sits under a dripping tap all night.' They heard rapping on the bathroom door. Moti turned the tap off to hear better. Titli snapped at him through the door. 'Don't waste water and hurry up with your bath.' In the brief silence that followed, Bhola visualized Moti feeling tense and unhappy while he rubbed himself down.

To Borkar, he said, 'It sounds like you, though, the sort of thing you'd preach to win yourself a following. Punishing the body hones it. Honing the body hones the mind and a

honed mind conquers the world. Its possessor gains
unimaginable success, wealth and power and lives happily
ever after with his wife who treats him like his mother.'

'Hahn—the wife-mother now.' Borkar sat up with a sigh,
as though he had finally resigned himself to being prevented
from sleeping. 'Ask the mother,' he continued good-
humouredly, smiling with his old eyes at Titli's contour as
she bent over to straighten the strip of mat before the door
to the bedroom-kitchen, 'why the idiot son-husband has been
trying for years to drill a hole in his head with drops of ice-
cold water.'

Something seemed to fit into place in Bhola's head
accompanied by the click made by the safety catch of a gun
in a slick gangster film soundtrack. In a dozen assignations,
he had seen Moti naked in the back room of Mrs Manchanda's
flat, shy and happy at being desired, yet with his face
suffused with blood, crimson with mortification at his own
eternally flaccid state. 'He can't get it up, so that's it.' Bhola
blurted out the revelation, and then tensed as he wondered
whether Borkar would be puzzled by how Bhola knew.

The doctor was however too pleased with how the evening
was progressing to notice. He slid off the stretcher and
proposed rum and a late dinner. Bhola, having sampled some
of Titli's preparations before, declined the food. In the space
of half an hour, he drank one glass of cheap rum and watched
Borkar down four. Titli and Moti remained in the kitchen,
ostensibly cooking something up. Bhola learnt from the doctor
that Moti's biological father had been some local shaman with
a cord attached to a ring in his foreskin who, before vanishing
from his life, had predicted a great future for his illegitimate
son.

'It's a sect of some sort. We had a servant once who must
have been a member.' He struggled with the images from his
past life that floated behind his forehead but could not focus
on Gopinath's face. In the haziness of his memory, it was

Moti who gracefully danced a step or two on the terrace of his childhood. 'My best friend and I wanted to sign up too but didn't know how.'

'It's a symbol, of course,' asserted Borkar knowledgably, 'of self-sufficiency.' He raised his right haunch, farted loudly and then, as though to maintain balance, looked concentratedly at nothing to induce an equally dramatic burp. 'The ring in the foreskin is the vagina.' Bhola, waiting for the eructations to pass him by and assault the rest of the world, stopped breathing.

'Moti!' barked Borkar suddenly without changing expression, continuing to look down at the Hindi newspaper beside the glass on his desk. The subject of their discussion appeared like a wraith at the doorway, wet hair parted and vengefully brushed across, large-eyed with misgiving, mistrustful of the conclusions that the two would reach after discussing threadbare his secrets. Borkar gazed at him for a bit and then said almost tenderly, 'Open the door, my man. It's getting stuffy in here.' Moti hurried to the front door. Bhola could almost see the cold air hustle in and bundle out the alcohol fumes and the smells of Titli's cooking. Moti waited, uncertain, alongside the window for further instructions. Smiling at him, Bhola elaborated, 'So he never gets an erection and has never ejaculated, is that it? Is that a medical anomaly? I mean, what happened at puberty? Doesn't he sleep with his wife at all? Something every now and then must at least stir somewhere.' Moti blinked at what he thought sounded like concern but, mindful of Borkar, tried not to allow his expression to change.

The doctor jerked his head towards the kitchen to dismiss him. 'A freak of nature. I don't think he has any fluid in him that could gush out. He'll die of a stroke before he is forty.'

'Poor thing.'

Bhola thought of his meetings with Moti and again felt ashamed. He had been so immersed in indulging himself that he had not noticed—not even once, not *really* noticed—his partner's body, whether he, Bhola, in turn was giving his lover any pleasure beyond making him grin and blush. Immediately, his sinister side reminded him with a smirk that Moti had always been paid for his services, that the unemployed, unemployable, illiterate cuckold preferred cash, no doubt, to any transient physical thrill.

'He wants me to operate on him and give him a cord, something that he can tug on to make his future look up.'

Gooseflesh ranged across Bhola's skin at the idea. The doctor however continued, 'I may not have a degree but I'm no crackpot quack. I know my medicine.'

It would complete the picture, give colour to the icon—a scarlet cord permanently traversing a dark and flat abdomen. 'It isn't such a bad idea. It would make the sonofabitch happy and his wife too. I could help, play your assistant nurse and wear a mask and hand you your scalpel and so on.'

The project of the operation helped Bhola finally to lay his hands on Titli.

'Look—it's not fully clear to me,' he whispered tenderly to the lice in her ear while they stood on the verandah in the chilly gloom of a subsequent evening, 'why he absolutely has to have this operation and why it's going to cost a thousand rupees. Can't we discuss this alone and in peace, away from them?'

Between the ages of eighteen and thirty-seven, when he died, Bhola had just eight sexual partners, four women and four males. When he reviewed his life while bleeding to death in The Calm Centre that Anin and Dosto had created, it pleased him that he had maintained a balance between genders in his choice of lovers. Of course, it was ridiculous that he should at the age of thirty-seven—and that too while feeling himself ebb away—be faintly and lightheadedly embarrassed about how few were the people he had slept with. Then he had reminded himself that that was nothing new, that he had always felt ridiculous, not to worry. Besides, the eight had all been top-quality, no doubt about that, even though at that moment, he could recall the names and vaguely the faces of just five.

The first had been Moti and the second Titli, first husband and then wife. Moti had simply been easier to get to. Titli had been a nightmare come true, obese, disingenuously demure, passively basking in his attentions, a voluptuous slab of fishmeat. She sprinkled talcum powder in her armpits and between her breasts but her loins reeked of the sewer, perhaps because Bhola's lips were the first to nuzzle them—or so she claimed. Initially, he paid her a hundred rupees per encounter. Practically his entire monthly pocket money went over to her and her husband. Each time after he saw her off, drained of desire and not wishing to meet her ever again, not at least for a couple of weeks, he would remind himself that their Hindi was improving in leaps and bounds.

She acknowledged only one previous lover, Moti's supposed cousin, the Electrician, referred to simply by his profession as Bijliwala, he who had ducked out of their lives more than three years ago in Gorakhpur. Dr Borkar didn't count as a lover. He was a saviour, an employer who also paid her to allow him, in moments of stress, to sniff her loins, rub his forehead against her buttocks and kiss her instep for a second before, amidst shivers and whimpers, exploding in his pants. 'Didn't Bijliwala—doesn't Moti—go down on you? Don't you try and suck him off?'

'Chhee!' She turned her face away in disgust. Bhola was surprised. 'Don't you even want to? Was Bijliwala's penis black, fat and smelly?' She claimed never to have seen it. They seemed always to have fucked in the dark, silently, guiltily and hurriedly. So no gasps of uncontainable pleasure ever issued from her mouth when Bhola got to work in the sewers. 'But aren't you enjoying this? You should be screaming with uncontrollable delight.' Just her lips (facial) parted and her entire face softened, came apart a little, reddened; when they had time to themselves, she—at the end of the afternoon, when she tucked away in her blouse the money that he gave her—looked smug with pleasure.

They spoke Hindi between themselves, naturally. Hers was more lively than learned. They had nothing to say to each other but he liked to refer to their assignations as their Hindi class. He enjoyed feeling disgusted, unclean, depressed and guilty after they were over. The smell of her loins, it seemed, remained in his nostrils for hours after her departure. He would say something dirty in a mix of English and his chaste Hindi and then prod her into overcoming her faked embarrassment to find the right colloquial expressions for it. 'Say, I like it when your tongue tickles—licks clean—my pussy—fat pussy.' She would blush, smile, nod faintly and swivel her head away. Sex sounded so much better in Hindi than in English. A fallout of upbringing, no doubt. She had absolutely no initiative of her own. How dare she pretend to blush, he would ask himself, when she is being paid for this nonsense? 'No, say it. Or say, I want to sit on your face, clamp my pussy over your nose so that that's all you can breathe. Say the full sentence while looking at me, into my eyes.' That was foreplay. It continued till she enunciated the full sentence at one go, smiling into his eyes and exhaling paan-breath into his nostrils.

It usually began at the door and sometimes, though rarely, on the telephone when they fixed date and time. There wasn't much to choose from, Bhola often felt, between him and Dr Borkar as sexual partners. He was twenty years younger, that was all. Perhaps that was not all. He was probably in better health and could almost certainly hold out for longer when the frenzy of desire possessed him. He had seen it himself—the doctor, when he got the hots for her, stopped whatever he was doing—eating, examining a patient's tonsils, shaving, bullying Moti—and went looking for her with dreadful singlemindedness. She liked being wanted, even bizarrely. It made her feel secure. On the days when she was to meet Bhola, she was careful to ensure that Dr Borkar was satisfied before she left his house. Once sated, the doctor, like Bhola, lost all interest in his nurse-housemaid for several hours and indeed, preferred that she remain out of sight for some time so as not to remind him of his unmanly, nervous incontinence.

She prepared herself for Bhola like women of her class do for an outing, putting on a rich sari and makeup that made her look like a prostitute. He could never tell for certain whether she ought to be categorized as one. She never failed to claim her fee and it had been she who had suggested it in the first place at the end of their first encounter. She had worn a sort of see-through sari—black with some pink flowers on it—and he had bruised the head of his penis while trying to enter her; it had felt like having a go at fucking hardened dough. While wiping off his spunk with *his* vest first and *then* with the edge of her petticoat, she, to assuage his dismay at spilling outside her, had continued to murmur some soothing noises and had then remarked that tea on the way back home would cost her a hundred rupees. Oh, so she is a prostitute after all, had been his first thought as he had watched her looking down her front to see if her sari fell correctly. It had for the moment distracted him from his depression at observing her treat his precious semen—mystically potent and ambrosial wasn't it meant to be?—as cat vomit. In all the literature on the subject that he had wolfed down, she was meant to slurp it all up greedily, and at the very least let the few droplets that remained dry lovingly on her skin till their next meeting.

Breathing deeply, with his abdomen, as it were, he allowed the revelation to sink into his system. He realized that he felt vaguely relieved and actually even impressed by her levelheadedness at defining early in the day their sexual relationship. One hundred rupees was a quarter of his monthly pocket money. He would simply have to tighten his belt and not meet her more than twice a month. Perhaps he could steal some of his money back if she ever swooned, aroused beyond sanity by what his tongue did to her orifices. That should take about a decade. Her husband fortunately cost less and, funnily, smelt and tasted better. Six months later, when his pocket money went up because his exam results had been good, he struggled with his conscience for a week and then (feeling foolish and certain that no other conscience would be harassed by such trifles) disproportionately raised her price to a hundred and fifty. She had looked neither surprised nor grateful, though, at seeing the extra note.

'May I borrow your comb?' Then her face had dulled when she'd sensed his faint, instinctive unwillingness to oblige, and she had added, 'I forgot to bring my own.'

Embarrassed at having revealed his reluctance to share his things with her, finding his own fastidiousness preposterous, marvelling at the change in his emotions that sexual climax could effect, making him feel disgusted at the thought of catching lice from the hair of a woman whose anus he, before being drained, had teased with his tongue, he had gone off to look for a comb that was not his in the bathroom used by his landlady and her son.

Yet if she were a prostitute, she was so horribly ignorant about what men want as to be comic. If he were to be asked how he was so sure about how prostitutes behave, he would have retorted, Well, not like her, I'm sure. And whether what he wanted from her was what all men want from whores, he, not being at all certain of the answer, would have blustered in response, But naturally, of course. He was young and she— her manner and her notions—had confused him. The first time when he had lifted up her sari and petticoat and approached her loins with his nose and mouth, she had been standing next to the spare gas cylinder in the kitchen. She had staggered and almost fallen when she had realized his intention. 'No no,' she had hissed in surprise, resisting his head with her strong hands. 'Dirty it is dirty.' He hadn't been sure whether she had meant what he was going to do or where he was heading for but he had stopped to enjoy the pressure of her palms on his cranium.

He wanted her to treat him as one of her own class and kind, to revile and abuse him in the way that he imagined she did her husband or any lover from her own world. The more ladylike she tried to appear with her lipstick and her georgette saris, the less attractive she looked. If she had had her way, she would have entered timidly by the back door, smiled faintly at him, plodded slowly and tiredly to the bed, sat down heavily on it, making it creak loudly, and simply waited, wrapped, as in a shawl, in her pleasure at being desired. 'Get up. Off with your clothes,' he would order, running his fingers down her sari-swathed mound and into her gully, watching her facial lips part as he stroked their vaginal counterparts. From her fourth visit onward, he began to greet her at the front door with a napkin and a bowl of hot water with some after-shave in it. While she undressed, he bathed the drains and her other zones with the warm, aromatic solution, all the while demanding of her whether she liked what he was doing to her and if yes, why she did not say so loudly, why she did not bite her own—or his—lips till they bled with passion. She, like her husband, found almost everything that he said embarrassing, comic, shocking and arousing—somehow all at the same time. Ditto he—and further, he saw himself—naked, on his haunches between her thighs, a wet dishcloth in his hand—as comically—almost powerfully—ridiculous, apt for a pornographic comic strip, needing simply a turban, funny ballooned-up pyjamas, a moustache and a couple of snakes to feel at home in an illustrated and uncensored *Arabian Nights*.

Yet they maintained decorum and followed the rules that from time to time one thought up and the other tacitly but willingly assented to. 'If Doctor picks up, don't say a word, disconnect. A good time to call is between 2.30 and 3.15 when he snores.' They were horribly intimate, yet between them grew no affection. Love, intimacy, desire, tenderness and passion appeared to be as distinct and separable as envelopes and notices in different pigeonholes. In the twenty years of their liaison, he never reminded her, even by an indirect comment, that he paid her each time for her time and services. He never once forced her to do something that she did not want to do. Rather, because it was ladylike, she routinely refused a couple of times each novel technique or position or trick and was game for it only after she felt that she had underscored anew her gentility. 'If it pleases you.'

'From the door, walk towards me slowly like an elephant with your index finger deep in your vagina. When you reach me, take your finger out, jab it directly into my mouth and order me to suck it like a mango.'

'If it pleases you.'

It pleased her too, that was certain, but to what extent Bhola in twenty years did not figure out. For one, he did not know the Hindi word for orgasm. He looked it up in a couple of Advanced English-to-Hindi dictionaries in the Reference Section of the M.K.M.Z.A.P. Library and encountered for the nth time in his life several unknown Hindi words. They were unfamiliar to her too. He then tried to explain in Hindi, to describe in the language of the literature that he had read in English, an orgasm. 'Your insides should melt and your pussy explode.'

'What?' Her brow furrowed in unattractive incomprehension.

She had more than one unflattering facial expression. He had seen none during the days when she had sold him vegetables from a cart but she showed him all of them as a fat nurse in a small town in the hills. When she laughed unrestrainedly for instance, she revealed as much of upper gum as teeth. In her presence, therefore, he restricted himself to witticisms that only he could follow and to the tone of which alone she could react in a half-smile. Then, whenever she contemplated asking him for an advance against future payments, she absentmindedly pushed her mouth out in a snout and wriggled it about so that her upper lip, writhing under her nostrils, itself seemed to render audible her exhalations. Again, when she did not understand a remark or a question, her eyes would narrow and her forehead wrinkle up so that she resembled for a while a fat, thoughtful rat. He had noticed for the first time that particular look on her face when, several months after he had first located her and her husband in the town, he had put to her one of his early harebrained proposals for facilitating her slipping away from both Moti and Dr Borkar for a couple of hours.

'You could say that for the special puja in memory of my mother on her eighteenth death anniversary, I would need the help of a lady like you—it's a requirement detailed in the *Sathapatha Brahmana*—someone who is married and can be a mother herself, is older than me but younger than my mother—had she been alive—and someone who can fluently and with pleasure recite those special Hindi prayers. They are originally in Sanskrit of course but it's okay to use a simplified Hindi version.'

'What?' Her brow had furrowed in unattractive incomprehension.

It had worked, though—that is to say, she surprised him the first time by appearing to be quite willing to spend an afternoon with him. For Dr Borkar, she concocted a cousin, a distant relative of some sort, a clerk, newly arrived in the town, who worked at the Inter-State Bus Terminus. To Moti, she stated mysteriously and solemnly that she needed to discuss with Bhola the financial and religious aspects of his operation. On that first occasion, in that silent Administrative Officer's flat with its windows of translucent glass, Bhola had served her tea and treated her like a lady guest. She had sipped it without making any slurping noises and—without showing any surprise at the absence of any prayer paraphernalia in the flat—had waited tranquilly for him to make the first move. When she refused a second cup, he suddenly sank to his knees before her, encircled her waist and mumbling, 'I'm lonely, I've never received a mother's love,' buried his face in her lap.

The trio finally operated on Moti two years later in the spring of 1979. It took that long to overcome Borkar's reluctance to snip off a piece of Moti's foreskin because neither Bhola nor Titli tried very hard to badger him. Bhola himself naturally was too taken up with the rhythms of his life—with attending class, wandering about with classmates, watching movies, playing chess, descending for a long weekend to the plains, jogging, walking correctly, laughing therapeutically like Santa Claus four times a day, stretching his pocket money to cover his sex life and alternating his assignations between husband and wife—too taken up with living to bother to listen properly to—and actually act on—what Moti, off and on and whiningly, said. Moti's and Titli's sexual life did interest him but only in bits and pieces. Further, it became clearer over the months that what interested him the most in it was what was absent from it—namely, all that they did not do to each other.

'Does beating up your wife turn you on?'

Moti blushed, grinned and nodded faintly in affirmation. With Bhola, he blushed and grinned virtually all the time.

'Where and when do you beat her? I mean, doesn't Borkar object to the racket? I want you to beat me like you beat her but not on the face. Here, spit on me.'

With Bhola, Moti was perpetually ashamed, scared of

being found out, excited, happy, tense and tongue-tied. To elicit any information from him, Bhola had to pose his questions in such a manner that Moti in response could make do with either a quick nod or a slow, ponderous shake.

'Will you beat her up once in front of me? Please?'

Moti farted in fear—*prrrrt!*—at the very thought. Disgusting, I deserve it, lamented Bhola, close to tears.

Not once in all those years did Moti evince any suspicion of his wife's relationship with Bhola. No doubt, privately, he considered Bhola to be a freak, safe because incapable of having sex with women, more to be pitied than spat on; no doubt, he also believed his wife's explanations of having been summoned to do the housework in Bhola's room or massage his landlady's back or plot a strategy in peace to convince Borkar to operate on Moti. In any case, the more time she spent away from the doctor, the better, so Moti felt.

Bhola liked cross-checking with Titli. It was fun.

'Isn't Borkar woken up by your screams and so on when Moti knocks you about? Do you hit him back?'

In the monsoon, Bhola rendezvoused less frequently with husband and wife in his room because he could never be sure when a sudden shower wouldn't bring Vivek and some of his noisy friends scurrying back home from the football field or the cigarette kiosk. As a substitute, he went over more often to Borkar's clinic to paw whichever object of desire was at hand when nobody else was in sight. It had its points as a source of entertainment and seemed to them to resemble some child's game, a variety of 'Touch', wherein he had to touch the body of one of two inmates of the place when the others weren't looking.

In fits and starts, while out walking in the hills with a classmate or staring blankly at a chessboard with the tock-tock of ping-pong in his ears, he wondered about the lives of his lovers, where and how they had met, how their marriage had been arranged, what made them laugh, what they thought about when they lay awake at night, whether they considered him, Bhola, to be a complete weirdo or a sort of godsend. Asking them about themselves, though, reaped few rewarding answers. Moti was naturally inarticulate, reddening into speechlessness each time he felt upon him the eyes of someone awaiting a response. Titli too answered practically in monosyllables, flattered but puzzled that someone like Bhola should be curious about the minutiae of her existence.

'Moti shouldn't mind, you know, that you sleep around. After all, your body has its needs.' Speaking the Hindi of the Bombay film made him feel unreal. He enjoyed the role, though, the sensation of feeling fat like the seventies cinema hero.

She was very offended. In the yellow streetlight, her face became still—like pudding—with hurt. They were out walking in the gloom, he on his way back to M.K.M.Z.A.P., she to the nearby shop to buy potatoes, tea leaves and sugar. Even the little stroll had had to be contrived. 'In fact,' he continued hurriedly, 'maybe if he saw us together naked and so on, it might help to arouse him.' From the expression on her features, that seemed to be an even wronger thing to say, so he instantly changed the subject. 'But tell me—what was it like, your marriage? Did your family pay lots of dowry for a prize catch like Moti? Were the laws of Manu to be followed, if you wanted children, Moti's brother—that is to say, me, since I love him like a brother—Moti's brother could legitimately be appointed to sleep with you and the offspring would legally be Moti's, having been born—as they say—in his field. And man, what a field,' concluded Bhola, smiling at her admiringly.

She began to cry inaudibly and without any fuss. She didn't stop walking, though, and looking down, as though at her own ponderous, elephant's gait. She had had two children with Moti, first a girl and then a boy, but how was her young dolt lover to know? Her eyes were still glistening with tears

when he left her before the kerosene lamps of the grocer's
shack. He thought that he had been his usual clumsy,
unintentionally boorish self—nothing more—and that God
would forgive him for he had not meant ill. At the fork where
the lane fanned out in a delta of gravel and mud to join the
road on which Bhola jogged when the weather allowed him
to, he on an impulse suspicious of her sorrow, looked back to
catch a glimpse of her. Amidst the single-storey houses, the
wooden sheds and tin stalls, the occasional dim street bulb
and hissing kerosene lanterns, the evening shoppers and
strollers, she was nowhere to be seen. She has squeezed
herself, he thought viciously, into some bushes with the
grocer so that she can pay for a tiny packet of Red Label Tea
by lifting up her sari. Their grunts and rustles would be
swallowed up by the gurgle in the gutters and the drip of
drops from the leaves of trees.

Only in fragments, each sharp like the shards of glass of
a broken mirror, could he, as the months passed, piece
together their history from what the trio let fall from their
lips. They—Moti and Titli—had always been poor. That had
not been difficult to surmise even from the passive—almost
paralysed—way in which they waited to be made love to. For
them, sex did not appear to be an activity that they could
imaginatively indulge in at leisure, for they had never, it
seemed, had any time left over from fretting all night over—
and scrounging about all day for—money.

They had both begun as casual labourers in a gang that
built roads in the district of Gorakhpur. Even out of the
pittance that they earned per day, they had had to pay a
percentage to the contractor's lackey for continuing to hire
them. His only wealth being his offspring, Moti then unwisely
decided to sign up at a vasectomy camp to have himself
sterilized in return for a transistor radio and two hundred
rupees in cash.

'That was five years ago,' elaborated Borkar lazily, speaking to the wall in front of the stretcher upon which he lay face down while a sullen and nervous Moti massaged his calves and the backs of his thighs, 'and he has been impotent ever since.' He added in English, 'Psychological psychosomatic no doubt about it.' Without lifting his head, he groped behind him for Moti's wrist and relocated the masseur's hand on the upper portion of the rear of his right thigh. 'It doesn't help that his wife is so attractive and morally loose.' Borkar then swivelled his skull to wink slowly at Bhola.

Over the years, Moti had consulted as many quacks and swallowed as many potions and pills that resembled goats' droppings as his finances would allow. Then two summers after the operation, in the heat of May in the plains, their four-year-old son died of sunstroke and dehydration. Among other effects, Moti's sorrow permanently dammed up any chances that he might have had of getting his juices to flow again.

Bhola was young and the story affected him only fleetingly. 'You can have a son through me!' He hissed excitedly to Moti in his room in the chill gloom of an autumn afternoon, 'It's perfect! You in my mouth while I'm in Titli! It's allowed in the texts!' He held Moti by his biceps and willed him to pay attention. 'You pump away while I gurgle out a sacred hymn or two. C'mon! She'll agree if you order her. You're the master!'

Moti grinned and blushed so much that Bhola feared that blood would begin to seep out of his ears.

'And your daughter, Titli? Where is she? Which of you does she look like? When she grows up, I'll marry her so that all of you can come and stay with me and we'll all sleep together in one enormous bed. Promise?'

With time—and haphazardly—Titli and Bhola—prodded by her—overcame each and every one of Borkar's objections to operating on Moti. The doctor agreed to almost anything when badgered enough because it—the pestering itself—made him feel at the core of things. They even cornered him for a date and finally settled on the first Sunday after Bhola's final exams. Titli and Moti stole some of Borkar's money and went shopping for the ring and the braided thread as for the paraphernalia for a wedding. She also bought herself a new sari—red with a pattern of white flowers, sickeningly loud. For Bhola, the image of a penis with a rein was quirky and exciting. 'Had I a stomach as flat as yours,' he confessed admiringly to Moti at one of their subsequent trysts, 'even I would've considered going in for a cord.'

'But you can't,' objected Moti with uncustomary rapidity and emphasis, frowning at the blasphemy, 'it has not been foretold for you.'

'What about women?' Bhola demanded of Titli at their next afternoon assignation. 'Women don't need any emblems of divinity? A cord and a ring would look terrific on you.'

Borkar consented also because he was curious, needled by the itch to see for himself whether a bridled penis would effectively symbolize one of the notions dear to him—namely, the subjugation of the senses and the control of the lower self by the ascetic higher. The passive organ, with a slack cord attached to it, ought to be akin to the austere Shiva's jyahrod, his unstrung bow. Hence, if all went well, lived experience would make concrete and give meaning to the metaphors of myth and religion. Almost inevitably, therefore, as the date of the operation neared, the doctor was sucked into the preparations for it, pleasing Titli and flattering Moti no end. He made the prospective patient undergo a routine medical checkup and was pleased to discover that he shared Bhola's blood group. The cuckold was anaemic but then so was the rest of the country. He sent Moti off to buy two mousetraps to diminish the vermin population in the clinic and ordered from Dehradun some essentials—catgut, mercurochrome, extra

xylocaine, a box of surgical gloves, syringes. He asked Titli to
dust the photograph of him on the wall. In turn, husband and
wife readied themselves by becoming more solemn. They
filched less of the doctor's money. They undertook a bus ride
to the Shiva temple at Manaspeth, offered stuff and prayed
for the success of the operation. Indeed, it seemed to begin
to have its holy effect even before it took place, for two
weeks prior to the designated Sunday, Moti stopped meeting
Bhola, considerably irritating the latter because he needed
release from the tension of his exams.

When just three days remained, Moti began walking
taller and straighter, with a light in his eyes and a permanent,
gentle snarl about his lips, weighing each of his statements—
'Yes, I bathed this morning'—before delivering them, in
anticipation of the mannerisms of a member of a select tribe,
with the ponderousness of a sage or a statesman. He did not
fail to put out of humour the other three conspirators. The
evening before, he shaved his pubis himself and, following
Borkar's instructions, stopped drinking water. Bhola arrived
at ten-thirty the next morning and smelt rum on Borkar's
breath. At eleven, Moti lay down on the stretcher that till four
hours previously had been his bed, naked from the waist
down, vest, shirt and sweater rolled up to his nipples. Titli
beneath her white coat had put on her new red sari with its
white blossoms and arranged a garland of jasmine in her hair.
Muttering ceaselessly to herself—prayers, checklists—she
carried about everywhere with her—from bathroom to gas
stove to front door—a large yellow torch, gripping its briefcase-
like handle as though she were going to the bank with the
company's cash.

'Well, how do we do it?' asked Borkar, leering at Bhola
over the supine body of the patient.

He was justifiably startled. 'You're the doctor.'

'But not a quack,' Borkar retorted delightedly, a debator
elated at the opportunity provided for scoring a point, 'as I

have had occasion to inform you before.' In the pause that
followed, he continued to smile challengingly at Bhola, with
a malicious chuckle in his eyes, a Well-I'm-waiting expression
in his stance. 'I don't want to be held responsible, you follow,
for any deaths in this clinic.'

'Deaths? It's a bloody circumcision.' Indignant, feeling
befooled, Bhola glanced at Titli waiting, torch in hand, at the
foot of the stretcher. She was keyed up and passively unhappy,
afraid of unnecessary speculation and activity because God
alone knew what cause led to which effect. He then looked
down at Moti, who shut his eyes the instant that he saw
Bhola's gaze turn on him. Surprising even himself, Bhola
gently ruffled Moti's hair. Moti's eyes snapped open in
surprise. Bhola's fingers felt sticky with hair oil. 'Very well.
Let me try and see how we'll do it. We first pull this bed
away from the wall and to the centre of the room so that we
can move about freely all around it. Then you poke him with
a local anaesthetic and then we have some tea while waiting
for him to turn numb. Not permanently numb, though, I
hope.' He stared manfully at Borkar's face, daring him, as it
were, to sneer.

Moti willingly got off the operating table, pulled up his
pants, rearranged his clothes and set about carrying out
Instruction One. Titli, glad to be performing a familiar chore,
went off and returned with a broom to attack the dust and
spiders that were disclosed behind the stretcher. Borkar was
inexplicably enthused into concentrating on locating for Moti's
bed the geometric centre of the remaining space in the room.
The two of them pushed and nudged it till it looked perfectly
equidistant from desk and window. Bhola, having decided to
sit in the doctor's chair and wait for tea, in passing knocked
against and displaced a little the desk, thereby upsetting the
doctor's estimates. He sat down and watched from far away
the other three. It was quite possible that Borkar wanted
Moti out of his life but Bhola hoped that it was unlikely that

he would go so far as to kill him. It would be fairly simple to inject him with something stronger than a local anaesthetic. He thought in flashes of the other worlds that he from time to time inhabited—of his father's face, bewildered, ravaged with disappointment over his elder son marrying a Borah Muslim girl from Bombay, of his friends Anin and Dosto planning to set up a gym in a rented basement in their neighbourhood—and then of a possible future, of Moti groaning on the stretcher, drenched in blood and dying, and he and Titli on the run across the country and forever, with Borkar in pursuit, from small town to city slum, in tin bus and second-class train, he clutching for succour a scarlet cord that emerged damp out of the folds of her sari. You deserve the mess that you are in, he castigated himself and feeling heroic, immediately resigned himself to it; it was truly of his own making. Moti and the others were at least motivated by some sort of religious impulse, however murky, whereas he only wanted his homosexual lust to be tickled by the vision of a thread snaking across an abdomen dark and taut with having shed as much weight as was humanly possible.

'Here we are,' announced Borkar, jolly and smiling, holding up to the light—as for the camera in a TV soap—a full syringe. 'Is that enough or should I bung in two of them? And where do you want me to push this in?'

Bhola pointed to Moti's groin. 'There, at the base.'

Chuckling, Borkar directed Titli to daub the spot with cotton soaked in disinfectant, and then homed in. Moti flinched once, then continued to stare nobly up at the dangling flakes of whitewash on the ceiling. The doctor's amusement irked Bhola. 'I hope you know what you are doing,' he remarked coldly.

'I hope *you* know what you are doing,' laughed Borkar in response, throwing his head back and reeking into the air rum and paan fumes. Gritting his teeth and willing himself to think of other things, Bhola moved closer to Moti and asked,

'Feeling all right?' Moti nodded but did not speak. The tip of his tongue flickered out snake-like to wet his lips.

He brushed a wisp of hair back from Moti's forehead. One grows into desire. He remembered that five years ago when he had first seen the man behind their vegetable cart, it had taken him weeks to become aware of him sexually. Moti's attractiveness had stolen over him insidiously, like a fever—when he hadn't been looking, as it were; he had been eyeing the contours of the wife and then suddenly one morning had woken up leaking at every pore with desire for the husband. On his stretcher, Moti sensed Bhola's affection for him and tried to smile back but his dry lips would not part. For reassurance, Bhola squeezed his bicep and asked, 'Have you stopped exercising with my dumb-bells?' Moti in response broke into a more successful smile.

The dumb-bells were small and had intrigued Moti. 'Is that a toy for children?' Moti was innately well-mannered and Bhola had noticed that he did not pick up or touch anything unless he was sure that he would be allowed to.

'Not at all. You hold them in your hands and you run on the spot with them.' Moti had been amused at the notion. Nonplussed, Bhola had struggled to continue, 'I use them when it's raining or it's too cold and I can't go out.' He had watched as awkwardly, weights in hand and grinning in embarrassment, Moti had tried to jog on the four feet of carpet beside the bed. 'On the spot,' Bhola had repeated, 'and lift your knees up at least till your waist.' Moti had tried for a while, laughing at the clumsiness of his effort. His laughter had been pleasant to hear and on an impulse, Bhola had given the dumb-bells away to him. The cuckold had mantled with delight and Bhola himself had felt buoyant, eased of a burden. He had surprised even himself by his generosity since there had been a time not so long before when those dumb-bells had travelled everywhere with him, ripping the stitching of several bags with their weight. On other occasions, because of them, the rucksacks that they had been in could not be pushed into the overhead luggage racks in buses. Once, a suspiciously helpful, ex-Army Officer type— probably homosexual, Bhola had decided but had not been interested since he had been fat, English-speaking, garrulous and socially of the same class—the ex-Army type had even stumbled and almost fallen because of the unexpected weight.

'What's in this bag, goodness! Bombs?'

Bhola had been briefly distracted by the 'goodness', not having actually heard the word outside the Mary Poppins kind of film. Roundly embarrassed nevertheless, he had plumped himself down in a window seat with the bag before his feet, feeling as though it was full of severed human heads. After an hour of the night journey, he had taken the dumb-bells out and dumped them under the seat in front of him and had then felt considerably saner and lighter but only for a brief while since with the reckless lurching and pitching of the bus, they had begun to trundle about in the darkness like an engine of some medieval war. Cursing them, he had put them back in the bag, failing to convince himself fully of the idea that the entire incident had been the work of God—that globule of blue perfumed air at the core of his heart—God pointing out to him that it was not correct to jettison useful things just because they were for the moment inconveniently heavy. Besides, he should view toting them around as a bonus exercise, particularly beneficial for the forearms and biceps.

'Feel anything?' asked Borkar, making eyes at Moti and flicking his numb penis with a sheathed index finger. Moti glanced down, then away and shook his head. Borkar gave the organ a final, dismissive tweak and then demanded of Bhola with a snort in his voice, 'Now then, Surgeon General saab, what next?'

Bhola for weeks hadn't spotted the dumb-bells anywhere in the clinic. No doubt, they had wisely been sold for scrap. He could surely learn a thing or two from his lovers about travelling light. He should stop daydreaming and focus instead on the immediate. 'Look, Borkarji, you are the best judge. To me, it seems that you should pull the foreskin forward and somehow hold it in place.' When he was feeling happy and at peace, he did not fantasize or daydream. As part of the uncontrollably mushrooming Secret Seven activities, he had learnt to check himself whenever he had found that he was slipping into a reverie (or riviera, as Borkar called it whenever he wanted to talk psychology and felt that the Hindi equivalent was simply not weighty enough). Borkar nodded approval of his suggestion. Bhola helped Titli by pulling forward the foreskin while she—clearly uneasy and further upset by her own clumsiness—took long to tie tight the tip of the penis with some twine. Moti's organ began to resemble one piece in a string of dark uncut cocktail sausages. On his best days, when he was most in control of himself, Bhola felt tired of daydreaming, put off by how much time it ate up. His distaste for it then dovetailed neatly into his vow of silence, as far as possible not to waste breath talking to ghosts.

Titli returned from the kitchen with the aluminium pan that she used for boiling milk and in which she had sterilized the scissors, forceps, needle, tweezers and other implements. Borkar selected the scissors, tested them in the air above Moti's abdomen a few times and asked, looking from patient to nurse, 'Where do you want the cut? Any special preference? Side, under, sixty degrees?' Neither looked as though they had heard. Borkar bent over and inspected the dome of the penis puckered up like the petals, in human flesh, of a tiny, fresh rose. 'Here,' he, suddenly the authoritative physician, directed Bhola, 'flatten out and hold back the skin with these tweezers.' Bhola watched the tip of the scissors, exploratory like the snout of a hound, approach Moti's groin and felt a sharp, anticipatory pinch in his own loins. Borkar snipped twice quickly and dumped the scissors in the enamel tray with a clatter that startled them all. Blood oozed out richly and instantly began to drip into the aluminium plate placed beneath. Bhola recognized it as one of the several out of which he had often eaten. 'Disinfectant.' Bhola swamped the bloody rose with a wad of cotton, cold and damp to the touch, that had been soaked in a brown liquid that had emerged out of a brown glass bottle. 'Needle.' Titli threaded it at one go. It's like watching a cobbler at work, thought Bhola as he observed the needle, like a tiny plane, the catgut its exhaust smoke, fly left, right, through and over Moti's loins with soft silken swishes. He once more enjoyed in his own body the keen pleasure of each puncture.

'Ring.' Titli took out her cloth purse from between her breasts, unclasped it and extracted from amidst the germ-laden notes and coins the golden ring. 'I'd asked you to sterilize it.' Sulking and pouting at being even mildly ticked off, she placed in the enamel tray the other surgical instruments from the milk pan and flounced off with it towards the kitchen. His lips parted absentmindedly in a grimace, hissing, almost whistling, between his teeth as one would to encourage an infant to urinate, Borkar, peeling off his gloves and dropping them on the stretcher—where one flopped on Moti's abdomen like a dead bird and the second settled on the blood in the aluminium plate beneath his loins—Borkar followed her and shut and bolted the connecting door behind them. Bhola stole a glance at Moti but his eyes were shut and his lips seemed to be moving in inaudible prayer. Suddenly tired, wondering how on earth he had dared to mess so with his sacred life, Bhola walked around the desk and sat down in the doctor's consulting chair.

He should tell his lovers, brooded he, dejectedly contemplating the knoll swathed in cotton on Moti's body, that if recent events were any indicators, he would probably be getting married soon—that is to say, at some point in the next few years. He had never discussed his other lives with either Titli or Moti, partly because neither had displayed an atom of interest.. He doubted whether they knew his full name. There were times, though, when he—even he, self-sufficient as he was—wanted to talk to someone about the things that happened to him and about where he was going.

In the preceding week, right between his Subsidiary Hindi and Supplementary Economics exams, he had received out of the blue, like blows on the jaw, two marriage proposals, one, half-comic and oblique, from Anin, and the second, dead serious and droll, from Mr Manchanda.

Anin's had been a Good-luck-for-the-exams card, with enclosures, that had arrived late, most likely because she had misplaced it and forgotten to post it in time. The enclosures, three clippings from the newspaper matrimonial columns, had introduced Bhola to a new world.

> *Gursikh Ramgarhia match for 24/50/182 M.A.(Eng) First Class even nature d/o retd Lt Col IAS/IPS/Defence preferred simple marriage first instance full details PN 873.*

> *Western or Japanese women over thirty but less than seventy intending to settle in matrimony in India with liberal non-vegetarian Hindu knowing advanced Yoga may contact Post Box 146.*

> *Status preferably working tall slim for Sindhi 176/27/3000 Delhi engineer own house Ambassador Box 6715.*

At the bottom of the card, Anin had appended in a postscript: *I myself should be getting married soon. And you? And to whom? Please refer enclosures.*

Bhola had not replied yet. He probably wouldn't, seeing

that he would go home in a week's time and meet both her and Dosto.

Mr Manchanda had dropped in with a nubile girl, his daughter from his second marriage, on the evening before the Economics paper.

Bhola had met him before, about a dozen times in all in the past three years. He drove a blue Ambassador car and wore black sunglasses—even indoors. He was taciturn—at least before Bhola, he typically did not utter more than a handful of sentences in the course of an evening. Vivek was almost a different person in his father's presence—more alive, fidgety, smiling without cause, humming his three tunes louder than ever.

Mr Manchanda didn't get much help from his ex-wife in presenting his case. She served the tea and fried crap and withdrew into the kitchen as into her shell, from which, however, the issuing bang and clatter of metal and china, unusual from one normally silently efficient, clearly emitted to Bhola the signal that she wanted the mission to fail. When he finally grasped the point of the visit, he was in turn—and rapidly—first taken aback, then mildly titillated by the wife-to-be and finally amused at visualizing his father's cardiac arrest at hearing the news. Vivek's half-sister aroused him because she looked like a painted-up servant girl trying to hide her origins. She was dark, and had put on red lipstick and grey face powder. After smiling frozenly and murmuring some greeting at Mrs Manchanda and Vivek, she sat with her back straight on the edge of an armchair and remained mute for the one hour that they stayed, staring fixedly at the cassette recorder atop the fridge, occasionally glancing surreptitiously at her father. Bhola would have liked her to sit on his chest and shower his face with face powder, spittle and Hindi abuse.

'It's early, no doubt,' admitted Mr Manchanda in Hindi, making sticky, slapping noises with his tongue and teeth as he strove to master the kilo of cheese pakoda in his mouth, 'but you should plan your marriage well in advance. If you can. All that you have to say at this stage is yes in principle.'

'I'd promised my mother—dear departed now,' responded Bhola, wondering with one tiny part of his head whether Manchandas were Brahmins in the first place, 'that I'd get married only after I master the vrischikkasana. Do you know it?'—looking affably from father to daughter to half-brother to father—'It's yoga, the pose of the scorpion. One balances only on one's hands and forearms. The body is sort of flung up into the air. The legs are then joined and slowly bent and lowered overhead so that the back forms an arc—a bit like a lower case e—and the soles of the feet come to rest gently on the top of one's head while all the time, the body continues to balance only on the forearms.' He was surprised that nobody seemed to be paying any attention. 'Very aesthetic, very backbreaking. I gave myself fifteen years to achieve my goal. Before my prospective in-laws, I want to pose only on my forearms, flip my back over, hold my head up with pride—practically sucking my toes—and trumpet: *Your progeny's achievements?! And what about mine!*'

Mr Manchanda looked like the kind of person who did not listen to what he did not want to hear. In response, he belched so loudly that even the dog looked up. 'Marriage settles you down, you know. It organizes your life and smoothens your eccentricities.'

O God fucka-fucka, lamented Bhola, his culpability leaping up as though electrified at the word 'eccentricities', he knows, the bugger knows that I swing like a ding-dong pendulum. This door swings both ways, sang the Hermann's Hermits in his head. Then: how could he possibly know, there was no oblique reference, merely my own guilt finding expression in the creation of phantoms. 'In any case, I thought that I should wait for some years and then ask my father's permission.'

Waiting. It was true—so he ruminated as the bedroom door opened and the doctor emerged with Titli in tow, milk pan in hand—that he felt all the time that he was simply waiting for something to explode all over and through him, to shatter and change and illuminate him. Borkar looked both spent and cynically amused. Smiling at Bhola, he announced, 'The gold ring has turned grey in colour.' Pale with bafflement, Titli held the pan under Bhola's nose. In a couple of centimetres of grey water lay the ring, glittering more like bellmetal than gold. 'I told Doctor that boiling it would not be necessary,' faltered she with trembling lips, rancour enlivening her face. 'Gold is gold and cannot carry any infection. What can we do now?'

For one brief moment, Bhola understood Titli's question to be an indirect invitation to coition. He tried to look sexily into her eyes but hers revealed only anxiety and spite at being tricked by whichever crook had sold them the ring. In the blankness of waiting between two sexual encounters, all the motions of action performed seemed fundamentally, in themselves, unimportant, only parts of the larger action of waiting, a means of better marking the passage of time to the next union with another brown body. When she read the lust in Bhola's eyes, with a frown and a 'tch' of impatience, she whisked away to the stretcher and tilted the pan over Moti's chest so that he could peek inside. 'He tricked us, that scoundrel,' she began in Hindi and then switched over to their dialect.

The fact of husband and wife having been duped had fully restored Borkar's good humour. 'Come on come on,' he, beckoning the milk pan, smiled avuncularly at Titli, 'Moti's golden foreskin awaits its crown.' He picked up his gloves off

Moti's abdomen and the aluminium plate, dipped and rinsed them in the water in the pan and put them on again. Then, palms facing outward, he flexed his fingers, and fisted and opened his hands as though signalling numbers in tens across some distance. 'We are ready for the further instructions of the Honourable Surgeon General.'

'Moti, drink the water in the pan,' ordered Bhola. 'It will prevent all infection.' He would have liked to see some distress on Titli's face, to hear her protest and then feel the pleasure of overriding her but, to his surprise, the pair seemed to like the idea. Titli gave a quick nod of approval and relief, Moti raised himself up on his elbows, she plucked the ring out with her left hand, held the pan to his lips and tilted it slowly forward, further and further, till he had swallowed the last drop. Borkar waited, a bemused half-smile on his face—as though jolted by Bhola's awesome knowledge of things—till Moti belched and lay down again. Then he took the ring, asked Bhola to hold apart with two pairs of tweezers the cut portions of foreskin, slipped the ring in place, directed Titli not to let go of the third pair of tweezers that grasped the ring and then, muttering that he couldn't see a thing because of the several hands hovering like hillocks over Moti's loins, began sewing up the last few millimetres of skin that he had snipped. Bhola noticed beneath him Titli's hands more veined and masculine than his, and in front of them, Borkar's receding hairline, the white roots at the base of the black dye, the large, square spectacles underneath the forehead gullied in concentration. He heard and felt on his hands Borkar's warm exhalations and again saw the needle mimic the erratic loop-the-loops of a tiny, acrobatic plane. The doctor finished in no time, asked them to remove the tweezers and swathe the area with disinfectant, dropped his gloves, this time in the milk pan, dug into his trouser pocket for his wallet and from it extracted a condom. 'Here,' he commanded Titli, enjoying her discomfiture, 'put this on him for some time, at least till

the bleeding stops.' Moti looked pale, too spent to be relieved.
Borkar beamed and chortled at him, 'A special case, you. It is
rare that the apple of his wife's eye has her tenderly swathe
him in a condom in public.'

'What is the Hindi word for condom?' asked Bhola of the
room as he took the contraceptive from Titli, tore off its
packet and unrolled it. 'We always used the word Nirodh but
that's like—' he paused for a moment to search Borkar's face
for an appropriate parallel—'saying Xerox for photocopy. I
mean, weren't there condoms in India before Nirodh was
introduced?'

Moti sat up to help the doctor's assistants. He held the
cotton in place while his wife taped it down. He then with
the fingers of his right hand tried to steer his penis into the
contraceptive that Bhola kept open for him. It was almost
impossible because of the dressing. Moti began to weep
silently. 'What is it?' asked his wife, waspish because of the
worry within her.

'I don't feel anything. Why don't I feel anything?'

'Garbhanirodhak,' announced Bhola in triumph,
abandoning the condom—but with tenderness—on Moti's
shaved abdomen. 'I am quite sure that's the dictionary word
for contraceptive but there must be something more
colloquial.'

'We used to call it topi,' said Borkar. He sat down behind
his desk, opened a drawer, fished out cigarettes and matches
and lit up. 'If you want to brush up your Hindi, you should
read a good Hindi newspaper. Keep abreast of both the
language and the times.'

'I don't need news. I don't subscribe to any.'

'Is that to save money?' Borkar laughed, some smoke
went down the wrong way and he broke into a fit of coughing
that threatened to disgorge his intestines on the floor. Bhola,
disapproving of the poor quality of his wit, looked coldly at
him and hoped that he would die. He picked up the condom,

dangled it in the air like a specimen of smelly fish and stated, 'The purpose of your post-surgical care remains mystifying, Masterji.'

'Really? Okay, give it back.' A little surprised, Bhola dropped the pink contraceptive in Borkar's open palm. With a faint simper, the doctor pushed it into his mouth and began to masticate it. 'Better than chewing gum,' he revealed wisely like an owl to nobody in particular, 'Less harmful. Whenever I go to the chemist to buy vitamins or cough syrup or paracetamol, I ask them to give me my change in condoms.' Bhola remembered remarking that whenever Borkar had taken out his wallet, he had flashed the condoms in them to everyone around him, like an exhibitionist airing his loins in the winter sun in a public park. Bhola had wondered more than once what possible use incontinent Borkar could make of them. Now he knew. 'Would you like to try one?'

'Okay.' Did he really want one? He was not sure even though he was in general truthful. Truth was a tactic of weight loss. One cut the crap when one spoke the truth.

He had torn the packet, taken out the condom and was looking at it, wondering whether he should unroll it before slipping it into his mouth, whether rolled up, it didn't simply look neater, more aesthetic and sort of professional, when Borkar broke in with, 'I'd suggested a contraceptive for Moti as a bag for any urine that catches him unawares, at least till the anaesthetic wears off and his penis begins to respond to the stimulus of the ring.'

It never did. Bhola turned and looked at Moti sitting up in his stretcher and sobbing mutely. Titli fussed around him, pulled his shirt and sweater down, pushed the hair back off his forehead, urged him softly to calm down, to go to the bathroom to wash his face and blow his nose, reassured him that the operation had been a success and that everything would turn out fine. Bhola stepped across to them, unrolled the condom and asked Moti to help him put it on him. 'You heard what the doctor said. Keep this on just in case. And wear a pyjama or lungi or something, something loose. Come on, you can get up now.'

Bhola bought a ticket on the bus home for the following Saturday. On the Wednesday preceding his departure—three full days had elapsed since the operation—Titli and Moti decided to go ahead with the Ceremony of the Maroon String even though sensation had not fully returned to his penis. The two invariably spoke of the rite in capital letters. 'Who knows? Perhaps I'll begin to respond completely only after the String has been fixed,' mused Moti in the philosophical tone used by the stupid when they wish to impute profundity to trivia. When he wanted to urinate, he felt only a vague twinge or two, akin to pins and needles, but that was enough—Borkar's chewing gum was not required—and that was all—he remained numb to all external and mental stimulus.

Bhola doubted very much whether Borkar himself knew what had gone wrong. 'A temporary nerve blockage. Not very serious.' Both of them pretended that nothing had, that the operation had been a success in that it had made Moti happy. 'I don't think that he has significantly less sensation than he had before.' Neither discussed the subject directly or at length even though it—and their indefinite sense of guilt—had thickened and rendered fetid the air of the clinic, making breathing difficult. 'The stitches are coming along nicely.' Bhola dropped in just three times in the entire week and didn't stay long on any of them. Belying the dull panic in her eyes, Titli spoke of hiring a priest for the Ceremony of the Maroon String and hinted that she expected Borkar or perhaps even Bhola to pay for his services. 'I pay for yours and that's enough,' muttered Bhola to himself in response to her. For that entire week, Borkar was virtually incommunicado—that is, he looked at the speaker when somebody said something to him but then turned away without a word even before he had finished, humming the bars of a fifties Hindi film tune, or answered completely out of context even while nodding intelligently and encouragingly.

In the end, the Ceremony of the Maroon String was performed by Bhola the Brahmin in three minutes flat in the presence of Titli and Borkar. Titli wore her new red sari again and Borkar once more drank rum. The new Moti, more assertive now that he was to be ordained, prepared himself for his luminous future by bathing in freezingly cold water on Wednesday morning and eating nothing but fresh fruit—that is, appropriately phallic bananas—all day. In the evening, after the last patient had left, Titli got down on her hands and knees and scrubbed the clinic clean. Both Borkar and Bhola followed her around to gaze at her bum because they had nothing else to do while waiting. Solemnly—and successfully hiding his embarrassment at being naked—Moti stood in front of the desk and stared straight ahead, the light in his eyes reflecting the incandescence of the days to come. Bhola fondled the cord that Titli handed him and allowed himself to be aroused by it. It was of the width of a shoelace, about a metre long and a rich scarlet in colour. While idly wondering how on earth one bought it and what one said when asked what it was meant for, he realized that it *was* a shoelace, three of them in fact with their aglets snipped off and their ends sewn together. He ran it around Moti's stomach like a tailor measuring his waist, and with Titli and Borkar behind him and concentrating on Moti's front, took the chance to stroke the cleft of his buttocks. That Moti's expression did not change annoyed him. He ran one end of the string through the ring, paused to let Titli sigh and mumble some incantation and then handed over the two ends to Moti. Moti, who had wished to tie the knot himself, trembled with the joy of fulfilment as he brought one chapter of their lives to a close.

LIPS THICK WITH REPOSE

Retribution—so it certainly appeared to be—exhibited itself within a week of their snipping at Moti's foreskin and playing doctor with his life. On Friday morning, the day before Bhola was to leave for his holidays, in the break between two halves of a guest lecture, he had trotted back to Mrs Manchanda's to quickly bathe and while humming and shivering and lathering himself, had noticed a red, splotchy soreness beneath his foreskin that hurt when he touched it with either finger or soap. He sat through the rest of the talk without hearing a single word, feeling a little like one of the sods in the Old Testament whom Jehovah is displeased with, and rushed after lunch to display himself to Borkar.

'Herpes,' announced Borkar, his face still and mottling up, 'I have it too.'

They hadn't met for two days, not since the evening of the Ceremony of the Maroon String that they had performed on Moti. Herpes? Bhola watched Borkar lean back and slump in his chair. Herpes was a school joke, wasn't it, a disease that the people whom one could joke about suffered from. What is the difference between true love and herpes? Herpes is forever. Before Bhola had fully digested the news, Borkar expressionlessly yelled for Titli. She opened the door of the kitchen-bedroom and paused, ladylike and enquiring. 'Come come, come forward, Titliji,' cooed the doctor—but with a face gorged with rage—as he arose, 'no need to be shy before we men of the world.' In one continuous movement, he picked up the empty bottle of Old Monk rum off his table, walked up to her and smashed it across her cheekbone. 'Bitch whore,' he muttered as, with a squawk that expressed as much surprise as pain, she staggered back against the wall, lost her balance and dropped to the floor. The bottle broke and its bottom half landed on her forearm, bounced off and splintered into several pieces on the cement. The varieties of noise brought Moti from the verandah into the room. Startled, with a gasp, he hurried forward to help his wife. Borkar looked at the part of the bottle that remained in his hand, then down at the figures beneath him, as though undecided which head to bring it down on when Bhola, finding his voice, warned, 'Careful, Doctor! The patients outside can hear us!'

Nodding wisely, neck of bottle still in hand, Borkar went to the front door, poked his head out and shooed the sick away. 'Clinic closed for the day! Away you go, all of you! An emergency! Go away! Tomorrow, tomorrow!'

Those inside heard out of doors the shuffling of slippers, mutterings of surprise, grumblings of disappointment, coughs that preceded demurely posed enquiries. 'Yes yes you continue the medicines till tomorrow. Three more days you take them!' By the time Borkar had watched the last of his clientele vanish through the gate and shut and bolted the door, Titli was sitting up with her back against the wall, holding up her head with both hands at the temples. Moti had disappeared into the kitchen. Borkar came up and stood over her, the broken bottle held casually in a dangling hand. Clumsily, he got down on his haunches beside her. His knees cracked. With his left hand, he held her right wrist and tried to prise her forearm away so that he could assess the damage done to her face. Titli continued to sit without stirring. Her arms did not budge. 'Come now, let me see! Come with me to the other room,' wheedled Borkar, almost involuntarily waving the broken bottle before what he could see of her features. Moti, silent, appeared at the doorway of the bedroom-kitchen, a small, lidless pressure cooker filled with water in his hands.

Bhola knew the cooker, a cheap, counterfeit product with a faulty lid, to be one of the most dangerous gadgets in a household already sufficiently menaced by violent and lunatic tempers, passions and temperaments. Four times a week, its lid flew off the handle and hit the ceiling, spraying the next meal of the trio all over the walls and bed. Moti found the antics of the cooker more amusing than dangerous. Bhola could see what he intended to do with it but was paralysed by the tension of waiting for the event. He opened his mouth meaning to alert the doctor; what emerged sounded like a saline, hot water gargle in the early morning. Positioning himself behind Borkar, Moti with both hands brought the cooker down on the back of his head with a thud that seemed to rattle the windows. Water splashed bountifully over the three of them. The bottle sank into the pleats of the sari at Titli's abdomen before bouncing on to and trundling— frightfully loudly—away across the floor. With a soft, sorrowful moan, Borkar slumped sideways and across Titli's legs. Moti flung the cooker down. It hit Borkar's shoulder, keeled over and lay on its side, pouring out its remaining water. Bhola watched the stream wind its way like colourless blood across the floor towards the front door. Moti helped Titli to disengage her legs and stand up. Her cheek was red and swollen already and her right eye half-closed but mercifully it itself seemed to have escaped damage. Bhola was sorry for her but considerably more sorry for himself for being where he was.

With his arm around her, in a new, manly way, Moti supported his wife to the stretcher—his own—bed and aided her to lie down on it. 'Get some cold water,' whispered Titli in a cracked, hoarse voice. Moti brushed past Bhola without looking at him, picked up the pressure cooker and vanished into the bedroom-kitchen.

'You seem fine, what a toughie you are,' announced Bhola cheerfully, stepping up to the stretcher. Her cheek had begun to resemble a large, overripe, almost rotten, red bell pepper. 'I mean, only you can tell whether you have any bones broken or anything.' He spoke brightly but hurriedly; he wanted to get to the point before Moti returned with—who knew?—a second pressure cooker filled with water to knock him out with. He abruptly remembered Dosto, when pressed for time, leaking into his pants with tension while trying to finish the last question in a school exam before the bell. 'And you should also have a look at Borkarji later, surely he couldn't be dead, I mean I hope not... And is there some medicine, some ointment or something that he used to take or apply to his penis?' Titli did not seem to have heard a single word. Moti reappeared with the topped up cooker. With his new, virile, at-the-helm manner, he began applying cold compresses on his wife's cheek and forehead. She went 'ooh' and 'aah' at each touch of the cloth. Leaving them to their fun, Bhola stepped back and went and stood over Borkar's body. Fortunately, he was still breathing and not oozing blood from any visible orifice. Titli of course should die immediately for having gifted herpes to all her lovers. Moti in any case was half-benumbed and Borkar probably in coma. He, Bhola advised himself, should get out before he went to jail or something. Nothing like herpes for curing lust permanently. How to become a Zen monk in one easy step.

He had to ask three times before his question registered. Finally, Titli asked her husband to give Bhola the ointment that they knew Borkar used to apply twice a day. Moti crossed over to the desk, rummaged around in each and every drawer with increasing impatience and finally found what he was looking for on the shelf next to Borkar's photograph. He handed Bhola a small bottle of Vicks Vaporub. While Bhola held it in his hand and reflected that some things, like Moti's obtuseness, would never change, Titli, frowning and laboriously sitting up on the stretcher and wiping her neck dry with the end of her sari, hastened to explain, 'There's something else inside. It's a balm that he used to make

himself with some herbs and roots and I don't know what all.'
Gingerly, fearing a genie, Bhola unscrewed the bottle. The
ointment was granular, very dark brown in colour and smelt
faintly of mustard oil mixed with very sour curd.

'I'll try my luck. I have to apply this twice a day?' He
raised the Vicks Vaporub at Titli. While she rearranged her
dishevelled clothes so as to look less ravaged, Moti answered,
'And you can also eat a tiny bit every morning, first thing on
an empty stomach. Doctor would pop a little—an eighth of a
spoon—under his tongue. Said that it kept him tip top.'

'That would depend,' murmured Bhola, glancing down at
the supine body of his fellow recipient of Titli's goodies, 'on
what you mean by tip top.' Neither of his listeners smiled.
They looked like hosts at the end of a long evening tiredly
and quietly waiting for their guests to depart. Bhola in
contrast was in high spirits and becoming perkier by the
minute. Liberated, at least for the time being, from his lust
for Titli and her husband, he suddenly realized that in all
likelihood he wouldn't see them again for some weeks and
that perhaps he should say adieu properly. 'Do have a look at
him soon, won't you? Douse him with water or something.'
Both Moti and wife nodded; to encourage Bhola to depart,
Moti even took a couple of steps towards the front door. 'And
you should sleep, take rest, whatever.' Outside, in the
afternoon sunshine, he inhaled deeply the fresh air of a new
world, remembered that he hadn't reminded them that he
was leaving the next morning for the long summer, then felt
that it would be impossible for him to reenter that stifling,
unclean prison cell of a clinic and, ointment in pocket and on
buoyant feet, began jogging Mrs Manchanda-wards.

He had a ticket for the eleven o'clock deluxe bus the
next morning. He reached by rickshaw the Inter-State
Terminus at ten-fifty, found his seat and gazing out of the
window at nothing, wondered whether he should go for a piss
right away or wait till the last possible minute before the

bus's departure. Eleven usually meant eleven twenty. He spotted between the fruit chaat stalls and the rickshaw pullers—relaxing squatting in the sun, smoking, coughing and tranquilly sharing their tuberculosis with the world—a familiar couple, the woman in a red sari with white blossoms. He ducked, leaned his head against the seat in front of him, gazed down between his feet at the grimy metalled flooring of the bus, stopped breathing and toyed with the idea of rewarding himself with his next inhalation only when the coast was clear. Behave yourself, he soon reprimanded himself sternly, arose, descended from the bus and wandered off in search of a place to leak. The options were limitless. He chose a section of the broken boundary wall behind some abandoned bus shelters. It was the region of the terminus furthest from the ticket booths before which—he could see—Titli, with Moti alongside her, had joined one of the shorter Ladies' Only queues. He wondered where on earth they were off to and why. Then he was suddenly sure that Borkar was dead and that they were running away. He tried but could neither urinate nor breathe. His entire thorax seemed to have become a gigantic, suffocating lump.

He was actually relieved to see them in the Deluxe bus, looking out of place and this way and that in the seat just in front of the rear door. They beamed, grinned and exclaimed with joy when they saw him, their faces lit up like the sun for an instant giving the clouds the slip.

'How is Borkar? Where are you going?' Some of their fellow passengers glanced momentarily in their direction at hearing the urgency in Bhola's voice.

Titli and Moti looked at each other before she replied with a hideously unconvincing smile, 'He is fine. He was sleeping when we left.'

Bhola had to move away from the door to allow the other passengers to get on. Yet he didn't want to stand too far down the aisle, yell out his questions and make public his disquiet.

As it was, the first thing that every person boarding the bus noticed was Titli's face with its bulbous, livid cheek, the weight of which had pulled her mouth down in a sneer and rendered her speech unclear. Then the second thing that they were all bound to take note of was how socially her interlocutor didn't belong to her world at all; then they would start paying even more attention to the conversation.

'I see. But how was he yesterday?'

As fine as he had been that morning, apparently. To hear the details, Bhola changed places with the pair immediately ahead of Titli and Moti, a teenaged girl and her grandmother who wanted to vomit but not to alight for fear that the bus would leave in her absence. The window of their seat was jammed shut. When Bhola offered them his, the grandmother immediately and without a word got up, navigated her way like a hunted animal through the other passengers to it, poked her head out of the bus and began to retch loudly. While he was being thankful for his shut window and absentmindedly wondering whether one could tell just from the *sounds* of heaving exactly what kind of indigestible food was being disgorged, Bhola learnt that Borkar hadn't regained consciousness for twenty hours. He had thrashed about a bit on the floor at night, as was his wont in his drunken, troubled sleep, so they had rolled him onto one blanket and covered him with another.

'I see,' said Bhola, though he didn't at all, even though he continued to nod intelligently. It was impossible for him to concentrate on the madness that he was being informed of. He couldn't bear to turn around and look at the faces of either wife or husband—Titli's like a prostitute's, thrashed to pulp and half to death for fun, with a couple of boils to boot blooming like spring on the edges of her upper lip, Moti's shining with a kind of crafty stupidity, with excited contentment at being alone with his most prized possession after having vanquished the ogre. Bhola stared instead at the granddaughter four seats ahead, standing behind the bent grandmother much as though intending to bugger her, munching some smelly mix of raw chopped onions and fried peanuts and whining peevishly in Hindi, 'That's simply enough of vomiting now. You just sit back, sip some water, shut your eyes and STOP IT NOW!'

The bus driver, wizened, unshaven, toothless, boarded through his tiny special door and blew the earsplitting horn for several seconds to signal the imminence of departure. *Get out of the bus instantly, you retard,* Bhola told himself, *and go and check whether Borkar is dead.* The notion depressed him so much that he felt cold. 'What if he doesn't wake up at all?' he asked without turning around.

'Some patient will shake him up. The front door is bolted from the outside but not locked,' explained Moti, grinning with accomplishment, fidgeting constantly with elation. A hirsute bus conductor, the top buttons of his uniform shirt undone, the hair on his chest resembling the torn stuffing, painted salt and pepper, of a coir mattress, reached them and, intrigued by Titli's face, first demanded of her her ticket. She dug out of her blouse her green purse and from it two mustard-yellow scraps of paper. The conductor examined them with a scowl and mumbled into his stubble that they needed to pay some more, that is, they had bought their tickets for the right to travel in that bus but not their reservations for the right to travel in particular, numbered seats. Bhola glanced at the notes, rolled up to the dimensions of cigarettes, that next emerged from the purse, noted with his mind elsewhere that Titli was richer than she looked and then, tingling with the shock of shame, realized why nurse and assistant had abandoned the doctor so suddenly. The driver pressed the horn once more, started the engine, briefly revved it up, experimentally declutched and allowed the bus to slide forward for a metre or two, grinned at the attendant shrieks and squawks of dismay from those passengers left behind at the tea stall and around the soft porn magazine vendor, put on at full volume a tape of some Bhojpuri devotional disco music on the audio system and then settled down to coaxing out of the engine the correct healthy roar. The music and the din of the engine made conversation impossible, so Bhola tried to compose himself into staring out of the window and wondering. The bus finally began to move, slowly at first, a sated anaconda, through the alleys and lanes of the town, its progress belying its roar. By the time that it had shaken off the huts on the outskirts and begun its proper descent to the plains, he had worked out that he would be in deep shit soup only if Borkar died, and *then* only if someone actually called the police, and *then* only if somebody else provided the cops accurate details of Titli and Moti, and then if the two were faithfully traced to the bus terminus, and finally only if some sharp idler at the depot could precisely recall them as having been passengers on a particular bus. He could perhaps breathe yet for a week. How long did a damn corpse take to rot in fine weather in the hills? Why did he never know anything useful?

The bus stopped after about a couple of hours at a nondescript market town for a piss, a puke and a prayer. Not wishing to be seen hobnobbing with them, Bhola declined to descend for tea with Titli and Moti. The music stopped too and the silence tingled his skin. Over his shoulder, Titli offered him a jar of Vicks Vaporub. 'I found some more that he had prepared. How is your health now?'

That she appeared to have left behind none of the ointment for its maker seemed to Bhola to be irrefutable proof that Borkar, cold and stiff, was at that very moment being sniffed by a monstrous black rat, the vanguard of an army. The jar felt warm and moist in his hand like a murder weapon. 'It's better. It pains much less than before.' That was not strictly true. He had applied some of Borkar's balm the night before and again that morning. It had burnt a bit, but bearably, and he had felt consoled at the thought that while he went about living his life, the wonder-working ointment would quietly set about doing its job and healing him. In any case, the herpes had not become more painful than it had been, that was something to be grateful for. It had, more accurately speaking, simply been overwhelmed by other crises. That was certainly one way of fixing it, like curing a heart attack by dropping a grenade in the neighbourhood of the sufferer.

'You have a place to stay in, don't you, in Ambedkarpuri?' He feared that they would follow him to his father's house like some monsters created by his sin out of his own tissue.

'Yes, we do,' answered Titli politely and primly. 'With Moti's uncle.'

Bhola reached home at five o'clock and soured his father considerably by leaving at six-thirty to meet Anin and Dosto. 'They've borrowed money from some bank, rented out a basement and opened a gym.' He paused to fabricate. 'Today's the formal inauguration. I'm already late.'

'But you haven't even told me how your Final Year exams went off!'

For an instant, he wondered what on earth his father was referring to. 'Oh those! A cakewalk in the breeze! I might not be back for dinner. Bye!'

Amidst the stationary bicycles, pull-up bars, barbells and rowing machines, he spent the first half-hour with Anin and Dosto praising their achievement and privately thinking that they had lost their heads. 'Oh yes, it's fantastic to go into business early, at twenty–twenty-one—but can't you do both? I mean, attend class during the day and get a post-graduate degree in Management or something and sit here in the evenings to rake it in?'

'Listen, you dolt,' retorted Dosto sharply in his recently

acquired, man-of-business, man-of-the-world manner, 'I'm going to be a graduate and that's enough. I've wasted enough time on this paper chase.' A few weeks previously, he and Anin had seen a Hollywood film with that title, *The Paper Chase*. He arose from his cashier's stool, strode over to the pull-up bar, braced himself beneath it, looked up, lunged, just managed to grab hold of it, tried to hoist himself up, exhausted himself midway and involuntarily moaned and farted at the same time with the effort. All three began to laugh. Dosto let go of the rod, landed and allowed himself to stumble on to the mat. He lay down flat on his back and continued to shake with mirth. His tight black teeshirt had ridden up to reveal the hair on his pale, hard paunch. He gravely addressed the ceiling. 'Health is in and all you need. We have hired two trainers who have to wear tracksuits to hide these tyres of suet about their waists. They can't touch their toes. *Breathing* tires them out. They pant instead. They remind me of those male spiders who are eaten up by the female after sex.'

'I know a man whom I want the two of you to meet tomorrow. He is the only person I know whose stomach is flatter than mine.' Bhola smiled at Anin to slow himself down, to drop from his voice all inflexion. 'He is dumb, he is innocent, hardworking, honest, a possible murderer and in search of a job. He could sleep here at night as a guard or something.'

It wasn't that easy, of course. Bhola had asked Titli to call him at eleven the next morning. She didn't. He spent the whole day roaming about the house with one ear cocked for the phone, exasperated by the waste of several hours and the way he lived his life. A line from an old Cliff Richard song, 'I keep waiting for the phone to ring,' entered his head and refused to vacate it, enervating him almost beyond endurance, particularly whenever he thought of whose call he was standing by for. She finally rang at seven-thirty in the evening when both his father and stepmother were at the dining table in the vicinity of the instrument. He barked at Titli guardedly and arranged a rendezvous for the following evening. He then contacted Anin to confirm the arrangement but she couldn't immediately recall what they were talking about.

'Oh that! I suppose we do need a full-time lackey but if he is as dumb as you say he is, he'll just sit around and gawk at everybody and make them conscious of how out of shape they are.'

He had given Titli and Moti the address of the gym. He himself reached there half an hour early because he wanted to try out some of the machines, the rower in particular. The basement was an ante-room, two identical halls and two toilets. The ante-room was Reception, locker room and office and each gender had a hall to itself for its groaning and grunting. Bhola smiled when he saw the trainers, for they fitted well Dosto's description of them. Even more, their faces were puffed-up, shifty-eyed and their glances venal; Bhola felt that if he looked them in the eye for a second too long, they would smile and drop their masks of civility along with their tracksuits. He was also surprised to see the size of the clientele. Each machine was occupied and in addition, several other exercisers waited their turns and bided their time by wandering about, smoking outdoors, limbering up, wheezing and snuffling and flirting with Anin. She sat at the front desk, greeting members, accepting cash from casual users, filling up, signing and doling out receipts, directing the trainers to provide towels and escort the more weighty habitués in.

Titli and Moti showed up twenty minutes early. Careful to address them as one civilly would one's servants, Bhola asked them to sit in a corner till Anin was free. They looked so uncomfortable that after a couple of minutes, he had a better idea and proposed to Moti that he get up and help the trainers in seeing to the towels, checking whether there were plastic glasses beside the drinking water filter, hanging up clothes in the racks, and opening the lockers for those too important to turn the key themselves. Moti shuffled to his responsibility with an enthusiasm that mingled so with his shyness that his manner made even Anin smile. She however was not enraptured by Titli in general and the by-then yellowish-blue bruise on her cheek in particular.

'No, I did not give it to her. She was hit by a stray cricket ball or something. It's true that she does look like Harlot Brontë but she isn't one, you know. She was a nurse and would probably be a great success massaging your female clients.'

'Lesbians, all of them.' Anin, grinning, stopped for a second as though taken aback at her own boldness, then plunged on, 'She wouldn't get a single night's rest.'

Step by step, patiently and determinedly over the next five days, Bhola wore nurse and assistant down and finally convinced them that for the brightness of their futures, they should agree to separate—though temporarily, of course, just for some months or so. Eroding away their apprehensions was an exhausting process. For one, the three of them couldn't even find a place where they could sit and discuss things in peace. They most often met in the Jahanpanah Public Gardens in the heat of the afternoon, between two-thirty and five, and sat and sweated in the shade of the tamarind trees and were harassed by eunuchs, itinerant ear-cleaners, and vendors of massage oils, incense sticks and digestive tablets. 'Look, jobs don't grow on trees, especially for not-so-young men who can neither read nor write. You should thank Heaven that you've found something with a salary. Borkar gave you nothing but dirty looks, remember? Work with them well and—who knows?—in a year, you might even be promoted to trainer and get to wear a jazzy maroon tracksuit.'

In tandem, he recalled to Titli the responsibilities that she had left behind. 'Up there, you have a job waiting for you.

You were a nurse, a doctor's assistant, dammit, how can you chuck that up and come down here to become a toilet cleaner?'

He advised Moti to wear tight teeshirts to work so that the well-heeled and well-upholstered regulars to the gym could have all the time before their eyes a walking, breathing vision of their goal. He also proposed that Moti hide for the time being the maroon string about his waist. 'The people here think only about money. They won't follow that by reining in your lust, you have become like the ascetic Siva with his unstrung bow. One can't explain that you are Ardhanarishwar, man above and below, the one in control of the source of creation. How would they understand?' Neither did Moti but he simpered and reddened with pleasure at the comparison. 'And for Heaven's sake, don't gain any weight.' He affectionately squeezed his shoulder. 'Here, just run after that chaiwala and ask him to come back and serve us all some tea.'

He watched Moti obediently amble off across the bald patches of undulating park. 'Does he have any problem urinating?' he asked Titli.

'No-o,' she answered hesitantly, 'I don't know. He doesn't tell me anything.'

'Does he get erections? Why don't you go off somewhere for a couple of minutes and I'll ask him.' She dutifully arose from the bench and began to see to the folds of her sari. 'We could take Moti to a doctor here but we might end up facing the police instead. What do you think?' Without replying, her face still with foreboding, she began to move off towards a clump of hibiscus bushes. She—all three of them—had till then preferred that forbidden subjects lie buried. With time, they would—God willing—have turned to dust. Bhola would not have raised one of them had not the unexpected untangling of another—the future of Moti—given him hope.

He observed with affectionate amusement Moti hop, trot,

skip and jump back across the intervening three hundred metres till he was close enough for Bhola to read the disquiet in his features. 'Where did Titli disappear to?' He heaved and gulped for breath between words.

'She? Oh, you see, Borkar suddenly turned up and asked her if he could have the honour of cleaning her ears. So they have gone off to those bushes.'

Without a word, Moti limped off in the direction that his wife had taken. Extremely irritated, Bhola raised his voice after him, 'You ninny! She's doing peepee! Leave her alone to breathe in peace for five seconds!' Moti slowed up and finally halted ten paces away, head down, but did not turn around. Still seething, Bhola got up, walked up to him, put his arm about his shoulders and steered him around and back to the bench. Moti continued to gaze down at the arid earth beneath their feet. 'Before your wife comes back, I want to know how you feel. *Your* peepee, does it pain when you piss?'

Sweat trickled down Moti's hot and red cheek. After a pause, he jerked his head in a sharp no. Bhola pushed him down on the bench and sat alongside him. 'Otherwise, someone'll usurp our places.' The chaiwala, with his enormous aluminium kettle and his small teacups on a string, had been waylaid en route by a courting couple. 'Do you get erections? Do you ejaculate? Any change by any chance?'

Moti glanced over his shoulder, as though to check whether Titli was eavesdropping, before replying in a tone meant to end the interrogation, 'It's fine.'

'No, listen to me, *look* at me.' Bhola held Moti's chin and turned his head to the right so that he could gaze into his eyes, 'Ejaculate? You didn't with me, ever. Your tool just stirred a bit, like a sleeping dog having a bad dream. Is it the same? Or worse or better?'

Even with his face level with and a foot away from Bhola's and his chin caught between the other's forefinger and thumb, Moti avoided his ex-lover's stare and looked tensely instead over his left shoulder into the middle distance. A passing eunuch loudly clapped her hands to encourage them. Bhola let go of Moti's chin and sat back to gaze absentmindedly at the dried-up, leaf-choked Municipal fountain. The antics of two monkeys on its bottom-most tier were just beginning to beguile him when Moti, looking down at his lap, muttered, 'No, it's the same but sometimes I bleed.'

Blood. Phrases from Manu, Shakespeare and the Rolling Stones whirled through Bhola's head as he gaped at Moti's profile and waited, as though paralysed, for him to elaborate. 'It's all right. Blood can be both holy and impure.' Without raising his head, swivelling it sideways much like a front-crawl swimmer does when he inhales, Moti glanced shyly at Bhola for a second. 'Just as the blood of menstruating women is unclean but that of menstruating goddesses is powerful and auspicious.'

Out of the corner of his eye, Bhola saw Titli emerge from the hibiscus bushes. Dangling his left arm over the back of the bench, he waved her back into them. She retreated like a denizen sensing danger. 'But you aren't either of them. Where do you exactly bleed from? We'd better see a doctor.'

Moti suddenly got up, arched his back, stretched, yawned and turned around to look out for his wife. He looked happier at having unburdened himself. 'Don't worry,' he smiled at Bhola almost avuncularly, 'it's just a drop or two, very precious.' Showing his teeth once more, he ambled off towards the bushes, clearly pleased at having stumped Bhola with some Borkarese.

'Your darling man can't stay away from you for more than five minutes, how on earth will he work at the gym when you go back to your nursing duties?' snapped Bhola at Titli when husband and wife sortied, smirking guiltily, from her lair. 'Let him start tomorrow—while you're still here. Let's see how things brew. I'll be going to a doctor myself this evening.

Moti should accompany me if he hasn't healed. He should shut up if he has. It isn't a laughing matter. I'll escort you back to the hills this Saturday. Is that clear?'

Neither wife nor husband looked awed at the efficiency and decisiveness of the man of action. 'Ah,' beamed Titli at a welcome sight beyond Bhola's shoulder, 'The chaiwala is here.'

That week passed by like water gushing out of a tap left open. A little to Bhola's surprise, Moti began work at the gym the next morning, spent the night there and seemed to get on well with his bosses. Dosto was attracted to him, that was certain; he touched his arm or patted his stomach or smiled into his eyes while speaking to him and allowed him, from the very first day, to bed down at the club with his wife, to swill down and shut the place up at ten in the evening, and then, in peace and privacy, even to pump iron to his heart's content.

Then on Thursday evening, Bhola risked his life once more in the murderous traffic of the city by repeating on his bicycle the ride that he had taken four years previously to Ambedkarpuri. On the earlier occasion, it had been an adventure; the second time, he felt merely underprivileged, poor, invisible to the buses and the air-conditioned cars. He was in fact almost broke. Shame and guilt prevented him from asking his father for any money over and above his monthly allowance, particularly to pay some cheap doctor's fees.

Ambedkarpuri chose itself as the appropriate setting for his search for the kind of quack before whom he could flash his loins without embarrassment. After all, he reasoned, it housed the low life from which Titli and his herpes had emerged. He found the right kind of clinic almost immediately, in the second alley off the main road, a one-room structure only marginally larger than the signboard atop its only door that shouted, in Hindi and English, in red and black letters on white, *Saraf Skin & VD Clinic. No Appointment Required*. The one room was further bifurcated by a wall of opaque glass. On a wooden bench, in the heat and stink compounded of summer sweat, anxiety and depression, Bhola sat amongst the prostitutes, unmarried minor girls, chauffeurs, hotel boys and shop assistants and shielded himself from them with his Penguin Classics edition of *Anna Karenina*. He read fourteen lines in one hour before he was called in.

The doctor was pale, fat, bespectacled and stressed. To save energy, he generally communicated binomially, through nods and non-nods—that is to say, when he wanted to express no, he merely decided that he had not heard what had been said to him. On specific occasions, he tilted his head and raised his eyebrows, as at Bhola's crotch. Bhola understood and stripped. Dr Saraf nodded and scribbled for thirty seconds on a prescription. Bhola zipped up his trousers and simultaneously tried to read what was being written but couldn't. The doctor jerked his head at the feebly active airconditioner. Bhola stripped again and clambered on to the stretcher beneath it. The doctor wet some cotton with some fluid from a small, dark and menacing-looking bottle and proceeded to cauterize the sore spots on Bhola's penis. With each dab, the small of his back contracted, his loins twitched, his bowels melted, his hips jerked up and he moaned in the manner of a soundtrack of a bad porn film.

'But what is it called? What do I have? Is it herpes?'

Dr Saraf permitted himself a quiver of the lips at his patient's ignorance. In response, however, he tapped on the prescription twice with his forefinger before handing it over with his right hand while accepting Bhola's money with his left. On the way out, Bhola again tried to decipher the doctor's handwriting. The diagnosis was in two words. The first looked like Zoon and the first syllable of the second was

perhaps Bal. Zoon? I'll see you on the dark side of the zoon.
Feeling like an illiterate fool, he asked the hoodlum who
shepherded the waiting patients, 'What has he written? I
can't make out.' It was a little like asking a football fan to
recite a poem of Rilke.

He was mystified, happy and completely broke. He
hummed to himself as he recklessly raced his bicycle in and
out of traffic. Even the thought that he didn't have money for
the two bus tickets on Saturday didn't dampen his spirits.
Titli could pay, surely, considering how much she had stolen
from Borkar and the amounts that he had given to her, on the
average twice a month, for three years. At the next red light,
panting gently, he totalled up. At least twelve thousand
rupees, minimum, because the hundred and fifty rupees per
meeting had been raised at some point—he couldn't remember
when—to two hundred. That was ten bicycles' worth of
money for a gift of Herpes Zoon.

She agreed to pay but not without a fuss. Bhola in the end
insisted that the bus tickets were his commission for having
found Moti a job. She sulked. Bhola spun a yarn for his father
and stepmother about a two-day camping expedition to
Hrishikesh with the college Mountaineering Club. It sounded
so feeble that he stopped in mid-sentence. He couldn't finish
it. Fortunately, he wasn't required to because they paid no
more attention than they would have had the reason for the
trip been genuine. He was sure that Titli would somehow—
either intentionally or without meaning to—miss the bus but
he was damned if he was going to travel south for ten
kilometres to pick her up and then north for thirty-five more
to catch the twelve o'clock deluxe. So in the end, that's what
he did on Saturday morning. He left by auto-rickshaw at nine
and took an hour-and-a-half to locate her in the alleys of
Ambedkarpuri. The low life stared hard at him. Titli was
flattered and smiling from ear to ear while he was in a
terrifically bad mood that, because of the heat and the

thought of the decaying, rat-eaten cadaver of Borkar, worsened when the bus trundled out of the terminus at twelve-twenty.

After an uneventful journey across the oven of the north Indian plains, they arrived at Chilkasa after five, parched, red, with heads throbbing with heat exhaustion. The late-afternoon light shown benignly on the parked buses, the dust, exhaust fumes, stray dogs, open drains and tea stalls. The moment they alit, a man, almost a beggar, mad-looking, with unkempt hair and clothes, and a rich stubble, snarling with a kind of fulfilment, pounced on Titli, making her gasp, exclaim and stumble, all at the same time. Bhola, barking at the man, had reached out for his shoulder before he realized that it was Borkar. He laughed out loud, dropped his bag, and from the side tried to hug Borkar, who hadn't let go of Titli's forearm, till the stench of his body made him desist. Borkar didn't take his red, panic-shattered eyes off Titli even for a second. Without saying a word or noticing Bhola's presence, he began to pull her towards the queue of rickshaws. Bhola, beaming, picked up his bag and followed them. Irrepressibly happy, he asked loudly of their backs in Hindi, 'Dr Strangelove-ji, what kind of infection is Zoon Bal, do you know?' Predictably, neither made any sign of having heard. Borkar did not release Titli's arm even to allow her to climb on to the rickshaw. Her face had been softened by the sight of what her absence had done to him. Bhola trailed them in a second rickshaw.

He didn't stay long at Borkar's. The two rooms were in a mess. The misspelt, practically-incomprehensible sign in Hindi that Moti had painted—*The Clinic Is Shut Today*—hung awry at the window. The first room was littered with bottles and stank overpoweringly of rum and vomit. None of the three demanded or required any explanations from the others. Now that he had seen that the quack was alive and well enough to have spent all his waking hours at the terminus waiting, with a lunatic's endurance, for all the buses on which Titli could possibly return, Bhola wanted to get away from the confined and hot concupiscence of their lives, to escape on winged feet into a Pink Floyd album cover, and lie down on an endless green lawn, in clean winter sunshine, and gaze up and see only bright blue sky. He was walking back to Mrs Manchanda's, his bag over his shoulder, exhausted by the day and even by his happiness at the way things had turned out, when he realized that he hadn't informed her that he would be coming up for the weekend. He hoped that she didn't have some of her thousand relatives up from the heat of the plains. He was relieved to find that on the contrary, she was alone and appeared to have been resting at the odd hour of six in the evening because when she opened the front door, her hair was undone and her lips looked thick with repose. She was delighted to see him. It was she who was going down to Lucknow on the following day. Vivek had already left. 'What a bit of luck, Auntie,' said Bhola, suddenly madly hungry, dirty and craving, 'I mean, that I turned up to catch you in time,' as he shut and bolted the front door firmly behind him.

WEIGHT GAIN

December, 1988. Bhola was twenty-nine, unmarried, a lecturer in Humanities at the M.K.M.Z.A.P. College, teaching *Othello* and Plato to nineteen-year-olds in Hindi, feeling middle-aged and cocooned—and even somehow content—in his depression and mediocrity. The winter fog hid the contours of the Himalayas and the rest of the world and made him feel that he lived underwater in a grey sea. Its ashenness was an extra hemming at the edges of the dark curtains. He woke up on a Friday morning not with a start but gradually, as though rhythmically and with graceful limb movements coming up for air out of a dream that might have been about sex but he had been happy in it. He woke up full and calm and absolutely ready for marriage.

The last was odd and like other morning things, not an outcome of reasoning. There seemed no cause for it and yet the passing moments did not lessen his conviction that he was at last ripe and ready. Slate-coloured cold steam tinted the walls of the room and roved about the furniture examining them, as it were, from all angles at a sale. It seemed an impossible time of day, as though the clocks wouldn't work. The noises of the world—the clink of cycles and the throat-clearing of humans wrapped up in blankets out for some crisis shopping—milk, bread, eggs—the noises of the world were absent. The greyness, beautiful and prenatal in some ways, was a day waiting to be born even at ten in the morning.

While making himself some tea, he remembered with dull, distant relief that he had no classes that morning. He

gazed out of the two square feet of kitchen window at the fog
that hid the identical kitchen window of the flat behind his
and above Mrs Manchanda's. With visibility that poor, one
couldn't make out whether the lights in other flats were on.
To signal to each other that the coast was clear, Mrs
Manchanda and he had arranged to leave their servant's room
lights on. Of course, he lived alone but when he didn't want
her to turn up, it meant that he hadn't finished his Secret
Seven activities for that day and that he didn't want her to
know what ridiculous things he was up to.

He liked his flat—or more accurately, what he had done
to his Staff Quarters. It was of the same tiny size as Mrs
Manchanda's, with a sitting room, a bedroom, two enclosed
verandahs, a toilet, a bathroom, a kitchen, a servant's hole—
but all minuscule, virtually for Snow White's companions.
But because he had none, and almost no furniture, it appeared
clean, airy and roomy. After struggling for eight months, he
had succeeded in coercing Maintenance to paint all the walls
alternately in bright yellow and white and to save its hideous
blue and rose for other apartments. Had he been married and
sharing the flat with another, it would have appeared different,
of course, more cramped with things that he himself would
have found no use for—a TV, a dressing table, a couple of
extra beds for guests. There was something scheduled for
late, late in the morning but the fog seemed to have clouded
his brain and he couldn't for the life of him remember what.

After he had turned twenty-six, his father—and later,
even his stepmother—had begun openly to write and talk
about his marriage. He had then blessed himself anew for
having stayed four hundred kilometres away from home since
the age of seventeen. They wanted him to marry someone
tall, fair, beautiful, comely, homely, of the right Brahmin sub-
caste, English- and Bengali-speaking, literate, preferably
actually educated. Boy or girl, they had forgotten to specify
but they said that they would nevertheless find the lucky one

for him. Getting him married off in the proper manner was like seeing their investments in a bank repay handsome dividends.

To gain time with his father and stepmother without offending them, he had proposed that to gauge the market, they should in all fairness advertise him in the first place. Without being asked, he had then sent them a draft that he had worked out while listening in a tutorial class to a Marxist interpretation in Hindi of *Robinson Crusoe*.

> *Stunning homely cook age no bar for 29/175 handsomeish tallish wheatish lecturer gloriousish prospects Kashyap Brahmin noble sincereish soberish cultured calm non-vegetarian occasional smoker real service accommodation own gas cylinder dowry strict nono but negotiable Apply with photo of Box*

He had had no wish at that time to get married. He liked living alone, a bisexual bachelor with some of the traits of a spinster. He enjoyed keeping house for himself, shopping, cooking, watering his plants. He knew every inch of his flat, where the pliers were and the rat poison, how backbreaking it had been to shift that potted palm to the spot beneath the window and when a female neighbour had remarked wittily that his drawing room could do with some colour, either bright red cushion covers or a wife, he had laughed affably but had been filled with a kind of awe at the extent of her presumption. He had a good idea of the kind of person he was and had more than once told his family that he wasn't thinking of marriage just then because he didn't wish upon anyone the misfortune of being married to him. His elder brother had agreed with his sentiments.

Jogging in the fog that morning didn't appear too attractive an idea. On the other hand, fewer students would be likely to spot him and chuckle and noisily clear their throats when he passed them by. It was their equivalent, he supposed, with a teacher of making a pass at a female fellow student. Besides, jogging no doubt would get his circulation going and drive the clouds out of his head and then he would be able to take better stock of that feeling that he had had on waking up of being ripe and ready for marriage.

For two months after his father had finally advertised Bhola in the papers—a modest paragraph of fulsome adjectives without syntax or punctuation—they—at home—had received from the newspapers weekly parcels of letters. His father had been hugely amused, and not cynically. His delight had been a kind of wonder at realizing that the world was not that faceless and impersonal after all, that beyond the house in which he lived in querulous retirement, some things actually clicked and connected. Bhola's father had contacted the newspapers only over the telephone and by the post but some chain reactions had really taken place, an inch-long advertisement had been inserted and lakhs of newspapers printed and run off one Sunday. They had been correctly distributed, hundreds of thousands of eyes had pored over the columns, some cursorily, some attentively; Bhola's fabled qualities had sparked off cogitation and discussion, corresponding lies had been worked out and carefully worded and at last letters written in response. The entire exercise had spoken to his father of linkages, of webs, of fingers supportively interlaced as an image of hope for the world.

He faithfully sent all the letters to his son four hundred kilometres away. Being meticulous about the unimportant, he annotated each letter in red; the significant phrases he underlined in green. He had a beautiful hand, neat and clear, like small plants in a well-ordered bed.

He did of course leave each decision to his son but his notes made clear where his own wishes lay. Out of more than a hundred and fifty, he recommended only six offers as worthy of pursuit. Out of whimsy, the son disregarded some of the warmest injunctions of the father, further shortlisted the six to three and himself followed up none of them. He finally married someone who hadn't seen the advertisement.

Cut up by his son's lack of enthusiasm, Bhola's father replied verbosely to the six letters that he had chosen. In a sense, he too was in it for the sport. Further correspondence ate up several months. For the three that Bhola had picked out, his stepmother proposed meetings at home—that is, where they stayed—and that Bhola take leave from work for them. He snorted at the idea both by post and over the telephone. 'Rubbish (pronounced roobish, after a British cricketing legend, a mumbler, whom he had once heard on television. He hadn't followed a single other word but had adored roobish). Can't rush these things. Ask for photos, frontals, profiles, full-lengths, photocopies of her bank passbooks, of the father's income tax returns, whatever, anything. Or we can postpone this to next winter. The Bible recommends marriage in the cold. Again, if two lie together, then they have heat: but how can one be warm alone?'

The fog had thinned a little by the time he set out for his run and—mercifully—was appreciably lighter when he returned at noon. He was roaming around the flat wasting time, wondering whether he should shave before or after his bath, and whether he should bathe at all, when the door bell rang once. Twice. Mrs Manchanda was a great one for codes. She looked her pale, composed self, except that her eyes shone behind her spectacles. Tears came to her quite easily. They were not fake, though. She simply cried like other people yawned. She carried beneath her shawl a large maroon diary. She placed it on her side of his bed. He pretended not to see it.

'Tea?' She asked brightly, took off her spectacles and put them on the diary. 'From my office window, I saw you run past on your way back. I recognized the blue cap.' She wore absolutely no makeup. He liked that about her. No lipstick, no mascara, even her eyebrows weren't tweezed, nor was her hair dyed. He smelt on her sometimes a faint lemony after-shower talc kind of perfume. He enjoyed seeing her fuss around—quietly but proprietorially—in his kitchen. He was happy that he had not postponed his jogging that morning and that he had run well. A kind of longing, like being homesick for a woman's body, welled up within him and brimmed over, exuded out of all his orifices, his ears and his nipples. He seized his ex-landlady by the hips, turned her around, pushed her against the fridge and, cupping her cold face in his hands, kissed her full and hard on the lips. Her mouth smelt of cloves. His fingers scrabbled about under her shawl and through sweater and blouse for her skin.

'Come to the bed. It's warmer.'

She kept her eyes averted and bit her lower lip when he entered her. 'Say that you want me,' he pleaded in Hindi as he thrust into her, wondering at the same time if she could see that the suggestion was nothing more than a soundtrack to enrich the joys of coitus. 'That you want me want me please that you want me.' If I can ram into her a hundred times before spilling, then she's understood—and liked—my auditory effects. Okay, fifty times. Twenty... three... times.

'You remember, I told you that I've maintained a kind of diary of letters to you?' She used the English word, 'diary'. 'From the day we first began—you know.' His face was warm in the crook of her shoulder. It was he who had coerced her to take all her clothes off when they were together. He didn't really believe that he was her first lover in the two decades since her divorce. 'And how strange it seems.' She turned her head away from him and wiped her eyes on the towel that covered his pillow to prevent it from being blackened by the wretched oil in his hair. 'As though it's not happening even now.'

He said nothing even though he agreed with her completely. They always seemed to meet in a time warp outside the routine run of things, in thick fog or on a holiday forenoon when the frosted glass of the windows protected them from the sharp sunlight and the sounds of the world going by. Besides, she spoke a mellifluous, cultivated Hindi that to hear gave him a pleasure that at times felt like lust and that compelled him either to keep quiet and enjoy its tones or to respond in like manner, in phrases that rendered unfamiliar the language of the streets. He dreaded what she was going to propose next. From personal experience, he knew how deathly diaries could be and simply wasn't up to reading hers about him but fortunately, before she could offer it as an item to keep beside his bed when she wasn't in it, the door bell rang once. Twice. For a moment, he thought that it was her again.

He went to the front door tying up his lungi and pulling on his teeshirt, with his lips swollen with lovemaking and his fingers reeking of Mrs Manchanda's vagina.

An elderly man of middle height, bespectacled, balding, stood in the doorway—practically inside the flat—smiling fixedly, his hand outstretched in bonhomie, his dentures seeming to reflect the light of the bulb overhead and giving Bhola the impression somehow of yellow-enamel clothes pegs in an ordered row. Two young women in resplendent saris and shawls stood respectfully behind him. One of them held the neck of a sitar that stood before them. The features of the second were dreadfully familiar but, befogged as he was, Bhola couldn't for an instant place them. He shook the proferred hand and then tried to will it silently to move up to the man's nose to scratch it or something so that he could be blessed with the smell of great pussy. Anin, of course, the belle not propping up the sitar was Anin. Oh God, he remembered then.

He invited them in, shuffled back to shut the bedroom door and then gestured vaguely towards his two cane armchairs and one dining chair. The visitors were nonplussed by his dress and unshaven face.

'Didn't your father inform you?'

'I thought that we were to meet tomorrow. Some misunderstanding but never mind.'

'Ah, not tomorrow. We go on to Lucknow this evening.' The father's manner and voice were affable but the eyes behind the spectacles were cloudy. 'My daughters, Kamala and Kaushalya. Kamala is my elder daughter.' Kamala half-smiled, glanced casually at the shut door of the bedroom and carefully laid the sitar down at her feet. 'Kaushalya I understand you already know.'

'Yes—we were neighbours for a while a good ten years ago. Then you moved away to Jaipur. Do please sit down while I—' he motioned embarrassedly at his clothes. Kamala smiled, Anin giggled and the father showed his teeth as his eyes took in the absence of wealth in the entire room. Bhola opened the bedroom door a fraction, tried to sidle in gracefully, got his lungi caught in some part of the woodwork, tripped, pushed the door wide open with his shoulder, and recalling the film roles of Peter Sellers, entered and shut the door carefully and politely behind him. Mrs Manchanda was in her blouse and petticoat beside the bed and putting on her sari.

'Can't you wait ten minutes? They won't stay long, I'm sure.'

'I need to get back before Vivek arrives home for lunch.' With grace and speed, she pleated the front of her sari. He in turn put on his track suit pants and, because he couldn't find its top in the mess of the bed, her cardigan—orange, with a black velvet coat collar and a row of black leaves at the bottom. He turned to leave the room, paused as in an amateur theatre production, looked back at her and announced, 'Our callers are candidates for the post of my wife. I could fob them off by speaking of large sums of money, some extreme and non-negotiable figure that would make all my suitors back off. Then we'd live happily ever after—my jogging shoes, my jock strap and me.' She paid no attention but sat heavily down on the bed to put on her woollen socks. He wondered what his visitors were making of these noises. He rejoined them, again shutting the door elaborately behind him as though he had just entered a room to be interviewed for the sort of personality test that begins with how one handles the bloody door. He brought forward a second dining chair and sat down on it opposite Kamala. Anin giggled at his sweater. The father noisily cleared his throat and opened with some pleasantries. Unmistakably, they all heard the bedroom door creak open a crack. They stared at it. Nobody appeared in search of a cardigan. 'It's Eavesdropperman,' revealed Bhola, grinning winningly at the sitar. Nobody followed.

'Why don't the two of you sing a couple of songs?' he then proposed hurriedly. 'Or before that, would you like some tea?' Stirred with my pussy fingers?

'Tea would be nice. Here, I'll make it if you show me where,' offered Anin with a secret smirk, getting up. Her new voice was pleasant and low.

Her sister's was gorgeous. It filled and beautified, beatified, the room like some emanation from a super high-tech, hi-fi Bose/Bang and Olufsen music system. It drew Mrs Manchanda out to the doorway of the bedroom. The singing transformed Kamala's face—similar to but plainer than Anin's—alchemically, the effort seeming to burn it of dross. The veins on her pale, long neck stood out like culverts. Bhola knew nothing about Hindustani classical music but the timbre of her voice, the skill and facility with which she conquered impossible notes, thrilled him and made him feel in an obscure way that life was worth living if the world, every now and then, produced a voice like hers. He loved the concentration, the frowning attention on her face when she approached a difficult part and then the way her features eased up after she had crossed the hurdle, like a blackboard being erased. He felt dimly ashamed of himself, of being incapable of bringing to living a little of that reverential tenacity that he glimpsed in her when she sang.

He glanced from the face of one sister to the other. Concentrating on their duet, they stared carefully at nothing. He couldn't even make out whether the grace with which Anin strummed the sitar in accompaniment was crab-like or divine. The father, both anxious and happy that things seemed to be going well, beamed frozenly at Mrs Manchanda's hips. If things worked out, Bhola pointed out to himself, he would have to start calling this bald satyr Father. He wasn't calling him anything just then because for the moment Anin's surname seemed to have slipped his mind. He couldn't even remember which of the two sisters was on offer. Vaguely both, he surmised. The choice of the bride is not left to the bridegroom, he could visualize his own father citing—usually misquoting—some ancient text while nodding his head in slow sage agreement. Sexual desire is an impersonal force. A man can satisfy his need with any woman. Any biologically normal woman can bear the children of any biologically normal man. Considerations of caste and propriety are more important than fickle romantic love. To choose a girl because one desires her sexually is to invite trouble. He would probably, thought Bhola as he watched the fingers of Anin's right hand flit back and forth across the strings of the instrument like the feet of a dancer, he would probably be happier off marrying his jockstrap, garlanding it and anointing it with ghee and circumventing a fire seven times with it tied to his kurta and dangling beneath his arse. He deserved nothing better.

The young women took a break after three lovely songs. Mrs Manchanda took the opportunity to smile shyly at them all, eye lingeringly the cardigan on her lover and glide towards the front door. The others wordlessly watched Bhola escort her to the head of the stairs. He re-entered, bolted the front door, smiled at the leer on Anin's face and complimented father and daughters on the performance.

'Thank you. Kamala of course has been devoted to her art since the age of ten. Kaushalya is more of a dancer.' He smiled—a sort of grimace—at his daughters, a signal to them to sit up straight. For the singing, they had sat crosslegged on the carpet, with backs upright and without support. That had in passing made Bhola uncomfortable. He much preferred—and somehow trusted more—people who slumped spineless against things. After having aired their most notable accomplishment, it was clearly time for the prospectives to answer questions. They waited for a while for Bhola to pose them but he appeared content to wait with them, snug in a companionable silence, simpering from time to time, encouragingly and in turn at Kamala and Anin.

'Would you like to ask my daughters something about themselves?'

'No, thanks.'

'Their likes and dislikes, what they feel?'

'Why don't you ask them, sir, on my behalf? You would know what to ask.'

The father laughed most heartily of all. 'My daughters are brilliant. Kamala has never stood second in any exam in her entire life. She even plans to write a book on the nutritional value of traditional Indian food, don't you?' Without waiting for Kamala's spiritless nod, he continued, 'And Kaushalya is already a successful businesswoman. At her tender age, she runs a first-rate, profitable health clinic.'

'That I'm aware of.'

'Are you sure that you have no questions to put to us?'

'Well, firstly, would any of you like some more tea?'

In the ensuing faked merriment, Bhola, trying to pin down a notion floating around in his head like a feather, realized that the other difference between the sisters was Kamala's increased womanliness. Anin, though prettier, was harder and more venal—the businesswoman, no doubt. Kamala looked older but also more complete and rested; in comparison, he himself felt shrivelled up and wry, as though if someone had there and then cut his skin, there wouldn't have been much blood, just some more skin of different shades of brown, like old bacon.

In the kitchen, Anin's eyes glittered as they made a second round of tea together. He couldn't make out whether she was sad or happy about the way the meeting had gone. Her unpredictability was exhausting. The father put down his cup with a theatrically satisfied sigh and then, placing his hands on his knees, made as if to get up to signal the start of the end-of-interview pleasantries.

'We'll keep in touch. I'll talk to your father this evening itself.'

'Yes, of course. A last question, if I may.'

'Certainly, certainly! You haven't asked any!'

'No, not that sort. I mean, however do you travel from place to place with that sitar? It doesn't even have a case. Why hasn't it snapped in two?'

Kamala was the quickest to respond. 'It's a tanpura, not a sitar,' she said mildly and then paused, unsure whether the questions needed answers, whether Bhola had been deliberately rude or unintentionally clumsy. 'It usually sits in front with the driver.'

'And in the train?'

'Another question! It generally goes to sleep in the upper berth.'

Bhola saw them out, grinning and carrying the tanpura to make amends for his gaffe. The father took his courtesy to be a good sign. All the way down the grey stairs and out in the cold December afternoon to the white Ambassador car with its orange, beacon-like light on its forehead, Bhola was thankful that his anxiety that he didn't bang the musical instrument against a corner gave him a reason to ignore the strafe of last-minute small talk from the father. When he turned to shake hands with Bhola—and while Bhola wondered whether he was expected to stoop to touch his father-in-law-to-be's feet, but what if, while he was in the process of doing so, the other, like lightning, leap-frogged over him, about-turned and buggered him from the back?—the uniformed policeman-chauffeur, who till then had taken the unshaven coolie in a funny sweater to be some sort of classy servant, woke up to his identity as possible son-in-law and saluted the handshake with parade-ground impeccability.

Bhola didn't have a phone in his flat because he was too junior in the college hierarchy. He received his outstation calls at Mrs Manchanda's. Whoever wanted to get in touch hurriedly had to call twice, thereby giving Mrs or Vivek enough time to inform him. They didn't seem to mind running across. In their place, he would have flatly refused had the summons been frequent. Fortunately, they weren't, not more often than twice a month, typically his father or Dosto or once in a blue moon, Bhanu his brother.

'Your prospective father-in-law is an albatross breathing down my neck at gunpoint.' Bhola's father's high good humour was discernible even on an indistinct, long-distance line. 'Well, what is your opinion of this morning's interview?'

Bhola explained his decision. His father sounded more taken aback than aghast, bemused, almost amused. 'I see. Let me see. I'll call you back.'

It was seven in the evening and extremely cold. The entire college was looking forward to the long winter vacations a mere four days away. Mrs Manchanda was alone in the flat, Vivek having left for his demeaning night-duty at the telephone exchange. It wasn't even a permanent job but it was all that he had found in nine years. The search itself had bottled him up and erected a barrier between him and Bhola.

'I've been wondering when you would get married. About time, I've been telling myself for the last couple of years.' Mrs Manchanda flashed at him a bitter snarl-like smile before turning back to the television. 'Since you are not a bottle of wine, your value in the market won't increase with age.' She, without seeing a thing, stared resolutely at the soap that inspired her dialogue and her morality. 'And marriage is great fun. It gives infidelity a touch of chilli and pepper.' Without taking her eyes off the box, she dabbed at them with the end of her sari.

'Why do you save your worst moments for me? All your sorrow and bad moods? It urges me to go away.' He had hoped to stay for dinner and make love, in that order. To give her a hint, he went out to the kitchen, found an apple, washed it at the sink and, wondering whether the droplets of water on its skin would give him jaundice or cholera or typhoid, returned chomping on it. 'People marry, you know, to complete the experience of the life cycle. Grihastha before vanaprastha and sanyasa. And if they don't, people like you will suspect them of being gay or something.' He spoke normally so as to be drowned out by the ferocious Hindi exchange from the TV. Clearly piqued by things, Mrs exhaled dramatically, got up and strode off towards the kitchen. He touched her elbow as she passed him.

'What's the matter?'

'Nothing. I should see to dinner.'

'Good idea. Do you want me to follow you like Shammi Kapoor follows Asha Parekh in I don't remember which film singing Deewana something or the other, ferociously wriggling his thighs to outdo her quivering bum?'

'Stop it,' she hissed, frowning, beginning to move away.

'But why are you blue?' He, trying to keep cool but rapidly losing it, held her forearm. She jerked herself away with a snappish, 'The curtains are not drawn, you selfish oaf.' He held her again, this time by the shoulders—and not very tenderly—and tried to respond calmly, 'The windows are of frosted glass and the fog outside is as thick as…' he paused because the only word that he could think of to complete the simile was semen, but fortunately, she began to struggle vigorously to escape his grasp, so he got hot and kissed her neck in passion. While she continued to squirm and shimmy in his arms, one part of his mind pointed out to another that his deportment could teach a thing or two to the villain in the TV film that had benumbed her for half the previous evening. Pretty soon, they were in bed and fucking away. They then shared a post-coital cigarette and attributed all of it to the peculiarity of the weather. He held the cigarette throughout in his left hand, even while bearing it to Mrs's lips, so that he could consider achieved at the same time his target of sinistrality for that day. She arose soon after and, munching cloves and cardamom, went about lighting incense in every room to mask the smell of tobacco smoke. He watched her. A compact had been reaffirmed and adultery confirmed even before the bride to be wed had been finally decided on. Laws could therefore be bypassed and untenable notions of duty abandoned well in advance. It was certainly one way of preparing for the future. He had woken up that morning ready for marriage but the first thing that he had slipped into was a triangle. Another life had been inaugurated. He would marry Kamala and on evenings like these, he would cocoon himself with Mrs Manchanda or some rickshaw-puller and then at the end of it, in the long, long run, he would pay for his transgressions; that seemed quite reasonable.

Opening the wooden box-like cupboard that was affixed to the wall alongside her dressing table and on which both Vivek and Bhola had cracked their skulls more than once, she readied herself for her evening prayers. He had at first thought that the cabinet held a second, tinier TV set but it was the roof over the heads of her gods and goddesses. Its insides were cushioned in maroon satin. Framed calendar pictures of Shiva and his wives, Krishna and his consorts, and even a Hellenic Buddha provided the backdrop against which pranced Nataraj and sundry incarnations of Vishnu in sandalwood and sandstone, and sat, comfortably sated, bellmetal and ivory idols of Ganesh. Arranged in the foreground, on a bed of flower petals, were the bric à brac of an altar—tiny bells, incense holders, a necklace of rudraksha beads. She began with the bells, tinkling them clockwise a mystical number of times in a circle generous enough to encompass the abode of the deities.

Her spectacles were off and her grey hair fell lush and unruly down her back. It seemed simply impossible that he had failed to notice when they had first met how attractive she was, a slim and pale mother figure, that he had actually lived for five years in her flat without even once thinking of her sexually—not seriously, at any rate. His feeling for her had grown and changed its contours over the years exactly as though his green ideas about desire had needed time to mature. One could be biologically ripe at thirteen but sexually aware, of oneself and the other, only at twenty-nine. Making love to her had made him feel obscurely—but tremendously— relieved, as though he finally belonged, and could now put down a heavy suitcase after having reached the end of an almost interminable railway platform.

'What day of the week is it?' she asked without turning her head. 'Friday?' Her prayers didn't last longer than some minutes—she would bow her head, mutter something, light some incense sticks and wave them about a bit, scatter some oblationary droplets of water on the pantheon, run her moist hand over her hair, light an earthen lamp, that sort of thing. The incense she chose depended on the day of the week. Thursdays for example was tuberose and Sundays honeysuckle—so the packets read. Bhola had been intrigued by those alien names, by how even the incense sticks that were fabricated somewhere in the country by underpaid, malnourished and illiterate labourers had suddenly been made fancy and posh by some pushy business person whose amoral, entrepreneurial skills must be akin to Anin and Dosto's.

'Friday. Fridays are usually good for me. I've noticed that Tuesdays and Fridays pass off well, Thursdays are usually unspeakably awful and the rest of the week so-so.'

His babble didn't register but she nodded and smiled without pausing in her routine. A subtle unhappiness welled up slowly within him, a sentiment that seemed to dribble out and reveal to the dim lamplit room that while he had been wasting his days analysing and pigeonholing them into good, awful and so-so, the rest of the world had simply moved on and each one in it had found his place, everyone except him. While he had discovered for himself the futile truth that the only way to face the day was to break it up and, annihilating past and future, move exclusively from moment to moment, he had missed out on the rhythms that actually constitute living. He was too underdeveloped. Instead of enjoying beautiful faces, he habitually looked for flaws in them. Finding them seemed to give him rest. It was his fault. He could have even proposed to Mrs Manchanda at the right time, why not? Is she good enough for me? had run through his head then and, You can't be serious, she is so dully Hindi-belt and middle-class.

'Which of the two this afternoon—sisters, weren't they?— is the bride-to-be?' Mrs Manchanda, having finished, placed the incense stand with its four glowing sticks on the dressing table and shut and latched the cupboard. 'They were both attractive.'

'Officially the younger one but it's complicated.' He picked up his woollen cap off the floor and pulled it down over his head to cover his ears. He looked ridiculous but he felt cold. 'The younger one is an old friend of mine. Perhaps you don't remember her but they've visited me up here when I was a PG with you. She's even phoned here a couple of times, Anin. She's—' He paused for a moment. Anin's insanity depressed him. To her, her own madcap plans seemed logical and original, merely a little daring. 'She's pregnant—

she was last month, or so she claimed. With her, nothing can ever be certain. I'm supposed to reject her elder sister whom she hates and select her instead. She once tried—' He stopped out of a feeling of loyalty to an old friend but nevertheless finished the sentence in his head—to kill her elder sister fourteen years ago, attacked her with a hockey stick while she was asleep. 'Then she will in return turn me down for not having chosen her elder sister and her father, moved by her fairytale-like devotion to her sibling, in tears will allow her to marry her business associate, another old friend of mine. They are both deeply in love with the appearance that they have kept up over the past decade.' Mrs Manchanda smiled at the plot without fathoming it entirely and left for the kitchen. Bhola straightened his clothes and the bed and followed her.

Some weeks previously, when he had last met Anin with Dosto over the Diwali weekend, she *had* looked pregnant, it was true; she had put on weight and the expression in—and even the colour of—her eyes seemed to have changed. Yet, behind the tanpura that afternoon, she had appeared slim enough. A personality test requirement, no doubt. On the eve of Diwali, though, when she—they—had unfolded their proposed future to him under the tubelights of their fitness centre, and when he had idly proposed that they rechristen their moneyspinner The Travelling Light Clinic, surrounded by those large, black, ugly, cumbersome, menacing exercise machines, at that time, her eyes, seemingly made smaller by fat, had glowed with a new, a sort of mad, secret triumph.

'Well, first of all, congratultions, though I'm not sure that that's the right word when you have a baby before marriage.' The flush of exclusive achievement in Anin's features—despite the difficulties that awaited her in her immediate future—inexplicably conjured up for Bhola a picture of mature village women huddled together in a clique over a veiled secret; we have borne sons and daughters, the image seemed to tell him, we have borne pain such as you will never even begin to imagine, we have borne you, now leave us alone.

In contrast, beside her, Dosto had looked horribly gross and clumsy, an ox meant simply to impregnate and stand by and smile vacuously. He? He is just a fat phallus; I have extracted from him to build my secret.

At a loss for words at Anin's increased attractiveness—and even vaguely embarrassed at her pregnancy—he had then tried to joke about her looking irresistible and his not having to bother with precautions seeing that she was with child. Though taken aback, mercifully she had joked back—also feebly—and in all that confusion, he had wistfully wondered a couple of times whether anything would come of it. To the right of her grinning head, he remembered distinctly, and above a treadmill that had cost sixty thousand rupees, had hung one of the first signs that he had suggested they put up to make the bare walls more attractive, to signal to their clientele that unlike other gyms, their health clinic took care of both body and soul. DO NOT LINGER, the framed poster had read, plain black capital letters on a pale yellow background with a line sketch, in black, in the bottom right-hand corner of two stick-like, folk-art figures walking—striding like Johnnie Walker on the bottle—the second carrying easily a third in his arms.

On his first visit after they had bought the new premises, he had looked around sceptically, searching for things to criticise. He had been from the beginning determined to hide how impressed he was with their business acumen. His envy abated in degrees—but never fully disappeared—only when they, over time—individually, together and repeatedly—asked him for bright ideas. Some of his suggestions had been quite intelligent, and none more unexpectedly successful than the first—his dumping Moti on them nine years ago as hireling. Indeed, he had even at times come to feel that the health club, the more it moved away from its inceptive aim—of providing at a cost a place where the unhealthy could chat and unwind—to other areas—yoga, mental wellbeing, therapeutic full body oil massages, arranging for men for the large number of homosexual patrons, darkroom meditation—the more the club enlarged its spheres of interest, correspondingly changing its name—and identity—from gym to Sports Arcade to Health Club to Wellbeing Clinic to Calm Centre, the more it became at least in part his brainchild. At most other times, he thought it to be vulgar, and his feelings towards it were comparable to those that he had for Hindi film music. Every once in a while, one could listen to it softly and behind locked doors but to admit to enjoying it openly would be shameful. And at all times, subcutaneously, their—Anin's and Dosto's—business sense awed, humbled and depressed him. While they, beginning with a pull-up bar, dumb-bells and weights in a rented basement, had, in nine industrious and fruitful years, moved up to buying a four-bedroom house for their Centre, he in that period had only managed to switch from paid sex with an ex-vegetable vendor and her husband to unpaid sex with an ex-landlady. When he thought of these things, he felt like killing himself. Then he decided that he would first just see what marriage was like and only thereafter—and maybe—slash his wrists or something.

'*Do not linger*, Dosto, is the message of a Buddhist parable. Zen Buddhist monks are mentally and physically as fit and fatless as cricket bats.'

'Yes, but can they bend over and suck themselves off, that's the question,' Dosto, his face puffed up with alcohol and an impure life, had asked, looking down at the fat discernible about his waist even through his loose, orange tracksuit. 'The yoga bugger whom we have coming in three times a week claims that he can. That show's going to be quite a draw for some of my clients.'

'These lusts and longings, this guilt and these taboos,

verily, verily, I say unto thee, O Horatio, truly we walk through life with a heavy burden. Thus two monks, returning home, came to a stream where a pretty girl waited, reluctant to cross, fearful of wetting her clothes. One monk picked her up in his arms, forded the water and, having deposited her dry and safe on the other side, strode on. The second was horrified and spluttered kilometre after kilometre his shocked disapproval. Remarked the first monk, abruptly aware of the other's indignation, 'That girl? I put her down way back at the stream. Are you still carrying her? My advice would be: Do not linger, my friend, over either pretty girls or the past.'

Dosto was impressed by the tale. 'That's the most pure pussy story that I've heard since that Magi shit that we had in our School Radiant Reader English course.' He shook his head a couple of times in admiration. 'I can even see them. The babe-carrier monk is a kung fu type, all muscle and more expression in his buttocks than on his face but swathed in saffron looks like ceremonial dignified moist erect cock and not a monkey. She is raw sex cream thighs muscle pussy but demure face rose lips. In his arms, her robe kimono whatever parts to show firm milk thighs. They are driving the world round the bend with their lingering puss aroma.'

Bhola's father phoned again that same evening. Bhola and Mrs Manchanda had finished dinner and he was helping her clear up. She hadn't really got used to it even in nine years. In her world, men ate, by themselves, heartily at table and then, wheezing and burping, munched some more—paan, cardamom, digestive pills—before the TV while the women, after clearing up and several hours later—nibbled at the leftovers in the kitchen. Mrs Manchanda had followed that practice for years with her son and her paying guest. Vivek continued to eat first and be served at table by his mother. In an obscure way, it made her feel the presence of a man in the house. The arrangement suited her since Bhola, a light switch away in the group of flats behind her, was on call to perform the remaining duties of the he-goat.

Bhola's father's high good humour was noticeably absent the second time. 'Hello! The elder sister has been married before! Did you know that?'

'Uhh...yes...yes. Anin had told me.'

'This is ridiculous. I don't see how you can choose to marry a divorcee or someone separated from her husband or whatever her present status is.' He was shouting into the phone, more agitated than angry. Bhola could visualize a livid vein in his temple, an overgorged worm, burst and blood beneath his skin inundate his face like red ink spreading across blotting paper.

'Okay. Your wishes are my command. Her marriage has not been consummated, though.'

'What? Yes, so her father claimed too but can they be trusted?'

'We could always ask for a certificate from a Registered Medical Practitioner. The first husband was some kind of Bengali nut from Hazaribagh.'

'Why don't you consider the younger daughter?'

'She is pregnant. At least she was at Diwali. Do you remember Dosto, my old school friend who is vulgar and whom you didn't like? She wants to marry *him*. She is a little unstable. She tried to kill her elder sister with a hockey stick several years ago. Then the sister went back to boarding school and Anin remained at home for a year to calm down and dance Kathak on the rooftop with a huge dog. They were our next-door neighbours then. That's how we met. You are not to let on to her father, though, that you know all this.'

Bhola's father took some seconds off to ask himself whether the difficulty that he seemed to be having in hearing was a heart attack and then, mindful of the expense of the telephone call, continued, 'We can't discuss this in too great detail over the phone. You are coming down next week, aren't you? On the other hand, you're never at home when you are here. Besides, you hide things from me, like the time you were expelled from school and I didn't know for years.'

'That was only to save you pain. You know, agony aunt, agony father, like that.' Father and son were both in their own ways gentlemen. There were things, no matter how true, that civil people simply didn't accuse each other of. Bhola knew that his father used to snoop around and read his sons' personal letters and diaries and having done so, the father knew for example of his son's sexual proclivities, and the son knew that the father knew, having read it a thousand times in the dark, puzzled sadness in his eyes, but these were not the topics for even serious conversations. They communicated with each other through their silences. Thus Bhola knew that his father was reluctant to let the present offer of marriage go. The caste, sub-caste—all that—was perfect. Particularly after his own second marriage to an office colleague who was Bihari and Catholic, and his first son's dramatic near-elopement with a practically underage Muslim girl, the father was even more anxious that things be done right, the traditional way, for his second son, who did not need an unconventional marriage to add extra spice to his already bizarre life. Perhaps a sound, properly arranged alliance might even set things right for him sexually, one could never tell.

'I refuse,' slipped in Bhola before his father could disconnect, 'to have a car in the dowry, have you told the cop that? It will remind me of the trauma that I went through last year when I didn't want one and you all pestered me to take the soft loan just because it was available. But I don't need a car! I screamed into deaf ears. As a concession, to ease the pressure, I upgraded my bicycle, traded in my old for a new one. Totally unnecessary, wasteful, almost immoral, economic activity.'

He used virtually the same adjectives to describe to

himself his wedding reception. It took place on the eighteenth
of October, 1989. It was the largest party that he had ever
been part of. The Prime Minister almost attended. Kamala
and he, and Anin and Dosto, got married together. Throughout
the inexhaustibly tiring evening, Anin, her eyes aglitter with
ecstatic nervousness—but with her exhalations seeming to
smell of sorrow—pressed his hand a thousand times and
breathed into his ear once, with a tiny hysterical laugh, 'I'll
get you for this.' There were over five hundred guests. He
himself had especially invited four. None turned up. Mrs
Manchanda, Titli and Borkar declined because the reception
was held four hundred kilometres away. It was not clear why
Moti was not present. Perhaps, like his wife, he too had
sensed that socially, he would feel terribly out of place under
the vulgar chandeliers of the banquet hall of the five-star
hotel that Kamala's father had chosen. In any case, Moti for
years had not been available at Dosto's Sports Arcade to be
asked why. In the July of 1980, the year after his descent to
the plains with a scarlet cord about his waist, he had left to
join the domestic staff of one of the richer businessmen who
frequented the club. In his new place of work, he had
officially been designated a personal security guard.

The reception spilt over onto the terrace lawn of the hotel.
Bhola's father and stepmother spent a large part of the
evening ambling about outdoors, looking warily at the others,
a little like guests at the wrong party. The father was not
especially happy over Bhola's choice of bride mainly because
he felt that the circumstances required that he play the role—
in a gentlemanly way, of course—of one who has undersold
his son. Besides, when his wife had bluntly asked her stepson
whether he truly found Kamala attractive, Bhola, airily
mimicking his father, had answered that she was passable,
but with a heavenly voice. Passable was simply not true, had

felt Bhola's father, she was short, dark and plain. His son might as well have married a nightingale. For Bhola's father, Ava Gardener had been passable. One must maintain certain standards, he had always felt. He didn't much like either the cynically amused manner in which Bhola got on with his father-in-law, clearly a rogue of a policeman with fingers in many pies. It boded ill for the future, the way in which he had taken all the reins into his hands.

'You can't remain up there in the hills, Bhola son,' had expostulated the Inspector General of Police with a smile, 'We won't then see the newly-weds at all!' He smiled all the time but never with his eyes. 'Doesn't this M.K.M.Z.A.P. College have a sister institution down here? We must see about your transfer. Why, they can create a post for you here, I'm sure, if need be.'

The two couples had had to take up vantage positions in the centre of the hall, to continuously smile, shake hands with the males, do namastes to the women, accept presents, dump them on the tables behind them and be photographed. Anin and Dosto were in charge of the chatter. In some ways, Bhola was grateful for their presence. Kamala didn't speak very much and surely two strong, silent types were one too many in a marriage? Time would tell. Bhanu, Bhola's brother, looking natty in a dark suit, dawdled for a while near the gifts, trying to gauge how many of the gorgeously dressed women were eyeing him. 'It'd be nice,' Bhola had wistfully expressed to him times out of number, 'if I could marry a maternal, illiterate, paan-chewing, foul-mouthed, Hindi-speaking, fat, big-breasted, warm, grasping, low-caste whore. She would cover just about all my requirements.'

'I doubt very much if you'd find one who could follow cricket,' Bhanu had responded, almost frowning. Seven years after his dramatic marriage, he had settled down to living a comfortable quadruple life. He was doing well professionally, they had two normal children, he had after six years of

patient wheedling succeeded in joining the Gymkhana Club
and was fucking around like crazy without rocking the family
boat that was the anchor of his existence and to which he
returned with something of the rhythmic predictability of a
domestic stray dog coming back to the kitchen of a restaurant
for its life-sustaining leftovers. Bhola glanced at Kamala's
profile, her smiling face wan and gloomy above the resplendent
black and gold of her sari and wondered how on earth they
were going to have sex together and that too in the next few
hours. Maybe they would do without it. After all, as long as
he could remember, his father and stepmother had slept in
separate rooms. When, at the age of ten, he had found out
about sex and looked around him and realized that the whole
world made, had made, or would make, love and that that's
what kept it turning, that everybody slept with someone or
the other, or had, or would, even that fat bespectacled
burping bus conductor and that rural-looking woman with a
fine face and bad teeth selling peanuts before a cinema hall,
everyone—he had nevertheless at that time felt that everyone
excluded his father and stepmother, and now perhaps Kamala
and him as well. She was smiling at him and introducing him
to some schoolmate of hers and her husband. Meanwhile,
fortunately, life was always there with its demands and
matters of life and death and could be shelved only for the
time being. He grinned, shook hands with the man, exchanged
namastes with the woman and was for the moment content
not to probe himself for reasons for his actions because he
was sure that he wouldn't find any. Things happened to him
at the wrong time, that was all. He would probably fall madly
and hopelessly in love at the age of sixty-eight or something.
He would be concerned no doubt even at that age about the
fat content in his arse. Till then, he would roll and pitch
through his days, oscillating between maddening lust and a
revulsion with loneliness on the one hand and a kind of
loathing on the other of the human body, of its implacable

and brutal demands.

A waiter with a hard, worldly face glided up with a tray. 'Drink, sir?'—in English—'Black or white?' With a gesture of his hand, Bhola indicated gallantly that he should first ask the ladies. Without following and continuing to be self-contained in his smugness, the waiter moved up to Dosto. Incensed, Bhola said to his old friend—with the waiter between them— 'Tell the dolt that he should first serve the women.' Dosto didn't hear but nodded and beamed, picked up a Cola, raised it in a toast to Bhola, downed it, put the glass back on the tray, picked up another and lifted it in a second salute to Kamala. Feeling foolish, like a failure, Bhola turned away to see his stepmother smiling shyly at him.

'You don't look too happy. I mean, you *could* look happier.'

'Well, let's just say that internally I'm beaming from ear to ear.' He watched, a little behind her, his father gulp down the homoeopathic anti-flatulence pills that he had been having for a decade. 'Would you like a drink, orange or grey?' The waiter smoothly slid up, Kamala behind him. She touched Bhola's arm. 'Come and be photographed.' Guilty about her, he broke into a smile that didn't work. Behind her, Bhanu was getting himself snapped with Kamala's classmate. But if they cannot contain—abruptly drifted like mist into Bhola's head—let them marry: for it is better to marry than to burn. Corinthians. No. But if they cannot contain, let them marry and two-time, for it is better to marry and two-time than to burn. As they straightened clothes and coiffures before the camera, he wondered whether his brother had any qualms about his quadruple life. Probably yes, he answered himself, observing Bhanu's thinning scalp and greying hair at the age of thirty-four, the pouches beneath the eyes.

'Aren't the lives and souls of the party imbibing?' suddenly bellowed at them a tall old man with a stoop, making them all—including the photographer—jump and ruining the shot. The alcoholic fumes that he liberally exuded at everybody

were almost visible like amber-coloured steam. Despite the
intervening thirteen years, Bhola recognized the paunch and
the bloated crimson face just before Dosto, assuming a
drunken manner to please his auditor, cackled in welcome,
'Swaraj Chacha! Come and join the picture!' Bhola wanted to
light a match under the noble nose and watch the entire head
go up in flames like an effigy's. That however was not
immediately possible and he moreover in the interim would
have to be civil to the rogue because apparently they—
Kamala and he—were to stay, for some months at least—in
one of the flats on the upper floors of Swaraj's sister's house.
'Here, let me introduce you,' Dosto continued to babble,
pulling his uncle forward, without touching him, by the
magnetism of his extended arm, 'Anin of course you already
know. Kamala here is her elder sister and Bhola is her new
husband—' Everyone save the speaker looked startled at his
use of 'new'—'I mean, my brother-in-law, or should it more
correctly be my sister-in-law's husband—'

'I remember him, your old friend,' Swaraj gazed balefully
at Bhola with his bulging yellow eyes, slowly nodded his head
and repeated, 'I remember him well, even though he's lost
weight. I was waiting for him to say hello first. He looks
gloomy, black and thin.'

'That's because the woods are lovely, dark and deep.
That's a quotation, sir, from a world-famous poem about the
female pubic thatch, which is construed, as in one branch of
our thought, to surround the centre of the world.' Kamala
muttered something and, pulling her sari more closely about
her, turned beaming to her classmate. Swaraj Chacha, redder
in the face than usual and mumbling to himself, followed
suit.

Before her first marriage, Kamala, along with her classmate,
had taught Economics at one of the city's better colleges. She
had had to resign to accompany her first husband, a medical
doctor, to Austin, Texas in the USA. She didn't drink. She in

fact detested alcohol because in part she associated it with her first husband who apparently used to imbibe and then become a beast.

'A vet, you mean,' Bhola had said. Mercifully, she had laughed. Like her sister, she had a nice laugh but it was more rare. It would be perfect, mused Bhola, as he absentmindedly sipped at a yellow drink—some sort of new artificial juice, dreadful—if she would arrange to get her sex elsewhere because he liked her. One possibility—in fact, the only person she met regularly—was her music teacher. She sang for hours every day. He came home four times a week. He was thin and old, with a face made out of parchment, a skull across which wandered a couple of strands of yellowish-grey hair and jowls adorned with a permanent white stubble. He lacked some teeth but fortunately could keep a tune. Bhola had been surprised how with her teacher, Kamala became a different person—demure, attentive and impressively grave. She addressed him as Guruji and touched his feet at the beginning and end of every session. Music was serious business. Perhaps for starters she could feel him up through his dhoti, send her short, squat fingers for a stroll up those hairless and fleshless, pale, almost translucent legs that the fossil displayed with the insouciance of a prostitute out of *Irma la Douce*. Things would have been different for all of them—and her music lessons solemn orgies—had she had, in contrast, someone gorgeous like Moti for tutor.

He—they—were never far from Bhola's thoughts, Moti and Titli, never had been. Out of sight simply meant that they had dunked their heads under water and were swimming around in the pool somewhere, occasionally and unexpectedly bobbing up in the features of other men and women whom Bhola met—in a cheekbone, a smile, a forelock, a ponderous gait, a lanky inability to stand straight. They were no longer merely Bhola's first lovers. They had also come to embody all that was wrong with Bhola's life. Ever since the day of the botched operation by which they, in their ignorance, drunkenness and incompetence, had futilely stitched a ring on to Moti's foreskin, he in particular had become a kind of permanent heaviness in Bhola's head, as though the latter's culpability had burst the arteries at the base of his skull, and the blood, fanning out like some contagion, had then congealed and become cold and numb like his lover's loins. As the days lapsed into months and years, and he moved on past a postgraduate degree to earning a living, the sense—quite independent of and unrelated to any events—just the sense of having transgressed moved—or rather, stayed—with Bhola, a thick and slow heartbeat at the back of his head. He needed to expiate without pause, to make amends, to accept and bear the retribution.

HEAVEN

Bhola had sex with Kamala just eight times in the three years that they remained together. They loved each other, though—at least he thought that they did—he loved her at any rate, or rather, when he couldn't be by himself, there was nobody else that he wanted more to be with. After the joint wedding, they honeymooned in Simla and Anin and Dosto in their gym. Bhola's father-in-law had waggishly suggested that they all go off together as a jolly quartet to the same place. No doubt, the hotelier had proposed even more reasonable rates for a quadruple occupancy. Mercifully, both his sons-in-law had refused. Bhola in particular didn't want to go up to the hills in the first place because it would be cold and probably raining up there and Anin, with her new sorceress's sneer that revealed that she knew exactly what the sex was like between him and her sister, would have been an added botheration, and Dosto hadn't wanted to leave his gym—metamorphosed by then into clinic—at all because they were about to launch some new operations—thermo therapy, body tapping and an ambitious, six-month-long, Success-Guaranteed-or-Money-Back programme called Workout Factory which was a mix of everything that they already had but at double the prices.

The newly-weds had spent the night of the wedding reception in the hotel itself. They had gone to bed at four in the morning and Bhola had presumed that sex at that hour with an unsexy unknown—for him as well as for her—was not a priority. She had locked herself in the bathroom to change, so he, droopy with fatigue, had pulled on his pyjamas with one eye on the TV film.

'You should have a slight belly,' she had said, 'You are too thin.' She had smiled to rob her words of any offence. They were the nicest that he had heard all evening. Her nightie had looked like a sleek black Occidental evening gown and he had wondered how women could tell the difference. They had yawned in unison, laughed and dropped off to sleep with the lights and the TV on.

Simla was cold, wet and cosy. They stayed three nights in a hotel that was in fact a private rooming house run by a long-nosed, crafty Army widow. Bhola and Kamala had a suite, a third of the first floor, to themselves. It comprised a sitting room, a bedroom, a kitchenette and a toilet. It rained every day. Kamala would get up frightfully early in the morning, potter around in the kitchenette, drink some honey-lemon-ginger-warm water concoction and, shutting the door behind her, sing in the sitting room for more than an hour. The door didn't latch properly and always remained slightly ajar. Bhola found that waking up to her singing in another room was a pleasure more sublime and restful than any that he could recall. Is it perfume from a dress that makes me so digress or is it the music from a farther room? immediately drifted into and lodged in his head. He felt silly that some famous lines from an English poem were all that he could find to relate his experience to. At six in the morning, the room was in shadow, illumined only by the lamplight that floated in like dew through the imperfectly fitting translucent glass panes of the door to the sitting room. He knew nothing about Hindustani classical music and didn't mind being ignorant. She spent the first quarter of an hour warming up, tuning her voice, doing epiglottal pushups, whatever. He lay dead still under the quilt, determined not to get up for a pee, not even to turn on his side for fear of making the bed creak and disturbing her. Her voice glided in like waves of butterflies on the wing. He was reminded of his Concert for Bangladesh record in which the audience had mistaken the sitar being tuned for some kind of overture and had clapped politely at the end of it. When she finished singing, Bhola, tired and at peace at seven-thirty in the morning, dozed off once more.

Even if it hadn't been raining, he would have found it difficult to go for a jog in an unknown place. On the days that he couldn't run, out of habit, he went, like a schoolboy on the last Friday before the summer vacation, a little mad and swung, almost Dr Jekyll-like, to the opposite extreme and did absolutely none of the things that typically defined his day. On his honeymoon, therefore, he lolled in bed, read Robert Ludlum, Dick Francis and Desmond Bagley, also in bed, instead of some elevating book sitting upright in a chair, did not try to meditate for a minute on nothing and took an hour to decide whether he should have those irresistible chicken cutlets for breakfast or lunch or both. When it stopped raining, they strolled about for a bit in the open air and took photographs. On the second night, Bhola asked Kamala whether she would sit crosslegged, in the nude, on the rug next to the heater, with her back to him and sing. 'Please.' Embarrassed, terribly shy, faintly excited, almost happy, uncertain, she complied. Naked, sitting behind her, he encircled her carefully in his arms. 'No, don't stop singing, please.'

On their return from Simla, they moved into the first floor of Swaraj's sister's house, a posh thing in the heart of town, a ten-minute walk from the Jahanpanah Public Gardens. The flat was Dosto's but Anin and he seemed to have exchanged it for Kamala's dowry, which was an apartment smaller but much nearer to the health centre. The details and actual purpose of the switch were a little hazy—for Anin and Dosto in fact stayed in a *third* flat, *Anin's* dowry—and Bhola suspected that Dosto needed, close to his place of work, a couple of cosy rooms for some disreputable activity. Kamala, it appeared, had pushed for the swap too, to accommodate what Bhola referred to as the rest of his dowry, namely, the ageing maidservant Ayama who had been with the family since Kamala had been six months old or something and had practically suckled her. For her, Swaraj's sister's first floor had a tinier, shabbier, extra room at the back with an attached hole of a toilet.

Despite Bhola's father-in-law's boasts and efforts, M.K.M.Z.A.P. College had declined to transfer one post of lecturer to its sister institution in the city. Bhola himself was quite thrilled with his bosses for having manfully resisted the wily police officer's influence. He thus, in the first few months of his marriage, fell into a rhythm that permanently dislocated and distanced him from his immediate surroundings. He would catch the Monday early morning bus for the hills, take his classes and tutorials for four days and on occasion meet Mrs Manchanda and Titli. After wheedling with his Head of Department for weeks, he succeeded in having his Friday classes and tutorials shifted to the afternoons of the other days of the week and so caught the Thursday evening bus back to his new family. Of the days on which Bhola was away, Kamala spent two or three per week at her parents' house. The sisters never seemed to meet, ever; neither ever asked Bhola of the other. When he met Anin and Dosto, it was usually in their new air-conditioned office at the gym.

He had noticed of late that Anin's eyes glittered continuously with a kind of secret, contemptuous smirk. She had lost weight and begun to resemble a small witch. He wondered how she could tell how infrequently he and Kamala had sex—twice in the first seven months of marriage—and was discomfited by the predatory, derisive challenge in her expression—I am going to sleep with you one day, you sap, and show you what you have missed by choosing the wrong sister. Later, when he thought back on that first year, the images that dominated his recollection were those of the black and excited disdain in her eyes and he trying to doze off while being rocked back and forth in a bus travelling long-distance, in the cool of the early hours of the morning or in the trapped heat of the early hours of the night, with his senses being choked by the roar of the engine, the smell of diesel and the stink of other people's sweat.

'Is Moti all right, by the way? His wife was complaining to me last Tuesday that I take up absolutely no news of him. He never phones, I told her, I don't even know where he's staying, and with whom, what work he does.'

Bhola sat for the first time in a flat the walls and ceilings of each room of which were all—without exception—painted in varying shades of red. The tones ranged from dawn pink and burning orange to dark scarlet. The flat was Kamala's dowry, the one in which they would have stayed had they not swapped it for Swaraj's sister's first floor. Bhola had arrived at the gym that evening a little later than usual and had just caught Anin and Dosto getting into their new car. They had hesitated for a fraction, a millionth, of a second before asking him to hop in at the back.

'Where are we off to?'

'Just around the corner, silly,' Anin had laughed without turning around, 'a getaway, a breather, tea, coffee, a sniff, a snort, whatever.' She still spoke her unpredictable mix of English and Hindi in each sentence.

The flat was ten minutes and three traffic lights away and on the second floor of a new and hideous apartment block. A sort of guard in a shabby brown uniform and a peaked cap held the car door open for Dosto. Bhola was surprised to see him exchange smiles with his friends. The flat was sparsely furnished. The sitting room had mattresses on the floor covered with red, patterned bedcovers and two low tables, on top of one of which sat a radio-cassette player and a candle in a stand made out of bamboo.

'Have you two noticed that neither the cassette recorder nor the candle are red in colour?'

Neither reacted. Both in fact disappeared through one of the two other doors of the room. Dosto returned a couple of minutes later carrying a small plastic packet. He asked in an elaborately offhand manner, 'Do you want to snort some coke?' He cleared his throat to make his meaning clearer. 'Cocaine?' He broke into a grimace of a smile.

'Uhh…no.' Bhola didn't fully succeed in keeping the surprise out of his voice. 'I have to catch that early morning bus tomorrow. But don't mind me.'

Dosto stooped and pressed the Play button on the tape. Loud, unfamilar eighties' Hindi film music hit Bhola almost like a fist in the diaphragm. Surrounded by those red walls and that blend of disco, North Indian folk and reggae, he felt as though he was entrapped in the den of some Hindi movie villain and expected at any moment a fat, Kashmiri-white, vamp-siren, dressed in a black, sequinned bikini, lipstick, eyeshadow, wig and some gauze over her thighs, to slink in through one of the two doors, swaying voluptuously, glass of whisky in hand, the ice cubes within it clinking in time to the dramatically slower and softer refrain of the song. 'Will you have a drink or something? Anin's a bit self-conscious about doing the coke in front of you. You don't mind? We won't be a minute.'

So when he asked them about Moti, they were lolling on a mattress in front of him, not touching each other, a maroon bolster a bulwark between them. Dosto's eyes were hooded and Anin's shining. She had a permanent half-smile on her face. He had aged, though, put on weight and lost some hair. No stranger would believe that he and Bhola had been in the same class at school. Dropping some ash from his cigarette into the enamel ashtray that he had balanced on his stomach, Dosto drawled, 'You tell her not to worry. Moti's going places. On that red string about his waist, he's going to climb all the way up to Heaven.'

Bhola sipped some Thums Up that he hadn't wanted in the first place and lazily, hazily marvelled at the ease—like warm sand slipping through one's fingers on the beach—with which friends became strangers. While he had been sniffing sewer pussy up in the hills, sneered he to himself in a sudden black mood, they had no doubt been sniffing coke down below. The different routes to maturity that people took were all puzzling, weren't they? Bhola felt foolish at having been surprised at being shown that he hadn't really known what his old friends had been up to for a decade. 'That doctor quack that Moti's wife is with hasn't been keeping too well. If he dies one of these days, she'll want to be with her husband, I guess. He should keep in touch, that's all.'

Anin shifted to a more comfortable position, pulled her kurta down. Her foot accidentally brushed against Dosto's thigh. Dosto pulled his leg away and then, after a moment, sat up and on his hands and knees crawled over to the unoccupied mattress next to the cassette recorder, lowered its volume and flopped down alongside it. 'If they want to, they can always join us at the Centre. There'll always be room for a quack and his ducky,' he announced to the roseate ceiling with a sigh.

In the silence that followed, during which it seemed that Anin and Dosto would continue to be horizontal and high for the next couple of hours, gazing at and saying nothing in particular, Bhola swallowed his drink, looked at his watch, realized that Kamala's music lesson would be getting over pretty soon, and decided to count till ten and then get up and leave. Just then, however, Dosto spoke, but in a tone that suggested that he at least thought that he had been speaking all the while. 'But that's the quack whom Moti doesn't like, right? Then maybe Borkar-Whorekar can pay *us* to get a job with us. All transactions should be based on an exchange of money. It keeps them clean.' He turned laboriously on his side and stared at Bhola as though from a great distance. 'We've been out of touch, friend. Because you don't seem to know that Anin lost my grandmother's necklace.' He paused, seemingly to allow Bhola to sink into coma with shock.

Bhola, regretting that he hadn't jumped up and left when he could have, looked towards Anin for illumination. Her face contorted with scorn as she retorted quietly and venomously, 'Ten years ago, you sold Moti for two lakhs of rupees to the builder thug who used to reek of scent. But you've kept in touch—we should tell Bhola our real secrets.' She glared at her husband for an instant, then jerked her head dismissively and shut her eyes.

'I have no secrets from you or from anybody else,' explained Dosto to Bhola without glancing in Anin's direction. He took pride in keeping calm. 'I've been wearing a gold necklace ever since my college days. Do you remember it? My grandmother had given it to me before she died. Twenty-two-carat gold, twenty-four hours a day I retained it around my neck swimming, bathing, pissing, fucking, running to catch a train, running to the toilet, whatever, always on me. Don't you remember it?'

'No. After my time, I'm sure.'

Dosto's features twitched in disbelief. He stared moodily at Bhola for a moment before continuing. 'Two years ago— in fact, just before Anin, Kamala and Papa Inspector General went up to croon before you and your mistress-in-the-cupboard, I gifted Anin the necklace. Well, she asked me for it and I gave it to her. She must have had it on when she sang that morning. Don't you recall seeing it?'

'No. But I wasn't peering down her blouse or anything, so it's possible that I missed it.'

Dosto picked up the ashtray and clumsily threw it at

Bhola. It hit the wall beneath the window and shattered into several pieces. Anin opened her eyes. Bhola turned around and noted with satisfaction that the ash had flecked, like the nails of a dog's wet paws, the immaculate orange of the wall. He arose from floor level with an effort, 'It's almost seven. I'd better go.'

Dosto, without getting up, raised his voice and quickened his speech like a debater determined to finish his full oration in the time allotted to him. 'Then exactly two months ago, in the evening, when she was changing into her tracksuit for her massage, I saw that her neck was bare. Boy. She had dropped it somewhere and hadn't even *noticed*.' Dosto closed his eyes, felt under his shirt collar with his right hand, pulled out a necklace and raised it to his lips for a long and fervent second. Bhola seized the opportunity to sidle closer to the front door.

'Don't skulk off in mid-sentence, lecturer sir,' drawled Anin, failing to cloak her annoyance beneath her affected manner of speech. 'There is a moral in the tale because the necklace has been found, hasn't it. Moti found it, didn't he. And now my husband-god wants him back with him.' With her left fist, she began rhythmically to pummel the bolster as she glared at Dosto and spoke. 'It was simple and touched the heart. Hold the red cord and believe, that is all that Moti said.' She glanced up beseechingly at Bhola. He was startled by the intensity of emotion in her expression. 'Believe that you'll find it and of course we didn't until we did. He explained it very clearly.' Suddenly, her head wilted onto her chest as some unexpected memory doused out her exhilaration. Her arm looked broken and lifeless on the bolster.

'Where was it finally found?' Bhola tried but failed to conjure up an image of Moti impressing two educated and intelligent people of the world with an explanation of anything. No doubt it was he, Bhola, himself who was retarded and too limited to see things. Since neither of his listeners answered his first question, he, mildly piqued, tried another. 'What did Moti explain so clearly? No, tell me on my next visit. It's like the question for the following week at the end of a TV quiz show.'

'You won't get anywhere unless you learn to wipe that sneer off your mind,' advised Dosto solemnly. He thought things over for a second, finally got up, swayed for a long moment before regaining equilibrium and belched without noticing it. 'You hold that cord around Moti's waist and think clearly about what you want.' He shuffled a couple of steps forward. His expensive-looking shirt popped out of his jeans like a plant recently uprooted. He raised his eyebrows and then stretched the muscles of his face in some sort of yogic yawn. 'Once you think clearly about what you want, you can then proceed towards obtaining it. This is no mumbo-jumbo. On the contrary, it is ascetic logic. The cord—or any other token object—is an aid to concentration.'

In the noisy auto-rickshaw on the way back home, getting high on the black exhaust fumes from the buses that careened past them down the left, the wrong, side, Bhola felt even more comically depressed and defeated than usual at the idea of Moti having become a kind of minor seer. There appeared to be truly no limits to the world's gullibility. Moti was clearly less imbecile than he looked if he had managed to retain and coherently regurgitate some phrases from Borkar's quasi-mystical babble. At the back of Bhola's mind was the fear that to increase his worth in the eyes of his fan club, Moti might have let fall hints disclosing the identity and the passion of his first lover. That knowlege—and the cocaine— and her life—would explain that permanent grimace of a smirk on Anin's face. The auto-rickshaw braked and swerved with frightening suddenness to avoid a family of cattle sitting around—very much at home—in the street's fast lane. Bhola cracked his head against one of the steel bars from which hung framed calendar paintings of Ganesh, the infant Krishna and Krishna the divine flautist. 'Drive carefully, you scruffy and sexy motherfucker,' he groaned in English. Evidently pleased at the adroit manner in which he had been able to avoid both the buses and the cattle, the driver sped up. There are no gods, Borkar—and now even Moti—sitting in the rear alongside me and leaning forward, thought Bhola, laying a distracting hand on the driver's shoulder, would have informed him, there are no gods to save you from your rash speed, there are only rites, and a rite is not one half of a bargain, of some reciprocal arrangement: Here, God, is something certain to please you; in return, please deign to give me what I want. How could that be when the god does not exist? The rite is an end in itself and meant to yield *apurva*, that which was not before. All that you need is concentration on what you are doing because everything in the world is connected—the cattle, your auto-rickshaw, the cricket match with the West Indies—and one thing leads to another if you follow the right route.

Bhola was glad to get back home, to see Ayama's handsome, immobile face at the back door. The tentative, conspiratorial smile about her eyes indicated that Kamala's music lesson hadn't yet finished. Bhola wandered about the apartment and inhaled deeply the aromas of normalcy—the warmth of overripe fruit from the dining table, the anti-mosquito incense lit near the armchairs before the TV, the special spiced tea that Ayama must have brewed for the guru. He, Amarendu Babu, had not come alone. Crosslegged on the carpet alongside him sat Francesca, the pretty Italian woman who was another of his pupils and whom he brought along from time to time because he found her Hindi only marginally less difficult to follow than she his English. Bhola liked Francesca; Swaraj downstairs liked her even more. No doubt encouraged by her evident love of Hindu culture, he had already waylaid her more than once to propose that she would benefit enormously from the yogic massage of her body that he could give her whenever she wanted. She could of course, he never failed to graciously add, retain her bra and panties during the operation.

While waiting for the singing session to get over and carrying a cup of Ayama's brew, Bhola went out and settled down on the verandah. He breathed in deeply once more the warm air of the April evening. The cocaine and the red rooms appeared in retrospect to be the enchanted castle of the ogre in the fairy tale from which he had escaped only because of his innate innocence and goodness. The squeaks and cackles of neighbour Chinmaya's teenaged daughters wafted up from the badminton court. Directly below, he could see Swaraj's sisters, one older and a spinster, the other younger and a widow, slapping at mosquitoes and gossiping at the low wall that separated the lawns of their two apartments. The widow favoured low cut blouses and, unfailingly flashing her rings and breasts at Bhola, in general spoke only of money—of rents and the prices of tomatoes going up, her previous electricity bill, how expensive her last trip to Bombay had been, and the costs of daycare for her doctor children, long since settled in America. Bhola and Kamala both preferred the spinster. Large, patriarchal, with a Roman nose and a discreet white beard, she comported herself with the dignity appropriate to an owner of property in different posh areas of the city that cumulatively was worth several crores of rupees. Her favourite subject too was money but she handled the topic with a decorum befitting her demeanour. Greed for her was a stately virtue. Early in their acquaintance—on the third day after Bhola and Kamala had moved in, in fact—and thereafter repeated on the average twice a week, she had informed them that the exhorbitant rents that she and her siblings were forced to charge from their several tenants dotted across the city were all gobbled up by the medical bills of their ailing mother.

Whom Bhola, from his first meeting with Swaraj thirteen

years ago, simply remembered as a benign presence, a perennially smiling, wrinkled, dried-up vegetable with silken white hair. She was now hundred-plus and had apparently been bedridden in the rear right bedroom for the last twelve years. Her existence was somehow substantiated mainly by the two nurses who turned up like clockwork, one at seven a.m., the other at seven in the evening. Dark, petite, cheerful, efficient, they enlivened the lives of the sisters and particularly the brother.

Amongst—and somehow emanating out of—the sounds of the evening—the teenagers happily arguing at badminton, Kamala singing magically in the apartment, the rumble from downstairs of Swaraj's elder sister's voice, a mother in some verandah demanding of her children that they cease their play and return home that instant, the deadening dialogue of a TV soap booming through a neighbour's open window—the thought floated into Bhola's head *out* of the sounds of the evening that it would be nice to have a child, to father a warm, living thing that would be part of the commonplace joys of the ordinary world, distinct and distant from that other distorted and arid universe of oppressive blood-coloured walls and intoxicants, where a guide to ethical living could be found in the shoelace that connected the penis to the waist of a manservant and who in turn had been loaned out to the lustful for a sum that equalled Bhola's salary in a year and a half.

'Good evening, Mrs Malhotra.'

'Good evening, Mr O'Brien.'

The flat above Bhola's and Kamala's was vacant and till recently had been an illegal workshop of the jewellery store owned by some other branch of Swaraj's extended family. All night, every night for months on end, the neighbourhood had suffered the whines of lathes, the hum of drills, the tap tap of discreet hammers and the subdued chortles and conversation in Hindi dialect of the workers till deliverance arrived next door in the shape of a bald, red, sweating Irish diplomat. He occupied the two floors above the widowed sister for two days and threatened to move out on the third. 'It's either me, Madam, or that devil's workshop.' Like a figure out of a nursery rhyme, he, morning and evening, fat in a white half-sleeves shirt and luxuriantly coloured tie, kept an open book between himself and his surroundings—doubtless in disgust at them—and read while walking to and back from work.

The sounds from within the apartment signalled that the lesson was over and Amarendu Babu and his Italian consort were about to leave. She stayed a few blocks away in Jahanpanah itself. It really was one of the posher areas of the city. Bhola had recently discovered that he liked living amongst the rich; he had also been faintly bemused upon realizing that it was only his birth, his caste—coupled with his father-in-law's—doubtless ill-gotten—wealth—that had granted him the leverage to ascend a rung of the social ladder. Those houses in the colony that had not been demolished to make way for apartment blocks were all huge, stately and fakely old-looking, having been built in the fifties by the wealthier refugees who streamed into the city after Partition. Poshness, Bhola had been pleased to learn, imposed its own rules over and above the standard Municipal regulations. The unsightly leper beggars, for example, who screamed and wailed for alms from their dog carts on rare sunny mornings were only heard and never seen in Jahanpanah, for the Residents' Welfare Association had decreed that they would be permitted to wander up and down only in the service-and-back-lanes. The police were called in if beggars were spotted either in the park or before any front gate. The police arrived quite promptly for the rich.

'Oof. I'm glad that that's over,' sighed Kamala as she sat down in the cane armchair beside Bhola, 'Francesca's nice but when she's around, Guruji becomes witty and cracks jokes. It's like seeing the ghost of your great-grandfather make a pass at your schoolfriend. What're you drinking? How was your day?'

'I'm so relieved that we don't stay in the flat that was meant for you—us. Dosto and Anin have painted it red— completely red, walls, ceilings, doors.'

Kamala nodded in the gloom as though she had expected nothing else from her sister, then laughed, a short, nervous bark, and suddenly pushed back her chair and got up. 'I'm going to drink a nimbu-pani. Do you want anything?'

'I thought that we could have a child. In the near, the very near future.'

He sensed more than saw the happy smile that illumined her face. 'Okay,' she replied equably before disappearing into the drawing room, as though he had asked her whether she wanted butter on her toast. He could hear her humming her way to the kitchen.

He felt glad, at peace, at having blurted out his wish for progeny. He had felt like honouring and fostering a rare, noble impulse within himself. As though to applaud his announcement, at that very moment, the handful of itinerant vendors who, both in the morning and evening, roved about the colony with their diverse goods—carpets, cane baskets, parrots, brooms, toys, quilts, miniature paintings—piled up to enormous heights on the carriers of their bicycles—the vendors at the widow's front gate began to holler in singsong the virtues of their wares. They were unfailingly punctual; their presence invariably denoted eight-thirty in the morning and a quarter to eight in the evening. On occasion, some of the more musical stray dogs of the neighbourhood howled along with them. They usually caught Kamala when she was in a tearing hurry to get to work and surrounded her more or less like the lepers harassing the King of the Jews outside the temple in *Jesus Christ Superstar*.

'Nothing can be done about them,' philosophized Swaraj from the lawn. He was always there in the morning, unshaven, in his sleeping suit of white kurta and pyjama, a cup of tea in his left hand, never letting slip the chance of a chat with Kamala for the eight seconds that she took to traverse the path from the stairs to the gate. 'They have been over-indulged by the French lady who stayed above Nirupama before Mr O'Brien took up residence with us. She was a charming person, very open to Indian ideas. Housing was a good sector those days, so we had upped the rent from forty thousand to sixty. She protested but we were polite and firm.' Swaraj usually shouted out the last few phrases to Kamala while she, still encircled by the stragglers amongst the sellers, was getting into her car. 'She then decided to vacate without giving us adequate notice. Moreover, in the last month, three of her friends moved in with her. So we were forced to shut off her electricity and water. She used to buy a lot of junk from these fellows. They loved displaying their goods to her.'

Swaraj was not averse to displaying his own goods either. On one of Bhola's visits in the following month, Kamala half-humorously complained to him, 'Swaraj has been flashing at Ayama. He waits at the gate till he spots her in the verandah, then he unbuttons his trousers and pretends to tuck in his shirt and adjust his undies and I don't know what else. She went down to borrow some cooking oil a couple of days ago and it seems that he grabbed her by the hand to ask her whom she was going to massage.'

Bhola predictably was more amused than scandalized. 'It's remarkable that his virility managed to pierce Ayama's defences. She's half-blind, deaf and lame and plots and plans all day long only on how to increase and improve the quantity and quality of her intake of food. Well, not for nothing is a male like Swaraj known as the loin of the Punjab.'

Kamala finally conceived in the April of 1991. Bhola's and her conjugal life had not improved in the intervening months. Though, as the days passed, he liked her more and more as an individual, she failed completely to arouse him. On her

part, she did not appear to miss sex in the least. Never
through joke or innuendo or gesture or expression did she
ever indicate that she had, at the end of the day, sex with
him—or with anybody else for that matter—on her mind.
There is something rotten in the state of Denmark, an
outsider would have judged. Of course, the subject had not
excessively bothered Bhola because he had been getting
quite a lot of it in Sweden. Kamala finally conceived only
because her husband at last included, in his lengthening list
of Secret Seven Activities, *Sex Once in Six Months with Wife*.

Kamala's parents were delighted at the news of their
daughter's pregnancy. Anin was offended that she was
informed by her mother and not by either her sister or Bhola.
'May your tribe increase,' however was all that she said,
smiling nastily and mysteriously. Kamala's father declared
that Bhola must try harder than ever for a transfer or consider
switching jobs. Why didn't he resign and start afresh in a
bank as an officer? He would earn three times as much. The
father also recommended to them a gynaecologist, Dr
Punchkuian, a female who had modern ideas and charged the
earth for them but not from them. Their visits were gratis
because 'your father and I are dear dear friends'. Bhola
understood her to mean that his father-in-law had helped her
to get the building plans of her nursing home cleared by the
Municipal Corporation.

The months glided by. Bhola informed neither Mrs
Manchanda nor Titli of his impending fatherhood. 'One
doesn't talk about it to anyone till the very end,' Kamala had
advised him. 'Superstition.' In any case, the ties between him
and the two women with time had slackened. In July, Mrs
Manchanda's distant relative, a female, gained admission to
the college and became her second paying guest. Her
assignations with her first automatically whittled down to a
couple of times in six months. Neither died of a broken heart.
Titli in her hole behind Fatman's Hotel was too taken up

with waiting for Borkar to die and wondering what would happen to her thereafter. The quack himself announced half-heroically to Bhola one day that he had cirrhosis of the liver; on another that it was cancer of the pancreas. It was true that he had lost weight and colour, that his eyes popped out more than ever and had become terribly yellow, that he brought up virtually all that he ate. Almost all his patients had deserted him. The remaining few were tended to by Titli. Bhola would wonder how she and Borkar made ends meet and whether she had finally and overtly taken to prostitution. His conjectures did not enliven their infrequent encounters. Her face had become sleeker and fatter and her eyes hard. She had taken to wearing only white saris in the belief that the colour reflected her soul. She had swollen up and her skin looked tight and overripe. No touch of Bhola stirred her. Everything inside her in contrast seemed to have withered; the little that remained appeared as alluring as garbage. She felt abandoned even by her near-idiot husband. Oblivious of Bhola, mindful only of the desolate sea that stretched before her to the horizon, she waited, cold, for him to finish so that she could pick up her earnings and trudge back to clean up Borkar's vomit.

Bhola was galled at her presumption that he was responsible for her future. At the same time, he felt guilty about how little she, at that stage of his life, mattered to him. 'Something will work out, don't worry. You can always join Moti.'

'If I knew exactly where he was. He sends me money orders once a month, that's all.'

'I understand that he's climbing up to Heaven on that red string of his.'

Borkar obliged Bhola by dying in winter, when the college was shut for the long vacation and he was four hundred kilometres away and emmeshed in domestic responsibilities—in phoning the gynaecologist for appointments, driving Kamala to them, making lists of what to ask the doctor, rearranging the flat to accommodate another soul, flipping through past issues of the Reader's Digest to learn about parenthood. It surprised him to know that Ayama was exclusively—and would remain—the cook and that they would need another servant, an ayah, for the baby. While he was in the midst of this new world and enjoying it, on the second Friday in December, Titli phoned him from the STD booth outside the post office. She was crying. He was moved most when he learnt that it was all over, that he wouldn't have to go up to help, that she had managed everything with the assistance of a couple of Borkar's ex-patients from the slums, from calling a real doctor to having the body ferried to the electric crematorium. 'Well done!' he shouted into the phone, feeling ashamed of himself but wondering at the same time what else he could say. 'Just get some rest and come down when you feel up to it. I'll make contact with Moti in the meanwhile.'

She never turned up. He waited for her all week and was quite relieved at the end of it. It would have been difficult to explain her away to his wife and their family heirloom of a servant. Perhaps she has set up shop as a doctor in Borkar's place, thought he idly as he prepared himself a pot of tea and later, limbered up for his run in the early morning chill in the Jahanpanah Public Gardens. Perhaps she has found some other incontinent charlatan to team up with. Once or twice, he thought of phoning Anin to ask whether she had any news of Titli through Moti but he desisted. He realized that he didn't really want to know where Titli was and what she was up to as long as she didn't turn up at his door. Perhaps she was deeply offended that he hadn't rushed up to take care of things at hearing of Borkar's passing, surmised Bhola as he watched Kamala bend laboriously to pick up a pillow that had fallen on the floor. Perhaps she will sulk forever and never see me again, or till I raise her fee to six hundred, whichever is earlier. Perhaps she went directly to the house where Moti

works and gets laid and has joined the staff as Night Nurse
or something.

Kamala was rushed to the nursing home on the evening
of the twelfth of January. It was a false alarm but close to the
real thing. Mentally and physically exhausted, Bhola returned
home just before midnight. Kamala herself had first insisted
that she would be perfectly fine alone; later, she had accepted
the suggestion, originally mooted by her and subesquently,
telepathically routed through her mother, that Ayama spend
the night with her.

The phone rang after midnight. Bhola, undressing,
thinking that it was the hospital, rushed. 'Hello.'

'Nobody picks up your phone or what. I've been trying to
contact you all evening,' said a male voice familiarly in Hindi.

'Who the fuck is this in the middle of the night?' asked
Bhola, also in Hindi.

Moti? Bhola's mind seemed to move like limbs mired in
quicksand. After having practically vanished for thirteen years
without a trace, Moti all of a sudden wanted to meet him
urgently. 'Not tomorrow morning. I've to go to the hospital
and will probably be there all day.' He didn't even know
whether he was excited but he did need to stall for time. 'Is
all well? Is Titli with you?' She was. That was what they had
to talk about. They arranged a rendezvous at five in the
evening in the Jahanpanah City Public Gardens. Bhola
explained roughly where, on the path that led into the park
from its third gate. He didn't sleep a wink that night. He'd
gone to bed too late, he had had two Nescafés with his in-
laws at the nursing home, he was expectedly tense about
Kamala and then Moti's phonecall out of the blue totally
knocked out of his skull any residual drowsiness.

He was in no condition to jog the next morning and felt
even more out of sorts for not being able to. To think of going
for a run and to fix a meeting with a male lover from his past,
to dawdle over a pot of tea at home while his wife was in

hospital expecting a baby at any moment—were sinful and irresponsible acts, all of them. You're having my baby. The song—but he simply couldn't recall the singer's name, just his thyroid-deficient eyes and neverending forehead—then slipped into his skull and wouldn't go away. What the fuck did Moti want, he had asked himself irritably without pause in bed, tossing and turning amidst the sheets; and the imp within him had leered in response, Perhaps your body, and what you did a long time ago with your tongue and lips to his. At that thought, a dyke within him had crumbled and he had remembered Moti's limbs and physique all night long, engulfed by longing like the white waves of dawn leaping upon an abandoned lighthouse.

PICKMEUP

January 13, 1992. The city at dusk was cold, dead and still. The mist and winter dust shut out the world and seemed to claw at Bhola's throat as he waited on the third bench before the third gate in the Jahanpanah City Public Gardens. Moti was an hour late.

Despite his tracksuit, windcheater, mittens and woollen cap, Bhola felt the chill. He pressed his knees together and hugged himself to fight it. He had been drained by the events of the past twenty-four hours. He would have liked to jog, to warm up, to clear his head, to get himself going. After a few steps, however, his will had failed him.

The lamps of the gardens, looming phantoms in the gloom, had been switched on half an hour previously. Any moment now, worried Bhola, the guards would come around with their whistles to signal closing time. He observed his fellow citizens on the paved path before him. A middle-aged couple, both grey-haired and bespectacled, an old Sikh gentleman with dog, a jogger who flayed his arms about faster than he moved his feet. Bhola felt both tense and in low spirits and partly attributed his depression to sundown, to the human body too finely attuned to the passage of the day.

He smelt someone just behind the bench. Sweat, fear, garlic, soured milk, the drains, the stench of a beast of the city. He knew before he turned that Moti stood behind him. He rose. 'You're late. I'd given up,' he said in Hindi.

Moti wore a foam jacket and a shawl swathed round his head and the bottom half of his face. He panted lightly and exuded his stench like steam.

'Come with me,' continued Bhola. 'Follow me, if you wish.' He turned and began strolling towards the exit. He hoped that he wouldn't meet somebody he knew. He casually looked back when he reached the gate. Moti was nowhere behind him. Walkers, lovebird couples, tai-chi practitioners, joggers, pet owners, peanut vendors, lonely hearts moved past him and out of the gardens. Its paired lamps glowed like the protruding eyes of some enormous extra-terrestrial creature. Exasperation mounting, he scanned each passing face. He walked back to the bench that he had just vacated and found Moti on it, slumped like the sculpture of a tramp.

'What's the matter?' asked Bhola. 'There's nobody at home. It'll be nicer.' He reached out for Moti's hand, large, calloused and chilled. They ambled back to the gate together, practically hand in hand, Bhola uneasy at the idea that in the parklamp-lit dusk, someone would notice the obvious class differences between the two of them.

Moti's reek filled the car. Bhola rolled down his window. In the streetlight that bathed them through the windshield, he looked long at Moti, at the yellow eyes set wide apart, almond-shaped, bright like a cat's. He watched him reach out for the cigarettes and lighter above the dashboard, jerk his shawl down a fraction and light up. His face was fuller. He had grown a caterpillar of a moustache. As he pulled long and fiercely on the cigarette, Bhola watched its tip glow more brightly. Thirteen years ago, Moti would not have touched the packet without first asking him. Bhola looked at Moti's black and full lips and wondered how many lovers he had had in the intervening span of time and how many of them had been male.

The apartment was a ten-minute drive away. Bhola was tense with renewed expectation at the prospect of the evening, the ease with which it was falling into place. While driving, he forced himself to remember to be calm, to retain in his head his life's objective of attaining a state of mind akin to a deep, unruffled pool, focussed, impervious to the multiplicity of things. He liked the way Moti sat in the car, relaxed but ramrod straight, small of back wedged deep into the seat. Glancing down at his lap, Bhola noticed that beneath his shawl and foam jacket, Moti also wore a green checked coat. He was reminded of a film sequence in which Groucho Marx first doffed, then donned, several layers of clothing, cigar in mouth, yakking all the while.

They reached Jahanpanah Bagh—the residential colony—without mishap. For years, one of Bhola's several fears had been that he would be involved in a ghastly traffic accident just when he was in the company of someone whom he didn't want to be seen with.

'Tch.' His favourite parking place—underneath the mango tree—had been taken by the widow on the ground floor. Bitch. He pointed to the stairs. 'I'll go up first. We are on the first floor, the door on the right. It's maroon in colour. You can't miss it.' Moti gave no sign of having heard him. He continued to gaze out of the windshield and puff away at his second cigarette. Bhola wondered if he had become a little deaf. 'Get out of the car. I want to lock it.'

The parking area was crowded. Children skipped rope under a streetlamp. Out-of-shape neighbours—males in expensive tracksuits, women in decorous churidaar kurtas—played badminton on the cement courts. Maddeningly loud music emanated from the open windows of a second-floor apartment.

Bhola had pushed the key into the door of the staircase and, with Moti waiting and smoking behind him, was coaxing it to turn when the door of the ground floor apartment opened and neighbour Swaraj said, 'Good evening and congratulations! All well on every front?'

'Yes, thanks very much. Will there be a bonfire at the club tonight?'

Swaraj raised his eyebrows and shoulders to express his ignorance. 'Just back from your jog, is it?' He glanced curiously at the caped and hooded Moti.

'Yes. It was too cold to jog for long.'

Swaraj laughed meaninglessly and shuffled past till the gate of the lawn, to lean on it, spit his opinion of the world on the road and wait for a few minutes for some excitement to pass him by.

Bhola unlocked the door, motioned Moti in and bolted it behind them. Indoor warmth enveloped them like a fog at sea. 'Wait.' He switched on a light, mounted with aching limbs the winding, cement staircase, unlocked the door of the flat with a second key, entered, drew the curtains of the two windows and then switched on two lamps. He stood before Moti, placed his hands on his shoulders and gently pushed him down on the cane sofa. 'Sit.'

He gazed down at him. Reaching forward, he unwrapped Moti's shawl and flung it on the floor. In a single, smooth action, Moti stretched out, picked the shawl up, arose, moved sideways a step, neatly folded and placed it delicately on one of the cane armchairs that matched the sofa. He then absentmindedly scratched his balls and cleared his throat with sudden dreadful violence.

For the first time that evening, Bhola could look at Moti face to face in full bright light. He had broadened, filled out and grown a moustache—no doubt to compensate for the thinning hair on his scalp. Bhola searched the stranger's face for any remnant of his earlier attractiveness. His eyes appeared darker in roomlight, even tawny, startling when framed by the salt and pepper strands that flopped on forehead and red, tanned high cheekbones. His smile had once been gap-toothed and open, sunny and at the same time sensual, but Bhola hadn't seen it that evening.

'Home sweet home,' and then in Hindi, 'What'll you drink?'

Without replying, Moti sat down again on the sofa.

'Maybe some tea,' Bhola answered himself. On his way to the kitchen, he stopped to stoop to switch on a room heater. At the doorway of the drawing room, he paused to look back. From the glass table beside the sofa, Moti had picked up *The Complete Illustrated Guide To Yoga*. He held the book from under, as one would a brick while gauging its weight by hand. It sat on his palm with its back cover up. Abruptly, he opened it at random and pressed its sides back till the covers touched, quite as though he wished, while aiding the book itself to perform one of the contortions illustrated within it, to snap its spine. Bhola hurriedly returned to him, passing on the way the bookcase by the window. 'Here, let me give you another book to read,' and handed him Kamala's copy of Linda Goodman's *Sun Signs*.

When he entered with the tea tray, she lay in two halves on the floor. He put the tray down, picked up the pieces, placed them on the table and handed Moti his teamug. He sat down in the armchair and squeezed some lemon into his tea. Abruptly, leaning sideways, so did Moti. They sipped.

'Sugar?'

Moti nodded but wouldn't say stop. Bhola put four spoons into the proferred mug. Moti took a noisy sip, then clearly dissatisfied, poured some milk into his tea. Interestedly, Bhola leaned forward to watch the tea curdle. Moti continued to sip away. Either he didn't want to waste the tea or he didn't care, as though because of some earlier deprivation, he could eat and drink anything. Food was both precious and at the same time so basic that it didn't have to be refined.

Bhola finished his tea, shifted in his armchair and gazed silently for a time at Moti's face. 'Business before pleasure. Why did you phone me? Is it money?' Moti stared at him steadily and without blinking, like a cat. Bhola smiled teasingly and added, 'You know that you and your ladywife have always been very special to me.' In response, Moti picked up the pieces of Linda Goodman and continued to tear her limb from limb, chapter by chapter. Bhola watched for a while the strong swollen hands at work before asking—and with a lover's plaint in his voice—'Where have you been all these years? You made no effort to keep in touch.'

Without warning, Moti arched his head back and yawned like a feline, as though he wanted to engulf the room. The book lay in a dozen parts on the carpet around his feet, like slim volumes of verse without either jackets or covers.

'Will you drink some rum? It'll warm you up.'

'No. Just some water.'

'What rubbish. Have a rum. I'll have some anyway. A pickmeup.'

A frown creased Moti's forehead. He shook his head vigorously and repeated, 'No, just water.'

'Don't be shy. Have a rum to keep me company.'

After a pause, with elaborate reluctance, Moti agreed. Bhola stood up. 'I'll be back in a minute.' He arranged the tea mugs on the tray and picked it up.

'I need to go to the toilet.'

'Through that door, straight ahead, the door on your right.' Bhola hoped that Moti was going to piss and not shit and leave behind a disgusting mess in the loo and a broken flush handle or something. Serves me right for trying to descend once again to the level of the lumpen. You couldn't nestle up to one of them without having some of him or her rub off on you.

He returned from the kitchen with a jug of water and glasses on the same tray. He fetched a bottle of rum from the locked cupboard of the bedroom and poured out two drinks. He was sipping his when Moti came back, carrying his foam jacket in a bundle under his arm. Bhola noticed that the green checked coat was too long and loose for him. Moti placed the bundle of his jacket tidily atop his shawl on the cane armchair. Bhola gestured at his drink. Moti picked up the glass and downed it at one go. Immediately—but with elaborate casualness—as though he had shifted forward mainly to be more comfortable on his feet, he lifted up the bottle and filled more than half his glass with rum. He added a couple of inches of water and tossed off the drink once more without pausing. He then seemed to rock back gently on his heels and belched like an explosion in the petrified forests of the post-modern novel.

'After we finish, will you massage my back? It acts up sometimes because of too much jogging.'

Moti swivelled his head slowly and looked long at Bhola without speaking. His almond-shaped eyes had become heavy-lidded and red. He suddenly nodded and turned back for a refill. Bhola noticed again his large, fleshy hands around the glass and the neck of the bottle. Moti's sandals too were enormous, cracked and of cheap beige plastic. Bhola felt that what he dimly recalled having read somewhere was correct, that both one's true financial condition and the state of one's soul were exposed by one's footwear. He set down his drink and went to fetch from the kitchen a plastic bottle of mustard oil and from the cupboard in the second bedroom the reserve blanket. He spread the blanket out on the carpet, flung down upon it a few cushions and looked a little peevishly at Moti fixing himself a fourth drink. 'Well, we can start whenever you're ready.' He then began to take off his clothes.

He lay down naked and shivering on the blanket. For a normal person, thought Bhola, Moti's intake would amount to some seven pegs in fifteen minutes. 'Can you hurry up a bit? I'm cold and waiting.'

Moti neither glanced at him nor gave any sign that he'd heard. He finished his drink, lightly chucked his glass on to the cane sofa and came and stood over Bhola.

'What do you want?' he asked, not very politely.

'I want you to take off your clothes, relax and massage me. Don't worry about money, I'll pay you whatever you need.' Bhola reached out and squeezed Moti's calf through his trouser leg. Moti moved back a step, took off his coat and heaved it carelessly on the sofa. It landed on the recumbent empty glass. He then sat down on his haunches beside Bhola.

'More. Like we used to. Take off all your clothes like me. There's only us.'

'And God.'

'He never says a word.'

Moti paused irresolutely. 'Please,' urged Bhola, 'I won't feel comfortable if you keep your clothes on.'

Shyly as of old, looking away from Bhola at the patterns on the curtains, Moti unbuckled his belt and stripped off his trousers. His legs were thin, dark and hairy and emerged like ink cartridges from his long, striped string drawers. Beneath his shirt, he wore a vest and an orange half-sleeve sweater. He peeled off the sweater and stepped forward to squat once more alongside Bhola. Beneath the cotton, Moti's paunch recalled for Bhola the enormous brass pot in which a cigarette-wala keeps his paan leaves immersed in water. In a flash, he felt tired, cheated, unaroused and low.

'No, everything. Your vest and undies too.' He dimly heard through the shut windows the din of the neighbour's Punjabo-Hindi rap music.

Moti frowned. 'No. I haven't liked being completely naked before somebody else for a long time.'

'That's new. Surely when you try and fuck?'

'It's always dark. Anyway, we always keep some of our clothes on.'

Sighing with exasperation and wondering who the we referred to, Bhola sat up and stretched out his hand for Moti's vest. Moti didn't protest as Bhola prised it up and off. Moti continued to gaze down demurely, at the carpet between his thighs. He had bloated up, become hairy and fat. He had almost a woman's breasts but with thick down on them. Bhola tugged at his drawers. 'Untie them before I tear them off.' Moti, depressed, did and stepped out of them. His pubis was shaved, his penis a black peanut. In its foreskin was embedded a golden ring; a faded red string led away from it only to lose its way under the overhanging flab of his abdomen.

Bhola sighed and lay down again. He wanted Moti to leave so that he could sleep and wake up in another world. 'Start with the legs. Massage always upward, towards the heart.' He waited with anticipation as Moti unscrewed the cap of the bottle and poured out a palmful of mustard oil. He began with Bhola's left calf. His hands were cold. Bhola stared at his masseur's face but Moti kept his eyes down. On his exhalations wafted to Bhola's nostrils the smell of rum.

'You look quite unhappy.'

Moti's brow furrowed. 'I don't like what we're doing.'

'Since when? You know, you've never told me, when you were younger, whom did you lose your virginity to?'

'To cattle.' Moti's hands began to rub Bhola's skin more vigorously. 'In our village, most of the boys grew up fucking cattle.'

'Oh I see. And the girls?'

Moti glanced disapprovingly at him for a second but did not reply.

'I was given to understand that one's foreskin simply falls off when one fucks cattle.' He caressed the inside of Moti's thigh with the sole of his foot. 'I must confess that even at the age of thirty-three, I don't quite know how one goes about fucking cattle. I mean, exactly where are the holes and so on. All that I can recall is—beneath the tail—a sort of open cabbage made out of cowdung. I prefer my tastes. When I was younger, what I longed for most was to be invisible.'

Bhola would have been the first to admit that as a longing, it had not been original. He very much doubted whether anyone had any genuinely original longing. Even a desire to sleep with cattle was not original. He himself had ached for years to turn invisible and slip into a lumpen household, to see how, when and where the lower orders had sex, whether they enjoyed it, how hurried it was and how he could join them.

He had always liked Moti for being taciturn, for keeping to himself. Thirteen years ago, he had been more or less familiar with the internal contours of Moti's skull, with the string of petty economic, personal and social tragedies that had helped to mould his mind. He had found Moti attractive as a physique, depressing as an individual and interesting as a type—rootless, totally adrift, mentally dislocated, illiterate, the quintessential constituent of a mob, waiting to be leavened by some demagogue, rabblerouser or saint.

Interrupting the masseur in mid-stroke, Bhola heaved himself up, turned right round and sitting crosslegged, leaned forward away from Moti. 'I'm cold. Please do my back.' In a few moments, Moti slapped some cold oil on his shoulder blades. 'As a rule, I love the cold, the winter. And you?'

Moti emitted in reply a sort of it-makes-no-difference-to-me grunt.

'W-h-i-i-i-i-t-e Christmas,' warbled Bhola and annotated for himself in classroom Hindi, 'By the grace of almighty God, not a single yellow, brown or black creature has been spotted this Noel.' He groped behind him for Moti's genitals. 'A cold peanut is best for winter.'

Moti frowned disapprovingly. 'I am slow to rise.' A tint of pride then cleared his features. 'I am now strong in my loins. I can hold on for hours. The longer one can retain oneself, the stronger one is morally.'

Bhola melted at the masculinity of the boast. He wanted to hear more to be aroused. 'Can you now enter a woman? And when inside and pumping away, how long can you hold on then?'

Moti didn't deign to restrict himself to a time limit. He

began lustily to knead the bicycle tyre of fat around Bhola's waist. The phone in the dining room rang, shattering their privacy. Moti stopped massaging. Bhola was in two minds about answering it but finally decided to for the reason that it could well be the hospital. He halted at the door when he realized that he was naked and that the curtains weren't drawn across the dining room windows. He turned back to see Moti bent over the neat pile of his clothes on the cane armchair. He picked up Moti's underwear from the floor and—his skin tingling—put it on. Enkindled by the reek of tobacco and sweat from the orange sweater, he had wheeled about to the door with it over his head when the phone stopped ringing. Tch. He slewed around to return to the blanket on the floor. He noticed then that Moti had taken out from the innards of his foam jacket what looked intriguingly like a revolver in one hand and a knife in the other and with furrowed brow was regarding them in turn. Perhaps they were toys. The phone began again.

The jacket now formed an untidy mound on the chair. Placing the knife beside it, Moti burrowed in it elbow deep with his left hand to retrieve the cigarettes—Bhola's—that he had pocketed while getting out of the car. Straightening and turning, he then lifted his arm and took aim at his own orange sweater on Bhola's chest.

'I think that you're laughing at me,' he muttered expressionlessly.

Bhola began physically to feel smaller, as though he had instantly shrunk just a little. 'The phone,' he whispered.

'Give me back my clothes.'

Altogether stripped of desire, Bhola shed Moti's sweater and underwear, picked and balled them up and tossed them weakly at the gun. They fell at Moti's feet. It was horrible that the mouth of the revolver, held by a naked man, should resemble a penis about to spit. They all had names, he recalled from the books of his past. Luger, Beretta, Colt.

Didn't India make revolvers of its own? Perhaps if he could recall one Indian gun name.

Instead, out of the blue, flashed into his mind without bidding an incident of twenty years ago. Then a boy of thirteen madly interested in General Knowledge, he had one drowsy afternoon telephoned Special Information at 176 to ask what the bore of the Smith and Wesson revolver measured. How long it had taken him to get through and how much longer to explain his question to the female operator who had sounded as though she had been chomping on peanuts, knitting and chatting all at the same time. She had however been a good-natured soul and had clarified, with giggles of genuine mirth, that Special Information could only tell him whether the new moon had officially been spotted for a festival, which train was running how many hours late and when the university examination results would be declared. Special Information was not, she had elaborated, a knowledge bank for the naive.

Innocent, practically mentally retarded in some respects, even at the age of thirty-three, Bhola did not understand either how human beings killed one another without sufficient cause or why millions of people on earth hated others on the basis of colour, religion and race to the point of slaughtering them. The evidence of man's savagery and ferocity that he constantly came across in books, the newspapers and on TV always made him feel odd, incomplete, as though there were some basic things about life—as fundamental as eating, sleeping, laughing and sex—about which he hadn't been told. If other human beings were in any way like him, it was inconceivable that anyone should consciously torment somebody else. Everyone would touch somebody else only out of affection or desire and would otherwise leave him or her alone.

'I'm cold,' he murmured almost to himself. 'I'll just put something on.' He registered dimly that the phone continued to ring. Stealing a glance at Moti's face, he moved sideways towards his clothes, stumbled over the heater and fell.

'You are very dirty.' Moti shut his eyes, frowned and jerked his head from side to side as though to deny a nightmare. 'How can I ask you to tie me a new sacred cord when you are so dirty?'

Keep them talking. Bhola remembered from the thrillers that he had read that it was vital to engross armed lunatics in conversation. His mind, though, was white with fear and incomprehension. He wasn't certain whether Moti had the guts and skill to fire. He was stung too by the loathing in the other's voice. 'Yes, I know that I'm dirty but so are you. I mean we all are.'

'Not me.' Moti's eyes gleamed in disagreement. 'Not me, you understand?' The snout of the gun stirred a little like a phallus. 'All those days for years when she used to go over to do the housework in your room.' He again jerked his head in a refusal to accept the knowledge of the wickedness of one of his wife's trusted clients. 'You're very dirty.' He glared at Bhola, not liking the expression of awed, near-amused disbelief on his face. 'First my wife, then me, sometimes on the same day with the same lips.'

However could the poor sod not have known? Bhola suddenly laughed. He didn't mean to, he certainly didn't find the situation comic, but he felt abruptly and explosively happy to find, so unexpectedly, innocence at the heart of things. Startled, Moti fired. Bhola felt in his chest the thud of the bullet and the most searing, unimaginable pain that he had ever experienced in his life.

TIE ME DOWN

Grey, swirling. Large hazy spots, yellow and red, like traffic lights in heavy fog. An indistinct sense of having gone astray in the inside of his own brain. A yellowish, thick taste in his mouth. His tongue heavy, unresponsive like an exhausted and pregnant beast. Lips dry, cracked. Thud thud. Thud thud, neverending the swollen, waterlogged drum in his skull.

A tubelight above the drawn curtains. A woman's face wan with worry. He knew who it was even though he couldn't remember her name.

The crash bang thwack from somewhere of a movie on TV. Off-white walls. White bandages on his chest. A glucose drip in his left arm. Lips dry, cracked. He thought that he heard himself groan for water but nobody responded. He shut his eyes once again.

Black save for the orange night light above the door. It didn't soothe at all, more like a warning. He wanted to scratch his back but found that he couldn't will himself to move. His head had been filled with soft, leaden wool. What he wished to do most was droop.

The next time that he saw Anin, it was noon and noisy. The sounds that registered were first that of the hum of a vacuum cleaner in the corridor and next of nurses chatting away in Malayalam. Some sun ventured in through the windows; all that he could see of the outside world without moving his head were some leafless branches against an uncertain sky. Drugged and exhausted, he waited for someone to discover that he was awake.

'You have a bullet in your chest.' Anin seemed to be crying and smiling at the same time.

'Where?' asked Bhola, looking down at the bandages. He wanted to stretch out his hand for hers but didn't know how to. His voice sounded like a recorded murmur being played back at a slower speed.

'Somewhere above or behind your collarbone.'

'Since when?'

'Monday evening.'

He looked at her tired eyes. 'And today is?'

'Wednesday.'

On the table beside the window, resplendent tulips in a vase. Bouquets under polythene heaped up in an armchair.

'How are Kamala and the baby?'

'Fine fine. They'll be going home tomorrow, I think.'

A nurse bustled in, a herald for the doctor on his rounds.

The policeman was Inspector Mudaliar of the Criminal Investigation Department. He was short, dark, bespectacled and dogged. 'If you aren't too tired, sir, why don't you tell me in your own words exactly what happened?' He spoke a sort of blend of English and Hindi that sounded like Tamil.

Bhola wondered where his watch was. Life was not unattractive without one, when one didn't know whether it was eleven-thirty in the morning or four in the afternoon.

'Sure, whatever I can remember.' Speaking and breathing with a bandaged chest was not easy. Each inhalation was short and inadequate and hurt. 'On Monday, at about five in the evening, I had driven down to the Jahanpanah City Public Gardens for my daily jog. I usually run in the mornings but on Monday—' He paused because all of a sudden, he felt mentally too tired to speak. Deep in a low chair beside the hospital bed, the Inspector waited impassively for him to pick up the thread again. 'Monday had been an Optional Holiday because of something—Makar Sankranti, I think. My wife was in hospital having a baby—our baby. I mean, I became a father last Monday. Ridiculous, at my age. I'd returned from the hospital at about two in the afternoon. I'd watched the infant being born and so I thought I'd go for a celebratory jog.' He shut his eyes, all at once nauseous with weakness.

He felt again that tremendous, breathtaking blow in his chest. He needed to slow down, to sift through things to see what he could conceal.

The birth of his daughter had till that point of his life been its most momentous event. Dr Punchkuian, a gynaecologist with modern ideas, had been rather keen that Bhola the father witness the childbirth. 'Bonding,' she had elaborated. She had a pleasant manner.

'I'll probably be more shaken than stirred,' Bhola had murmured in response.

In the delivery room, he, fascinated, had watched Kamala his wife, usually so reserved, turn into a howling, gasping and moaning unknown, and had felt the doctor and her assistants, strangers all, become intimate in the shared warmth of the event. For almost an hour, Dr Punchkuian had urged her on, calmly, rhythmically and with professional tenderness. With the hands of a potter, she had seemed to mould the contours of Kamala's stomach. 'No.' 'Please.' 'God.' 'I—'

'Can you see the head?'

For close to an hour, Bhola had been reluctant to blink for fear of missing out on a second of the process. 'Push.' Kneading. 'Push.' Brutal heaving. The gynae's hands all over Kamala's stomach like a geographer's on a globe. 'Yes. Now.'

During the pauses, Bhola had moved up once or twice to the bed to stroke Kamala's forehead and whisper words of encouragement—provide the noises off, as it were. The rhythm of the give-and-take between doctor and mother-to-be had slowly picked up speed. A coach coaxing his athlete to peak. 'Okay. Steady. Now! Push! Push!' At last, incredible fountains of blood as climax. Then tiny, wrinkled, ugly, all covered in slime and blood, a miracle, mewling like a cat. He had felt jealous, had wanted desperately to be in Kamala's position to feel all of it—the weight, the agony, the easing, the emptiness, the indescribable exhaustion, the achievement.

He had helped give their daughter her first bath. 'Hold her firmly, baba,' had ordered the nurse, a bully, 'as you would a fish.' No chin, he had commented to himself as he had fallen in love with the infant. His dreams of dispossession were going to go out of the window. There was a time to be born and a time to die and a time to hang around in the interim, tied down and wondering.

Bhanu, his elder brother, handed Bhola the phone. 'Here, speak to Kamala.'

Even bending an arm to hold a receiver against an ear sent stabs through his chest. 'Markandeya?'

'Hi hi. How are things?' She sounded weak, warped and distant.

'Fine. Much better. Almost clearheaded. And you? And Baby?'

'Fine. Fagged out but fine. My father went to see you this morning but you were asleep.'

'Ah. Don't you get out and go home today?'

'Yes, I think so, this evening.' He then heard a smile in her voice. 'She looks like you.'

Though physically exhausted, in pain, dulled and drugged, Bhola, when alone in the late evenings or at night, or when he shut his eyes out of tiredness, could remember every second of the encounter with Moti. He had stared at the barrel of the gun and known seconds before the event that he was going to be shot. Again and again he felt the sledge-hammer thwack of the bullet in his chest. He recalled distinctly the pact that he had made with God, his conscience, an instant before Moti had pulled the trigger. If I get out of this alive, I'll be good and straight hereafter. His bowels had seemed to churn with contrition.

From his hospital bed the following morning, he smiled at Kamala's haggard, concerned face. With perfect clarity, he saw that nothing in this world or the next could compare with being alive, with having teetered on and yet not tumbled off the edge. For that, he would have to remember forever to be grateful. When next he looked at her, his eyes had filled with tears.

She didn't stay long. She'd fed the baby and left her with her mother and the maid. They didn't speak much but the silence was cordial. For several reasons, she posed no questions about the events of Monday evening. She didn't particularly want to know. She was too tired out by the childbirth. There was only so much that she could handle at one moment in time. It was enough that he was alive.

Inspector Mudaliar returned at the end of visiting hours.

'I couldn't jog for more than a few steps. I felt more dead than alive. I sat down on a bench. I recall that a man came up to ask me for a light for his cigarette. He turned out to be someone—a coincidence—that I'd briefly known some thirteen-fourteen years ago during my college days at M.K.M.Z.A.P. He used to be the Assistant to the doctor whom I used to visit when I needed to. But he must have left his service more than a decade ago. The doctor himself died last month—last year.' Bhola paused to see whether he needed to continue. He had an impression from the Inspector's composure and impassivity that it might not be necessary for him to speak sense, that he could keep quiet, conserve his strength and that the policeman would still arrive at the right conclusions. 'Moti offered me a cigarette too. I accepted. I don't usually smoke but I wanted to celebrate in some way my daughter's birth.' His head began to throb energetically.

Cigarette smoking, like a couple of other things, had seldom failed to make him feel weak and guilty. He had often ratiocinated that nicotine lowered his mental guard and therefore caused unpleasant things to happen to him. To counterbalance his guilt, while on cigarettes, he had tried to be nicer than ever with others, continuously considerate. The posing had tired him out. It had made him feel virtuous but secretly dull and passively unhappy. On the many occasions that he had stopped smoking and drinking, he had felt fit but irritable, and aggressively unhappy.

'An interesting recovery,' commented Dr Ratra, long-nosed, pale with stress, mumbling softly to his own moustache, seemingly ready to move on from Bhola's bed even before he had fully stopped in front of it.

'I understand, Doctor, that the bullet is still there inside me, somewhere behind my collarbone.'

The doctor looked slowly and uncertainly up from the report in his hand to the face of the nearest assistant. He seemed unused to patients posing questions about themselves directly to him. 'Once you recover, you won't feel it at all and the muscle will heal nicely over it,' answered the tall nurse who headed the doctor's retinue. She was fleshy, fair and pretty and appeared, by her abrupt, jerky movements, to be attached by an invisible cord to the rear loops of the doctor's belt.

'I don't want it.'

Subdued merriment rippled through the group. 'Of course

you don't,' smiled the doctor at the X-ray that an assistant handed him. 'But no surgeon wants to perform an unnecessary operation. You get my point?'

Roses, tulips, lilies, blue somethings that Kamala clarified were orchids that had been sent by Francesca. Bhola was not sure either whether he had ever seen orchids before or whether they were grown in India. No orchids for Miss Blandish. The flesh of the orchid. With the flowers, visitors from some police organization under his father-in-law, a couple of badminton-loving neighbours, Kamala's friends, Dosto who had got in that morning from Hong Kong. To all, Bhola gave the impression that his memory continued to be a bit fuzzy. To Anin and Dosto—the second fatter, more venal and venturesome—he omitted to mention that the man with the gun had been a visitant from their common past.

Inspector Mudaliar was present in the room at nine-thirty the next morning. Bhola pretended to be asleep till eleven.

'I haven't seen my watch since I came to. Does someone have it? Perhaps Moti took it. Unlikely though, since it was quite ordinary.' He curled his lip and raised his eyebrows to express a shrug of the shoulders. 'In the gardens, Moti asked me flat out whether we could chat about old times over a cup of tea. There hadn't been any old times of course but it appeared to me from his demeanour that he was desperately hungry and broke and wanted somebody to feed him. I agreed because I didn't want to say no to anybody that evening. I couldn't, I was so exhaustedly content.'

Not entirely untrue. On the evening of January 13, Bhola had been too exhaustedly content to run. Had he managed to jog, he would have felt fitter and more heterosexual, more in control of himself.

'I proposed that we go back home because I had no money with me in the park. Quite naturally since I had left the apartment with the intention of jogging and not of buying someone his dinner. Once indoors, he somehow changed and became more sure of himself. We had tea at first. He then began belching away and prowling about the house. How much money can you lend me? he asked. Well, how much do you want? Ten thousand rupees. Ten thousand rupees! Well, okay, as much as you can spare. I don't think I can part with more than fifty. He found the alcohol that we keep in the bedroom. I asked him then to stop snooping around. He didn't like it.'

The tubelight above the windows suddenly began to blink, on-off, on-off, distracting Bhola from his fabrications. He needed to concentrate even though Inspector Mudaliar behind his spectacles looked as though he was daydreaming nonstop about some steamy stripper in a highway bar in Madras. Bhola would have preferred, in place of the tubelight, the red, illumined EXIT sign of an old-fashioned cinema house or one that winked with the throb of a heartbeat, WAY OF ESCAPE, WAY OF ESCAPE. As a child and even as a young adolescent, in a movie theatre, he had usually watched more often the glowing EXIT signs than the film. It, the picture, had almost always been frighteningly loud and generally incomprehensible and in contrast the EXIT signs bewitching. He hazily recalled that he had often been tense that the signs would be switched off when he wasn't looking or even that they would change in a wink to EVIL or ENTER—but only when his attention was elsewhere and not, never, if he kept an eye on them.

He sat up so that the bandages could be changed. He was scared as the layers of lint began to be peeled off. The last couple hurt. 'Can I get a hand mirror so that I can see what the wound looks like?' The Malayali nurse of the brisk movements didn't seem to hear his request. He gave up. After she had removed the dressing completely, she left the room without a word. She returned a few moments later with a vanity mirror in a pink plastic frame. 'Thank you, sister.'

The scar was huge and dramatically ugly, puffed up, purplish yellow, located just where the collarbone met the muscle of the neck, pulpy, like the lips of a bovine vagina. Medical science however was rather pleased with it. 'Near perfect. You can probably go home tomorrow,' announced a bespectacled, moustached male whom Bhola hadn't noticed before.

'I don't *feel* near perfect. When I try to turn my neck, it in fact hurts like hell.'

'Naturally. There aren't any bullets in heaven.'

Bhola's father-in-law strode into the room just when Inspector Mudaliar had taken off his spectacles to clean them with his handkerchief. He was therefore slow to recognize the visitor. He heard him greet Bhola, put on his spectacles, squawked mutedly in surprise, scrambled to his feet, boomed his boots on the floor and rocketed his forearm to his forehead in a high-tension salute. Bhola's father-in-law nodded and smiled briefly in response.

'Much better, thanks. I learnt this morning that I might be discharged tomorrow.' Bhola noted that Inspector Mudaliar continued to stand at attention, gazing straight ahead at nothing. 'Home sweet home. Will Inspector Mudaliar follow me there?'

'Probably.' Bhola's father-in-law unhurriedly lowered himself into an armchair and waved at the Inspector to sit down. 'How is it going, Mudaliar? Pieces falling into place? Or is our theory all falling to pieces?'

In reply, the subordinate gurgled something vaguely encouraging.

'What's the theory?'

Bhola's father-in-law, pale, soft-spoken, civil, bespectacled, slim, an industrious walker, more godfearing than religious, was humbly ashamed of his baldness. He possessed the unpredictable gentility of a snake. The education of the spirit was an important issue with him and a recurring theme in his conversations with everybody. 'Like the typical anglophone educated man of your time, you are practically an atheist, certainly an agnostic. Why?'—a typical parley from his side would run—'Why is it that education inevitably encourages the growth of an underripe rationalism that scoffs at religion? Why can't we hear it said of someone, "He became educated and therefore began to believe in God?"' Bhola disliked being alone with him.

He smiled briefly and humorlessly at his son-in-law. 'The theory is almost a fact. Even though you might have known him years ago, the man who shot at you very likely is an ex-police constable who has killed at least once before. Last June, he knifed a Station House Officer whose gun he then stole. A .22. That's why Mudaliar here would be very keen to look at the bullet that the doctors prefer remains tucked away in your sternocleido mastoid. It does look like a .22 though from the X-rays.' Bhola gulped as though trying to dislodge the slug in his neck.

From the tiny diary in his shirt pocket, Inspector Mudaliar took out a much-folded sheet of paper that seemed to be falling apart at its creases. He opened it out carefully and tried to show it to Bhola's father-in-law but reading on his superior officer's face a disinclination to be associated with a document so stained and untidy, changed tack in midair and arrived with it in one smooth movement under Bhola's nose. It was a xerox of an ancient official form, completely illegible and faded. The original had had a much-stamped-on photograph affixed to its top right-hand corner; in the smudged, excessively blackened photocopy, one could just about tell that the snapshot represented some sort of human being. 'Yes, that does look like Moti,' declared Bhola at once with a note of finality, 'he appears to have changed his name, though, for his life as a constable.'

There still remained several unanswered questions but Bhola was ready for at least some of them.

'You were found naked?'

'After I had ticked Moti off for snooping around, I went to the bedroom to change. I'd just taken off my tracksuit when he opened the door and walked in with his gun. He asked me to shed my underclothes as well.'

In the new world in which he found himself, the questions seemed to reach him as through a colour filter. His sense of being blessed, of having been reborn—a feeling that coalesced the wonders of both his resurrection and his fatherhood— tinted all that was said to him.

'When did you drink?'

'I can't remember, not precisely. I know that he had many drinks and at some point insisted that I drink too.'

'When was the last time that you saw him, that is, before January 13?'

'Years ago, I should imagine. Not after I finished my graduation in 1979.'

'Would he have known your address?'

'Our meeting in the Jahanpanah Gardens was a coincidence, I think. He just emerged out of the dusk to ask me for a light for his cigarette.'

'Frankly, you can do what you want,' advised Dr Ratra on Saturday morning, 'Cut your toenails, stand on your head, climb a tree. Your body itself will be the best judge. Don't be intimidated by these bandages. Think of them as an extra vest to keep you warm. I shall see you next week.'

Stepping out of the hospital into mild January sunshine felt heavenly. Conscious of a faint dizziness, Bhola treaded carefully. For the first time in his life, he understood and sympathized with those who on momentous occasions kiss the ground that they stride on. His father-in-law had sent him an Ambassdor car, a driver and an aide. The humans saluted him. He was tired by the time that he reclined in the back seat. Breathe deep, he advised himself, with your abdomen, like a child. Remember that you can reach anywhere if you pace yourself. The area around the wound felt hot and sticky. He tried to wriggle his shoulders a fraction. It hurt appreciably. He felt as though he had become a condensed article in the *Reader's Digest*.

Outside the gates of the hospital, the city hit him like a slap. He'd forgotten in five days how noisy, crowded and ugly it was. At the traffic lights just beyond the gates, the car stopped beside a blackened, burnt-out shell of a Metropolitan Transport bus. A riot, he presumed—some display of public disaffection with the way the world worked, perhaps even with the rotten good luck with which he had gotten away with his life. Its windows had been shattered, parts of its body smashed, its tyres burst, its seats broken and dismantled. One long bench even dangled out from a jagged hole to the right and rear of the vehicle, some six feet away from his nose. He could read the anti-terrorist advice stencilled on its back:

1) LOOK BENEATH YOUR SEAT

2) DO YOU SEE A BOMB?

3) NOT TO PANIC

4) RAISE ALARM

5) WIN TAX-EXEMPT AWARD

An urchin on heroin at the car window tried to sell him a box of paper tissues for twenty-five rupees, and five boxes for a hundred. The aide in the front seat snarled at the boy both to disappear and to join the minimum-wage labour force somewhere far away. As the lights turned green and the car tried to inch forward, honking more than budging, the rates for the paper tissues began to plummet. Six boxes for a hundred, saab. Eight. Ten. Ten boxes for a hundred, saab. Fuck your mother.

Ayama—ageing, maternal, matriarchal, handsome, self-contained—opened the door of the apartment. There were tears in her eyes. Bhola smiled at her, both surprised and touched and walked in. The familiar drawing room, the cane armchairs, *The Complete Illustrated Guide To Yoga* on the glass table, the room heater, brought back with a thud the evening with Moti. He paused for a moment to steady himself.

'Where's the carpet?'

'The police took it away.'

Kamala, cigarette in hand, met him at the door to the dining room. They hugged gently. He lightly squeezed her upper arm through her kurta.

'I wanted so to go over to the hospital this morning.'

He waved her good intentions away. 'How are things?' He trailed her to their bedroom. She gestured with her cigarette hand at the crib beside the bed. Bhola walked over and lifted the mosquito net. 'I thought that they didn't have any hair at birth.' He smiled at the little that he could see of the baby amidst the covers and the headgear.

'She looks like you.'

'I think that I'll have a cigarette in celebration.'

Civility of manner and an on-off addiciton to tobacco were two of the few things that Kamala shared with her husband.

She smoked more though, sometimes as many as ten a day. She was the one who, at certain moments in the day—in the loo in the morning, for example—simply couldn't do without a cigarette. Both of them would remember for years thereafter an incident from one of the first few months of their marriage. On a weekday, early in the morning, both had wanted to use the toilet (different toilets, it should be clarified) and then discovered that there remained only one cigarette in the entire apartment.

'I'll go out and buy a packet.'

'No kiosk around here opens before eight.'

'We can snap it into two. You smoke the part with the filter.'

'That's no fun. We need a full cigarette each.'

'Thy need is greater. Take it.'

'And you?' He was a little taken aback that she had not demurred.

'With a ballpoint pen in my mouth, I'll make do with reflecting on the conquest of mind over matter.'

Tired and queasy he felt; nevertheless, he made himself a pot of tea. He had missed decent tea at the hospital. He felt happy to be back but at the same time tense and depressed about picking up again the pieces of his old life. Four spoons of top-notch Darjeeling tea—two of Flowery Orange Pekoe, one of Champagne, one of Mist Queen. They all tasted the same. Fresh water, boiled on the gas stove and not in the electric kettle. Taken off the fire just before boiling point and poured from a height of not less than six inches above the pot. Let it brew under an old tea cozy for seven minutes. A maximum of four quality cups a day after day after day for fifteen years while outside, the good life had quietly passed him by.

'My mother wants to drop by and actually stay with us for a few days to help with Baby. Mindful of your sensitivities, I

said, no, thanks, I'd manage with Ayama. My mother was
upset but in my state, I don't think that I'd have been able
to stand her nitpicking while going without smoking for days
on end. What do you think of Karuna for a name?'

'Terrible. Is it because of K? Kamala, Kaushalya and
Karuna? O God and your mother Krishna. Who suggested it?'

'She did but I quite like it.'

Face to face at the dining table across the tea things.

'You need to shave.'

'It hurts when I pull at and stretch my skin. I could grow
a beard. Certainly simpler.'

'No-o, I think. No.'

'In these past few days, I really haven't spent much time
thinking about my face and what I look like. A few inches
higher and the bullet would have turned it into bloody
vomit.'

Her face dimmed. She looked away at the Dances of
India calendar on the wall. He was sorry for having ruined the
intimacy of the moment but didn't much feel like expressing
regret. He pushed a tea cup across to her.

'My parents are in any case going to stop by to help,
harass and boss over everybody. Would you like to sleep
alone for a few days in the other bedroom? Baby can be
nightmarish sometimes.'

Bhola smiled but said nothing because he hadn't been
much listening. Pouring himself out his second cup of tea, he
marvelled again at how much he had missed it in hospital. In
bed recuperating, characteristically, he had thought of the
little things and not of the big. Think of the little things and
the big would take care of themselves? More likely that he
was incapable of thinking of the big things. Darjeeling tea,
yes, but what of ruminating on time, life, space, the universe,
biorhythms, purpose? 'Tis the small drops of water that make
up a bucket? No quotation could possibly have bucket in it.

He had always been irritated by 'tis. A pity she's a whore.
Tits the small drops of water that make up a bucket; surely
he thought of the little things—titties then—even at the age
of thirty plus because he was retarded.

How else could he explain that he had noticed pretty
early in his marriage that his parents-in-law usually contrived
to drop in round about mealtimes and departed only after
eating? It should be the maids-class, shouldn't it, the Ayamas,
that should think of such little things. Perhaps only when one
was physically, mentally and emotionally secure and snug did
one move on to the big.

'All three of us are going to sleep badly,' continued
Kamala, 'for the next few days. I'd thought that you might
like to be alone so that you can rest.'

'I've had enough of sleeping alone.'

Even the most unintended and indirect of sexual remarks
made Kamala uncomfortable. She sipped her tea and changed
the subject. 'You were of course in the news. My parents
have kept the clippings.'

'Aren't they going to go to the temple to thank Lord
Shiva Naipaul that I'm still alive? He—for lack of more
accurate identification—was with me. Had he not been, I
wouldn't be here.'

Slowly he unpacked and put his things away in the large,
plain, wooden chest that he used as a cupboard. Kamala and
he had had separate storage spaces from the beginning.
Ayama had packed the bag for him and had also put in his
only dark suit. 'How thoughtful of her,' he murmured to
himself, 'just in case I had torn off the glucose drip and
sneaked out of bed and the hospital to boogie, bleeding, with
some fashion designers.'

He was exhausted. Whenever he felt more tired, the
memories of Moti with the gun and of the excruciating jolt to

his chest seemed to gain ground against the efforts of his will to keep his bogeys at bay. Moti crouched on the edge of his consciousness like a calm and watchful beast, waiting only for the victim's defences to waver. Bhola lay down carefully on their double bed and repeated to himself that since he had been blessed with a second life, he must strive to be worthy of it, to find out what matters most, what comes second after the gift of life. God, that is to say, one's conscience, one's tranquil mind, would know the answers. One would have to be prepared to listen, though, to peel away the unnecessary questions.

One couldn't tell whether they were unnecessary until one had asked them. Time pointed out the answers to most of them. For want of belief and guidance on what constitutes the good life, Bhola, like a million others before him, had come to search Time's passage, the haphazard fall of events, for presaging signs. If X happens, then it indicates that Y (quite unconnected with X—that is to say, they *might* be connected but he for the moment didn't see how) too will happen. If that green light doesn't turn amber before my car reaches it, then I can go ahead and make a pass at the servant girl next door. If my wife gives birth without mishap to a normal infant, then I can cruise for entertainment this evening in the gardens. Were he to be asked how he could organize his life on principles so unscientific, he would have retorted that being retarded, he didn't know of any better. Some of the great confessions of the world were memorable because their utterers too had honestly admitted to being retarded, a few steps behind their time. Give me chastity, but only not yet.

One's notion of the good life partly depended of course on one's religious upbringing. Bhola had had none. He had spent eleven pleasant years in his Jesuit school playing cricket and lusting after diverse male and female teachers. He was Hindu by birth certificate and according to his father, a

Brahmin to his toenails. He himself couldn't have cared less. For him, godhead was mercurial and defined entirely by one's mood. God was a nice guy on one's good days and an absolute devil on Mondays. He was quite willing to pardon one for one's transgressions and everready to lengthen the rope that He had given out to His children. After each infidelity, each misdemeanour, Bhola's initial panic slowly, as the seconds ticked away, relaxed into relief—yet God has not said a word!—and then mellowed into a belief that the misdeed had never been judged as wrong because God had been with him all the time—perched on his shoulder, as it were, watching him throughout the process of its commitment, even guiding him here and there, or else however could he have enjoyed it so much?

To be nearly killed is the price that one pays for all the fun that one's been having. After all, it could have been worse. One dutifully thanked God that one was still alive. At times in the last few days in hospital, when he had ceased for the moment to feel contrite, it had seemed to him that he bowed his head not to acknowledge but to ride the punishment, to conserve himself so as to bounce back, not so much repentant as heedless, forgetful. Finally, all that had happened, he would then reason with himself, was that because of the bullet in his neck, he had gained mass by a few grammes. That would have to be taken into account in his future programmes of weight loss.

All is illusion. All is vanity. One needed to adopt the appropriate philosophical and religious approach to things. Then ethical questions of right and wrong, particularly those that concerned sexual peccadilloes and marital infidelity, shrivelled up to their correct size.

Bhola was woken up from his catnap by a sound that he took some seconds to identify. He gulped down the saliva that had accumulated in his gorge. It hurt. As always when he swallowed spit, he recalled Borkar the shaman holding forth on the theory that spittle, sexually such a potent bodily excretion, was particularly susceptible to contamination by action and thoughts. Miasmic vapours and toxic fluids were constantly being generated within the cavern of the mouth because all thoughts driven from the mind took shelter there. The first long step towards transcendental sex therefore was to vacuum up the inside of one's head. The sound that had tweaked him up out of sleep was like the whine of an enervated toy, quicker and more frantic than the mewls of a kitten stuck in a tree. Kamala entered the bedroom, deposited her cigarette in an ashtray, pushed back the mosquito net and, cooing hurriedly, picked up the baby. She sat down with it at the foot of the bed and gave it her left breast. Like a record player playing rock just when the electricity fails, the wailing dropped to a gurgle. Bhola watched his wife's face become more tender as she gazed down at the infant. He moved his left foot under the blanket so that it could rest against the comfort of her body. He heard the sounds of the winter afternoon outside the room—children at tennis-ball cricket, Hindi soap dialogue from a neighbour's TV, the disapproval of a distant car horn. The interior of the room itself was immersed in a lamplit liquid silence. He heard sounds—like the slurps, gurgles and sighs of the baby—as though filtered through water. Minutes passed. Quietude seemed to swathe him slowly from head to toe, like a second blanket of wool. To cease upon the midnight with no pain, that's what he felt like, as though he had peaked and in this life could not be more content. He wished never to speak any more. There was nothing left to say.

He watched Kamala change breasts, later walk around with Karuna to burp her and then put her down on the bed beside him to check her diaper. He smiled at the baby and offered her his forefinger to hold.

In the drawing room that evening, Bhola's mother-in-law reluctantly handed him a plastic folder of newspaper clippings. Clearly, she would have preferred passing them on via her daughter. 'You can read them at leisure.' Even after more than two years of his marriage, she was as uncomfortable in his presence as she was speaking English. Neither gave her any discernible pleasure.

'Thank you.' She was cold, pale and pretty. 'I must also thank you for footing my and Kamala's hospital expenses.'

Embarrassed, she sort of grimaced in reply, murmured something and left the room in search of her granddaughter.

He had said Thank You only to have something to say to his mother-in-law. He would himself have quite willingly paid the hospital bills. Not that he was terribly rich—it was just that money made him feel guilty and uncomfortable. It was like a burden that one needed to shrug off at the earliest, or food stuffed into a full stomach, rotting because there was too much of it.

For the birth of their grandchild, Kamala's parents had given them a gift cheque of eighty-four thousand rupees. The amount had been arrived at after some severe astrological computation. Bhola did not wish to know whether the sum would have been more had the grandchild been a boy. It was to be invested in some bank thing that would mature when the child turned eighteen and inflation made the accumulated amount worthless. The cheque discomfited him. He knew that he needed to get it out of the way, like pushing things out of sight under a bed. He would probably put it in some term deposit fiddle and thereafter misplace the receipt. That, he had found, was a good way of dealing with large sums of money.

His attitude to wealth and its indices had been one of the several features about him that had perplexed his parents-in-law. 'I don't understand, Bhola,' Kamala's father had confessed some six months before the birth of his granddaughter, 'why on earth do you want to buy the Maruti Van when there are other cars to choose from?'

'Actually, my first choice is a bicycle. Failing that, the Van is cheap and utterly reliable. From various newspaper reports, one concludes that all the dacoits of Ghaziabad, Faridabad and south Delhi use it for smooth and effective getaways. No one respectable drives it. Long-distance unregistered taxis, professional murderers, film crews, wholesale dealers in textiles and underwear. It must be good. Besides, I don't want to draw attention to myself on the road.'

'You should consider the Ambassador. A solid car, comfortable, reputable, symbolic. It can be repaired in any village in the country.'

'It runs on incense and correctly chanted hymns from the Rig Veda. Dosto bought one of the first Vans some five years ago. He says that he still doesn't know where its innards are.'

Which car to buy, especially when one didn't want one, was a decision that could stump anybody. His parents-in-law clearly wished their daughter to possess a car. Well, why didn't they buy one for the newly-wed, reasoned Bhola to himself, so what if they had already—and quietly—given her an apartment for her marriage? Contrary to received wisdom, the strength of one's love, for want of a more accurate measure, needed to be computed and notched up in material terms. He sensed that they believed him to be a bit miserly. He wasn't really; it was just that he preferred a bicycle to a car. If the whole world cycled, then it would automatically lose weight and gain shapely calves while going about its business. While there had still been time before the wedding, when everybody had been cautiously negotiating while circling about and sizing up everybody else, he should have added an Atlas—full-size, adult, no-nonsense—bicycle to his list of demands, right there at number two after Kamala herself, the sort of sturdy, strong-as-an-ox boneshaker that peons and postmen could use to breeze through the Tour de France with. He was certain that Kamala's parents would have agreed like a shot and deemed it to be an adequate measure of their regard for him.

He glanced at his in-laws over the rim of his teacup and wondered what they all—his wife, her absent sister, her parents—actually thought of his being shot at and almost killed while in the nude, in the apartment that they had exchanged for the one that had been part of her dowry. He couldn't see them discussing it. He felt dreadfully and deeply ashamed of himself. Well, what did they privately think of the incident, each to himself? Kamala, he was certain, wouldn't dwell on it for long, would shy away from its images as a hand from a hot plate. She would simply wish the unpleasantness to disappear and things to revert to normal. In one sense, she did not care. She was certainly unhappy about it but it exceeded what she for the moment could take. Maybe after she had got over the childbirth and the presence of the baby, she would begin to probe but he doubted it.

He did actually need to thank his father-in-law for having kept the police at bay.

'No no please don't mention it.' His father-in-law's waxen face melted into creases. 'In any case, in your condition, it would have been impossible for you to make trips to the police station and so on.'

Ayama came in with a second round of her special tea for Kamala's parents. It was more spices than tea, crushed cardamoms, cloves, cinnamon, ginger. Its waft as always made Bhola feel slightly sick. In honour of their visitors, she had put on a new sari and shawl. It hid her warm, motherly pillow of a thorax.

'Did the doctors indicate how long it would take you to get back to a totally normal routine?' asked Kamala's father and then answered himself, 'It all depends, I suppose.' He was not just making polite conversation; out of habit, he was also cross-checking information culled from elsewhere. It was his wont affably and circumspectly to cross-examine everybody. Everyone has committed or will commit a crime; it was better to be in the know as early as possible.

'I did meet the hospital physiotherapist though, a sort of South Indian Baywatch person. He taught me how to rotate my wrists for maximum benefit.'

Kamala's father nodded. He had probably met him too. 'In a week's time, you should be back at work. We all realize, of course, that this is a Heaven-sent opportunity for you to arrange for your transfer to one of the institutions here.'

Bhola held his child at home for the first time the next morning. Rather, he sat upright in a comfortable armchair in a rhomboid patch of grey winter sun in the verandah and Kamala placed the bundle in his lap. Its eyes were open, it seemed to smile. 'I want to practise today. I haven't now for almost three weeks,' she sighed as she leaned against the iron railing.

Behind her, he could see the cars parked all anyhow around the badminton courts. 'Sure, whenever you want to. Why not now? It would unwind you,' responded he, smiling all the while at his daughter. Lady housewives in nightgowns that looked like batik kitchen gardens surrounded the laden carts of two vendors of vegetables and fruit. He spotted Ayama among them, shortsightedly examining a capsicum held an inch away from her nose. Two young things—sisters—from the opposite block of flats, a diplomat's daughters, raced each other on roller skates. He wondered why they weren't at school and couldn't immediately remember what day of the week it was. His own daughter—how tiny she was, how like a pink baby monkey, fragile, cuddly, a miracle of pollution created out of semen and blood, the fluids of lust—she evoked in him all the expected parental wonder. Carefully, with his left hand supporting her neck, he lifted her up a little so that he could kiss her on the forehead. She seemed to frown at the graze of his stubble. He stroked her minuscule fingers with the tips of his own. 'Ka-ru-na. Ka-ru-na.' He leaned back in the armchair.

Chinmaya from the second floor verandah of the adjacent block waved. Bhola raised a Buddha-like palm in response. 'Good to see you back—and with an added burden in your lap,' shouted Chinmaya, grinning, gripping hard the verandah railing to raise himself, over and over, on his toes in the involuntary calisthenics triggered off by his elation at Bhola's return. His second wife and Kamala were friends. Kamala was quite popular amongst the neighbours, perhaps because, unlike her husband, she kept in touch with people.

'It gets heavier as they grow older.'

Through his moustache, Chinmaya chuckled appreciatively. He himself had teenaged children. 'They weigh you down and then tie you up in knots.'

'Or tie you down.'

Leaving behind him in the air a second chortle, Chinmaya disappeared into his flat. Bhola noticed for the umpteenth time how much nicer Chinmaya's verandah was when compared to some of their neighbours'. Theirs—his and Kamala's—had old armchairs and unimaginative potted plants mantled with dust. Most others were used as a storeroom for trunks, bicycles and unwieldy desert coolers. Some had even been walled up to create extra living space, usually a den for a teenage son.

He shut his eyes and gently traced the contours of the baby's face with his fingertips, idly wondering what germs they were transmitting. Tie me down. The warmth of the weight in his lap made him feel blessed, bonded, at last as though he belonged. Then, to complete his happiness, Kamala began to sing in another room.

To allow oneself to be tied down by filial piety went against one of the basic virtues of Hindu ethics, namely, *tyaga*, which was loosely translated as 'sacrifice' but more literally meant 'ignoring'. *Tyaga* was dutiful and passive renunciation, calmly letting go of things. It was one of the paths to release, to achieving one's true desires. In the murky idiom of Hindu scripture, what was renounced was in fact gained tenfold. *Tyaga* was mystical weight loss; it subsumed several of the notions that had intrigued Bhola for over a decade, about which he had mused a lot and done precious little: *ahimsa* or non-injury; *aparigraha* or non-possession, the owning of nothing; Nature no longer hides her secrets from those who own nothing; *asparsha* or non-touching, keeping aloof from the worldly and carnal life; and *mauna* or silence, abstinence both from speech and revealing facial gesture.

Quite distinct from *tyaga* was the sterner and more austere renunciation of *tapas*. *Tapas* in fact wasn't renunciation at all; it was heat, ardour. It was difficult, ascetic and heroic. Its concomitant virtues were *dhairya* or endurance, *dhriti* or fortitude, and *virya* or heroic acceptance of pain. The world was created and is sustained by the *tapas* of Brahma.

Every time—or almost every time—that he had stumbled on the *tyaga* path, that he had felt violent, venal or lustful, Bhola had told himself that he was probably more cut out for the passion of *tapas;* he would sink into the scalding morass and then burn, burn; he would at last emerge in another life, pale, whittled down to the bone, thin and light, bleached of all desire.

Both Chinmaya and neighbour Swaraj—his eyes luminous with gin and curiosity—dropped in on the second evening after Bhola's return from hospital. 'Thank God, you know, that the lights went off that evening because it was then that I noticed that our battery inverter had come on automatically and yours hadn't. Do you remember that we met outside the stairs door when you returned with your—well, one can hardly call him friend—from Jahanpanah?' Swaraj sat on the edge of the armchair and played with a cigarette lighter. His left leg vibrated—bobbed up and down in tremors—with a life of its own. 'Where's the carpet?'

'The police took it away for drycleaning.'

Both Chinmaya and Swaraj smiled uncertainly, prepared to laugh but not fully sure that the remark had been witty. 'It was soaked, soaked in blood. You know, I'd knocked because I'd wanted to ask you whether you needed help with your inverter. It was Chandrika—my mother's night nurse—' he elaborated to Chinmaya in an aside '—who then pointed out that your front door was bolted from the outside. Perhaps he's on the roof. Just go and check, I asked her. I've better things to do in the dark, she retorted. Impossible, this new lot, and getting worse day by day.'

Ayama placed on the tables beside the visitors cups of her sweetened and spiced tea. Chinmaya, out of the civility bred in him by his years in the diplomatic service, thanked her unthinkingly and in English. Swaraj glanced at him and then at her thorax as she bent over the table before continuing. 'Thank God for inquisitive neighbours, I say. I banged on the door for a while before unbolting it. All dark, of course. The nurse saw you first on the carpet in the torchlight. Ooooooooh. It's the first time in my life that I've actually had to call the police. I dialled 100, not quite believing what I was doing. It actually works! My sisters were a little apprehensive about getting involved. Unbelievable, I tell you. Fortunately, I remembered that your father-in-law was a high-ranking police officer but unfortunately I couldn't recall either his name or his post. Inspector General, Prisons, I told them airily. You see, neither could I remember the name of the hospital in which Kamala was. I rushed around myself to his—' he pointed at Chinmaya with—appropriately—his chin '—flat but they weren't home and his daughters were having a party with music so loud that he could have shot you with an AK-47. Anyway, the police seemed to have got to your father-in-law fast enough.'

'Have they caught the devil yet?' enquired Chinmaya circumspectly between sips of tea.

Bhola looked at himself in the bathroom mirror and fondled the rich stubble on his face. Though he didn't much feel like it, he needed to shave, to pick up the leftovers of his old life as fast as possible. The skin of his chin and jowls felt strange, as though it was someone else's hand that stroked them. As a rule, consciously, deliberately, he did not touch his own face or body except when unavoidable—to wash it, to brush his teeth or comb his hair, for example. He never rested his chin on his palm or absentmindedly sent straying a pinkie up a nostril or fiddled with cheek or chin or ear while speaking. An excessive concern over one's looks was narcissistic, vulgar and a sign of insecurity. One touched one's own face often to reassure oneself or to hide a mole or scar. He ought to be grateful that Moti had not shot him elsewhere. Seven inches above and to the right, said he to himself while daubing his face with warm water, and he could have sung in refrain one of the English pop songs that he had grown up with and would probably never outgrow, *Can You See the Real Me, Can You, Can You?*

Mrs Manchanda phoned, long distance. 'Some well-wishers even want to drop by and see you over the weekend.'

'Please ask them not to. Please tell them that their prayers have been answered. I will still take some more weeks to get back to work. The doctors have advised complete bed rest. No movement, no visitors. I'm sure they'll understand. I'm going to send the Dean an application for leave. Till the end of the month, for a start. Medical leave, I suppose. What else could it be?'

'I had given up hope of being able to speak to you. This is the third time that I've phoned since you left hospital. Did you or did you not get my earlier messages?'

Bhola hadn't but said that he had. He lied—everyone lied—to his father all the time. Telling him what he wanted to hear made him fractionally easier to deal with.

'On both occasions, I spoke to some female servant. She sounded old and a bit wanting in the brain. I shouted myself hoarse and lost my voice trying to explain to her who I was. At first, I mistook her for your wife and began speaking in English. I am the father and I'm calling long-distance, I yelled. Instead of stating that she didn't follow English, she kept parroting tremulously, "Heelo. Heelo," making me shriek louder and louder.'

'Yes, she is a real Dostoyevsky. And useless with the baby.'

For a second, Bhola heard nothing from the other end of the phone, then abruptly a short, wild bark of a cackle. 'Many women are. It's a myth that they instinctively connect better with infants. Bhanu told me that you were perfectly fine and that the newspapers had exaggerated the whole episode.'

'I feel fine. Right as hard rain. A sound mind in a healthy workshop.' Bhola felt ashamed that he hadn't thought of his father even once in months and struggled to subdue his guilt. 'Wish you were here.' It sounded ridiculous. 'Life, I am beginning to learn, is both a gift and a challenge and one has to struggle to give it value.' Cease this babbling instantly. 'How are things with you? When do you get back? Won any bridge tournaments lately?'

'We've started going out for walks in the morning. The resolution is three days old. But I phoned to ask about you,

Bhola. Are you eating enough protein? Fish? Don't starve yourself. The thinner you are, remember that the more susceptible you become to various, potentially fatal, sexually transmitted diseases. It is better to be fat than dead.'

'I'm not so sure.' He smiled as he weighed whether he should describe to his father on the phone his envy at his first sight, seventeen years ago, of Moti's wiry, fleshless physique. 'Life must also have a meaningful, untranscendental purpose. Strength, health and good looks mean nothing unless they conduce to self-control. One gets rid of physical and mental flab to achieve focus, the *dhyan* that the sages of the world modified to Zen by wisely sidestepping the tonguetwisters of Sanskrit. The distractions that prevent one from honing oneself should either be surmounted or immediately succumbed to. What do you think?'

'Good. You certainly sound your old self.' Bhola's father tired easily. Self-centred, fragile and nervous by temperament, he had been made even more unsure by a hint of a heart attack that had half-frightened him to death several months ago. 'Do you meet your father-in-law often? Please thank him on my behalf for his telegram. Are you happy to be the father of a daughter? When I first heard the news, I thought for a moment that you had shot yourself in disappointment. Daughters are nice, you'll find. They are more faithful than sons.'

'Hey Ram, not bisexual sons,' replied Bhola but not loudly enough for his father to hear.

Eleven in the morning at the hospital. He felt that he could have driven himself but his father-in-law sent him a car and an escort. It hurt when the bandages came off. In the hand-mirror, against his badly-shaven jowls, the wound continued to look hideous—yellowish-grey, livid, a tiny, sated snake curled up and hibernating above his collarbone. Dr Ratra's bespectacled, moustached, nameless assistant was however quite pleased with it.

'Nice, nice. Are you sleeping well, by the way?'

'No, not very.' He couldn't elaborate that whenever he shut his eyes, the orange haziness behind his eyelids coalesced into a naked, hairy male body with a gun and silencer in lieu of loins, stiffening, rising to point at him.

'I can suggest a sleeping pill if you feel it absolutely necessary but I don't want to. Once you begin to lead your routine life, everything will revert to normal. How old are you, did you say?'

'Thirty-three. I really should look and act more my age.'

He couldn't because—as he had often told himself—he was retarded. Very few thirty-plus-year-olds that he knew had his goals—of jogging so many kilometres per week, of increasing the number of chin-ups that he did every day. On his blue days, he pointed out to himself that he should accept that for him, the game was over. His contemporaries had crawled over, clawed and scratched one another—and their own selves—in their neverending and purposeless struggle upward but he seemed to have begun, slowly and without pause, to slide even before starting the ascent. When he notched up, all that he had to his credit were an agreeable, undemanding job, a ditto marriage and the number of push-ups that he could do per minute.

'Perhaps you ought to see our psychiatrist. I can arrange an appointment.'

Bhola had never been to one. He felt that they would be full of tricks.

'No, thanks, not immediately. A good friend of mine is one herself. When do you think I can start jogging again?'

The doctor smiled at the question. 'Whenever you want to, whenever you can. Have you tried?'

'A couple of steps at home. My chest hurt with each.'

'Begin walking in the park first,' suggested the doctor

lamely, clearly nonplussed by the banality of Bhola's anxieties.

What he wanted to hear from the doctor was that it was okay—and more, beneficial—to run even when your chest hurt sorely with each step and that a fortnight's holiday from physical exercise because of a bullet in his chest hadn't made him less fit in any way—had in fact made him pinker because his body had badly needed the rest. 'You know, when I don't jog and do the rest of my routine, I—my ankles, knees, even my wrists—become stiff. It's like one's arthritis or gout acting up.'

The doctor perked up a little, like a torpid dog when it hears an unfamiliar and worrying sound. 'Are you arthritic?' Though in his mid-thirties too, he resembled a boy, bald and overgrown, plump, shapeless, with an intelligently-contoured head that was too large for his body. 'Your immunological system is working well, otherwise you wouldn't have recovered so fast. Your bodyache is simply the corpus protesting in outrage at the illegal entry of a tiny foreigner. Not so tiny actually.'

The surly, attractive Malayali nurse whom Bhola remembered from his stay in the hospital bustled in just then with a tray of bandages and disinfectant. He watched her long, dark fingers deftly daub the scar of the wound and thrilled to her touch. If he bent his head a little, he could have kissed her knuckles. He wanted to out of a kind of mix of tension and depression. He decided not to because among other things she didn't much like him. He had confused her with the cleaning woman who too had been tall, dark and attractive and had been swabbing the floor once when he had surfaced out of sleep. When the nurse had next entered, he, to make polite conversation, had asked her whether she had to change her dress each time she swept the floor or whether she mopped up only in the morning and put on her white uniform thereafter just once. She had presumed that he, ill-mannered and clumsy, had tried to make a pass.

'I should've imagined that it's been on the whole quite smooth, in fact—how the body has accepted the bullet.'

'It lodged itself in muscle tissue which simply closed around it again.'

The doctor waited a little impatiently for Bhola to slip on his shirt and pullover. He shook hands, said goodbye and left even as Bhola stood chattering away. 'I'm glad that I'm not overweight—and there are other things to be grateful for too—I don't suffer from either anorexia nervosa or bulimia, for example. Those afflictions apparently are triggered off by a person's inability to cope with adult life.'

He watched the doctor waddle—and the nurse lope—off down the corridor on twinkling feet. He was ashamed at how self-centred and adolescent his concerns were when compared to those of others. Perhaps, had he made the right choices when younger, he could have invested his life in probing the mysteries of the human body or the universe instead of spending hours a day thinking about his own weight and the shapes of the bodies of others.

On the way back from hospital, he asked the chauffeur to drop him off at the NCSC. 'I'll walk home from there.'

NCSC was the Neighbourhood Convenient Shopping Centre, forty grey single-storey concrete boxes constructed by the City Corporation around a square patch of wasteland that it had officially christened MCP, the Municipal Children's Park. It was the unofficial latrine for stray cattle and the residents of the vicinal slums. Each shop had invaded, settled its wares in and thus annexed parts of the corridor in front of it, so that Bhola, wending his way to the Let's Talk Shop shop—a hive of phone booths, computer terminals and video game stations—had to snake his way past plastic buckets, second-hand refrigerators, baskets of potatoes, gas stoves frying chicken chowmein in some sort of used engine oil, stacks of cheap audio cassette players, racks of shoes and Hawaii slippers and mounds of aluminium cooking utensils.

He was careful to avoid bumping into people. To circumvent an ill-intentioned stray dog, he turned and stepped out into the weak sunlight and in the process noticed, several shops behind him and in the corridor to his right, his police escort of the morning.

In none of the known parts of the world have policemen ever been known to look embarrassed. Tall, burnt red by the sun, moustached, thickheaded, the escort gazed stonily back at Bhola while waiting for him to move. Bhola bypassed the dog and continued to meander down the corridor till he came to a shop that maintained—illegally—two fronts. He stepped in, past the racks of fruit and vegetables, out the other end and turned along the rear wall of the shops. He walked briskly past a refuse dump, a fetid urinal, a circle of single-minded stray dogs around an exhausted bitch in heat, reached the end of the row, turned right to regain the corridor, glanced briefly at the back of the escort waiting before the vegetable and fruit shop and slipped into Let's Talk Shop. Shutting himself in the phone booth furthest from the main entrance—it stank of heat, boiled cauliflower and stale cigarettes—he dialed Anin's city code and phone number.

An unfamiliar woman picked up after twelve rings. Anin? Do you mean Madam Anin? She had her own phone now in the cottage next door and didn't hop across any more for calls. Who was speaking?

Bhola gave her his name. Ohh, hello how are you? She had heard so much about him. He hadn't about her. He was fine. How were things with her and could he have Madam Anin's phone number if it wasn't too much bother?

'It's me, Bhola. Our phone at home is tapped. They both stay with you, don't they? I suspect that it was you who put it into that cretin's head to shoot me.'

She didn't understand. But he thought that he heard a smile in her voice. She explained that Moti and Titli had been away at Gorakhpur for several weeks for their daughter's wedding and were due to return sometime that month. When they get back, you tell them that I want to see them again face to face, he said.

A walk in the sunlight in the Jahanpanah City Public Gardens with Kamala and Karuna in her pram. It was their first outing together. Kamala drove.

'You don't mind if we return to Jahanpanah, or do you?'

'No, I don't mind. There are no ghosts that have to be laid to rest.'

Kamala was not the sort to waste time scouting around for parking. She left the car half on the pavement and the keys with the driver of the police escort jeep. They strolled down the ordered path from the third gate. It was composed of octagonal tiles of Kota stone. Bhola pushed the pram. The bandages were off. He felt mild twinges above his collarbone only when he wriggled vigorously his left shoulder. It was only to be expected that some of the walkers would eye him, a perambulating headline, a little too curiously. They passed the bench on which he had waited for Moti. He had willed a metal shutter in his head to slide down with a click and block off the images of his previous experience. Besides, he was on the second occasion with wife and daughter and it was a rare February afternoon, almost warmish, with the earth turning over under its quilt before rising from its long sleep.

'What is sudden death? It's either a term in some sport or something unspeakable that actually happens to babies.'

'The second, I think, like being asphyxiated or choking on one's own vomit.'

'That's American rock stars.'

'It's particularly horrible, I find, to die within a few weeks of birth.'

'Well, it depends. Think of all the unpleasantness that

one escapes. The binomial theorem, relatives who can't speak English, North Indian summers. It's good to be a masochist in this world. One then also becomes a practising Buddhist. What else is one to do with this goodly frame, the earth, O Gautama, that contains so much suffering?'

Kamala paused to exchange greetings with two stately women in tracksuits. Bhola glided on with the pram. He couldn't spot a single unoccupied bench. He stepped off the path on to the grass, rearranged the mosquito net over the pram and flopped down beside a flowerbed. He was faintly dismayed at how tired he felt. He watched Kamala approach them. She was short but held herself well, as though she had taken lessons in posture.

'That policeman following you—us—around sticks out like a hairbrush tucked in amongst white lilies in a vase. Is he your father's doing or just my karma?'

Kamala smiled politely, said nothing and seemed grateful for the opportunity to sit down. She began to rummage in her handbag. He liked the fact that she hardly ever made the effort to be witty. That was restful.

His karma, doubtless. For it was true that everywhere around him, wherever he looked, he saw cyclical motion—so why not in the events that befall one in one's life? Ups, downs, round and round, winter, spring, day, night, sin, punishment, transgression, fall? A water cycle, a food cycle, the earth in motion, birth, death and a circuit for souls the path of which was determined by conduct—it was perfectly possible. As one sows, so one reaps at the other end of the diameter. On the circumference, down the path from sorrow and suffering lay the urge to be happy. The movement from one to the other and round again to the first was natural and inevitable.

'Would you recognize the man with the gun if you saw him again?'

The question, unexpected, hit him like a bullet in his

chest. 'Yes, I think so. His eyes in particular.' With a sigh, he lay down flat on his back so that he wouldn't have to look his wife in the face. 'They were yellowish, bright and widely-spaced. He might put on weight and lose his hair but his eyes wouldn't change.' He noticed that the sky was an even, grubby blue.

'Ayama has suggested more than once that we get a second maid, an ayah for the baby and everything. She has somebody in mind, someone from her village—or someone known to someone from her village. Prospective is a young thing desperate for a job.'

'Ayama couldn't attest to her honesty, I'm sure. Young Thing shouldn't mind if we register her at the police station. And medical tests, VD, TB, Hepatitis B. Have you met her?'

'We both can this week. Yamini she said her name was. Either Yamini or Mona or both.'

Sudden, soft wails of discontentment from the pram made Bhola sit up. He unveiled the baby, grinned at and cooed to her, lifted her out and ensconced her in his lap. He felt more protected. A jogger went by, one of the park regulars. He raised a hand in greeting but didn't stop. Bhola watched his figure recede and all at once felt an almost irresistible urge to join him, to hear himself huff and puff rhythmically again, to land on his heel and propel himself off the ball of the foot, step after step after tireless step, to narrow down, to reduce, the universe and the future to the correct placement of the next footfall, like a Buddhist monk being trained to be continually aware, fully conscious, of himself and each of his acts.

'Shall we walk around a bit? Briskly? The movement would lull her back to sleep.' He was rapidly proving to be the sort of young parent who loves his children most when they are asleep. 'Actually, no. I'm too fagged out.' Even the thought of jogging had made him feel more tired.

'Yes, I'm amazed that you can even propose the idea.'

Their relationship was pleasant, companionable and cold. He hardly ever knew what she really thought about things. In truth, he hadn't made much of an effort to find out. She was attractive—large-eyed, full-lipped—but had never really aroused him—certainly not in the bestial manner in which Titli could; perhaps a peculiarity, even a deficiency, in him emasculated him from responding as husband to wife—that is to say, what seemed to kill desire was the conjugal relationship itself—above-board, respectable and mortally dull.

Yet he liked her very much. She was intelligent, straightforward, unfailingly well-mannered. It was inconceivable that she could be persuaded to do, for instance, what Titli used to—sit naked on his face and rocking herself gently, sedately intone after him as he, periodically wriggling his nose and mouth free to breathe in fresh air, translated from out of his head into textbook Hindi:

'Passages from the Brahmanas and the Upanishads speak of coition as a form of sacred rite and draw close parallels between the two. Thus, woman is equated with the sacred place; her hips and haunches with the sacrificial ground; the mons veneris to the altar, the pubic hair to the *kusa* grass, the moist labia to the soma press, the yellow vulva to the readied fuel, the red-tipped phallus to the ember, lust to smoke, penetration to the mystic chants, voluptuousness to sparks, movement to the burning heat, orgasm to the living flame and semen to the oblation.'

Short, shrill bawls from Bhola's lap made them decide to resume their stroll. 'She had her feed just before we left home. What's her problem?' muttered Kamala, enjoying playing the disgruntled mother. She stooped to peek into the pram. 'Maybe we should leave the mosquito net off. Then she can—you know—see the sky and the trees and so on.'

'God knows what she will make of them.' Then, feeling on a sudden confessional, he blurted out, 'We left it behind, the bench where I met the guy with the gun. I wanted to show it to you.'

Her face stopped looking serene. 'On the way back—and that too perhaps. Unless you intend to pick somebody else up today.' She smiled to hide—but in effect to accentuate—her rancour. It was the first time that she had been so open about his misadventure.

He was stung by the unexpectedness of the barb and looked away at a dog on a leash sniffing the anus of another. By the time that he had composed himself enough to glance slyly at her face, she had tears in her eyes. 'It's a miracle that you're still alive. Your experience should make you fall on your knees and kiss the hems of the pyjamas and saris of all the gods and goddesses of the world. Instead—I know you—all that you're bothered about is when you can start jogging again.'

'Jogging is worship.' He joked feebly, at the same time—and without warning—feeling extremely sorry for her for having landed a husband like him, 'I think that I'm still alive because I was aware all through the incident—the booze, the gun and everything—that I—we—were being watched by an ET whom out of affection one prefers to call god. Like a child snug in a protective father's arms, one trusts and therefore knows no shame.'

Finally, Anin and Dosto once more looked Bhola up together on a mid-February evening, more than a month after the shooting. Dosto had again been away—health tourism conferences, selling gymnastic equipment, canvassing new hotel sites on supposedly virgin beaches, buying enormous tracts of agricultural land in the Deccan to expand the retreat that he and Anin seemed to have invested their lives in. The retreat, begun two years ago as an aggrandisement of the idea of a health clinic, was the one venture that had kept the two together. It would continue to do so till death did them part; that apart, even death couldn't snuff out their married life any further.

Bhola wasn't certain of exactly what Dosto did for a living. When he wasn't flogging treadmills and exercise machines, he was some sort of financial speculator, buying and selling and juggling around other people's money—but precisely what that entailed, Bhola—whose interest in money and how it works was minimal—did not understand. All that he could follow were the effects that his profession had had on Dosto. His old schoolfriend was always stressed, almost always—even when the weather was forty degrees plus—dressed in suits and always on the phone. He had put on weight, lost hair and at the end of the decade after they left college, had his first heart attack, a subject that simply could not be mentioned in his presence.

He was openly delighted to see Bhola. 'When I dropped in last time, we couldn't talk because you were still on your funeral pyre. But this is the first real thing that's happened to you, Retard. Was it sexy, I mean, did it turn you on? Couldn't you have knocked the gun off with your kung fu kick?'

Friends tend to hark back to a shared past when there is not much else left in common. When Bhola had been twelve and Dosto thirteen, in one of their fights in the school bus that they had got into principally to attract the attention of their teacher Miss Jeremiah, Bhola had leapt back to take up what he imagined was a kung fu position. That had been some time before the country had been overwhelmed by the hit songs *Dance the Kung Fu* and *Kung Fu Fighting*. Fists close to chest, head down, thinking quite obviously that if one simply assumed the posture and didn't do anything else, one won the fight merely by virtue of the aesthetic menace of the stance. While Bhola had stood poised on the balls of his feet, Dosto had danced up the aisle and, to commence the bout, slapped him on the cheek with an open palm.

Kamala wasn't in. She took care not to be whenever her sister dropped in. She had complained to her husband more than once that Dosto's witty flirting tired her. 'Not even particularly witty,' she had modified, 'He told me that he found women who smoked irresistible.'

'What he really meant was mannish women. Women who ride horses wearing white cowboy hats, cigarettes dangling from lips, attractive crows' feet at the edges of narrowed steely-blue eyes, jowls like tanned, lined and badly-shaven leather. That's what he meant. Come to where the flavour is. Come to Marlboro Cuntry. That was his favourite—his only—line during our schooldays, whispered, accompanied by heavy breathing, whenever he saw a woman. It took me ten years to realize that he meant "cuntry" and not "country". He'd stop whatever he'd been doing and—practically barring her path—try to light a cigarette in a Marlboro way, head curved over the lighter, eyes contracted, one hand cupping flame, fag pendent like magic from lower lip. The lighter flame was often on maximum and he then unfailingly singed his eyelashes. Then for several days he resembled a serial killer in a Z-grade film.'

'Does my sister know,' asked Anin, crossing her legs, leaning back in the armchair and gulping down almost half her rum and Thums Up, 'that I visited you twice in hospital?'

'She was shocked to learn that Dosto still—even after fifteen years or something—calls you Bitchie Rich. She doesn't think it funny in the least.'

'Neither do I. Since she isn't here, why don't you tell us what really happened between you and whoever it was?' And she smiled with her bright eyes.

Bhola blinked and sighed to give himself time to dissimulate, to get into the game, determined not to be the one to blink first. 'January 13 was—or almost was—Makar Sankranti, wasn't it—and therefore particularly auspicious—or inauspicious, I forget which. For me, the odd years have always been better than the even. Just as some days of the week are unfailingly terrible in themselves. When I analyse the incident, I've to keep these facts in mind.' He smiled at them to show that he was changing the subject. 'What news of Titli and Moti? Shaping well?'

'Great. Everything is great,' replied Dosto automatically. He hesitated for a second before continuing, 'We now have clients who insist on a drop or two of blood of a particular group in their cocktails. Moti is O Negative or something. He's in demand.' He then briefly glared at Bhola, as though daring him to disbelieve.

Bhola refused to be impressed, to be drawn into the trap. For a trap it was; Dosto would use his reponse—twist it, whatever it was—to turn on Anin; she would snap back and he would burst into drunken tears. 'How times have changed. In our last years in school, we made do with tap water.'

Raising his glass, Dosto began to weep, happily, silently and sottishly, in memory of the days that were no more. Bhola doubted whether he even remembered them. Dosto in those days had thrown riotous parties that had begun in the afternoon at three, right after the school bus had deposited its charges in stifling heat and amongst frequent power failures. They had ended at six in the evening so that his mother, on returning from work, wouldn't raise hell at the mess. At those parties, Bhola and the others had drunk Dosto's father's cognacs and cointreaus diluted with tap water and had later filled up the bottles with more tap water. Risking heat exhaustion, they had also on the terrace determinedly smoked to the filter and beyond the father's nauseating Cuban cigarillos. Girls at those parties had meant Dosto's unattractive younger sister whom he would bark at out of habit and apprehension that she, while enjoying the company of males, was nevertheless merely waiting, to squeal to their parents, for her next routine fight with her brother.

Dosto got up to leave after his third whisky. 'Take care. I'll see you around—' he abruptly added, comically and in an undertone, slapping his abdomen, his right and then his left thigh in a rapid circular series around his pubic region '— the mulberry bush the mulberry bush.' To his wife, he continued, 'I'll send the car back for you at nine. Would that be okay?' He claimed to have a business appointment but his fidgeting emitted the whiff of extra-marital ardour.

'Don't borry. I can drop Anin back.'

They cackled dutifully and drunkenly at borry. 'Have you started driving yet?'

'No, but tonight is as good a time as any to start.' Bhola gently pushed his right fist into the lard that overflowed out of Dosto's trousers to cover his belt. 'You have either stopped believing that sex is the best weight loss programme or you aren't getting much of it.' He saw that he had embarrassed both his friends and regretted the remark. 'To think that I envied your swimmer's physique when we were kids.'

Theatrically, Dosto pulled in his stomach, puffed out his chest and with his arms bent inward, fisted his hands just before his testicles and then flexed all his muscles in a bodybuilder's pose. 'I am a rock—'

'You'd better send the car back,' said Anin. 'We wouldn't want Bhola to pick somebody else up after he dropped me off.'

Neither friend had expressed a wish during the entire evening to see the baby. Bhola had a couple of times considered carrying her in so that she could be praised but had desisted out of pride. Now and then, he felt the need to have her head rest on his shoulder. The bullet encased in tissue a couple of centimetres away from the baby's ear then seemed to dissolve in warmth into his bloodstream. Mercifully, he had thought, neither Anin nor Dosto had any children of their own. To him, the infant was literal proof of the fruitfulness of his marriage, a further cementing of the bond. Her nurture would be a welcome addition to his list of daily responsibilities. It was his way of dealing with the day, with time. One decided every morning as clearheadedly as possible one's objectives for the waking hours to follow and then pegged away at attaining them. Some goals of course remained on the list for weeks and seasons, and some forever—knock a minute off your four-kilometre run by September-end, wade through Darwin, pace yourself, take it easy without wasting time—and some were more ephemeral—an escapade with an urchin in the park, a film show with the wife. He simply kept at them all with some of the Zen discipline of a long-distance runner. That perseverance itself willed the future to bear fruit, to respond favourably. Of course it didn't always—but by the time that one found out that it wouldn't, one had become so immersed in the plugging away that the final objective appeared blurred, as though it had merged with the steps towards its attainment. Then one fine morning the grand end was achieved, suddenly, serendipitously, accompanied by a sense that the touchdown seemed to have lost some of its promised savour.

Quite often, some of his daily targets were fanciful, comic and unworthy of being listed as the aims of a rational human being. I must listen to all my rock music albums by midnight, otherwise I'll never make it in any way anywhere. Such self-challenges were silly, unachievable and demeaning—yet they too served a purpose and goaded him to act. Even the rock albums—listen to sound, do not ignore your sense of hearing, calm down and hear the murmur of the world beneath the racket of that electric guitar. Since everything had a purpose, he would have to keep going to find out what this gift of a child was for.

'It's a marvel,' laughed Dosto, 'that your car didn't pack up on you and your killer boy that evening. He would've then shot you while you were behind the wheel. Tchhee, what a mess. Your brains all over the windshield.'

'He could have anyway and then stolen the car. But I don't think that he needed money. I mean, he asked me for some but then finally didn't take any.'

'Since you're rolling in it, perhaps you haven't yet noticed a missing wad or two. Had you told Killer Boy that when you'd bought the car from your father-in-law, it had even at that point of time been a steal?'

In the preceding year, soon after his marriage, Bhola's father-in-law had tried to sell him his third-hand Ambassador car.

'Why don't you gift it to us?' Bhola had asked politely.

'At thirty thousand rupees, it's a steal.'

Some months thereafter, Bhola had been amused to learn from Anin that her father had tried the previous year to sell the same car for twenty thousand rupees but hadn't found a buyer. The world was divided, Bhola had then pointed out to himself, into the cheats and the cheated and everything was fine as long as the dupes reminded themselves that they were needed to make the world go round. He was fortunate that he found money—both in itself and with its rig—interest rate, disinflation, liquidity, deflation, lemon, stagflation, depreciation, reflation—neither interesting nor comprehensible. However, a couple of times after the sale, he had murmured in his father-in-law's presence, just loud enough to be audible and apropos nothing, 'It's a steal.'

'Since you said that you were—but now don't seem to be—leaving,' asked Bhola of Dosto, 'would you like another drink before you go?'

Not surprisingly, the offer was accepted. Dosto then asked Anin to fetch him a bottle of soda from the fridge in the kitchen. 'You know that I'd have gone myself but that old sexbomb's cooking away and she's just too much for me. One glance and I'd be on my knees blubbering before her thighs. What on earth is she up to? She's been frying and stewing ever since we've arrived. You have guests for dinner and you haven't invited us, is that it?'

Bhola watched Anin walk to the door. She too had put on weight at the hips but attractively. 'She cooks all day just for herself. She also talks to whatever's on the fire—potatoes, eggs, coconut rice. Zen again, because it improves her cooking.'

Dosto subsided into an armchair, belched at full volume, grinned and idly and nervously began to riffle through the scrapbook of newspaper clippings that his—and Bhola's—mother-in-law had made of the episode with Moti. '*Inspector General's Son-in-law*— should be Sonofabitch—and, what the hell, they should specify which son-in-law—*Shot by Unidentified Intruder... IG Relative Attacked in Bizarre Encounter.*' He skimmed through the pages. 'How come none of them mention that you were found naked?'

'Officially I wasn't.'

Anin returned with a bottle each of soda and Thums Up. Her kurta was a little tight across her breasts. For the first time since the hospital, Bhola felt the stirrings of desire. She poured the soda into Dosto's drink and added some Thums Up to her own. For the past few weeks, because he had been free of the burden of lust in his skull, of the sensation that his blood had been dammed up in his forehead, he had felt light and incomplete. The feeling was akin, say, to roaming about naked when alone in a familiar apartment—one feels airy—almost invisible—and peculiar. In general, he would have agreed with the view that mere physical control, abstinence, with sexual longing all stoppered up in one's veins, was injurious to health and one's general well-being. Sex was therapeutic for physical and mental weight loss, for burning up calories as well as for ridding the mind of distracting junk so that it could better focus on things. He was quite sure that he had no false notions about sex. Unlike Borkar the late shaman, he did not believe that sex was a mystical, impersonal, creative and sacred force, as natural as water in a river bed, as restless and prodigious as the sea. No, sex was a fucking headache. When one wasn't getting it, one became irritable and snapped at everybody.

He couldn't deny that he had now and then found insidiously attractive the bull about sex that Borkar dinned without respite into the unreceptive skulls of Titli and Moti and which Dosto and Anin tried in their retreat to put into effect—swathed in mystical mumbo-jumbo, of course, for not even a booby would pay that kind of money to be told matter-of-factly that, for example, what on the physical plane was called sex functioned on the affective stratum as artistic impulse, zest and emotional power and in the domain of the mind became that creative urge that has engendered all that man has ever produced, including his ideas of himself. Sublimation meant not so much selecting the channel through which one wanted the force to flow as enabling them, through ceaseless vigilance and self-control, to intertwine.

Most of the time, though, Bhola privately felt that some theorists upgraded sex because they were discomfited at the idea that something so good was at the same time so base, so basic and so fleeting.

'It doesn't say anywhere either that your boy was also some serial killer,' Dosto slapped the scrapbook shut and tossed it on to the side table. Its pages flapped like the wings of a wounded bird. It landed untidily. 'Did somebody make that up?' He lunged for the day's newspapers that lay on the armchair to his left. He bent over to spread *The State of The Times* out before his feet. 'You haven't even *read* today's papers. They are all crisp and unfolded. Why do you subscribe to three when you don't read any?' The sheets on the floor looked like the plains from the ramparts of a medieval fort.

'Well, Ayama needs sheets to line the kitchen cupboards with and wrap clothes to be sent for ironing in. More recently, to roll up disposable diapers in before chucking them into the garbage.'

'Listen then to what you are missing. "A Bangladeshi woman, the wife of a trucker, on Friday committed suicide in Chittagong. Depression at Cameroon having lost the Cup football to England was alleged to be the cause."'

'I suppose we all have our principles by which to live.'

'What Dosto wants to know,' broke in Anin at that moment, speaking slowly and clearly as though to a foreigner, eyes bright with drunkenness, 'except that he hasn't quite worked out how to ask you, is how much you have told the police about Moti, Titli and us, where he is at the moment, and where we go from here.' Her smile was like a leer.

'He must have scuttled back to your farm.' Bhola exhaled audibly. He instantly felt better at having things out in the open. 'To the police, I had nothing to tell. I insisted that I didn't remember clearly the sequence of events that evening. I have to encourage myself to forget them, so I told a more senior policeman, like pulling down a shop shutter at the end of the day. He was a Deputy Commissioner, I think—sleek, moustached, fat-cheeked—and didn't want to hear any metaphors in English from an injured citizen. You'll catch him, I'm sure, were my parting words. We're on the job, let's hope for the best, was his retort. He was the sort who, to ensure his own peace of mind, must have the last word in a conversation. Hope, I wanted to needle him, was an utter waste of time. Only the losers hope. The winners simply get ready for the unexpected.'

'We are your oldest—your only—friends, Bhola.' Anin gently reminded him, smiling tenderly over the rim of her glass. 'Surely you can trust blindfolded people whom you're so close to.'

He gazed at her for a couple of seconds before absentmindedly repeating the phrase, 'Trust blindfolded.' He abruptly arose to switch on the lamp above the bookcase by the window. 'Blinded by the light. In school, during the sports period, some of us were almost blinded by our loonily right-wing Physical Education teacher.' He turned to Dosto. 'You couldn't have forgotten Anthony.' Dosto stood with his back to the room, facing the settee on which lay Kamala's tanpura. He had unbelted and unzipped his trousers, pulled them down to his thighs and was occupied in tugging down

and straightening out his shirt so that it could be tucked in
perfectly. Bhola turned back to Anin. 'Week after week, for
two years running—till he was thrown out for walloping a kid
almost to death—Anthony would make us face—stare at—
the sun. Keep your eyes open, he would shriek into our ears
while boxing them so hard that our heads sang. Naturally, no
one could. I still remember the heat on the eyelids, the
orange glow behind them.' Dosto guffawed all of a sudden.
Bhola broke into a smile.

'This retard—' Dosto jerked a thumb at Bhola '—this
joker—I'll never forget—tried to escape one PT class by
feigning blindness. He blundered about the field, snivelling
and boohooing, "Help me! I can't see!"—all the while flaying
his hands about trying to grab a fistful of Anthony's bum.
After he was thwacked around a bit, he began to shriek,
"Thank you sir for slapping me to death! Now I can see!"'

Joker. Bhola hadn't heard himself being called one in two
decades. He had remained one, though, more or less, and
Dosto it was who had lost perspective. 'All lies,' he objected
smilingly. 'It is true, nevertheless,' he continued, deflecting
the topic, with something of the humorist's need for diversion,
to matters more befitting a funny man's curiosity about the
ways of the world, 'that in certain circumstances, the more
the light, the better the vision. After the rains, for example,
when the light is washed and spick and span, one just *sees*
better. The shapes of leaves, the crow on the dish antenna.
In the dark, conversely, one is as blind as the blind and
infinitely clumsier. One needs perfect sight only for an
unfamiliar world. When I'm lying down with my eyes closed
and someone known to me enters'—he glanced at Anin—'I
know who it is even before he or she speaks. It's the whiff of
intimacy, of camaraderie.'

'Of stinking feet, if it's you,' butted in Dosto with another
drunken snigger. 'During one of those Anthony classes,' he
elaborated to a smiling and inattentive Anin, 'Bhola, while

performing a yoga contortion, discovered a kind of green
fungus thriving at the base of the nail of the big toe of his
right foot. Saw it an inch away from his nose. Did he yell.
Anthony, showing off a perfect headstand, lost his balance.'
He chortled with deep contentment at the memory.

'I must clarify. I gave voice not to disgust or fright but to
a fascination at the secret life feeding on one's body of which
one is made aware only by chance. I remember wishing later
that the fungus would sprout all over me so that I could then
slip into the Legion of Super Heroes.'

Ayama was in the doorway, the baby's milk bottle in her
hand. Bhola put down his glass, rose and went towards her.
She fidgetted and mumbled shyly, 'I thought that she might
be hungry. Her rhythm is disturbed.'

'Hers or yours?'

Ayama smiled and blushed at being joked with. Her lined
face lost its grimness and looked completely different, younger,
alive, more shining.

'Will they eat here?' she asked audibly, wriggling her
eyebrows at the guests.

'No, I don't think so. They aren't sure of what meat we
eat at home. Bits of human muscle tissue gored off by bullets,
I explained.' He took the bottle, upturned it over his palm,
tasted the milk for its temperature and handed the bottle
back to the maid. He wondered why he was cracking bad
jokes with a servant and what else it could be other than
flirting out of habit with a mother figure. He felt depressed
and disgusted with himself.

'We will stay for dinner actually, thank you, Ayama.'
They did. Bhola would have liked them to depart before
Kamala returned. He opened the windows of the dining room
to let in the temperate night air, the noises of the
neighbourhood and the pre-early-spring mosquitoes. He
remembered that during the evening with Moti, the curtains
of those windows had not been drawn and that he had been

about to put something on to go and pull them across when Moti had pointed at him his gun.

He went through dinner with his mind elsewhere. His being grazed by death, he had decided upon reflection, was intended to show him that he needed to be broken so that he could mend. It fitted in with how he viewed things. He never threw anything broken away without trying to repair it first— umbrellas, teapots, tape recorders, jeans, fountain pens. More than buying new things—wretched conspicuous wasteful consumption—he liked old objects that, accidentally cracked or marred, were mended well enough to be used again. It seemed to him a parallel to the Christian ethic of revering more those who have strayed from and then returned to the path.

This preference for the blemished and imperfect he saw as part of a masochistic creed that coloured every aspect of his thinking. In an argument, he preferred the underdog's point of view; in a hierarchy, he wished the subordinate to enjoy the struggle to rise. He was more comfortable when he chased a target, when he ascended from the depths. On the rare occasions when he reached up to attain a goal or was particularly blessed by fortuity, he wanted thereafter to descend in some other way so that he could again look up to the future looming above him, vast and heavy like an unaroused lover. At such moments, his last meeting with Moti seemed a fall from the climax of the birth of his daughter; at the remembrance of the thwack of the bullet in his chest, he would even feel wander over him the gooseflesh of a thrill at the prospect of the future hiding in the folds of its flesh the consummation of that unfinished business.

Right and wrong, good and bad, were like the right and left hands of the buffoon Lancelot Gobbo in Shakespeare's *The Merchant of Venice*, all the time beckoning to Bhola from either side, making him swivel his head this way and that, non-stop, in his efforts to decide what course to follow. Pacts

with the devil were of course pacts with oneself. Occasionally
therefore, when one was blue, tired, weak, bored or unhappy,
one told off one's good right hand and indulged the sinister
parts of oneself.

Declared Swaraj to him at the Mother Dairy Milk booth one
evening in the middle of March, 'I know what you were up
to with that man who shot you'—an avuncular squeeze of the
shoulder—'but your secret is safe with me.' He smiled at
Bhola and waited for him to collapse, blubbering with guilt.
Swaraj looked wild-eyed. Spittle had edged out of the corners
of his mouth. He hadn't aligned his shirt buttons with their
holes while buttoning up. The top button near his right
collarbone looked noticeably forlorn.

Bhola put down the milk can and squirmed his torso to
adjust the weight of the sleeping baby in its kangaroo pouch,
a thoughtful gift from Anin and Dosto. He loved the feel of
Karuna next to his heart. 'It quietens me even more than it
does her.'

To get back as fast as possible to whatever could be
called a normal life, he had begun, after recovering from the
shooting incident and before returning to work at
M.K.M.Z.A.P., to do the domestic shopping. One should
handle as much of one's own life as possible. One feels more
in control, one sees more clearly both where one's money is
going and the petty thievery of the servant types.

He smiled at Swaraj and said, 'Of course it is. That's what
good neighbours are for.'

The reply pleased Swaraj no end. He turned to walk a
few steps with Bhola. 'No milk today?' Bhola teased him.
Almost the entire neighbourhood knew that Swaraj dawdled
around the milk booth on many evenings only to eye the
servant class. Of late, of course Bhola had attracted all the
attention as the one who had been shot.

'No. Too expensive,' retorted Swaraj, happily falling into playing the game, 'what with the recent price hike. I always find February and March—the period around Holi—the dreariest and most expensive of the year. The stars, perhaps, who knows?'

'It's the weather—this grey, dull cold—that, following a complex economic law, seeps into the cost of living. I like price hikes, though. As a rule, all economists like them as well. They indicate that the economy's on the move and has arrived.'

'You sound happy. Good.' Swaraj pointed with his chin at the baby's head in its woollen cap. 'Thanking God that you are alive?'

'Well, thanking the baby's ayah more than God, actually.' It was true, though, that with the birth of his daughter, Bhola's contentment with his life appeared complete. The bullet embedded above his collar bone was the price that he had paid for that contentment. After all, why should he get anything for free?

He grinned at Swaraj, 'It's amusing—and pathetic, really— how a good ayah becomes the most important person in the household, quickly superseding both husband and wife.'

Swaraj chortled obligingly, displaying yellow-brown teeth. 'You have had quite a few of them already, haven't you?'

That they had, four in the nine weeks of the baby's existence. They seemed to have run through them as through a box of tissues. The first, arranged for by Kamala's mother, had been sixty-plus and had lasted three days. She had on the whole slept more than the baby. She had been wrinkled, bespectacled and a masseuse. She had offered to massage Kamala on the very first evening. Kamala had proposed that she take care of the baby instead. Not to be diverted from her theme, the masseuse had then disclosed the nugget that she herself had a smooth, hairless, young girl's pubis only because of vigorous and regular rubdowns.

On the third day, conversationally in her Hindi dialect, she told Bhola that there was shit in the baby's cunt.

The second ayah, recommended by Nirupama the widowed sister of Swaraj, had been too good to last. She bathed and fed the baby, cleaned her, played with her, sang to her, all with a smile. She herself looked cleaner and more respectable than both Bhola and Kamala. Life with her was so comfortable that it made them tense. Bhola was reluctant to promenade the baby with her for fear that she would be mistaken for his wife.

'Are we classy enough for her, that's the question. And when will the bubble burst?'

It burst after five weeks. After she had picked up her salary on the second day of the following month, she simply stopped coming. For two days, Kamala was frantic and Ayama and Bhola fatalistic and depressed. On the third morning, a Wednesday, a gruff male voice telephoned, introduced itself as that of the ayah's husband, and stated that she was ill.

'Oh I see. What with?' TB, AIDS, VD, Hepatitis B, the Ebola virus, ran through Bhola's head.

'She's been advised rest for a couple of weeks by the doctor.'

'Overworked, is she? You mean that we'd better look for somebody else.'

'That would be the most reasonable thing to do, sir.' In the voice could be discerned a sort of amused relief, even admiration, at Bhola's having got to the point directly. 'I'll drop by myself, sir.'

'Whatever for?'

'To receive the one day's wages that are due, sir.'

Bhola disconnected before he could lose his temper. On hearing the news, Kamala had a nervous breakdown for half an hour and then asked Ayama to locate the maid whom she had spoken of, the one from her village or part of the country or whatever.

She, Esther Yamini Mona by name, turned up the following Saturday. Bhola had gone to the Jahanpanah park that evening for his first full jog. When he returned, he found Kamala in the drawing room, chatting with a short, trapezoid-shaped woman standing in front of her. Bhola's heart sank when she turned to greet him. She looked like a coelacanth doing namaste. He wondered whether his infant would enjoy waking up to find herself in the fins of a fish of great antiquity.

'Have you handled babies before?'

'I had one myself.' To the discomfiture of Kamala and Bhola, tears formed in Mona's eyes. Bhola and his wife exchanged a We-don't-want-a-fucking-nut-in-the-house glance. 'I lost him within a week of his birth.'

'We are sorry to hear that. How long ago was that?'

'A fortnight ago.'

'Oh. Is your name Mona or Yamini?'

'I've already asked her that.'

'My name is Esther.' Bhola and Kamala exchanged glances again, then looked at her with the same expression of grave doubt. So she continued, 'For Hindu households, I adopt a Hindu name. It's simpler.'

'And Mona?'

'For modern households.'

'And …uh…your husband?'

'Joseph. He'll come sometimes to protect me but not to worry. He won't disturb us, he won't stay.'

'He's downstairs at the moment,' contributed the usually taciturn Ayama.

'Oh well, ask him to join us.'

'I'm not so sure that we can employ a fish to look after our baby,' opined Bhola as soon as the front door had shut behind Esther Yamini Mona. 'What do you think?'

Kamala said nothing but looked tired and disappointed at having to agree with Bhola's assessment. So as not to have to smile at his wit when she didn't feel like it, she buried her face in the infant's stomach and began to tickle it with her nose. Bhola went to get out of his jogging clothes.

Joseph turned out to be small and swarthy, large-eyed and moustached. While Kamala ignored him and Bhola wondered what to ask him, he took out his wallet and from it a card that he offered the master of the house. 'My place of work,' he added in explanation in English. The card advertised the firm of Anthony and Alvarez, Undertakers and Funeral Managers, Town Hall Chowk. *With Us, You Aren't Lonely When You're Dead*, it read above the phone and fax numbers. 'If there's any problem, you can call me there,' asserted Joseph, jabbing at the card with his finger.

'Why should there be?' objected Bhola mildly, loftily and automatically. 'We haven't decided yet, though, whether we'll take on Esther Yamini Mona.' He liked the sound of her name. It had the rhythms of John Gabriel Bjorkman.

'You keep her. She is good. She likes you. Both Joseph and Jesus have been watching her ever since she lost her baby. I know that she's told you. She tells the whole world. Like Hindus say Ram Ram. You'll give me your card in return?'

'By Joseph, did you mean yourself or Jesus's Papa?' While Joseph, frowning, mulled over the implications of the question, Bhola turned to Esther Yamini Mona. She had sat down beside the baby without being asked and was cooing to it. 'You won't mind if we get some blood tests done? We'll pay, of course.'

A frown traversed her face like a shadow. She shrugged her shoulders after a brief pause. 'Okay, I suppose.'

'And we'll have to register you at the police station. It's mandatory these days for all servants.'

She flinched and paled as though she had been insulted. Her lips formed an O of outrage. Joseph intervened, 'That won't be necessary. We aren't criminals out on bail.'

Bhola disliked dealing with members of the lower orders who had clearly risen above their station. He lowered his head and stared at Joseph over invisible reading glasses. 'It's absolutely nothing, as far as I understand. *We* have to fill in a form with your home address, your photograph, that sort of thing.'

Esther Yamini Mona suddenly exchanged a few sentences with Joseph fiercely and intensely in what to Bhola sounded like Konkani. Joseph hissed and snapped just as much as her. 'This is incredible,' murmured Kamala to the world and prepared to gather up the baby and leave the room. Joseph then recomposed his face, turned to Bhola and stammered, 'This police identification, I don't think it would be easy to accept. It would be like having a police record.'

'Look,' Bhola sounded far more decisive than he felt, 'get yourself photographed and turn up tomorrow with your things. We'll begin with the blood tests and see how those go. We'll save the police for later.'

'Have you registered her,' Esther rolled her eyes in the direction of Ayama, 'with the police?'

Ayama's face flushed with resentment at the question. 'No, of course not,' replied Bhola, taken aback at the acuity of the demand, 'she's been a part of my wife's family for the past thirty years.'

'I will go now,' announced Joseph with his feet together, inclining his torso a little forward as though about to bow in farewell, 'but Esther will stay. You see, she is ready to perform her duties from Day One. Look,' with a flick of his hand, he indicated a plastic shopping bag at his wife's feet. Hardeep Stores, it said in green beneath three cupolas of gold. 'She has brought her night things with her.'

'Okay,' agreed Bhola, suddenly fed up of ayahs, undertakers and dissimulators, and wanting to get on with his evening no matter what. Esther and Joseph glanced at each other and then looked away to hide their smirks of triumph and relief. Esther was employed for all of six seconds because Bhola at that moment saw Ayama's sullen face and remembered that the flat only had one servant's toilet which the difficult old woman was not willing to share twenty-four hours with a stranger. With the earlier maids, she had coolly proposed that they go outside the flat and wander about on the roads to piss. Bhola was amazed that Kamala wasn't firmer with the human component of her dowry.

'She can't leave the baby and roam about from pillar to post looking for a pothole to relieve herself in.'

'Ayama is worried that she will dirty the toilet.'

'Look. It's an Indian-style toilet. Only the soles of your feet touch the floor when you squat. I can't believe that we're having this conversation.'

Before the master of the house could proclaim to Esther and Joseph that he had changed his mind and they in fact did not want a live-in, Ayama whispered conspiratorially but loudly enough for all the assembled to hear, 'They look insane. They'll steal the baby in the middle of the night.' The accusation set off a slanging match between Ayama and the other two that did not cease even when Kamala returned with a red-faced, shrieking infant who, choosing well, threw up over Joseph's leather shoes some expensive Lactogen.

BLOOD SUGAR

The fourth ayah was found on the day preceding the one on which Swaraj met Bhola and Karuna at the Mother Dairy Milk booth. Anin had sent her over. It was Bhola who opened the door when she rang the bell at four in the afternoon. At seeing her, he oozed into his pants with shock and uncontrollable joy, right there at the door, and didn't even notice.

In the four months that he hadn't seen her, Titli had come to look like a ladylike keeper of a brothel. 'It's nice and peaceful down there in the south, green, but Madam Anin said that you badly needed help at home so how could I refuse?' She wore an expensive-looking, blue-checked sari, lipstick, even a hint of sindoor in her hair, and new fat bellmetal bangles at her wrists. There was nobody at home save Bhola, Kamala having gone off to her mother's with the baby and the maid. Yet he felt safe for the moment, emptied of desire by that first overwhelming explosion of his seed.

'Naturally.' Feeling horribly uncertain and vulnerable, he went to the phone and stared at the instrument, wondering why he had crossed the room.

First things first. He called Kamala and asked whether she wanted to see the new ayah, who seemed all right, immediately. Kamala said yes and that she would send back the car to pick her up. They all had at their disposal white Ambassador cars with police constables as chauffeurs. Titli sat in front with the driver, looking down at her lap, carefully arranging her sari about her. He began to paw her while driving during the first ride itself. Foreplay was him humming increasingly loudly a risqué Hindi film song. Later, when she got into the rhythm of things and didn't feel up to being felt up by the other police constable who drove Kamala to work, Titli would demurely propose that she take Baby out for an airing. Then she regally lolled in the back seat, thighs spread luxuriously, paying as much attention to the infant in her lap as she would to the groceries.

'I'm disappointed in and worried for Anin, I must say,' declared Anin's father over dinner, smiling beatifically at Bhola across the table while his eyes behind his spectacles darted repeatedly across the room to Titli sitting on the carpet before his grandchild. 'To sell out a successful business enterprise only to sink all your capital into another even more venturesome is highly risky. They could easily run *both* the health clinic here and the farm or whatever it is down there.'

Mercifully, Bhola's mother-in-law shrilly broke in and prevented him from having to mouth some sort of reply. 'Gently! Slowly! Don't stuff her mouth she'll choke or vomit what's the hurry you have all the time in the world arrey!' Her husband gratefully accepted the opportunity of pushing back his chair and leaving the table to get closer to Titli. As he crossed the room, he continued to address Bhola in his mild snake's hiss. 'What is a retreat exactly? They gave me the impression that it was a kind of religious gym.'

'I haven't met them in ages,' replied Bhola defensively. It was a Sunday evening early in June. He was not looking forward to leaving the following morning to return to work at M.K.M.Z.A.P. College after a gap of six months. Following an established pattern, the rest of his family would move in with his mother-in-law for the days of the week on which he was away. 'I've spoken to them on the phone, though, a couple of times. Out of the blue, Dosto called sometime last

month and in passing asked me to ask my father to translate
into Sanskrit the phrases "All You Need Is Love" and "Love
Is All You Need". He needs to attract the foreign tourist, he
said, with some Sanskrit combined with beards—for the men
of course—and long, unstitched, brilliantly coloured but
monochromatic robes. Then the dollars will flow in like the
muck surging out of a drain during the monsoon. I suggested
to him the phrase: *Vatsaha, Tvam Shrimantaha Manushyaha
Asi.*' Neither his father-in-law nor anybody else was listening
to Bhola. His father-in-law had squatted down beside Titli,
taken the spoon out of her hand and begun to amuse his
granddaughter by repeatedly approaching her mouth with her
feed and withdrawing it at the last moment.

Titli was a hit with the whole masculine world around her.
Neighbour Swaraj for instance met her so often before the
stairs that it was obvious that for her, too, he lay in wait all
day behind the front door of his sister's flat. Titli flirted with
him with decorum and skill. With Bhola, in contrast, she
behaved as correctly as he with her. As always, she waited
patiently for him to make the first move. He on his part
didn't even hint at it in her first three months with them.
Things were close to being near-perfect and he didn't want
to rock the boat, to relive those frightful days when he had
had to help to take care of the baby. Of course, his notion of
the near-perfect was quite loose and flabby. Moreover, he
would be ashamed to look gaga with lust like his father-in-
law. In fact, he desired Titli considerably less also because he
saw about him hideous old and middle-aged men like Swaraj
and Kamala's father—whom he did not wish to resemble in
any way—make no secret of their itch for her.

Last of all, he hadn't had many chances. Titli arrived
from Ambedkarpuri at about eight in the morning carrying
her handbag and her small steel flask of some homoeo-yunani

medicine—or so she described it—that she kept, after having initially taken Kamala's permission, in the freezer compartment of the fridge. Bhola had no wish to learn the details of the malady against which the contents of the flask were an antidote. He simply imagined the worst. It helped to make Titli noticeably more resistible. After Kamala had hared off to work, Titli did remain with the baby in the house all day and so did Bhola, that was true, but so did Ayama the spy, at least for the hours when she wasn't dead to the world during her siesta, when the snores from her room sounded like the grumbling of a vicinal dinosaur, or when she wasn't summoned to Kamala's mother's, on the average three times a week, to cook one of her dishes for some special occasion. 'You don't have much of a home life, do you,' Mrs Manchanda, who had become Mrs Kapoor in April, commented later in the year on his tiring weekly commuting.

'No,' Bhola agreed, 'not even when I'm with my wife and child.'

'On some afternoons during the week,' disclosed Swaraj to Bhola and Kamala over samosas and tea at a weekend open-air Tambola get-together of the Jahanpanah Residents' Welfare Association being held vaguely to celebrate Independence Day in mid-August, 'when neither of you is at home, I've heard the baby shriek for an unrelenting half-hour as though the world had come to an end. Last Thursday, I remember that I couldn't stand it and even went upstairs to enquire. The ayah—the younger one—answered the bell and without making it obvious, barred the doorway and wouldn't let me enter. "No no the baby is fine," she grinned, "Just a bad dream." I couldn't notice your cook anywhere—the older fatter one. Her afternoon nap, I suppose.'

'Horny old Swaraj,' annotated Bhola to Kamala when they were alone, 'anything to get a peek at Titli. Good thing she didn't let him in.'

Because they had a maid to look after the infant and because the baby looked, well, normal and appeared to be growing up the usual way and according to pattern, Bhola considered the first few months of his daughter's existence some of the best of his own life. True, he had been shot by an ex-lover during that period but things could have been far worse. He had proof of that in the enormous sense of foreboding and consequent depression that filled almost every waking moment of those best months of his life. When will things go haywire for me? he would ask his wan reflection in the grimy window pane of the Monday morning bus as it roared into the dawn without actually moving very fast. Not, why *aren't* they going haywire but *when* will they. A second bullet from a passing stranger could finish him off. He could get AIDS, hepatitis B, gonorrhoea and herpes Zoon as birthday gifts from another. Kamala could have a ghastly car accident on some new, badly constructed and ill-lit flyover. Titli could kidnap the baby and demand a stupendous ransom. Some other villain could do it before her nose while she was busy soliciting in the Jahanpanah Public Gardens. He felt abased but couldn't help himself, on some of the days when he was in town, from, without even telling Kamala, secretly following Titli and the pram as they went promenading in the park with other ayahs and babies. He was not sure whether he wanted to protect his child from mishap or snoop on the ayah's other life. He didn't like the look of any of the other maids that their own chatted with. He presumed that they discussed their respective salaries and perks and that their conversation continued to give Titli bright little ideas about abduction or quitting her job to take up something more lucrative elsewhere.

On the first Thursday in September, he was packing in his college flat for the routine weekend trip when the phone rang. He had had it installed on his return to work, citing on the application form, mainly because no one ever read them, Mrs Manchanda's marriage as a reason for an allotment on priority. It hardly ever rang and sometimes when it did, if he was in the midst of something, he didn't answer it.

'You are coming down this evening?' Kamala calling him was indeed a rare occurrence. He tensed and stopped breathing. 'I might not be in because Ma ...is not well. I'm going back to the hospital right now.' Her voice sounded distant with strain.

'Oh I'm sorry to hear that. What's happened?' He would have much preferred to sound less formal but was as usual at a loss for words.

'I'll tell you when we meet.' She seemed to speak to somebody else for a moment. 'Ayama is with me in case we need her. I phoned to say that Titli will be alone in the flat with Baby. She said that she'd wait until you arrive.' Once more her voice became feebler as though she had moved away from the instrument. 'She's at the same time scared of being alone so we've locked the door from the outside because she doesn't want the Swaraj types dropping in. The reason I phoned was to remind you not to forget your keys.'

'Don't worry—and good luck at the hospital—which one is it, by the way?' But she had disconnected.

For four hours in the bus, he, even more depressed by his sore throat and the monsoon chill, could think of nothing but Titli waiting for him with the baby in the flat and how voluptuously he would fall from the state of grace that he had attained in the preceding nine months. Maybe Kamala herself would somehow die in the hospital and he would never have to exit from the spider clasp of Titli's limbs. He curled up into himself in his seat beside the window and felt his eyelids, heavy with dejection, droop and blot out what must have been his soul. In his struggle to better himself, in his mind he had already been routed, he had lost both the battle and the war. He had fallen and would continue to fall till the

bus at last stopped somewhere. First of all, he would ask Titli
to take off all her clothes and, naked, continue to do whatever
she had been doing while he sat down somewhere, had
something refreshing to drink, spread his thighs wide and
watched her.

From the lane, he noticed that the lights in every room in
the apartment were on, as though they were preparing for a
wedding in the family. From Swaraj's lawn, he heard the
screams of the baby. He rushed up the stairs, stumbled,
banged his shin sharply against a step, cursed, fumbled with
the keys and finally got the front door open. The shrieks
were deafening inside the flat. He bolted the door and
dumped his bag on the floor. He heard Titli trying to soothe
the baby but in a different, her real, voice, louder, less
considerate, more vulgar and bossy, on the verge of snapping
at her charge to shut up. Bhola paused at the doorway of the
bedroom to take in the scene. Titli sensed him before she
saw him. Even before she, standing by the bed, turned to
look, she slid under a pillow what had looked like a red
plastic tube in her hand.

'What's wrong? Why is she screaming like a nut? Did she
fall off the bed or what?'

'No, nothing,' Titli simpered embarrassedly. 'Just bad
dreams.'

The infant was naked save for her diaper. Bhola noticed
her sleeveless vest lying in a heap on the floor. As he picked
her up, he saw on her left forearm, just below the crook of her
elbow, tiny livid swellings around two black pinpricks. He
pressed his child to his breast, hugged and kissed its neck,
strolled around with it till it slowly began to calm down. Not
stirring from her place beside the bed, Titli watched them
with a fixed, patient smile.

'Does she have these attacks often? You never told us.
And those bites on her forearm, what are they, do you know?
Mosquitoes? Bedbugs? Spiders? But we did pest control

before she was born, I remember.'

'Heat boils, probably. They've been there for a couple of days.'

He spotted behind the pillow on the bed Titli's steel flask. He didn't put Karuna down even when she stopped whimpering completely. Still circling about the room with her, patting her back and soothing her, he said to Titli, looking her in the eye over the baby's shoulder, 'Take off your clothes, Titli Devi. Pick up the baby's vest off the floor and put it on as an undie.'

She looked relieved, flattered, pleased, embarrassed. Obediently, with her back to him, she divested herself of her sari, blouse and under-blouse, which was less like a bra and more like a blouse, smaller, tighter, more cottony and sleeveless, laid them on and around the pillow, turned, sat down on the edge of the bed and pulled up her green petticoat to demurely cover her breasts and incidentally display her fat white thighs. 'Take off that petticoat, Titli Devi.' As though she had only been waiting for her cue, she stood up, let the garment slide to the floor, perched again on the bed, bent down, knees pressed together, breasts decorously dangling before her shaved pubis, picked up the petticoat and laid it beside her atop her under-blouse on the pillow. 'Squeeze into Baby's vest, Titli Devi.'

She held aloft the vest and examined it dubiously. 'It will tear,' she announced finally.

'The armholes are for your thighs, Titli Devi, and the neck-hole is for my tongue. I want to see your fat flesh bubbling and oozing out of all the openings in that top.' It got stuck at her shins and would mount no further. She looked ridiculous—plump, nude, smiling without pleasure, crouched over in a struggle to use as an undie a vest that was fifteen sizes too small for her. Unable to restrain himself any longer, feeling like a skydiver just before he starts his freefall, Bhola gingerly put the infant down in the playpen that it detested, popped its soother into its mouth even though it was against house rules, unzipped his trousers, pulled down his shorts and leaving them in a tangle around his ankles, lurched forward towards the maid. He thrust her back on the bed with his body, lay on top of her, picked up her discarded clothes and swathed their heads in their aroma and bruised with his lips and bit her neck and face till he had spent himself. He lay quietly atop her, his face in the crook of her right shoulder, waiting for the guilt to rise and ravage him. A foot away from his nose, partly visible beneath the pillow, lay the red plastic tube that he thought he had spotted in her hand from the doorway. Without shifting his body, he stretched out his left arm and pulled it out. It was a hypodermic syringe full of blood.

He sat up on her stomach and held the needle above her nose. Her face wore the watchful expression of a crafty old beast. Unblinkingly, she waited for him to make the first move. Behind him, he could hear his child contentedly sucking on its soother. He reached over her head for her steel flask, unscrewed its top and overturned a cupful of blood on her breasts. She wriggled and exclaimed—an 'aah'—in discomfort. He grabbed her tightly with his thighs and, grasping the syringe like a dagger, jabbed it into her left breast above her nipple. The needle snapped off in her fat just as he depressed the plunger. The blood of the baby sprayed over her as water from a pistol during a festival. 'Ughh... aargh!' With her eyes screwed shut, she, in disgust, jerked and twisted her head this way and that. He balled his hand into a fist and hit her hard on the mouth. Something cracked, his knuckle hurt. He got off her and the bed, wiped his daughter's blood off his stomach with Titli's sari and put on his underwear and jeans.

She sat up. With an outstretched arm and an open palm, he commanded her not to move. Bending down, he dragged Karuna's vest off her calves, checked it for bloodstains and dropped it in the playpen. Gathering up her clothes about her, Titli shuffled off clumsily to the bathroom. Before she could bolt the door, he yelled, 'Don't shut it! I want to know what you're up to in there!' The sound of water drumming into an empty bucket seemed to explode in his head and burst a blood vessel. His temples began to throb. Not knowing what he was doing, he bolted the bathroom door from the outside.

He picked up his child from the playpen. She looked delighted to see him again. Her eyes lit up like light bulbs in a cartoon film. Drooling and slurping frantically over her pacifier, intrigued by his bare skin, she clawed at her father's shoulder. He held her tight against his chest and began to weep silently. He wanted to die, to atone, to have his semen drained out of him by an enormous syringe, to give up his body and his life for her.

With the child in his arms, he phoned Kamala with absolutely no idea of what he was going to say. The constable-cook answered. He couldn't understand who Bhola was. All he had done for over a decade was to cook stupefying vegetarian food and say either *Yes sir?* or *Yes sir!* to everybody, including women. He did not have any idea either which hospital the family had gone to or when it would return. Before he lost his temper and started to abuse the cook in Hindi—in response to which too he had been known to say *Yes sir!* in an alert military manner—Bhola disconnected and looked around for the address book in which he could search for the paediatrician's number. He didn't find it. He returned to the child's room, put the baby down in the playpen, and dressed her in the top that he had flung down a few minutes previously, all the while ignoring the polite, persistent tapping on the bathroom door. He wore his shirt before finally opening it.

'Just a minute. You aren't going anywhere until you tell me a few things.'

Titli stepped into the room, stood uncertainly beside the playpen and waited for instructions. Her expression was harsh and sullen, her upper lip swollen.

'How often have you sold the baby's blood? How much of it and to which wretched, disease-infected blood bank?' He stopped and blinked with fatigue. The question that he really wanted to ask was, However could you do it? but posing it to a person with a face as prison-like as hers was impossible. He shook his head and tried again to arrange his thoughts in order. 'Your...relationship to this house has been...special...We trusted you with our most prized possession...How could...' His head jerked convulsively as though telling him that he had got the words wrong and ought to begin afresh.

She relaxed visibly when she realized that beyond paying an ear every now and then to his mumbling, she didn't really have to respond to anything. She moved over to the bed and cautiously began to arrange her things, the steel flask, its lid, her comb, handbag.

'...a vampire...you damaged her...you could've killed her...'

'I know how much blood to take,' she turned to retort a little sharply, as though her professional competence had been doubted. 'And you don't understand. It's part of the cure. She has too much sugar in her blood.'

Her tone momentarily silenced him. Her next question nonplussed him even further. 'It's late. I should be going. Should I come at the usual time tomorrow?'

Simply to gain time to find the right words with which he could fire her without loss of dignity, he asked in response, 'Has Baby been fed? Why don't you make her bottle before you go?'

Simpering, she made a move to hasten off towards the kitchen. Not believing what he was doing, he asked her when she was at the door, 'Do you know what the paediatrician's number is? It's written down somewhere.' Careful not to grin too openly, she returned to the night table, rummaged in the paperback edition of Spock and handed him a slip of paper. 'Ah, thank you.' He carried his daughter with him when he went to phone.

He got through on the third try and explained that it was an emergency. The secretary gave him half an hour on Tuesday afternoon, five days away.

'So bloody fucking busy making money that all these weeks she didn't even notice the needle marks on the baby's forearm.' He had discovered quite some time ago that one could say just about anything to anybody if one spat it out fast and in BBC English. Then in a normal voice, he wheedled, 'An emergency case, Madam—' and added, inspired for a moment, 'A child abuse matter.'

He called a taxi. While feeding the baby, Titli asked him if he could drop her off en route at the Main Post Office Bus Stop. He did and absentmindedly waved goodbye to her when she alit.

'Were you the one who had phoned? Child abuse case, you'd said?'

He had forgotten that Reception at the paediatrician's clinic was invariably tubelit, ugly and crowded. Karuna didn't like it either and began struggling and screaming in her father's arms the moment they entered. Heads turned at the loud question posed by the pert nurse at the desk. 'Dr Chipmunk Shenoy, please,' muttered Bhola in answer. He meant Dr Champak but neither he nor Reception cared. They were ushered in, on the ground floor itself, behind a strip of dirty blue curtain. It was not wide enough to shut out the prying eyes. Bhola wanted to keep his back as buffer in the gap between doorway and curtain but couldn't because nurses and male attendants kept wandering in and out carrying glucose bottles and enamel trays.

Dr Champak was tall and moustached, with an easy manner and a pleasant smile. 'What happened?' he asked, examining the red, puffed-up and evil-looking punctures on the baby's forearm. Bhola started to narrate the events in order but halted after a couple of sentences. The doctor did not seem to notice. It is my fault, mumbled Bhola to himself, yet hoping that someone with the power to cleanse and forgive was listening. I allowed a creature of the drains into our house because I was neither prepared nor equipped to rear my own child.

'Should I call the police?' enquired Dr Champak, baring his teeth cheerfully at Bhola. In the same breath, he turned to glare fiercely at his assistants and snap at them to wheel Karuna's stretcher away. He then swung back once more to Bhola to curl his lip and ask, 'What is the child's name? And where was the mother when it happened, by the way? I'd like to talk to her please, if you don't mind. You may kindly now wait outside, please. Thank you.'

Reception would not allow him to use its phone and directed him to the two public booths outside, before which he in a daze joined the longer queue. Kamala was fortunately available at her father's house and almost out of her wits because her mother wasn't out of danger yet and she had incessantly phoned home to check if things were okay but no one had picked up.

'Can you come over to Chipmunk Shenoy's clinic? No no Karuna is fine I mean nothing serious just a couple of injections no just come over and please without your father if it's possible and if you don't mind, please.' Then, pointing out to himself that the circumstances were extraordinary, he permitted himself to smoke three cigarettes while strolling about on the pavement outside the clinic and waiting for his wife. She turned up in record time with her father in his car, its red official light on its forehead winking wickedly, and a handful of policemen behind them in a jeep. Kamala heard the first few phrases of his story and walked rapidly, almost skipped, into the hospital. Bhola's father-in-law softly ordered one of the policemen to follow her.

Kamala emerged forty minutes later with the child. She looked frozen, stared straight ahead at nothing and remained silent. The grandfather cootchie-cooed to the infant. 'Is she all right?' Kamala nodded briefly and got into the car that, wrongly parked, had caused traffic behind it to pile up. Bhola sat in front feeling guilty. Just as they drove off, he enquired after his mother-in-law.

After a long pause in which Bhola felt that the upper crust in the back seat had decided not to answer his question, his father-in-law responded in his gentle hiss of a voice. 'It is very strange. By accident, she drank some Baygon insecticide or something this afternoon. We don't know yet what happened.' Then no one in the car had anything else to say. The baby fell asleep. They dropped the father off first.

Ayama was at home, as usual preparing dinner for herself and the others. Bhola followed mother and daughter to the child's room; at the doorway, he remembered with a jolt the sight of Titli slipping the filled-up syringe under the pillow. He half-expected her to be in the apartment somewhere, modestly waiting to explain to Kamala how long and how well she had known the master of the house. Kamala laid the baby down on the bed, removed its top and flung the garment violently towards the bathroom door. Bhola helped his wife to change the diaper and dress the infant in its sleeping suit. Kamala then sat back alongside her daughter and after a while turned to Bhola with eyes red and filmed with tears.

'The doctor said that there were semen stains on Baby's vest. He wanted to check with me first before he called the police.'

'My God how disgusting.' Then he remembered how the stains had been caused. In a voice considerably less outraged, he continued, 'Whoever could it have been, do you think? One of the attendants at the clinic, or Chipmunk himself, perhaps? But is he *sure*? One never knows. But this is monstrous.' Kamala left the room without a word.

She that night slept with her daughter in her and Bhola's room while he dossed down on a mattress beside the playpen. He woke some hours later with a start, an aching head and a terrible thirst. It took him a few minutes to realize where he had gone to bed. His head and hair felt strange, like a destroyed wig. He arose for a glass of water. The lights in the flat were all off. A dog howled somewhere in the neighbourhood. He looked at his watch but couldn't make out the time.

He was about to switch on the kitchen light when he thought that he heard a human sound, a sort of sigh, from the servant's room. The door to it was ajar. He crept up and peeked in to see, in the streetlight diffusing a white glow through the window, Ayama sitting crosslegged on the floor, yawning and caressing and calming down Kamala suckling at her left breast. The sound that Bhola had caught was that of his wife shuddering and weeping. Fabulous breasts, a fraction of his brain filed away, more so for a woman of her age.

He backed away in utter silence. It was important to him not to disturb them or anyone else, to leave the whole world in peace. The drink of water forgotten, he returned to his daughter's room and lay down again. In a few minutes, sleep crept up on him like mist.

He awoke late, after nine, bright, fresh and happy, ready to welcome a new world. Rare sunlight lit up the room and his innards. The flat was tidy and silent. Wife, daughter and wife's surrogate mother appeared to have left several hours ago. He made himself his ritual pot of tea and wondered when he would see them again.

He spent a long, quiet weekend all by himself. He phoned his father-in-law's house twice and left messages

with the cretin-cook. He enquired of him—and immediately
regretted asking—whether his mother-in-law was dead yet
and *Yes sir!* he heard in reply. He toyed with the idea of going
back to work a day early, on Sunday—maybe even on Saturday
evening—and wondered, with his family having abandoned
him, what would happen to the balance that he had always
tried to maintain at the heart of his life. It had for years
seemed the sole object worth pursuing and he had got used
to its keeping him from feeling blue. Consolidate your family
ties. Try and learn something new every day. Read every day.
Do not gain weight in the wrong places, for the body mirrors
the soul, whatever that might be. In his daily round of
meaningless activities, each seemed significant and worth
doing mainly because it contributed towards his maintaining
his deals with God. His lifestyle in fact helped him to define
God. God was the balance within, the mean between his left
and right sides. From where He lived, in his vitals somewhere,
God occasionally prodded and aroused his guilt, the guilt that
blurred focus and prevented one from functioning with pure
attention. It was necessary to efface it along with all the vices
and weaknesses that distracted one. God was truly that state
of pure attention.

THE CALM CENTRE

Then for the next four years of his life, till October of 1996, Bhola lived out in the hills the life of an old, dried up, abandoned bachelor. He even found a sort of contentment in his deadened unhappiness, in waiting to steadily shrivel up further and further with each passing day. He rearranged his classes and tutorials so that neither Fridays nor Saturdays were any longer free. Impulsively, two or three times a year, he wrote letters to Kamala, chatty, informal but impersonal efforts—about the howler that he had heard from a student the previous week and how there were fewer tourists that year. Early in 1993, when their daughter turned one, he asked her to send him a photograph of herself and their child. He received neither any letter in reply nor any snap. From Anin, round about that time, he heard the extraordinary news that her father had begun looking around for another husband for Kamala and that only when he found someone suitable would he set about effacing Bhola from the record of his family.

He was half-tempted to advertise himself anew.

Stunning homely cook masseur age sex no bar for 34/175 abandoned tallish wheatish lecturer abandoned Kashyap Brahmin noble takemehome abandoned takemehome own gas cylinder Apply soon

He missed the feel of his daughter's head on his shoulder, of the fleeciness of her hair in his fingers. Looking back at the people who had formed his life, he wondered how, twenty years ago, Titli and Moti had not died of grief at the death of their infant son. Perhaps they had and it was only he who had not seen the corpse in their eyes.

He missed Kamala too and, while their daughter in the background whined and fretted incessantly and refused to be calmed down, carried on several imaginary and important conversations with his wife.

'Your home is here, not in your parents' house. You're thirty-six years old. Every time that you're unhappy with your life, you scurry off to your mother like a child rushing back home from the playing field before it gets dark. Grow up. Or be like your sister—she's insane but she doesn't beg for help to go her own way. You reserve your best behaviour for your music teacher and are inattentive, insensitive, to your home and husband and then once a year, you also wish him to make love to you.'

'Neither to me nor to our daughter.'

'That's ridiculous. I can explain those semen stains on her teeshirt.'

He even regretted not having posed to her in time the questions about music that he had postponed for an indefinite future for fear that asking them would embarrass him. Increasingly, her singing, floating out through an open window, had nudged loose in him a vague longing for knowledge that would hone his appreciation of her talent. What kind of song do you sing in the mornings, Kamala, and why a different type in the evenings? Where do they connect—the brash rock that I've enjoyed for decades and your heavenly melody? Is a khayal a thought and a thumri a lilt? And an alaap an appetizer or the precursor of a mood? Is it too late for me to learn to sing with you?

He maintained his rhythm, his regime. He read, he wrote his diary, he tried to think of nothing, he laughed therapeutically four times a day, he jogged, even when his legs felt like warm yogurt and his stride became a leaden wobble, he still jogged.

Bhola's father-in-law began revenge proceedings against him and Titli quite early during that period.

The first of October, 1992. Bhola had been separated then from his wife and child for just over three weeks. After his classes were over, cold autumnal rain kept him indoors all afternoon. The flat felt empty, chilly and so depressing that he actually thought that he would die, that he couldn't possibly outlive the night. At five-thirty in the evening, he, caressing the nine-month-old bullet scar beside his collarbone, was roving about from room to room switching on lights and mosquito-repellent mats when the doorbell rang. It was a stranger who had got wet in the rain. *He is so dumb that he doesn't even have enough sense to come in out of the rain,* ran disconnectedly in Bhola's head as he noted that the man's moustache, coarse swarthiness and obstinate manner made him a policeman. He disliked them. They spelt trouble and made him feel uncomfortable, womanish and guilty. In the drawing-room, looking around him at the Grundig radiogram and the prints on the wall, the sub-inspector took his time to settle down before divulging the reason for his visit.

'Back there in Jahanabad, there is a woman in one of the general wards of the Civil Hospital who was brought in half-dead, unconscious, a couple of days ago. Rape case. She was found in an abandoned sandstone quarry just off the Altafgarh Road. She came to this morning and mentioned you. It'd be simplest if you accompanied me back to see if you recognize her.'

Bhola had no idea about the regulations of criminal procedure, whether he could tell the policeman to go away and never come back. He doubted it very much and besides, wondered whether he truly wanted to. A seven-hour drive was one way of trying to escape the frigid emptiness in his skull.

'I have to be back, though, for class day after tomorrow. And where'll I stay in case I have to spend the night or something?' For one heart-exploding moment, he thought that it was a kind of trick, like a surprise birthday party, and that wife and daughter were waiting for him as before in the old flat.

The policeman did not consider Bhola's question worth responding to.

They travelled in a jeep and, crushing sundry fowl and other fauna en route, covered the distance in five hours. The satellite town that they arrived at was unfamiliar, ugly, noisy and crowded even at midnight. At the Civil Hospital, they walked through buildings, courtyards littered with broken beds and abandoned cupboards and length after length of corridor, picking their way past the supine bodies of insomniac patients and sleeping relatives till they arrived at a hall at the entrance of which half-dozed a constable on a chair on guard duty. He took his time to register their presence and follow them in.

Titli shared the ward with five others—that is, if the form under the hospital sheet was indeed her. Its head, right eye and upper thorax were bandaged. Its face, lips and eyelid had ballooned up and cracked and were the colour of potato. It didn't seem to be breathing and indeed looked dead, like a corpse obscenely bloated and stuck against a fence in a flash flood. It was inconceivable that such a cadaver would wake up, assume an attractive human visage and mouth his name and those of others he knew.

'Whoever assaulted her has worked very hard. She has lost her right eye, it seems,' offered the occupant of the next bed, a dark, bald man with a youngish expression and several gaps in his teeth, sleepless and happy even at that hour, 'She is not going to name anybody, I can give it to you in writing. She'll reveal nothing, she will have nothing to do with the police. She'll say that she remembers nothing, that her head hurts, and will keep weeping till her bed is needed for the next road rage victim.' The man beamed his approval of his own assessment of her strategy.

Bhola moved up to the bed and gazed down at the grey, puffed-up features, the mouth gaping like an arid wound, the bandages stained all over with yellow, as though some sloppy person had lunched on rice and dal while holding the plate just above her head. He would have liked to squeeze her hand but, mindful of his two escorts, desisted. Then for one incredible instant, he imagined that he saw her open her left eye and stare straight at him, conscious, alert and crafty. He blinked and turned to the policeman. 'Yes, I know who she is. When I last saw her, she was a maidservant in my father-in-law's house. He is an Inspector General of Police. There was some—' he appropriately lowered his voice at the euphemism '—tension in the family over her and as a consequence, the almost-late Mrs Inspector General even drank some Baygon instead of coffee after lunch. She too was in hospital but a private one, of course, much posher than this and commensurate with her status and all that.'

He spent the first part of the rest of the night on a concrete bench amongst the mosquitoes and under the flickering tubelights of the town's Inter-State Bus Terminus. The earliest bus to the hills was at six the following morning. At three a.m., shivering with cold, he got up, wandered off and returned from a piss to find that his place had been taken by two rock-star-type beggars. Hugging himself, he ambled off to look for another spot, found none vacant, and finally settled down against the side wall of a closed ticket booth, idly wondering whether he had seated himself on and was rubbing his back against a stranger's dried urine. He remembered Titli's left eye opening and gazing steadily at him for a second. He imagined his father-in-law weeping prayers for her moral upliftment with his lips nuzzling her loins while a constable beat her head into pulp with a pressure cooker shouting all the while *Yes Sir! Yes Sir!* Yes sir, that was what had happened. Were she—succumbing to bribes or threats or both—to denounce Bhola as her assaulter, he would simply, discarding his past, set off on the world's longest non-stop jog.

Everything in those four years—his state of mind, his memories, his friendless, dead, disciplined life—everything seemed to help him to lose more weight. He began to look gaunt, older than his years. Acquaintances—those whose idea of brimming good health was a thirty-nine-inch waist and hairy tits to match—unfailingly exclaimed and commented on how haggard he looked and asked—with eyes shining—whether he was ill. He started to avoid them. When he couldn't, he acknowledged that yes, he had had a problem with his blood sugar. It satisfied them because it sounded exactly like a respectable camouflage for some vile disease.

He kept in touch, in a manner of speaking, with Anin and Dosto. They sent each other cards every now and then, at Dussehra and the new Year. From their side, Anin wrote the news and Dosto the incomprehensible witticism scrawled illegibly at the bottom. All three were careful to steer clear of information that mattered. Bhola would have been glad after a fashion to hear, for instance, that Moti and Titli were both alive and well and contributing to the wellbeing of their employers' wealthy clients. Bhola had reached that state of depression—a sort of nirvana—when he could bear nobody in the world a grudge, neither the person who shot him nor the person who extracted his infant's blood for sale, nobody. He had returned to the mental condition in which impatience is inconceivable and waiting is an end in itself.

In December of 1995, in an end-of-the-year issue of a popular weekly newsmagazine, he, sitting numbly tranquil in his flat in the winter gloom at two in the afternoon, came across a picture of Dosto and Anin, featured together as a couple in an article on India's Fifty Most Influential Behind-the-Scenes People.

On a lush, ochre-toned carpet, Anin, smiling shyly but with eyes aglitter, dressed in a gold and blue sari, and with her hair cut short and framing neatly her face, sat with legs crossed in a cane armchair. Behind her, hands resting lightly on her shoulders, her head hiding part of his paunch, Dosto, in some kind of brocaded maroon princely outfit, with hooded eyes and patronising smirk, stood gazing regally into the camera. Beneath them in red letters and between blue quotation marks was inscribed: *Mantra: Health meets Wealth and exerts its weighty influence on people of consequence.*

It thrilled him, chancing upon their photograph in that manner. He gazed at it for a while, smiling in remembrance of other times. The accompanying writeup was badly composed but fulsome in its praises of the luxuries and peace of mind—the two seemed intertwined—made available at the Calm Centre.

On an impulse, he wanted to write to his friends to ask whether he could hop, skip and jump across time and space and with a sigh of homecoming snuggle out of sight under that wonderfully warm-coloured carpet.

Sex with Mrs Manchanda became almost impossibly infrequent. In her husband's presence, she had taken to calling him Brother. It never failed to nonplus him, to make him wonder whether privately she thought of him as Sisterfucker. She herself was about to retire from service and was trying hard to inveigle an extension of tenure. When he wanted to find out whether she was willing, Bhola would pass by her office desk between classes. She usually slotted their assignations between lunch and her return to work. Her husband was a small, bald, bespectacled, plump and jolly hypertensive in his late sixties. A couple of times a month, Bhola played chess with him and once in six months, mainly to please Vivek who had taken to the bottle because he did not find it easy to accept his stepfather, he drank himself silly with the son, usually on a Saturday evening.

It was the third Saturday in October 1996 when he heard in his head the phone ring all night long. At three in the morning, he got up to vomit, splashed his face with cold water and then picked up the receiver. 'Hello?' He heard nothing in response except a woman sobbing, distant but clear. 'Hello?' He disconnected. It rang again, shrill and demanding in the night. Once more nothing but the gasps and sobs of a woman breaking.

'Who is it?' in Hindi. Somehow he knew that she was someone out of his past, that if he could only clear his head and focus, her identity would be clear from the sound of her sorrow. 'What is it?' But she wouldn't speak. He gripped hard the bakelite of the receiver, benumbed even further by the hushed, trembling ululations of wretchedness.

His forehead pulsated like a heart. In the kitchen, he sipped some water and then lurched off to wander about the flat. In the drawing room, he put a record on the gramophone, a family heirloom that a police van had brought up unexpectedly some months after his separation. In his daydreams, he was to bequeath it to his daughter on a subsequent birthday. She'd be deeply touched, but he in his heart of hearts would be convinced that she'd think it cheap, that her child's jaw would sag with disbelief at the sight of her father sweating to install the monster in some other corner of her room. It stood there beneath the window, dust-laden, solid, a Grundig, in perfect working condition despite having been ignored and buffeted about for decades. He riffled through the records in the rack below with a confused sense of guilt, of having been unjust both to his past and the gramophone itself.

Hindi film music of the sixties and early seventies, British pop, American rock, jazz, blues, soul—he sifted through the albums in the dust and finally selected The Moody Blues. He cleaned the disc with the sleeve of his kurta and placed it on the turntable without enthusiasm. Yet, at the same time, he had no wish to listen to anything, new or difficult, that would make demands on him. 'Isn't Life Str-a-a-a-ange,' sang The Moody Blues. He glanced around at the tidy void of the drawing room. He had now no future left to petrify him. A million times, he had visualized his daughter and himself, in the years to come, saying and waving goodbye to each other in different situations—she from the doorway of her friend's house or the window of a school bus, the entrance to her music school, the gate of the park where she skipped rope or the arch of some ghastly multinational fast-food restaurant; and each time that they would part, involuntarily the thought would squirm into his head: This might be the last time that you see her. While you plod away at your work and your adultery, she might during the same half-hour be kidnapped, raped and murdered. So look at her long and carefully. Neither bark at her nor touch her violently because you'll rue it for the rest of your muddled and insignificant life.

The phone rang again. He never picked it up, never, when there was somebody else in the house. He usually let it ring. It didn't bother him. He considered it proof of the superiority of mind over matter. For him, it, like in his youth the telegram in the middle of the night, existed mainly to purvey catastrophic news—deaths, murders, kidnappings, rapes. A harsh, northern Indian voice speaking street Hindi: 'We have your daughter and will kill her by this evening if you don't pay—shut your silly mouth, bitch!'

Vivek had left the bathroom and kitchen lights on. Bhola poked his head in to see what else he hadn't switched off. The geyser, the Aquaguard water filter. He had sometimes chided Kamala too on her carelessness. Some residual nugget of scientific information—on the amount of living matter contained in a drop of water—that had lodged in her skull ever since her student days had goaded her into asking for a water filter even in the bathroom. The topic had cropped up again in her muted conversation with Ayama on one of the last nights before her departure. Reliving and relocating it helped Bhola to imagine that she in her heart of hearts had not wanted to leave.

'Here we have an Aquaguard even in the bathroom and I'm now used both to brushing my teeth and washing Baby's hands and face with filtered pure water—so I even drink a little straight from the Aquaguard spout after rinsing my mouth. But at my mother's, there isn't any Aquaguard anywhere and I'd have to brush my teeth with plain tap water. And I'm now in the habit of drinking just a little, a sip, straight from the tap just after brushing. I'm sure that I'll absentmindedly drink some tap water there—or someone'll sponge Baby's face with it—and we'll both catch some horrible disease—cholera or typhoid or something.'

Bhola tumbled into his dishevelled bed at four thirty. When he awoke, it was past ten in the morning and the phone was still ringing. He waited for it to stop, then he dialled Mrs Manchanda to tell her that he couldn't come in that day because there had been a serial killing in the neighbourhood and the police weren't allowing anyone to leave the area. She softly reminded him that it was Sunday.

He then made himself some tea and took his weight. He noted that he seemed to have lost another kilo in a fortnight. He reminded himself that he had found in general that he could lose weight more easily when he lived alone. In any case, he seemed to have lost everything else. It sounded like a witticism and, wandering about from window to window, he repeated the phrase to himself more than once.

Living alone was simpler and emptier. He ratiocinated that Kamala had left him because of her psychological need to wander. It was her way of remaining young. In the same manner, she had misplaced her phone and address books once every three years and, before her marriage, changed houses every fifteen months.

He needed to renew himself too, to shake off his depression the way a good jog tones one up. That very week, he would seriously ask at the office for what his father-in-law had proposed four years ago, a transfer to another institution in another city. That would wake him up properly and vacuum clean the inside of his skull. Sipping tea, he gazed at the geyser for five minutes, wondering whether he should switch it on, at the back of his mind trying to will himself to put on his running shoes, till the cleaning woman came. She picked up the phone. 'It's for you.'

'Hello.'

'It's me, Titli.'

His flesh tingled. They hadn't spoken in four years. 'Oh hello Titli how are you?' He felt dully sick, apprehensive.

'Could you...come down here for a few days?' Her voice sounded thin with exhaustion. 'Dosto...passed away last night. He...passed away.'

This is the end, sang the Doors inside Bhola's head, my only friend, the end. He was—as often—embarrassed at the quality of the first thing that he had thought of. 'How what happened? Was it his heart?'

'He overdosed.' From nowhere a second female voice on

the line, louder, hoarse, distraught, made him jump. 'If you had any feeling at all, you'd come down and see why he overdosed.' 'It's okay, Anin-ji, get off the line, I'll speak to him,' he heard Titli say.

'Yes, I'll come,' he listened to himself respond, 'I'll have to take a train though. I mean, I don't have the money for a plane ticket.' It seemed as though he was sitting on his haunches at the corner of the ceiling like Spiderman, watching himself speak on the telephone.

After a pause, Titli, still sounding distant, said in her stilted Hindi, 'I'd have imagined that you would rush. Well, let us know when you will arrive.'

He didn't want her to disconnect. He wanted to continue conversing till the news sank in and he felt grief so that he could react correctly. 'I'm not in very good shape at the moment so I mustn't be blamed for saying the wrong things. Is there anything I can do here before leaving?'

'There? Like what?'

'I don't know.' Tie a yellow ribbon round the old oak tree, proposed the jack-in-the-box in his head. 'I don't know. I'll see what my bank account looks like and whether I can fly.'

He took the Deccan Express from the plains the following evening. He had some money in the bank, sufficient by his standards but not enough for a return plane ticket. As a rule, whenever he checked his bank balance, he found that it had gone up by a fraction, a phenomenon that both puzzled and reassured him. He was neither a miser nor a spendthrift. Money didn't interest him, that was all. There should simply be adequate amounts of it but in the background somewhere, like the presence of a discreet, efficient and impersonal servant. In fact, there had been times—rare though—when he had viewed a fat bank balance as an unhealthy heaviness, as the overeating that causes indigestion and acidity. When, due to the payment of salary arrears or an increase in the dearness allowance, his account had shown a respectable full figure, he had become as alarmed as a villager when the river that ran through his life crossed in the monsoon the danger mark. Careful, son, he had cautioned himself, when you have money, your children are kidnapped, your servants and chauffeur fleece you till you bleed, your car is attacked by your ex-employee dacoits at a crossroads in broad daylight and the police know what you have been up to just because you had money enough to waste on a mobile phone. Not worth it, son.

One of the virtues of having a family was that one was then surrounded by people whom one could make happy by spending money on them. There were then fewer chances of being accused of being the cause of unhappiness. When left to himself, Bhola found nothing worth buying save vegetables, fruit and running shoes.

'But I don't *want* a CD player,' he had protested to Kamala, 'we have that ancient Grundig radiogram collecting cockroaches, geckos and dust. When I want to listen to music, I can play my records.'

Periodically, in the old days, when his bank balance had begun to weigh him down, he had gone out and bought a toy for his daughter or a CD for his wife. He had then felt well, much lighter, virtuous, as one does when one successfully sticks to a diet. It was wise, he had always felt, not to let money sit, to keep it in circulation like one's blood during a light jog. The more one spent judiciously, the more one got— from God knows where, though—and the freer one became. To cave in to the yearning for money made one naked and weak; it allowed one's vitals to ooze out; at the same time, it bloated out one's face and abdomen as though one's skin itself had stretched out to grasp and tuck things inside itself. Really, one's goal needed to be: to be civilized and *not* to covet, voilà, to prove that refinement leads not to the upgradation but to the pruning of one's wants.

Before leaving, nervous and unsure of what he was doing, he phoned his in-laws and spoke in turn to a new constable-cook, his mother-in-law and finally his wife. 'I'm sorry about—' he had begun but his mother-in-law had abandoned him in mid-sentence. 'Come back, baby, come back,' sang he softly and absentmindedly into the receiver while waiting for his wife. He thought he heard in the background his daughter wailing. To Kamala's dull 'Hello,' he responded with the news of his departure.

'Yes, that's good. Papa has already gone. Will you be away long?'

'Just three or four days. Till the weekend, maximum. I also asked at the office this morning for a transfer. I thought that another city would make more sense. I mean, this apartment is dark and dead with me alone.' He paused for her to react but she didn't. 'How are things otherwise?'

'Karuna's a little cranky today. She has a kind of rash at the base of her neck. Perhaps it's a delayed reaction to the medication that she's been having for her viral fever.'

'It's probably her body protesting against the accumulated dirt of weeks. Or you take her to some fashionable paediat who will charge five hundred rupees to tell you that it's nothing, just a seasonal allergy to airborne pollen. Just get her bathed properly and soaped like a normal human being.' But Kamala had put down the phone.

He sat down heavily at the dining table and gazed blankly at the stains on the tablecloth. He had married without love and apparently just a little above himself. Allergies, for example, were a sign of upward mobility, weren't they? He meant that neither he nor his brother had ever had them whereas Kamala hadn't lived even one fortnight of her life without having her lips swell up or the skin of her stomach bloom with a rash like a field in spring. Perhaps he should have detained his wife and child from departure by promising that he too would sprout hypersensitive allergies in the future. Tears abruptly filmed his eyes. At thirty-seven, he had nothing to share with his wife or the rest of the world. He wanted to lie down in the cold under a warm quilt, never open his eyes again and allow forever the sun-dappled world to pass him by outside a firmly shut window.

He almost missed the train. He had been in two minds all day about catching it. It was his first journey since his trip to see his ailing father three winters ago. Dosto had been cremated the evening before. Locking up the apartment, checking doors and windows, taps and light switches, the gas cylinder and the geyser, had seemed laborious and fruitless. He saw that he had one of the narrow, lower berths that lie lengthwise between the aisle and the wall of the bogey. He hated them. When one lay down with one's eyes open, all that one saw were arses in transit. When one shut them, one felt the pummel of travelling bags and smelt passing farts. Fried caulifower, moong dal and radish, butter chilli chicken.

He ordered from a vendor tea that he didn't particularly want to drink. In the magazine section of the day's newspaper, he read of a white resident of Milwaukee, USA, who had been a murderer, a molester of male children, a necrophile and a cannibal and he was only thirty-one. Here he himself was thirty-seven and going nowhere; in contrast, Bhola felt like a boy, an adolescent not waiting for the adventures of life but one whom they—and life itself—had quietly bypassed. All that he had to boast of at the end of almost four decades were a series of petty misadventures and the scar of a bullet wound. Even when they had been dangerous, they had been petty. Now it was simply too late for adventures. He had once believed that they weren't worth it, that the thrills that one enjoyed in the name of experience didn't offset the damage to one's heart and honour. Two decades later, however, he wasn't at all certain that he had earlier been right. Now that his ties had shrugged themselves off, it seemed as though he had been freed—by Time the lord of all—to explore, much like an unleashed dog that, with his nose to the ground, scurries about for unsavoury smells.

For years, the games that he had played with himself had made it easier for him to forget his biological age, to remind himself that how one felt in one's skin was more important than the tell-tale signs of one's years—the difficulty in achieving a good night's sleep, the aches and pains of the morning, the inability to lunge for a ball while playing with a child. Increasingly in the last ten years, the newsmakers that he had read about in the papers and magazines, particularly the sportspersons, had turned out to be considerably younger than him. Flipping through their achievements usually disoriented him, made him feel that if at thirty-five, one momentarily envied someone of twenty-two, then age, the process of growing old, was a farce, a trick. Complementarily, all human exploits appeared trite when the ghoulish acts of a thirty-one-year-old subhuman murderer and the achievements of a twenty-year-old footballer impressed a sane, intelligent and older person with the same intensity.

'Dinner veg or non-veg?' asked the train attendant, tall, uniformed and hirsute.

Bhola was most likely to make a pass at another man, invariably of the lower orders, when he himself was blue. Men of his own background and class did not interest him in the least. To bolster his virtue, he shut his eyes and·reminded himself of the purpose of his journey. That helped him but unexpectedly because the memory of Dosto warmed him and made him smile. Whenever possible, Dosto had succumbed immediately to temptation. 'Men of action never put off for tomorrow what can be had today,' he had maintained.

'What is non-veg?' His own question dredged up in Bhola another recollection, making him grin, puzzling the attendant into letting his jaw hang loose in an idiot's smile. In the vocabulary of their schooldays, non-veg had been code for those companions of whom it was alleged that they lapped up palmfuls of their own semen. A classmate's innocent admission that he was a vegetarian on Tuesdays and Thursdays had often catapulted Dosto into mystifying near-hysteria.

'Chicken, saab.'

Bhola spotted in time the contents of the dinner trays being served to the family across the aisle and passed altogether. The first law of weight loss, he recalled, was not to eat when one was not hungry.

The family had ordered four trays, one presumably for each member, but it appeared that the father was going to gorge his way through three. He began by popping whole into his mouth, one by one, the six gulab jamuns, two on each tray, that had been meant for dessert. 'Come down, you two,' trilled the mother in what sounded like Oriya, 'before your father finishes everything.'

The children, two girls in the age group of eight to ten, ignored the summons and continued their card game on the upper berth. It seemed to involve the slapping down of some and picking up of other cards at tremendous speed, the tempo of the hands punctuated by hisses and restrained shouts, every few seconds, of what sounded like 'Lutt!' and 'Tonkay!'

The child whose face Bhola could see was pale and thin, serious, with curly hair kept in place by a pink Alice band. Her elder sister was broader and more jumpy. Children. Each time that she rocked forward to fling down or snatch up a card, the berth creaked and her ponytail bucked and pranced on her back like a black towrope. Bhola wanted to join them but desisted from asking. He had off and on thought even about their having in a year or two a second child. When he had suggested it to Kamala, she had hedged, 'At my age?' With reason, since she had been thirty-five when she had conceived their daughter. 'I doubt whether there's any gynae who would advise it after the age of thirty-eight.' He remembered that at hearing her response, he had felt uncertain and fuzzy, as though he had again become the seventeen-year-old who had been massively impressed by the masculinity of Mike Rossi of Peyton Place. Mike Rossi had been a very manly thirty-eight. Bhola too had wanted to rest his head and eyelids against his forty-eight-inch chest. Or had it been an eight-inch penis (when limp)? At seventeen, his own chest, despite his prodigious efforts, had measured thirty-two inches even when puffed up like Popeye's. He supposed that he would remain young as long as he retained his gift of recalling useless detail.

'I suppose the done thing would be to have the second time round a boy,' he had nevertheless mused. 'Though I'm sure if Karuna's opinion on siblings is sought when she is older, she'll say that she'd prefer to have a cat. Even though a younger brother or sister is much easier to beat up.'

Children at least imposed upon life a semblance of a sense of duty, if not purpose. As extensions of oneself, they took one out of one's skin. Anin and Dosto ought to have had them perhaps. They drew out the mother in the male, they made one whole. Without his child, Bhola wasted the whole day on himself and ruminating about the bleakness in himself, and within that bleakness on his fifty push-ups and forty-five-minute jog, on whether he had eaten enough fruit that day and drunk two litres of water before sundown.

The sisters, card game abandoned, now lay on their stomachs, one on each upper berth, with their heads jutting over the edges into the aisle, and observed down below their father wheeze his way through three dinners. Bhola willy-nilly watched too, as always half-mesmerized by gluttony. The man seemed to be just a commodious stomach to which were attached four limbs and a head.

'No food later, huh,' he warned his daughters in Hindi, in a voice in which one could hear an index finger wagging in admonishment. 'No chips, no Coca, no Kitkat.' Bhola had the impression that he was spoofing someone, perhaps a TV emcee or a character out of a soap.

'Okay, not for us, but why not for yourself?' asked the elder one, her ponytail swaying gently before her father's face. The younger sister began to titter. She suddenly didn't look serious in the least. Wiping damp hands on the edge of her sari, the mother returned and joined the banter. Feeling deprived and depressed, Bhola inhaled when her large buttocks passed his face.

His bio read as the life story of a man to whom some of the usual things had happened but all at the wrong time. He had almost died at thirty-three. He had been intrigued by yogic meditation not at sixty-five but at sixteen. He had left home at seventeen not to fend for himself or seek his fortune but, driven by lust, to sniff out a woman of the streets and her husband. He had toyed with celibacy at nineteen. He had experienced a sort of calf love at thirty-two for his mistress and ex-landlady only when he learnt that she was getting married again. What remained? An early death? Or perhaps a second childhood filled with the radiant innocence that his first had never had.

Even at thirty-seven, he puzzled like an adolescent over the mysteries of the world. His bewilderment made him feel retarded and prevented him, out of embarrassment, from seeking counsel for his questions. He couldn't understand how, at the end of the twentieth century, people could still die by the millions out of poverty. He spotted the wretched everywhere. They were outside the window when the train stopped at an unimportant station, two young girls in scraps of clothes, squabbling and pulling each other's hair in between begging, one carrying an infant brother in a sling. These sights never failed to dampen him, to evoke in him, as in the Buddha of fable, a profound disgust, an overwhelming urge to renounce things completely, to run away to some hole in the hills where, in the silence and peace of a decade of solitude, he could think things out. Perhaps the destitution of the two girls was his fault. In an indirect Marxist way, perhaps his style of living compelled them to remain where they were and prevented them from rising. Perhaps he should invite them into the bogey, make them sit with him on his bunk, share their lice, offer them some tea and Marie biscuits, wash their feet and drink that water thereafter. Eeeeks. Saints were rather kinky. He then wondered—as always—whether the difference between the beggars and him had been effected by his education alone. When he considered how worthless and paltry it had been, the thought of its being deemed a privilege depressed him to the point of tears.

The rhythm of the train finally petted him into a doze. He drowsily mulled over whether there existed a method by which one could ready oneself for the future in the manner, say, in which one prepared oneself for exams. One studied the syllabus and the probable questions. But beyond becoming more and more thickskinned to the slings and arrows, he didn't seem to have gained much from his past. Perhaps it had nothing else to offer. Even his memories were unspectacular, bubbles in a thick, sluggish—almost stagnant— flux the colour of mud.

The train was two hours late. He observed from the window the chaos on the platform. He was the last to alight. Titli had confirmed on the phone that they would send someone to pick him up but he didn't see any probable face. It was impossible in any case to spot somebody in that confusion. He repulsed the suit of a couple of coolies, hoisted his grip on his shoulder, sidestepped a gaggle of urchins, instinctively checked his pocket for his wallet and keys and moved off towards the stairs.

Behind the policeman at the main exit, he saw an unoccupied phone booth. The instrument worked. He pressed the buttons of the number that he had but a tape-recorded female voice from Telecom said in three languages that it didn't exist any more. It did not however add what Bhola should do next. He then phoned Enquiries but couldn't get past a second tape-recorded voice that told him, also in three languages, to kindly wait in a queue. While he hung on, they made him listen to the version of Mozart's 40th Symphony that he had heard in a stationary aeroplane awaiting for ages the clearance of traffic control. Then they disconnected. That happened four times. The fifth time, the music stopped and he got through to a woman who seemed to be cleaning her infant's bum while talking to him. He gave her Anin's old number and asked her for the new one. She requested him to hold on forever and replaced herself with Mozart.

The day was bright and pleasantly warm. Its tropical October air had a little in it of a Mediterranean summer. It made focussed thinking seem unnecessary. He sauntered off the platform and into the muddle of the cavernous ante-hall. Amidst the coolies, passengers, touts, beggars, Armymen, pilgrims, tourists, vagrants, backpackers, lost souls, doves, hawks, birds of passage and the pieces of luggage dispersed like rockpiles all over the floor, he spotted a placard with his name on it. The man who stood holding it looked slightly stooped and shrunken and wore the kind of spectacles that become sunglasses depending on the light. He wouldn't have been less than sixty-five. He was incongruously dressed in white churidaars and a maroon kurta. His ill-fitting, bright white dentures stretched the skin above his upper lip. Even in repose, his mouth remained slightly open as though everready for a kiss. The care with which his white hair was brushed indicated that he was proud of it.

Bhola was in that frame of mind in which he would have preferred to be received by someone more obviously sexy. 'That's me,' he said in Hindi, pointing to the placard and added a little coldly, 'My name's been misspelt. I expected to find you inside on the platform.'

The man smiled disarmingly and responded, 'I waited here because there would be fewer chances of missing you.'

He spoke a terrible Hindi, the sort usually associated with Anglo-Indians. He extended a hand—but lukewarmly—to take Bhola's bag.

'No thanks. You can carry the placard and walk in front of me like a herald.' So that I can observe your arse twitch, added Bhola to himself, even through that kurta. The man smiled uncertainly. He wore a shiny dot of an earring in his right lobe. They walked off towards the car park. Despite— or because of—his age, the man's gait was a parody of the lithe and mannered stride of a mannequin.

Bhola spotted at the taxi stand the family that had been across the aisle from him in the train. The younger sister saw him. He smiled and raised his left arm in farewell. She grinned ecstatically and waved back. Her elder sister turned to stare and after a moment limply lifted a hand to the level of her shoulder, fingers crumpled and inert, and jerked it sideways a couple of times.

Anin had sent him a posh, air-conditioned, Japanese jeep the size of a cottage. The driver, dark, shrivelled, middle-aged and red-eyed, wore a white kurta and churidaars. Bhola sat in front beside him and his escort at the rear. They hummed through the congestion of the old town. The fine weather made all the difference to Bhola's spirits. The windows were down and they didn't need air conditioning. He remembered that five years ago, it had been Anin who had stressed that they set up shop in a place where the weather remained near-perfect all the year round. It took them half-an-hour to reach the suburbs and a further twenty minutes to break free of them. The driver drove barefoot, patiently and well. The feet on the clutch and accelerator pedals, Bhola noticed, were pale, long, shapely and effeminate. The hands on the steering wheel in contrast were large, hard and prominently veined.

Gradually, at its own pace, the landscape changed from urban to micropolitan and pseudo-rural. The cosmopolitan farms were fortresses behind twenty-foot-high concrete walls designed to withstand both the pickaxes and the bullets of the next revolution. Which could well begin, mused Bhola, in the matchboxes at the gates that housed the sentries of the mansions. In sleeveless vests, they basked on stools outside their kennels, there evidently not being enough room within for the intercom, the single chair over which were draped their civvies, the visitors' book *and* their bodies. The traffic had thinned but become more heterogeneous. They passed bullock carts and open trucks, both monstrously overloaded with diverse fruits of the earth. Everybody, including their chauffeur, drove a little more rashly. Every hectare for dozens of kilometres, it was rumoured, had been sold to the film financiers, diamond merchants, underworld dons, property developers and entertainment barons of the city. Periodically, the farmhouse walls made way for the emblems of the life of the hinterland—an inter-state bus depot, an open-air vegetable and fruit retail market, sugarcane fields, a garish cinema hall, a cattle fair. The drive helped Bhola to keep the core of his self calm and rested, emptied of expectations.

They arrived quite suddenly. The jeep veered off the road to stop before iron gates painted the same attractive ochre as the boundary wall that off and on had caught Bhola's attention for the preceding half a kilometre. Varieties of trees—well-watered and lush gulmohar, jacaranda, laburnum— had half-hidden it. Parts of it had been painted on in a childlike style that Bhola presumed was a chic tribal art form. The figures had sticks for limbs, isoceles triangles for torsos and globules for heads and had reminded him of the murderous pictographic messages that Sherlock Holmes had deciphered in *The Dancing Men*.

'This is a private entrance,' explained the escort with the tinted spectacles. 'The public gate faces the north,' he gestured vaguely through the windshield, 'and is off the highway.' The driver switched off the engine and they alit from the vehicle.

Unlike the escort, the guard who walked up to them was young. He too wore white churidaars. His kurta however was sea blue. He smiled a hello at the driver, said 'Good afternoon, sir' in English to Bhola and took the car keys. Bhola, bag on shoulder, followed the escort upto and through a door in the left gate to face the greenest, most restful and pleasing gardens that he had ever seen in his entire life.

The tiles of the paths were triangular, haphazardly laid and of varying shades of red. Like trails on a hillside, they meandered across the lawns to cottages of different sizes that all had tiled sloping roofs of the same ochre as the boundary wall. They were bordered by several varieties of flowering shrubs, bushes and creepers, amongst which Bhola, being botanically illiterate, could put names only to bougainvillea and hibiscus. The grass, mown like an Armyman's crew cut, was bright, almost luminously, green, as though it had been spray painted. He tramped contentedly along behind the escort. Every hundred metres or so, young trees, all but a grove, provided a chiaroscuro of shade for wrought-iron benches. 'Peacock. I just saw a peacock.' Appropriately at that moment, the sky above was a cloudless, breathless blue. He felt as though he had strolled into a very real film set.

They passed a couple of gardeners cooling off after having lounged about all morning, a waiter bearing a tray with the stuff on it hidden by a napkin, a white couple, in goggles and arm in arm but in Indian dress, cotton pyjamas and overshirt. 'Not too many people about. Is it the off season or just the wrong time of day?'

The escort turned to smile. It said to him, 'This is a health retreat, you jerk and not a Mediterranean beach at high noon in midsummer.' Aloud, he spoke, 'They would be at meditation or at a discourse.' Bhola noted with quiet joy that because he had twirled around to patronize him, the escort walked straight into the spray of an automatic sprinkler.

They headed towards the porch of a cottage larger than

the rest. The escort pushed open the main door, led Bhola into an airy and simply decorated reception room and with a valedictory simper, disappeared by way of an arch through which Bhola glimpsed a corridor and a sunny patch of lawn, terribly green.

Two large windows were open to the light and the summery buzzing of wasps. He let down his bag and watched two of them explore the sockets of the electric switchboard. The room, more a hall, had a high ceiling and no fans. He sat down on an uncomfortable wooden bench. Gazing about him, he noted and approved of the absence of inessential furniture. The walls were painted a warm yellow. He heard from afar some therapeutic choral chanting in an indistinguishable tongue and beneath it, from even further away, faint shouts of forced, purgatory, health-giving, bellowing laughter. They augmented the cushioned silence around him. He looked at his watch. One-thirty in the afternoon. He hadn't eaten for twenty hours but was neither hungry nor thirsty. He felt as though he had entered a different time zone halfway round the globe. His shoulders slumped forward as he sat.

The squeak of new rubber-soled sandals in the corridor beyond the archway announced Anin's arrival. She was alone. 'Bhola.' She flung her arms out and bustled up to him. The squeaks mounted in pitch and tempo. They hugged warmly. She held him by his biceps and beamed up at him. He felt a bit silly and resisted the urge to shrug her hands off so that *he* could hold *her* by her biceps and beam down at *her*. 'Bhola. Sala.'

With a quick, secret giggle, she bent down and touched his feet.

'Really, Anin, what *are* you doing!

'But you *are* my elder brother-in-law, at least till divorce do you part!' She clutched him by the arms and smiled into his eyes again.

In the four years since they had last met, she had changed

her hair and her eyes. 'You must be dead tired after that train journey. I don't think that I've sat in a railway compartment since 1980. But look at you. Just as thin as ever.' Her fingers trailed across his left cheek, his neck and the scar of the bullet wound above the collarbone. In all the years that he had known her, the pupils of her eyes had been black. They were now a tawny yellow. They made her a different person and her face difficult to read, as of a person with sunglasses. 'Are you in touch at all with Kamala and—I'm afraid I've forgotten my niece's name.'

'Karuna. KKK runs in your family.' Anin's hair had been dark brown and was now pitch black and silky. Parted at dead-centre, it flopped down on either side till just beneath her ears. It was the style that she had had in the photograph that he had seen in the newsmagazine the previous December. When her head moved, her hair swayed with some of the vigour of a bead curtain in a doorway in a breeze. Her earrings too—they resembled wooden talismans at the end of keychains—clicked and clacked with each shake and nod. He wondered what they hit to produce those sounds. Perhaps her noggin.

'I like your hairstyle, Anin. It suits you.'

'Thanks. It's a wig.' She released him, sat down on the bench and gazed up at him. Her yellow contact lenses however robbed her face of expression and made her appear like a villainess in a Wonder Woman comic. 'I lost all my hair to chemotherapy.'

His mind was so befogged that he couldn't for a moment recall what that was. 'Oh. Sorry to hear about that.'

'Come.' Suddenly she arose to a squeak of her sandals and a clack from her earrings, 'I'll show you your room.' Obediently, he picked up his bag and followed her out through the archway.

He sensed more than saw rooms with shut doors on his right and alongside the courtyard of lawn on his left a white wall with figures painted on it. They ascended the spiral stairs at the end of the corridor. Anin climbed stiffly, almost pausing for rest on each step. The corridor on the first floor was a replica of the one below. It ended in a terrace directly above the reception room and below the roof. From enormous ochre pots, creepers trailed their way up the wooden lattices against the walls and across the mesh beneath the tiles of the roof. Anin allowed Bhola to admire the terrace for a minute, then led him back to the room closest to it. Its door was shut but not locked. She opened it and preceded him in.

The room was large, with a crimson, clean cement floor. The bed in the middle had a wooden frame for a mosquito net but no net; he noticed pale saffron walls and a window, open, that gave on to a luxuriant pipal tree. Beneath the window stood a desk and chair and against the wall alongside the door a wooden bench of the type that he had seen downstairs. 'Would you like to nap, wash up, rest, bathe, shave, jog, whatever?'

'Yes, I think. I mean, I'm meant to, aren't I? I'm sure that you have things to do and don't want me following you around like a nagging thought.'

She agreed to return at four-thirty. He, with a faint but genuine smile of pleasure, half-murmuring, half-humming the line from the song *Lovely To See You Again, My Friend*, shut the door softly behind her.

He unpacked even though he had no wish to see and arrange his shabby belongings. He placed his manual alarm clock beside the lamp on the bedside table and noticed the photograph on it. He sat down on the bed and picked up the frame. Moti's face had filled out. Its expression, no longer hunted, had become feline, sensual, almost venal. The cheeks had no hollows, the lips seemed to have swollen, almost as though stung. His eyes, all-knowing, tawnier than Anin's lenses, gazed at the world in drugged tranquillity. A black bandana tied tight over his head kept his untidy hair off his forehead. The collar of his buttoned-up, black silk kurta seemed to cut into the red flesh of his neck. He was fairer in the photograph than he had ever been in life. At the bottom of the likeness, on an ochre band, was printed in black: *Vatsaha, Tvam Shrimantaha Manushyaha Asi.* Bhola went to the bathroom and tenderly placed the photograph face down on the floor beneath the waste pipe behind the WC. He then returned and stretched out on the bed. The pillow was thin and uncomfortable. He doubled it up and stared at the ceiling. He noticed around the ends of the tubelight the smudges of some electrician's grubby hands and wondered, just before dozing off, how Dosto had died.

Anin knocked on the door at a quarter to five. She still wore her white churidaars and long, bottle-green khadi kurta but looked brighter, more refreshed. Her eyes seemed to have become yellower. 'So? Feeling better? Did push-ups for a couple of hours?'

'You haven't told me yet how Dosto died. An overdose of what?'

'Do not linger.' She stroked the rings on her left hand with the fingers of the right. 'Cocaine.' She smiled, a brief grimace. 'Are you hungry? The last meal with us here finishes well before sunset. I'm going to have a bowl of soup. Would you like some too?'

The terrace glowed orange with the last light that filtered in through the mesh of foliage. In a minute, Bhola realized that the effect was partly created by coloured lamps concealed behind the ochre-coloured pots that sustained the creepers. The soup was delicious, whitish, vaguely like chicken sweet corn but tasting of ginger, onion and something else that his limited culinary knowledge could not identify. When Anin proposed a second helping, he did not refuse.

'It does one good, this soup. Full of nutrients and goodness, I'm sure. What is it?'

'It's Chinese. Fortunately, we haven't yet rejected

altogether the wisdom of China,' commented the new Anin primly. She drained her bowl, wiped her lips daintily with a napkin and continued to speak—a little schoolmarmishly— while folding and arranging it and her bowl on the tray. 'Aborted human fœtus soup. Have you ever been to China? I developed a taste for it in Shen-zhen. At one of the state-run health centres there, the doctors regularly took fœtuses home. The best are the first-born males of young mothers. That's only natural in our sexist society, I told him.'

As far as Bhola knew, the closest that she had got to China was Calcutta, but he had other things on his mind. 'Whose fœtus have I just eaten?'

'How on earth should I know?' She frowned at the stupidity of the question. Her tone became faintly acerbic. 'Don't be squeamish. No doctor would carry out an abortion just to have a go at the fœtus.' Then she paused to resume her classroom manner. 'On the other hand, a fœtus would be wasted if not eaten. They are even richer than placentas in nutritional value and are particularly beneficial for the kidneys and skin tone. One just has to be careful about the strong medicines used in abortions.'

Bhola put his empty bowl atop the other on the tray. He thought that he felt the soup rising within him and determinedly fought the sensation down. Their eyes met briefly.

'Tell me, sala sir, when do you intend to start flirting with me?'

'Sorry?'

'I need to know so that I can plan my evening.'

The escort of the morning glided out from the corridor and up to them. He simpered—familiarly but not disrespectfully—at Bhola. In response, Bhola flexed his facial muscles for half a second. Anin emitted a short and unexpected giggle. Then in silence, they watched him depart with the tray.

'What would you do if you suddenly learnt that a falling meteorite or nuclear bomb gave you just five more minutes to live?' She gazed at him seductively and long. 'I understand— Dosto used to tell me—that such were the questions with which you used to amuse yourselves in school.' If he was going to vomit, it would be right then and there, in a fountain on to the table and her. 'Five minutes is too short, one would suppose. You and Dosto would masturbate, I should think, out of stress. Or would you go out of the room, look up at the darkening sky and wait, awed like children?' She wriggled down and forward in her armchair till the nape of her neck rested against the top of its back. 'And suppose death were not five minutes but one hour away? One more day? One week? One month? Six months, which is what doctors in books give your cancer? Mine gave me two years after glancing at my bank balance. You can't take it with you, so you might as well give it to me.' Think of it as chicken sweet corn, grains of enriched maize floating in warm semen. 'It's almost five-thirty. We should go down now. Does growing old bother you?'

'A few months ago, I remember that while shaving, I noticed a white hair in my nostril. That nonplussed me completely and I took half an hour to shave that morning. That apart, no, I don't think that ageing bothers me particularly. My stepmother, for example, plucks out the grey hair on her head. She is half bald therefore but with naturally black hair. Far too many people dye their hair, don't you think so? Why don't they jog instead?'

He felt sluggish and could not stop himself from saying oafish, clumsy things. Anin had become another person and he wondered why he had made the journey. They descended, left the cottage by the main door and turned left towards the interior of the complex. She nodded and smiled at several passers-by. They skirted a couple of crowded grass tennis courts and a tree house, dense with children and dwarfs, built in the lower branches of a prodigious banyan. A pair of huffers and puffers jogged by. Bhola could not resist and ran after them for a couple of steps. He then stopped for Anin and smiled winningly at her. A ripple of a response glided across her face. A cottage on the right, from the posters pinned to its noticeboard, looked like the auditorium of an arty film club. They crossed a lawn exploding with bougainvillea and opened a door in a wooden lattice wall that cordoned off the swimming pool.

At forty-four, Titli looked sixty. She sat in a white plastic armchair facing the water, alone. In the four years since she had been beaten up by Bhola's father-in-law's goons, she had swollen up impossibly. She had shaved her head and its stubble shone silver. She didn't turn around when they approached her. He noticed large blackheads on the nape of her neck. Shit, AIDS was his first thought.

'I'll leave you with her for a while,' said Anin without bothering to lower her voice. 'She's blind in the right eye and acutely diabetic. Munches spoonsful of sugar when she thinks no one's looking.' Bhola watched Anin recede to the wooden lattice. She made an effort, it seemed, not to slouch, to make her back look attractive. He turned around, picked up a red chair, placed it alongside Titli's and sat down. He reached out and touched the obese arm.

'Ohhh.' She feigned surprise unconvincingly. 'All well at home? Baby?' Though her face regained some of its maternal attractiveness when she smiled, her pupils remained unfocussed and mentally she seemed far away. Her face had softened, become gentler and infinitely older, as though she had finally understood the wisdom in giving up the struggle. Invisible fingers seemed to be continually and firmly tugging her jowls down, stretching the skin over the swollen cheeks.

'Yes, Karuna has survived you and is probably fine.'

She pretended not to understand and looked away at the water. One of the two swimmers had stopped splashing about in the shallows. They watched him place his palms flat on the matting that hemmed the pool, and try to jump up and jack himself out cleanly. He failed twice. He then reclined on his left forearm, hoisted his right foot over the edge and rolled over and out. He stood up, automatically dusted his hands, sucked in his stomach and ambled off towards the changing rooms, feet splayed outwards.

'Have you had dinner? Would you like to go and rest?'

'I'm off food for the moment, thanks.'

Titli got up as though he had said yes. In her kurta, she resembled a gunny sack crammed with pumpkins. She steadied herself with a bamboo walking stick that had been tucked away on her blind side. 'What about watermelon? Chikoos? They seem to follow your advice here on matters of food. "Respect your stomach as you would yourself"—that kind of rubbish doesn't agree with me at all. I've suffered terrible loose motions and flatulence from the moment I arrived—'

'Spare me the details.'

They began to plod towards the water. 'On some days, there isn't any rice at all! I mean, there's just some soup that looks and tastes like baby vomit, followed by fruit. I sometimes feel as though I've become a monkey.'

There were more English phrases in her speech than before, even though it was clear that with him, she was happy to revert to her odd Hindi. They moved slowly down the length of the pool, rounded the corner and sidestepped the diving board. Titli paused, swayed on her walking stick and sluggishly waved goodbye at the female in cap and goggles intent on swimming till dawn. The pool itself indefinably depressed Bhola—perhaps because it reminded him of his school days, perhaps because of the light. By the time they reached the door in the opposite lattice wall, Titli was panting gently.

He pushed his hand underneath her kurta, stroked the

cleft of her buttocks and then gently began to pump her anus. He would have to remember to whip his hand away in time in case he activated her bloody loose motions. Her respiration became more audible. Man does not breathe freely through both nostrils at any one time, thus out of the blue he remembered, from almost twenty years ago, Dosto reading aloud to the world from one of his, Bhola's, yoga books on a holiday morning in the sun on the terrace outside his room. Breathing, like everything else in this world, is cyclical. Titli's mouth was slightly open. Her nostrils quivered faintly and she gazed straight ahead at nothing. Humans use nostrils alternately, switching every four hours from one to the other. The polarity observed in all nature may be found in the human body in the eyes, ears, limbs, hands, feet, breasts, buttocks, testicles and nostrils, and even in the rhythms and mystical syllables of respiration, in the *hum* aspirated and the *sa* vehemently exhaled.

They moved on slowly through a kitchen patch and a nursery for potted plants. In the twilight under the canopy of wire mesh and creeper, amidst the screech and squawk of birds, Titli stopped, leaned her stick against the crook of her thigh and tried to swat a mosquito.

The cottage that she inhabited was tiny and pink, with a deep blue front door. They entered, she sighed and immediately moved to the two windows to shut them. Their panes were of frosted glass. She deposited her walking stick in a cane basket by the door, walked slowly but without difficulty to a table against the opposite wall, found her bidis, matches and a tiny brass ashtray in its top drawer and lit up. She then sauntered to the mattress on the floor between the windows and exhaling luxuriously, collapsed on to it. Bhola walked up to kneel beside her, prised her feet out of her sandals and kissed her right instep. Her foot was small, strong and shapely. He liked its hard and wrinkled feel against his lips.

'Look at me in the eyes and take off your clothes.' It was something that she had never been able to do. Four years ago, in another life and another planet, he had vowed to himself, with an earnestness that had seared his insides, that he would never ever touch or talk to her again. He hadn't forgotten his promise; it had simply been squashed underfoot and thrown out of the window by lust. He didn't enjoy being untrue to himself; he was thus almost always unhappy while having sex—and distracted throughout the fun by his yearning to be mentally fitter, to possess a will with more muscle and less fat.

She sat up slowly, as always both pleased and pretending to be embarrassed and with the bidi dangling from her lips, yet demurely looking down at the buttons of her kurta, began fumbling with them. His left hand pattered up her thigh like a lizard. He parted wide her legs, raised her kurta and snuggled his nose and lips against the warmth of her vagina. 'Hurry hurry Hari Om Hari hurry up please it's time,' he urged her. He caressed and tenderly kneaded his fists into the enormous folds of her stomach. They were cool and faintly damp with sweat. Her kurta came off and was folded and placed behind the bolster. He reached for the strings of her churidaar. He noticed that she still wore her peculiar style of bra, more like a man's capacious sleeveless vest than a woman's undergarment. 'Take off take off,' he mumblingly ordered, 'let me taste your body in my mouth.' She picked her bidi up from the ashtray, relit it, inhaled twice, stubbed it out and began to remove her bra. Her breasts, vast and cumbersome, tumbled out like papayas. He abandoned the churidaar and reached out to chafe her nipples with his palms. 'Suffocate me.' He massaged her breasts, fat, slippery and overflowing in his hands, teasing with his fingers, rhythmically with each circular stroke, her damp armpits. 'Get up. Take off these silly pyjamas.' Obediently, she raised herself up on to her knees to undo the strings. She stood up completely to wriggle the churidaar off her hips. She sat down again with it crumpled up around her ankles. One by one, he took her feet in his lap and eased the garment off. As usual, she wore no pantie. He sundered wide her legs. To lift each one of them was akin to pumping iron. 'Ah. You have shaved your pubis along with your head.'

'Lice. An invasion. Even in my armpits. Perhaps it was the humidity of the monsoon.' She rarely spoke of her own during sex. But she liked the game that he had taught her to play, of chatting away normally, while copulating, on any subject under the sun.

'When I saw you at the pool, I thought that you'd shaved your head for Dosto.' He knelt between her thighs, his feet tucked away yoga-like under him. 'In memoriam ahh.' Her sticky, sweet-sour smell drew his head down. He guided her hands to interlock and grasp his skull at its base.

'Why should I shave for him?' she retorted a little sharply. 'He wasn't my husband.'

'How exactly did he die? You and Anin were a little vague—naturally—on the phone.' He then began to fuck her with his chest. It was a great exercise, he had discovered by trial and error, for the entire body and particularly for the upper torso and shoulders. In the golden days, he had done eight rapid rounds of fifty humps each. Time would soon reveal what the years had done to his physique. He rubbed his forehead against her clitoris till they both felt moist and comfortable. Then he parted her legs till he could flatten his sternum against her vagina. His arms went under and around her hips, pushing her buttocks up so that his hands landed on her breasts as on dunes of rubber. Her feet lay calm and inert on his shoulder blades. 'Squeeze me with your thighs. Make some effort. And warn me in advance if some explosions of either kind intend to issue from your great tum.' He wanted to feel like a six-foot prick imprisoned not so much by the strength of her body as by its weight. Then he recalled that he had felt like one all his life and began to snigger to himself.

'Heartfail,' she responded laconically in Hindi, that is to say, she used the two English words but uttered them as one, pronouncing the f as the ph in tophat.

Thirty-seven...thirty-eight...thirty-niiiiine...Where are you from Jesus what do you want Jesus tell me...forty-four...forty-five...His hands left her breasts to delve into her armpits, maul her cheeks, to wander over her body. 'Light up a bidi. Exhale over me.' Her face had flushed and softened and exhibited again that expression—sad, slightly idiotic—characteristic of her when she lost control. Obediently, she let go of his head to try and reach her matches and packet. She had to wait for him to pause after his second round of thrusts. He sat on her abdomen, rocking her periodically and watched her light up. He couldn't even remember whether she had regularly smoked earlier.

'I have to finish this one quickly,' she said and began inhaling and exhaling deeply and rapidly. 'We can't keep the windows shut for too long.' He observed for a moment the bidi end glow fiercely and fade. He got off her stomach and pushed the sole of his right foot deep against her perineum. 'Take in my whole leg deep deep deep.' He sat down on her right foreleg and teased the tyres of her stomach with the toes of his left foot.

Half an hour later, when Anin knocked on the front door, the windows had been open for a while and aromatic incense sticks lit at several points in the room to dispel the odour of tobacco. Titli munched on a mixture out of a silver box and offered Bhola some. He distinguished the tastes of areca, clove and cardamom. 'You didn't pay me this time,' she protested with a smile, pausing on her way to the front door.

He was taken aback but sought to control his surprise. 'I wasn't sure of what the rates would be.' Since she continued to smile faintly and wait, he took out his wallet and extracted his single five-hundred-rupee note from it. He rolled it up into a cigarette and pushed it into the breast pocket of her kurta. In response, her features congealed into pudding, her eyes narrowed and she smiled slowly, hurt and contemptuous. 'Thenkew, you miserly flysucker.' She lifted out her stick from its basket and, walking again as though she needed it, continued, 'Dosto was generous, a king. He gave me a gold necklace. You follow me? Have you ever thought of giving me gold as a present? Any silk saris? Woollen shawls? Your life will ooze out of your orifices at the very idea.' She reached up to unbolt the door.

He flopped down again on the mattress on the floor. He needed to enjoy what remained of his post-coital lassitude, its emptiness, to let go, allow his life—as the fat, grasping, graceless bitch had suggested—to ooze out of his orifices. Abruptly, he missed the sounds of his wife singing and the sad, gentle twang of her accompanying tanpura, the stillness infused in him by the fulfilment that her music expressed. Anin glanced at him once, supine and abandoned, before replying to a question that Titli had posed. He was filled with the void of contentment, the vacuity that was not the lack of anything. Truly speaking, he needed nothing; he realized anew that all things were best appreciated in their absence. Negated by their opposites, they left behind just the nothingness that the world had begun with. The music, with its plaintive notes and restful pauses, would have reflected in its silences the beauty of that void.

'Well, rediscovered your old selves?' Anin stood above him with her feet apart and her hips thrust out—a little like a man pissing—and smiled at him with her yellow eyes. 'Are you still hungry? If you want some more soup, you'll have to wait till the morning because the kitchen shuts down at sunset.' He struggled up to a more respectable position. He had had an absurd—but overwhelming—impression that if he didn't move, she would lift up her kurta, undo her strings and start urinating on him. He shook his head to clear it. 'Tell me,' she continued, settling down beside him on the mattress and decorously arranging her kurta over her knees, 'If I were to commit suicide in a day or two and were to mention you as an abetter in my Goodbye-cruel-world note, would you be flattered or offended?'

'Offended, I think.' He shifted his right leg slightly so that it could rest against her left foot. He watched Titli hobble through an open door and switch on a tubelight to reveal a kitchen. Anin's hair did really look like a wig from close quarters. Yet being unobservant, naive and immersed in his self, he would never have realized it had he not been told. Her perfume was faint and lemony.

'I've seen you often in my dreams,' she confessed, smiling at him tenderly. 'In my dreams, you always sleep with your back to me.'

'That's because as far as possible,' he opened wide his mouth, stretched his tongue out to the maximum and rolled his eyes up and inwards in a yogic drill meant mainly to exercise the facial and throat muscles and secondarily to unsettle passers-by, 'one should avoid inhaling other people's exhalations. As for your death wish,' he continued chatting to the back of her thighs, for she had suddenly risen, smoothening down her kurta over her hips, 'it is not—' surprising in the circumstances, he had wanted to say just for the sake of blabbering away but didn't. For one, even by his standards, it would have been an exceptionally tasteless remark. Besides, she had stepped off the mattress and stumped off towards the kitchen, no doubt to lend Titli a hand.

For all the years that they had been together in school and college, Dosto on the average had contemplated suicide twice a month. Whenever he hadn't had his way, or had been depressed, or yelled at by his father—'I'm going to kill myself,' he had announced in a hiss through his tears and rushed out of the house or away from the cricket field. On each occasion, en route to killing himself, he had stopped to snack, smoke a cigarette or chat with a stranger. Forty minutes later, when a servant had been despatched to bring back the corpse for its homework and dinner, Dosto had been found either laughing and swinging on the gate with an acquaintance or lounging about at the end of the lane before the chaat vendor, snickering at passing girls.

Suicide or accident, no matter how Dosto had died, Bhola saw that he would gain nothing by pressing for details. He had wanted to be reassured that it had not—not even in some remotely indirect way—been his doing, that Dosto had not succumbed to the ill effects of some ghastly experiment that Bhola, letting his mind ramble and thinking aloud, might have—weeks or months or years ago—suggested in some dreamy, idle moment—but he—Bhola—realized that he would simply have to remain content with suspecting the worst. It was over, after all. In a similar manner, Anin, despite the length of their friendship, had not asked how the years had treated him. On their faces were etched quite plainly the broad contours of their wasted lives and it would have been in poor taste to demand that the blanks be filled in.

Men without love think only of self
But the loving strip themselves to the bone for others.

Owing to his prodigious memory for the unimportant, he had never forgotten those lines from a Tamil work that he had come across in a history book in his last years in school. Slowly, almost insidiously, they—with time, his marriage and the birth of his daughter—had come to express what he wanted to achieve with his life, namely, to strip himself (in a sexually liberating, exhibitionistic way) to the bone (almost religiously, after suffering privation) for others (and thus to escape from himself). With the discipline of decades, he had succeeded in attaining some measure of calmness at the cold centre of his heart that he now wanted to expose and shatter.

Anin emerged from the kitchen with a teapot and cups on
a tray. Titli behind her switched off the tubelight. Beneath
the single light bulb under its maroon shade, they arranged
themselves on flat cushions around a low square table. With
the rest of the room in gloom, they resembled conspirators or
psychics preparing to rap with spirits. He noticed that Titli's
tea—dense, brown and creamy, with a skin on its surface—
had already been poured out. It looked irresistible, as though
it would be heavy with sugar. He wanted to gulp it down and
with a warm thick sweet milky tongue tease open her labia.
Anin remarked, almost as though following his thoughts, 'It's
herbal tea for us, light and soothing.' She lifted up the tea
cozy and the lid of the pot and stirred its contents with a
spoon. With the steam arose a warm fragrance of cinnamon
and lavender. 'Have you drunk it before? I hadn't until I
arrived here. Now I hardly drink anything else.' She poured
out two cups.

He sipped. 'It's very nice. What fœtal excretions does it
contain?'

'Our Dr Borkar,' said Titli abruptly, noisily slurping from
her cup, 'sometimes used to drink your kind of tea, neither
milk nor sugar. He claimed that it helped his incontinence.'
She drained her cup, put it down and licked off her lips some
residual cream. 'It's quite popular here in the retreat too.
Only Moti and I seem to have stuck to milk and sugar, and
tea leaves boiled with the water.' She belched gently but
unabashedly.

'When do you want to see Moti, now or tomorrow
morning?' asked Anin, sipping her tea and looking at Bhola as
of old over the rim of the cup.

'If I have to meet him at all,' replied Bhola rapidly and in
English so that Titli wouldn't follow, 'I'd prefer to with a
knife in my hand.'

Anin's face became more careful and formal, as when one
composes oneself before a camera for a passport photograph.

'Would you know how to handle one?' she asked in a murmur. With a sigh of effort, she then got up and trudged out through the third door that led to the rest of the cottage.

Well, there's always a first and last time, he answered without opening his mouth. Gulping down his tea, he returned to flop down on the mattress. Titli watched his every move with a fixed half-smile and her small unblinking eyes. Her allusion to her doctor paramour had brought back to Bhola the suppressed vignettes of another life. Years ago, in response to his probing, she had revealed some of the details of her early experiences of sex with Borkar, from the days when she had first given up selling vegetables from a cart and joined his household as a domestic to mop the floors, scour the toilets and do the dishes and laundry. With her short-sleeved blouses that showed off her strong collarbones and robust and fleshy upper arms, she, by her very presence in his surroundings, had made the good doctor ooze into his trousers. In ten days, much against his mother's wishes, Titli had graduated to helping him in his clinic. In three weeks, he had suggested that she wear a nurse's cap and uniform because he wanted to see her calves. In return, she had proposed that he quadruple her salary. He had accepted. Humming to herself, she had begun to gain weight. Four or five times in the course of a day, the doctor, unable to contain himself, had hissed at her playacting his nurse, with the blurred outlines of the waiting patients visible through the frosted glass, to show him her breasts, to lift up her uniform so that he could press a cold, surgical knife flat against her genitals. He would smack her in a frenzy of incontinence when she refused, delayed matters or even looked reluctant. He flooded his trousers in seconds. He was otherwise cold and correct with her. He had suffered his lack of sexual self-control ever since he could remember. In his school and college days, for instance, if the bell rang during the last answer of an examination, he would routinely climax in his pants with the tension of trying to finish before his paper was snatched away.

'Did Anin mix something in that herbal tea? I'm a bit high.'

'Very likely.' Titli lifted the lid of the teapot with a clatter, leaned forward to position her nose above it and inhaled audibly and deeply in a snort. 'Everyone here seems to be high on various kinds of substances. Nice.' She looked up to smile knowingly at Bhola. Fat, like the beaming moon, and crowned by a silvery stubble, her face above the teapot seemed to enact a nursery rhyme or a fairy tale. At any moment, he expected the spoons in the saucers to upend themselves and waltz off the table.

They heard the rapid squeak of Anin's sandals well before she entered. She carried an incongruous, maroon canvas school satchel. Ponderously, she sank to her knees beside the mattress, unclasped the bag, and held it up commandingly under Bhola's nose. Her eyes seemed to gleam with sorrow beneath the fronds of her false hair and her lips buckled in an involuntary, humorless grimace but she did not speak. Bhola sat up, dutifully peeped inside the satchel, saw part of a black leather case that could have contained a knife or spectacles or pens, raised his eyebrows, twitched his lips and nodded to look impressed and, duty done, collapsed again on the mattress.

'Lesbo lesbo let'sgo,' he murmured too softly for anyone to hear.

The camp was carved up—or fell—into three divisions. Since his arrival, Bhola had seen parts of only the right flank. The elongated central portion, called The Middle Way, was devoted to Natal Promise discourses, Dream Yoga meditation classes, Sufi whirling, Enlightenment Therapy and bio-etheric healing.

Dosto's domain was the smaller, extreme-left, section of the retreat. From the outside, it looked like the end of the road, for the front wall of the large cottage was part of the boundary wall of the park. They rang the bell and waited. Bhola glanced at his watch. It was only seven thirty-five in the evening even though it looked and felt like two a.m. All the cottages that they had passed had been dark and silent. A few stray lamps in the lanes and on the lawns glowed spectrally in the thin vesperine mist. The main door was opened noiselessly by another fine young man who too was dressed in churidaar and maroon kurta. They entered a large, simply furnished and dimly lit hall. Bhola smelt the fragrance of incense in the air. On the walls could be discerned enormous, intricately-painted murals of concentric circles, triangles, spoked wheels and other geometrical figures with Devanagari letters and numerals inked in in some of them. With their dominant colours of yellow and orange, the walls glowed with warmth in reflecting the lamplight.

Anin muttered something inaudible and with her red school satchel disappeared behind a thin bamboo curtain. Titli with her stick followed more sedately. Bhola, presuming that he was to wait, sat down on a cane stool and absentmindedly picked up a glossy pamphlet from the occasional table beside him. The young man, fit, dark, lithe, waited, with a half-smile and seemingly on the balls of his feet, beside the bamboo curtain, as though on guard. The incense, reminding Bhola of the perfume of his father's hair oil, distracted and depressed him. He felt high, as though the herbal tea had touched off and on and off and on and off tiny, multicoloured, fairy lights behind his forehead. He widened his eyes and then glared to focus them on the foldout in his hands.

The Circle Of Health, read the cover. He noticed that it mirrored the designs that he saw on the walls surrounding him. He flipped through the pages. *Mandala is Sanskrit for circle. At the end of the course, each participant can design a circle that will provide her/him a visual portrait of her/his state of mental health after she/he has systematically analysed her/his mental, physical and spiritual functioning.* The course sounded like group sex. *Mandalas have appeared throughout the ages as symbolic representations of a culture's worldview, an artist's inner life or the energy of the Mother Goddess. Many indigenous peoples create round earth shields with shells, feathers, leather and other materials sacred to the tribe. Even during the European Middle Ages, mandalas were evident in the stained glass windows of great cathedrals like Chartres and Notre Dame. Closer to the source, Tibetan Buddhist monks create short-lived, exquisite mandalas of coloured sand representing both their entire cosmology and endless impermanence.* He looked about him. The attendant continued to smile at him with a light in his eyes that could clearly be construed as an invitation. Dazed at the twists and turns that his life had taken to arrive at that moment and shutting himself off from thinking about the immediate future that he seemed to have committed himself to, Bhola beamed at the young man and patted the stool next to him as an offer to him to sit down. It was smirkingly ignored. Smiling to subdue the spurt of bitterness at the rejection, he returned to scanning the pamphlet. *Your personalized mandala of well-being will serve your imagination as a tool, spurring you to adopt and enjoy more healthy activities and eventually to create within yourself that calm centre that is the ultimate aim of existence. You will create and colour your own wheel and make it evolve into a many-tinted pictogram that will depict exactly where you are focussing your time and energy and where you might need to pay more attention. It will help you to identify imbalances in your daily life. Do you spend too much time fantasizing? Masturbating? Remember that none of your other activities metaphysically is more wasteful. Do your daily responsibilities crowd out areas of self-care? Do you let rhythm and music move you? Think of the mandala as a living wheel always in flux, constantly readjusting to the shifting demands and desires of your life and helping you to see yourself more clearly. Remember that there are important questions that we never ask ourselves. Why not? Do you reserve a portion of each day for the divine? When each moment is seen as precious, then life becomes a long, long course to be run. Are you travelling light? Are you able to express hurt and anger without blame? Do you sense purpose and meaning in your life? Do not forget that life's greatest achievements are gained through the accumulated sum of small daily disciplines. Out of the many possible lives that you could be living, your small, daily actions determine the one you have.*

The bamboo curtain rustled and Anin entered, face expressionless but wet with tears. She waited at the doorway for him and then preceded him through it to the corridor. The cottages seemed to have been constructed all on one model; he again noted on his left the square of lawn that ended in a wall. It too had been painted over with geometrical shapes that looked brightly coloured even in the dim light that reached them from the corridor. On his right, one after another like sentries at parade, the shut doors of rooms presented their blank faces. The spiral staircase at the end of the corridor was barred by a low gate. The attendant slipped past them to unlock it and then mounted the stairs barefoot, pausing at the curve to swivel and bestow on them a beguiling simper. In a maroon pigeonhole clamped to the wall on the right, Anin left her squeaky sandals and Bhola his canvas shoes and followed him.

On the floor above, they stepped in at the only open door into the first of six similar and interconnected changing rooms. They were all minimally furnished. The participants proceeded from one to the next in a certain order. Each room had occasional tables, clotheshorses, and a bamboo pole horizontal along a wall with hangers dangling on it. The incense sticks in the first room gave out the scent of jasmine and in the subsequent rooms those of sandalwood, pine, rose, orange blossom and lavender. Similarly, the walls of the first room were painted a pale violet and those of the following

descended delicately through the colours of the rainbow. The
electric lights were off. Earthen lamps and the fat wax
candles that Bhola could never see without being reminded
of the dirty jokes of his adolescence cast an aptly lambent
glow. Diminutive speakers set high up on the walls emitted
pseudo-religious music appropriate to the mood—conch shells,
drums, bells, strings and some resonant Sanskrit recitation of
which he could follow just the stray word. The atmosphere of
the rooms instantly made him feel calmer and sleepier.

Two white women turned at their entry and smiled
briefly at them. Neither Titli nor the attendant were to be
seen. The older woman, with grey short hair and a square
face, took off her spectacles and began polishing them with
the end of her short kurta. Beneath her Bermuda shorts, the
younger woman's calves were waxen and shapely. With a
second glance at Bhola and Anin that did not quite meet their
eyes, they exited through the door that led to the indigo
room. Bhola checked his pockets and, hoping that his undies
didn't look too grey and elastic-less, stepped out of his
trousers and into a pair of churidaars that had no pockets.
'What am I to do with these?' he asked, holding aloft his
wallet and keys.

'Don't yell. There are lockers in the next room,' replied
Anin in a hiss, looking at him sceptically while he struggled
with the strings of the churidaar.

'What am I to do with the key of the locker when I don't
have pockets?'

There were no lockers in the indigo room. The musical
chants sounded louder. The younger white woman admired
in an undertone the shade on the wall. She wore no bra. To
avoid being blinded by the outline of her nipples under her
polo shirt, Bhola focussed with discreet intensity on the
contour of the pantie of the older woman under her slacks. It
appeared to be the size of a man's waistcoat. 'There aren't
any keys. The lockers have combination locks instead,'

answered Anin, turning her face to an indigo wall to grapple
with an imminent sneeze.

Placing his wallet and keys on the floor, Bhola divested
himself of his shirt. 'What am I to do when I forget the
combination code? When it's a four-digit number, I use my
year of birth but I am always confused between my actual
and official year of birth. Strictly speaking, unless one
undergoes a DNA test or something, one can never be sure
of one's age, you know.' He slung his shirt on a hanger with
elaborate clumsiness for he had been distracted by a sudden
recollection of the sunny morning when he, aged seven, had
been casually informed by his father that he was actually
eight.

'We reduced your age when we filled in your school
application form. It should give you a headstart in life.' His
father had spoken more to his own reflection in the shaving
mirror propped up on the parapet of the terrace. 'So we filled
in your year of birth as 1960 instead of 1959. But I don't think
that you should discuss this with anyone because it makes
your parents look like cheats—although for a cause, of course.'
His father had massaged his cheek partly in self-love and
partly to check the quality of the shave. 'Think of yourself
forever as seven and not eight, okay? Not forever, naturally,
but for the time being, for a year or so.'

That had been the golden age of fraud. The registration
of births with one or the other arm of the government had not
been mandatory. Lying about official things had therefore
been easier. The date given on one's school-leaving certificate
was accepted everywhere as one's real date of birth. Well, it
was as valid as any. One was as old as one felt and as old as
one's memory. Bhola himself didn't remember anything of
his life before the summer of 1963, when his elder brother
had been pushed from the top rung of the ladder of one of
the slides in Children's Park, had landed head first on a small
stone and got up with it embedded in his skull and blood

streaming down his face like water from an overflowing
bucket. Well, 1963 made him more thirty-three than thirty-
seven.

He preferred to trust his own memory to that of his
parents. When they stated that he was actually eight but
officially seven, he realized upon reflection that biologically
he could just as well have been six or even five. His father
was notoriously forgetful about matters that did not concern
him.

The lockers, bright turquoise in colour, took up one wall
of the blue room. He climbed a stepladder to deposit his
belongings in one of the vacant boxes at the top. He clicked
the door shut but did not lock it. Dumping one's personal
effects somewhere counted as a stage in the gradational
process of weight loss. He watched Anin take off her yellow
contact lenses, drop them in a tiny white plastic case and
place the case in a locker. She did not bother either to spin
its wheel. As her old self, she looked less unfinished, more
accessible and attractive. He smiled at her with genuine
cordiality.

He was in a purplish kaftan by the time they reached the
orange room. His skin tingled and stirred at the novelty of his
dress. Another attendant, also young and smiling, came forward
with a tray on which stood a pile of earth-coloured saucers,
cups and a jar of what looked like milk. He had long
luxurious sideburns that drew attention to themselves like a
sudden vulgar wink. What is the height of fashion?—Bhola
suddenly remembered a joke from his adolescence. Sideburns
on the cock was the answer.

Titli sat on a cushion on the floor in a corner, cowed-
down, glum despite being carefully expressionless, gazing
mindlessly down at nothing, knees up and pressed together,
her left arm protectively encircling her forelegs, her right
hand enfolding a cup of milk. Anin nudged her shoulder, she
looked up, drained the milk, got clumsily to her feet, hobbled
over to a table to deposit the cup, returned to them, picked

up the maroon canvas school satchel that Anin had earlier carried and glanced briefly at Bhola. The three took a couple of steps towards the exit. The attendant shimmied up before them once more with the tray. Bhola took up the jug and poured himself a cup. It *was* warm, sweetened milk, soothing.

The last, the red, room was a hall, the open, foliage-vaulted terrace of the other cottages covered in concrete and converted. Unlike the uniformly muted, lulling pastel shades on the walls of the changing rooms, the reds in the hall, though different from one another, were each of deep and vibrant tints; stippled in yellow on the scarlet and crimson were the geometrical designs of the reception room downstairs. The incense sticks diffused a mild fragrance that seemed to blend camphor and lime. Mattresses covered in orange-maroon- and rose-coloured sheets were arranged along the walls. The three settled down on one. Bhola rested his head on Titli's thigh and, thinking that she would like all that togetherness, pulled Anin's legs across his abdomen. She didn't notice.

From the corners, a sort of lustre was diffused across the hall by means of lamps that intensely beamed their light at the walls alone. There were five other human forms present— the two white women whom they had encountered in the changing rooms, the attendant whose sideburns looked like Matthew Arnold's and who had sidled in behind them, a supine male form on a mattress and a young, dark woman, crosslegged in yoga fashion on another mattress, applying some unguent on her upper arms from a jar beside her. The two white women lay on one mattress with eyes shut, arms folded across breasts, in some symbolic inverted position, that is to say, each head lay close to the feet of the other. They appeared to be enjoying the music. It indeed had become more enjoyable—faster, more urgent, and the chorus had been replaced by a sole female voice with an enter-me-right-now in her tone. The language sounded like Hindi dialect.

'Welcome.' The young dark woman came to kneel before their mattress. Pushing her hair back from her forehead, she collapsed flowingly onto her haunches. Her knees cracked faintly though.

'Nothing for the present, thank you, Lopa,' said Anin in Hindi, politely but firmly. 'We've had the milk.' Lopa gracefully moved on to the two white women, bent over their stomachs, mellifluously and in bad English whispered a sweet nothing and lifting up the garment, began to rub some unguent on one creamy abdomen. Bhola noticed that she dipped her fingers into the jar, touched them to her left armpit or the back of her knee—presumably to add, in a symbolic way, her own sweat to her labours, so she must have been instructed while being trained in the mumbo-jumbo of the Retreat—and then, in a steady, lulling, clockwise motion, massaged the pliant flesh. The belly under her hands swelled and dipped like a rollercoaster. Bhola didn't want to know what bodily by-products had gone into the making of the unguent. The toejam of a low-caste menstruating virgin, at the very least. He could see Dosto thinking them up and seeing them through, could picture to himself Dosto's drugged, waggish glee and behind it, his razor-edged and simultaneously corroded brain, pulsing away without pause to find ways and means of striking it rich, having a laugh and pleasing the world, ideally all at the same time.

If Bhola had surmised correctly, Dosto had died—or begun to die—in that very hall. He had lain on one of those mattresses and, defeated, had waited for sleep. Bhola saw just then, beyond Anin's knees, the lone man nearest the door sigh suddenly in his drowse and roll over to face him. The feminine, smooth and almost rounded way in which the unconscious figure moved jolted loose in his head another image, a memory of a lover in another time. It was the manner in which the body had turned more than the face in repose fifteen feet away that made Bhola realize that the sleeper was Moti.

He nudged Anin's legs off his stomach, got up and, before padding across to take stock of how Moti had weathered the years, glanced down at his companions. Titli's head lay at an almost impossible angle on the bolster. She seemed to be virtually comatose in her slumber. Her mouth was slightly open and her breathing the faint and rhythmical whistle of a kettle. Her canvas satchel reclined comfortably in the crook of Anin's arm much like a favourite doll against a child's body. Anin herself gazed through a film of tears at nothing.

Moti had become a dark and bald skeleton. A thin tuft of sharply white hair stood atop his scalp like wild grass on a road shoulder. In his eye sockets, deep and black, his wrinkled eyelids seemed barely visible. The skin stretched unrelentingly tight over his forehead and cheekbones. Ensconced by the holes of his cheeks, his mouth stuck out lewdly, his lips so taut over his teeth that he seemed to be grinning like a skeleton even in his sleep.

'What is it?' No one heard. 'Anin, what does he have?'

'TB of the intestines,' he caught her voice from far away. He listened to her order someone else politely, 'We should have him taken back to his room.'

Going down on both knees, Bhola stared through his tears at the strands that remained of Moti's moustache. Only when he scanned earnestly the dormant form before him did he glimpse—but faintly—like an additional contour, an accretion of ether around the dying frame—the flabless hermaphroditic physical ideal that had been a dream of his own, a need, an aspiration worthy of the labours of a lifetime. In his lithe frolicsome body, Moti had had no brain but that had never mattered. Indeed, it had given him some of the attractiveness of a child; being trusting and gullible, he had half-believed both in the role that he had often had to play for Bhola and in the accompanying hocus-pocus that he had been teased with. The Supreme Being, Bhola had tried to din into Moti's head, gazing smilingly and deep into his eyes to infuse in him some self-esteem, is of one composite sex, possessing within himself both the male and female principles. Think of Shiva as Ardhanarishvara, fused with the form of his consort Parvati. Think of Krishna, who as the godhead is the one true male entity and the world and its creatures are all female in principle, created for his pleasure. In the mundane world too, all men and women combine the same duality. One is complete when one accepts within oneself the qualities of both genders. It is inevitable therefore that our masculinity harmonizes best with our femininity during sexual intercourse. During coition, through the conduit of another body, the man within you experiences and enjoys his own womanly counterpart and thus achieves enlightenment and bliss before he becomes a bag of bones. A black bag of bones.

Bhola felt tired and extremely sleepy. He wanted to go home and back in time and try and win back his old life with his wife and daughter. He arose dispiritedly. Matthew Arnold touched his forearm and with his habitual simper and a jerk of the head, indicated Anin, with her back to the room, standing before a table in a corner, busy laying out before her what looked like a set of surgical instruments. Somewhere in the back of his head, Bhola noted that Matthew Arnold too in the interim had donned the yellowish contact lenses that were evidently the totem of some inner cabal.

The white women, like Titli, were asleep. The masseuse stepped out through a door alongside the table, leaving it to fan back and forth. Bhola walked over to stand beside Anin, looked down at the array of knives and said, 'I'm going to nod off for a bit on one of these mattresses—if that's okay with you. I'm not yet in the mood to be part of whatever you intend to do. It would've been impossible even if they hadn't been diseased and dying.' She neither looked up nor spoke. He caught beneath the fragrance of the incense a hint of her perfume and noticed behind her right ear a scar like a lush, livid worm. The door swung open towards them. A stretcher trundled in, followed by the masseuse. She stopped alongside Moti and stooping, pushed him, not very gently, onto his back. Then she grasped him by the knees and Matthew Arnold held him by the armpits. Together, smoothly, they hoisted him onto the stretcher. As it rolled out of the hall, Moti in his benumbed state grumbled incoherently a couple of times.

'There's nothing to be done, really,' advised Anin conversationally, 'Everything is on course—even though it's not the course that anyone here either foresaw or planned. Dosto escaped with an overdose and left me in the company of servants.' She finally selected three knives, resheathed the others in the case, snapped it shut and put it away under the table. She rolled up the chosen three in a large white towel and tucked it under her arm. 'And wealth. *Vatsaha, Tvam Shrimantaha Manushyaha Asi.*'

He touched her forearm. 'That's funny. I mean it's funny how it works.' He cleared his throat to cease his mumbling. 'Dosto had asked me to translate the phrase *All You Need Is Love* and instead as a joke I did *Baby, You're A Rich Man*. And yet it works.' He stopped, fearing that the white women would overhear and that he sounded nonsensical. 'Where are you going? Should I accompany you?'

Anin paused, shut her eyes and put the back of her right hand to her forehead as though checking her own temperature. 'I need to see to things,' she murmured vaguely, 'get rid of people. Those men—from his past, from his School Old Boys' Association—that Dosto gathered around himself for his second childhood.' She opened her eyes and smiled wanly at Bhola. 'Anthony from your school. He waited for you all morning to recognize him and call him sir and all that. Instead you apparently were quite rude to him at the station. Should I send him in to massage you? That was what Dosto liked the most after his fix. Stay here. I'll be back.' She disappeared through the swing door through which Moti had been trundled out.

Anthony. That white-haired dried-up old cucumber with the ill-fitting false teeth had been the same Anthony after the memory of whom he had lusted without hope for God knows how many wasted years. He frowned with the effort of trying to find even one point of commonality between his escort of the morning and the physique of the man of his dreams. Unmanned by the power of Time, by its impassive, inexorable brutality, Bhola sat down on the mattress on which the rotting body of Moti had lain.

At some point, Lopa the masseuse materialized to hover over him.

'Would you like to be massaged? Or maybe drink something first?'

'Drink something first. Darjeeling leaf tea. No tea bag, no blood, no urine, no saliva, just tea.'

'With breast milk?'

'Whose?'

'Or whisky?'

'I'd planned not to touch it for some time.'

'Johnnie Walker Blue?'

He wondered whether his good resolutions were expected to evaporate when the whisky too was good. Perhaps it would be laced with a toxin and his goodly frame would turn an appropriate blue. The large-bolster-like contour of the supine Titli on the other mattress, beneath a wall the colour of blood, distracted him. In a daze, he wondered how much blood was required to be drained from the human body for the scales to register a significant loss of weight. He suspected that the masseuse had no clue either. Wasn't seventy per cent of body weight blood? Or was it water? Or was that volume and not weight?

'Everyone here—and everywhere else, I suppose—is either ageing, dying or dead,' he commented conversationally to the back of the masseuse as she moved off towards the bamboo curtain across the archway. He arose clumsily and with trembling calves crossed over to plump himself down beside Titli. 'Here, when someone dies, you say that he has entered samadhi, I suppose that that's one possible line to take,' ruminated he aloud, testing the warmth of Titli's cheek with the back of his hand, abstractedly groping for a pulse on the right wrist, then in her neck, pushing back an eyelid to confront her eyeball to eyeball. 'Death and killing are both natural. The natural cannot be transgressed. What do you think, Titli?' He teased out from beneath her shoulder and the bolster the red canvas satchel. He unclasped it and took out Moti's knife. 'We have consistently advocated nature's way. The most natural acts can be the most meritorious: eating and drinking that sustain life—bread and wine—sexual intercourse that propagates it, the natural functions that give it ease, dying and killing that cease it either because one's time has come or because one wants it to.' For a brief second, he held the blade of the knife flat against the fat of her cheek. 'Even when we are butchers,' he mumbled snivellingly and distractedly, as though mugging up lines for a role in a play, 'it is not without purpose. Killing gives one an aura of strength that is really the radiation of the forces from another world. Soldiers and butchers and hangmen have it, this latent occult potency that needs to be channelized and orientated, awakened.' Sighing, he stood up and trudged back to the rose-coloured mattress on which, on first entering the room, he had seen Moti.

The music had been shut off without his noticing.

The silence was sudden and overbearing, accentuated by the gentle rhythmical sighs of Titli's exhalations. She slept with mouth partly open and forehead a little furrowed— perhaps by the load of her sins. Even the scarlet wall behind her with its geometrical designs in yellow and black appeared too dark and oppressive. Bhola shut his eyes. The room, seeming to loom in towards him, became even more intolerable. He opened them again. He glanced around, arose and shuffled across to reposition himself on the mattress which the white women had abandoned a while ago.

The changed perspective altered both his mood and his impressions of the hall. He wondered why the symbolism of its red walls, its warmth and balmy odours had not been immediately clear to him. It had in addition the form of the sleeping Titli, tousled kurta revealing the contour of her hips. Yoni, holder, the vulva, also used to mean origin, nest, lap or womb. Yoni refers specifically to the female organ as a symbol of sexual pleasure and the matrix of generation. Bhola could practically see Dosto and Anin standing in the middle of the hall and designing the core of the calm centre. The designs on the walls jumped to life. Yoni, my dear, includes i) the *bhaga*, the dispenser of delight, the pubes, ii) the *vedha*, a breach, opening or cleft, the labia, iii) the *yoni* or vagina, often compared to the interior of a mollusc or conch-shell and believed to possess a life of its own; of the twenty extra muscles that the female body is supposed to have—at the notion of sexual muscles, Dosto's face would have become flaccid with desire; to mask his emotion, he would wrinkle up his nose and inhale in a long-drawn-in sniff—five each are in the two breasts and the remaining ten are in the yoni, iv) the *garbha*, the womb shaped like the *rohit*, a kind of fish, narrow at the opening and wide at the upper end. The yoni is a sacred area, a soft pad of bliss, a zone of felicity, an occult region of cosmic mysteries, an *axis mundi* worthy of reverence, a vessel of delights. It is the honey that attracts the male organ, the mouth that wafts out a silent and irresistible command to men to come and sip, the ruler of the universe to whom all men are subject and from whom they all originate, the sacred field in which the seed of all creatures is planted and nourished by the vital pulsations of the Ultimate. It symbolizes in its shape the mystical *sunya*, zero, the emptiness in which all things are inherent. Om. Amen.

Abased, Bhola wished obscurely to atone for what he felt was his final conquest of desire. He rolled up the sleeves of his kurta and unsheathed the knife. Since ambidexterity had been for years one of the objectives of his retarded life, he chose to cut open first his right wrist. It was odd that the knife unlocked no memories in him. You can do it, just me and you, with a little luck, he sang to himself in encouragement and involuntarily pulling in his testicles and tensing his abdomen, pushed down hard with his left hand. He gasped with the pain. He watched the blood well up and dribble over onto his purplish kurta and wondered what on earth he was up to. Before he could change his mind fully, he transferred the knife to his right hand, placed its blade against the artery in his left wrist and pressed down. He felt that he hadn't thrust hard enough but didn't have the courage to try again. The two red wrists in his lap, limp, palms wrinkled, fingers curled up, looked like someone else's, sacrificial offerings before an object of worship. He lay down, careful to keep his wrists on his kurta. He shut his eyes, opened them and, unsure even of which of the two he preferred, shut them again.

The bamboo curtain across the archway clacked gently as somebody entered the hall. He slowly twisted his head to look and saw the two white women with a man in jeans and polo shirt who looked like Bhola himself ten years after. Fatigue, no doubt. One must build not on the past but on the future. Where had he read that? Or had he cooked it up himself? Quite possibly. In his limited way, he was a good cook. Build an image of yourself ten years in the future and work towards that goal. Ten years? Even ten minutes was an eternity when desire and will were seeping out of one. Who was it who had slashed himself at the crook of the elbow just so as to bleed better? Rothko? He raised his red forearms in the air to draw attention to his distress. He was still in two minds and like Shakespeare's Lancelot Gobbo, felt that his hands could fight the matter out for him. The white women smiled, clapped softly, perhaps at his feat, bowed low in Japanese fashion and exited without turning their backs on him. The man smiled apologetically at Bhola and followed them. Bhola wondered whether in that dim light and that distance, they had noticed at all the blood. Peaceful moments passed.

Before the blurred orange-dark veil of his eyelids, a child's face, moon-like, grinned ecstatically at him. It was his daughter, he was sure of it, from the world to come, reassuring him that all was well. He had the impression that she wanted to pummel him for several minutes into waking up from the life that he was in. Never in all his years or in his dreams had he seen anything more welcome, more beautiful. At the sight of her, some metal in his forehead seemed to descend into his body and dissolve into the calm at its centre. Everything became perfect, even his slit wrists. Then his daughter stopped smiling. Her face crumpled up instead. Do people really weep for God as they do for their wife and children? Now who had asked that? Sri Ramakrishna? And why on earth should they? retorted Bhola, gently mussing his daughter's hair, careful not to bloody it as the life dribbled out of him.

ACKNOWLEDGEMENTS

Quotations—verbatim, modified, partly twisted, turned upside-down—from Benjamin Walker's readable and informative two-volume *Hindu World*, published by Munshiram Manoharlal, abound in *Weight Loss*. Examples can be seen on pages 24, 61, 62, 83, 137, 142, 143, 146, 147, 149, 251, 298, 305, 309, 317, 325, 326, 391, 410, 413 and 414. I should add that the occasional ironic or comic use of a passage from Walker, required by the demands of the context, certainly does not reflect its intrinsic worth or my appreciation of its value.

References to the *Manusmriti* are to the Penguin Classics edition translated by Wendy Doniger.

The nugget of information on Chinese soup on page 387 is based on a news item in *The Statesman* of Saturday, 15 April 1995.

The anecdote on page 229 of two Buddhist monks is based on one found in Christmas Humphreys's *Buddhism*.

The passage on pages 401-02 on the Mandala is based almost entirely on Peggy Jordan's column on the same subject in *The Hindu*.